With love,



# *Fortuna*

CARAGH BELL

First published in 2024



ISBN 978-1-3999-9027-1

Printed by Inspire, Skibbereen.

*For Kathleen*

# THE AUTHOR

Caragh Bell is from Skibbereen in west Cork. A graduate of University College Cork, she has a degree in French and English. She also has a postgraduate Diploma in Education, a Masters in Education and is currently doing a PhD in Education. She teaches at Sacred Heart Secondary School in Clonakilty where she produces the SHSS Podcast.

Caragh has published six books with Poolbeg Press in Dublin: Indecision, Regrets, Promises, Echoes of Grace, Gabriella and Mosaic. Her stories are filled with drama, heartbreak and lots of romance. Described by the Irish Examiner as light, funny and fast-moving, her novels are page turners with memorable characters.

She has published an article in the Irish Journal of Technology Enhanced Learning entitled Tweetez-Vous Français? which explores the use of social media in second language teaching. She has also contributed to 'Perspectives on the Teaching of English in the Post-Primary Education' published by Cork University Press.

Caragh regularly has articles published in various magazines and newspapers, and gives workshops on creative writing. She has been the guest on various podcasts and radio shows. She has also written a play entitled 'One in Four' which tackles the subject of miscarriage.

Fortuna is her seventh book.

# ACKNOWLEDGEMENTS

This book is dedicated to my late mother-in-law, Kathleen Daly, who passed away in May 2024. She read the first draft and was always so supportive of my writing. I miss her every day.

Thanks to my parents, Ann and John, are truly the greatest. Without them, I would never have followed my dreams. I love you both so much.

To my gorgeous children: Fódhla, Aoibhe, Lughan, Oscar and Feidhlim. You are my raison d'être. Special thanks to Fó for editing this book with me.

To my siblings who all feature in my books. Try and guess which characters are based on you.

To my father-in-law, Eugene, who thankfully has never read my books.

To Daniel O'Driscoll, my confidant and supporter. You're the best.

To Katy Salvidge. Thanks for letting me mirror parts of your story in Emilia. That day we met in O'Neill's Coffee was truly the beginning of this book.

To Justin Grounds. Thanks for all the orchestra and strings info. You made it all so real. You were so generous with your time and expertise.

To Sheelagh. Thanks for reading. Your opinion always means the world.

To Sylvia and Michael. I love you two.

To Inspire (especially Fintan) for printing this book. Your expertise and professionalism were fab.

To my work buddies. Love you all.

To David Louks (Chicken Dave) who sadly passed away recently. You were always my biggest fan, writing sweet messages on bags of chicken, and I miss you terribly.

To Jilly. You are my greatest inspiration. Thanks for being so kind. I included more dogs in this book x

To Romeo Cedric Fitzwilliam Daly. My baby. You make me so happy.

To all who read my stories. I'm glad that my books provide a small bit of escapism in this crazy world. It was nice to continue Caspian's story and to bring back other old characters. When I get my movie deal, you can party on my yacht.

# Baptiste

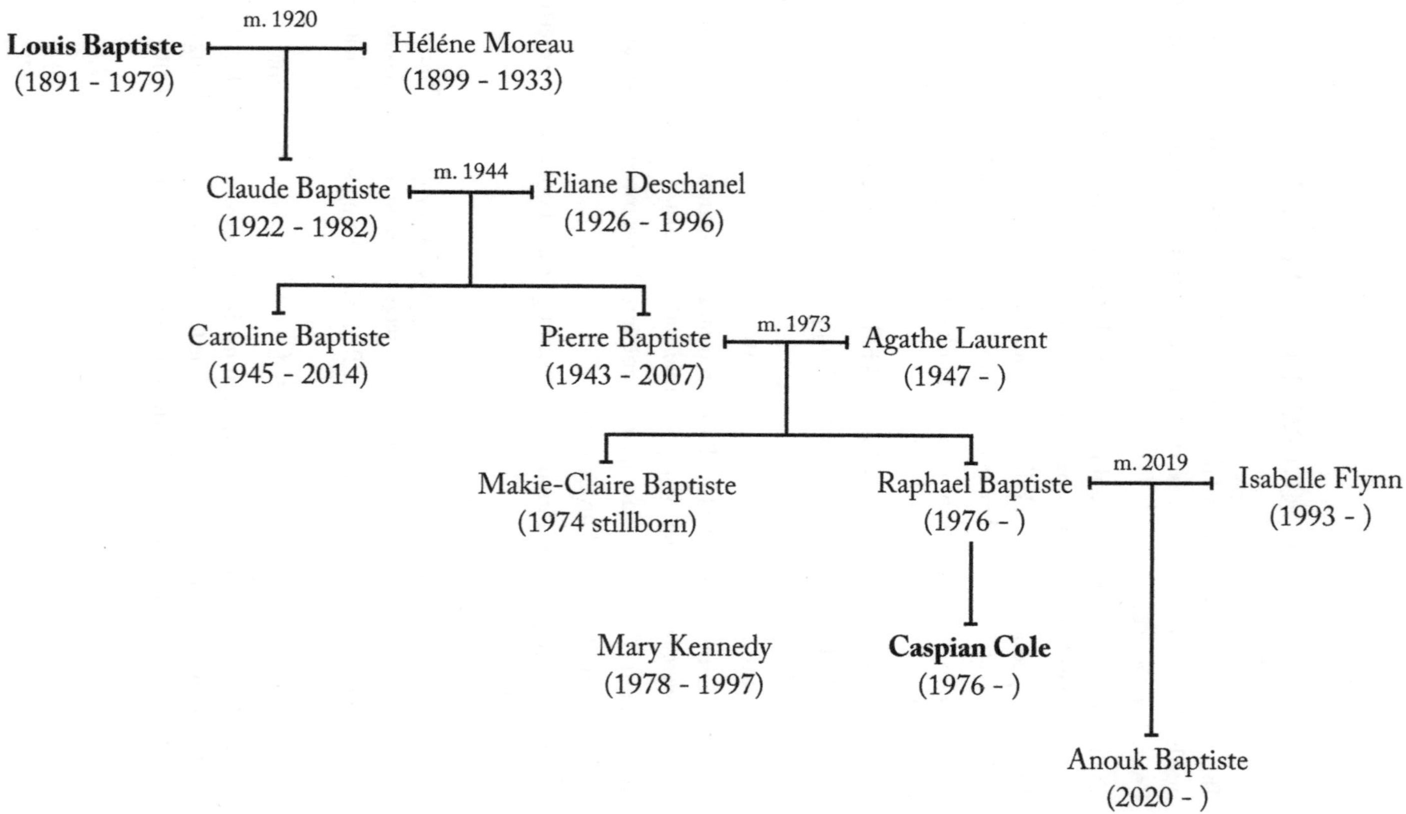

**Louis Baptiste**
(1891 - 1979)
m. 1920
Héléne Moreau
(1899 - 1933)
Claude Baptiste
(1922 - 1982)
m. 1944
Eliane Deschanel
(1926 - 1996)
Caroline Baptiste
(1945 - 2014)
Pierre Baptiste
(1943 - 2007)
m. 1973
Agathe Laurent
(1947 - )
Makie-Claire Baptiste
(1974 stillborn)
Raphael Baptiste
(1976 - )
m. 2019
Isabelle Flynn
(1993 - )
Mary Kennedy
(1978 - 1997)
**Caspian Cole**
(1976 - )
Anouk Baptiste
(2020 - )

# Weber

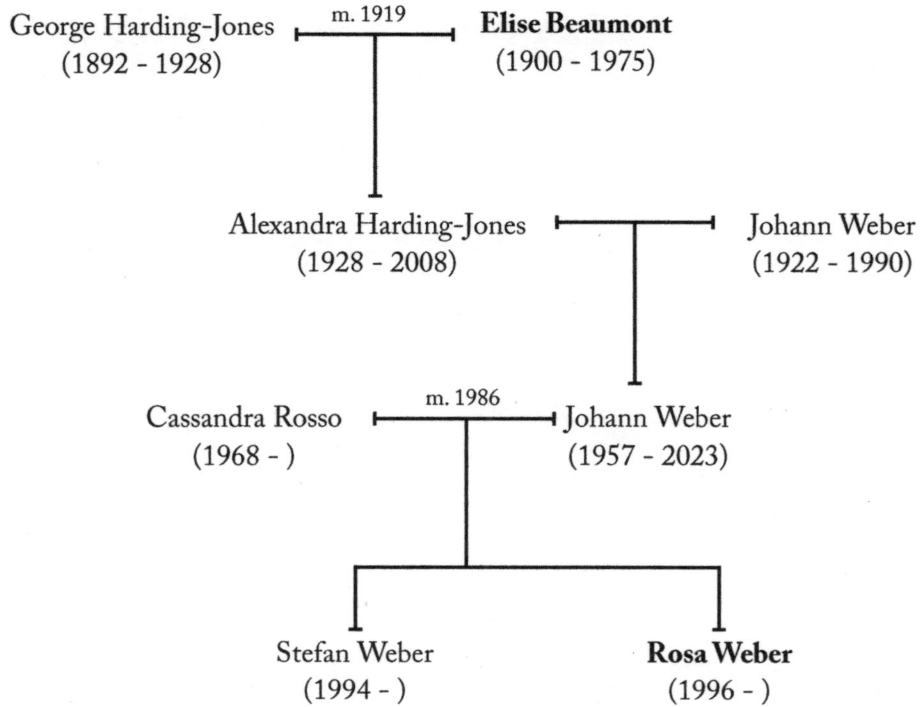
George Harding-Jones
(1892 - 1928)
m. 1919
**Elise Beaumont**
(1900 - 1975)
Alexandra Harding-Jones
(1928 - 2008)
Johann Weber
(1922 - 1990)
Cassandra Rosso
(1968 - )
m. 1986
Johann Weber
(1957 - 2023)
Stefan Weber
(1994 - )
**Rosa Weber**
(1996 - )

# CHAPTER ONE

## 2002

"Emilia? Would you like a coffee?" Alfie propped his cello on its stand. "I can't play another note without a hit of caffeine."

"Yes, please." She smiled absentmindedly as she twisted the pegs her violin. "One sugar."

"I know that." Alfie made a face. "I am the overworked coffee mule, you know. Anything else? I fancy a cinnamon bun."

She shook her head. "No, no. Just a coffee." She played an arpeggio and the sound reverberated through the room.

"Back in a sec." The door shut quietly.

Emilia closed her eyes and played the notes on the sheet music in front of her. Something was not quite right. She could feel it in the pit of her stomach. It needed to be tweaked. She just needed to figure out where.

She sighed and rested her jaw on the chin rest of her violin. The love theme was the last part of the film score left. The submission date was close to two weeks ago and she still wasn't ready. Even though this was her twentieth time working on a project of this scale, she still didn't get complacent. She still felt nervous at the thought of it being rejected. She had seen it happen many times in the movie industry. Composing was a fickle business. She was renowned and well-respected, but you were only as good as your last concerto.

Her living room didn't have a television like most. Instead, it was dominated by a grand piano near the bay windows, a violin stand, a shelf filled with music books and sheets of notes scattered all over the floor. This Victorian house which she had purchased ten years before was her greatest joy. Its pokey rooms and classical fireplaces had attracted her instantly. It was almost in ruin when she found it, so she had hired an interior designer to restore it. The peeling wallpaper in the parlour was analysed and traced back to a company in France. Luckily, they were still trading and, for a hefty fee, reproduced the same oriental style. This pattern was popular in the 1840s, they told her. It was a sign of prestige.

It took three years to renovate the house and make it habitable. She glanced up at the frames on the wall above her piano. Various awards for different films over the years. Oscar, her imaginative name for her Academy Award, stood proudly on the mantelpiece: a symbol of excellence. Yet, she never got complacent. Her father taught her that.

"Pride comes before a fall, Emmy," he'd say in his gravelly voice.

Her darling dad. How she missed him.

Standing erect, she played the music once more, her brow furrowed. She would crack this. She would figure this out. It was almost there. Almost.

So engrossed was she in this task that she didn't notice Alfie coming back into the room.

Alfie Fletcher. Her oldest friend.

He placed the polystyrene mugs on the mahogany coffee table and wiped some cinnamon sugar from his lips.

"Any progress?" he asked when she lowered her bow.

"Nope."

"You'll figure it out," he said. "I rang Miranda. I said I'd be home by dinner time."

"Of course." Emilia waved him away. "I monopolise too much of your time. Go home to your family."

"She understands," he said, brushing his sandy-coloured hair from his eyes. "We are *artistes*, after all. She likes being a long-suffering wife." He picked up her coffee and handed it to her. "Take a break, Em. You look exhausted."

She forced a smile and placed her beloved violin on the piano.

"Thanks, Alfie." She took the cup from his outstretched hand and sat down on the armchair. Folding her long legs underneath her, she sighed. That love theme would take over until she was happy with it. She couldn't imagine eating or sleeping until it was right. She looked up to find Alfie watching her.

"You're biting your lower lip."

"So?"

"You do that when you're worried."

She sipped her coffee. "What if I can't do it? What if it doesn't click?"

Alfie rolled his eyes. "Emilia! How long have we known each other?"

She shrugged. "Twenty odd years?"

"Exactly. And how many times have you failed in a task like this?"

"Never."

"So, relax." He sat back. "We'll take another crack at it and see where that takes us."

"Thanks, Alfie."

"Now drink that coffee. I had to queue for ages."

"Really? I don't know why you insist on going to that barista."

"No offence, but the instant coffee in your kitchen does nothing for me. Why don't you invest in a proper machine?"

She smiled. "I wouldn't know where to start."

"Well, it would save me walking into the village for sustenance."

Her fingers moved up the armrest of the chair as a melody played in her head. The notes danced around in her mind's eye, rearranging themselves rapidly on imaginary sheet music.

Suddenly, she started. She could see the problem clearly.

Getting up hurriedly, she put her cup on the coffee table.

"I think I have it," she said breathlessly.

"Already?" He raised an eyebrow. "I thought we had at least forty-eight more hours of suffering left."

"No, no. This is it." She sat at the piano and played the tune. "You see! Look at the difference a few notes make."

He got up and walked to the piano. "Play it again."

She obliged and a slow smile spread across her face. "That's it, Alfie. I can feel it." She exhaled. "Oh, the relief."

He jerked his head towards the discarded cups. "If this isn't proof that you need to buy a decent coffee machine, nothing is. It was the roasted Colombian beans that did it."

"You could be right." She beamed at him.

Alfie left at seven.

Darkness was falling which was typical for March. She walked to the fireplace and was gratified to see the coal bucket was full. Bending down, she poked the ashes from the previous day and emptied the grate. Striking a match, she ignited a firelighter under a pyramid of kindling and blew gently on the flame, causing it to dance upwards.

The love theme was the final part of the puzzle. She had been working on this particular score for eighteen months. It was for a historical film about the arrival of the pilgrims in Massachusetts by Carey McGrath, a young American director. Alfie was her talisman. His cheery attitude and can-do approach to life calmed her.

Walking to the piano, she sat on the upholstered chair and played the love theme again. The music emanated out of her fingertips and she closed her eyes. She could see the heroine on the deck of the ship, en route to the New World. Carey would be pleased. He had called two days before saying that filming was to recommence in the summer after a long sabbatical and lockdowns.

The fire crackled in the grate as the flames came to life. She carefully put the lid down on the piano keys and stretched. When she was working, she didn't even think about food. The music consumed her and everything else faded away into insignificance. Alfie chided her about her erratic eating habits.

"You're too skinny," he'd say with a frown. "You're like a string bean."

She smiled to herself. She'd always been tall and slim, and 'string bean' was an accurate description. Her stomach rumbled. Even string beans needed to eat.

Her kitchen, although refurbished and filled with mod cons, still retained the Victorian look. The dresser on the far wall was filled with fine china plates and had jugs hanging on hooks. There was a large oak table in the centre of the flagstones, scrubbed clean. The black stove, which served to heat the house, was cold. Emilia shivered. It would heat the house if she ever deigned to light it. She opened the fridge and was dismayed to see nothing but out-of-date yoghurt and some congealed ham. She glanced at her watch. She could order in some take away. She fancied an Indian. Some curry with a naan bread on the side.

Just as she re-entered the sitting room to find her phone, the doorbell rang. Alfie stood on the steps outside, holding a Tupperware box.

"Miranda made far too much lasagne. I knew your cupboards would be bare, so I thought I'd drop some over."

Emilia's face broke into a huge smile, the curry forgotten.

"Oh, Alfie. What would I do without you?"

He grinned. "Here. Reheat this and get it down you."

"Thanks."

"Let me guess, you've no decent food in the house."

"Well…"

"Are you trying to be frugal? You're not poor anymore, Emmy. You're rich. Keep your fridge stocked." He blew her a kiss. "See you in the morning."

Emilia waved. "I'll order off Waitrose right away."

# CHAPTER TWO

Emilia Thomas was born in Birmingham in 1977. Her father worked at MG Motors in Longbridge and her mother cleaned bedrooms at a local hotel. Her upbringing was modest – they lived in a small red-brick terraced house near Solihull and ate minced meat with gravy most days.

From a young age she displayed musical talent. Her mother claimed she had inherited it from her father, a Welsh miner with a powerful voice. At the age of five, she learned recorder at school and picked it up easily. Without any practice, she could play a tune effortlessly. Her teacher, a kind old lady called Mrs. Davies, offered her private violin lessons after school at her house. There, she grappled with scales and arpeggios. Then, she progressed to piano and, by the age of thirteen, she was proficient in all three instruments. She borrowed books about famous composers from the library and pored over them, her passion for music all-consuming.

When the time came to attend university, her rich contemporaries at school were encouraged to apply for Oxford and Cambridge. Letters were sent to various wealthy families with all the application details. Emilia, with her modest background, didn't receive a letter. Like her mother before her, she was expected to work in a hotel or a bar. Incensed, she applied to Oxford by herself, determined to prove them all wrong. She sent applications to five colleges and sat an Oxbridge exam. To her huge surprise, she was called to an interview and, a few days later, she received her letter of acceptance. She would attend Christ Church College and was granted a choral scholarship. The only catch was that she had to sing at services each week. Mrs. Davies, now in her seventies, was thrilled that her protégée had beaten the odds. "And a bursary too!" she said in delight. "Well done, Emmy!"

Her parents didn't own a car so when the day came to go to university, they hired a large van and filled it with her things. Together, they sped up the road to Oxford, singing *My Old Man's a Dustman* at the top of their voices. When they reached St. Aldate's, they approached the college and parked right in front of the main entrance. The road was filled with huge BMWs and Jaguars so their rental van stuck out like a sore thumb. Her father insisted that the family pose on the grass for a photo and asked a passing student to take the shot. With a pained face, he took three photos of Emilia, her dog and her parents standing on the grass. "I should tell you that one doesn't stand on the Quad," the young man said in his posh voice, handing the camera back to her father. "I thought everybody knew that."

Emilia spent three years at Oxford: three happy years. Most of her classmates were alumni of prestigious schools like Eton, Harrow and Malvern St James, and admitted to having been coached to pass the entrance exam. They found it amazing that Emilia had been selected on her own merit, not because of her background. The mid-nineties was a great time to be a student and she dressed in torn jeans and graphic t-shirts, her long hair in a ponytail and a silver ring on her index finger.

Despite her lack of connections and her limited funds, her talent shone through and she excelled in her classes. She lived in college rooms throughout her course and ate her meals in the famous 16th century hall. She joined the Cathedral Choir and became a well-known part of the music scene. She loved composing music and often got inspired while walking along by the river next to the Christ Church Meadow on the other side of the college.

Tall and willowy, she had long auburn hair and bright blue eyes, with a number of boyfriends throughout her time at college. All the relationships fizzled out in the end as she was not the type of girl these boys would bring home to their snooty mothers.

It was at college that she met Alfie. He played cello and together they joined the Oxford University Orchestra. From a privileged background, he often bankrolled Emilia when she didn't have enough funds to buy a dress for the Christmas ball or strings for her violin. He understood that she didn't have the contacts and connections he had so he always looked out for her. One night, in their second year, he worked up the courage to kiss her, but she gently pushed him away.

"Oh, Alfie," she said softly. "If only I fancied you. You're wonderful and kind and giving. It's just that it's like kissing my brother."

A few awkward weeks followed, but then they slipped back into their relationship of old. He made sure that she woke up on time for exams and services on a Sunday. She was notorious for sleeping in and there was many a morning he would bang incessantly on the door of her room, yelling at her to get out of bed.

After graduation, she moved to London and became the assistant of a composer called Tony Donoghue who wrote catchy songs for advertisements. He called her Emma, despite her correcting him umpteen times, and only required her to make lunch and coffees. To her chagrin, she didn't get an opportunity to write music and play. She just got to watch him tap out repetitive songs on his keyboard, high-fiving himself when he cracked what he called 'a new classic for our times'. Tony was a good boss but had a huge sense of his own importance, deeming his work on an advertising campaign for carpet cleaner on par with Beethoven's Choral Symphony.

"It's all about the jingle," he'd say in his London accent. "That's what sells products, Emma. The jingle."

Then one day, Alfie called her up and asked her to accompany him to a job interview in Oxford.

"You should tag along as there might be something for you too."

"What's the job?" she asked. "Playing music?"

"It's to be a orchestrator. You know, you arrange the score before it's sent to a copyist. You'd be great at it."

"A score for what?"

"A film. Look, it's for a guy called Johann Weber."

"Who?"

"Doesn't matter. Just meet me outside the library tomorrow at three."

Emilia's train from Paddington Station was delayed at Didcot Parkway, so when she arrived at Oxford Station, she rushed to the bus stop in the city centre and prayed a bus would arrive promptly. When she got there, breathless and apologetic, Alfie was waiting outside the library.

"Christ, Emmy, I can't believe you're late," said Alfie in annoyance.

"Sorry."

"And what the hell are you wearing?" he asked in horror, pointing to her red hot pants and spaghetti string top. "Look at my shirt and tie! We'll look ridiculous together."

"I was planning on changing into a dress when I got here. It's not my fault I'm late. Give me five minutes to switch outfits…"

"No, no. We've no time. Come on."

Alfie knocked on the large oak door of a small room to the right of the main library.

"Come in," came a deep voice.

"Please say you printed out your CV like I asked," hissed Alfie, straightening his tie.

She pulled out a crumpled handwritten page from her bag and showed him. "Will this do?" she asked sheepishly.

"Emilia! I give up."

Walking into the room, they were confronted with a man of about forty, poring over a score. He was handsome with sallow skin and an athletic body. He wore half-moon spectacles on his nose and an open-necked shirt. His eyes widened in surprise when he saw Emilia's attire.

He waved them forward. "Come in," he commanded. "I'm Johann Weber."

He had a foreign accent and pronounced his surname 'Veber'. Emilia didn't recognise the name but he said it in such a way that she felt she should have.

Alfie pulled out his CV and rushed forward. "I graduated this year and I play cello. I have an honours degree and..."

"You play cello?" Johann interrupted.

"Yes, sir."

"Have you orchestrated any pieces?"

Alfie nodded. "Three times, sir. Once for the Beeb. It's all there on my CV."

Johann threw the pristine typed pages on the desk.

"And you?" he said, turning to Emilia. "Have you experience?"

Emilia raised her chin upwards. "Not really," she replied. "I'm too busy as an assistant for Tony Donoghue."

"Who?" he asked puzzled.

"A famous composer," she said. "He writes very famous jingles." She sang a song from a washing powder ad on the television.

"Right." He smiled slightly. "Do you play an instrument?"

"Yes. I play violin, piano, recorder and I'm currently learning the harp."

"Do you have a CV?"

"Yes." She handed him her handwritten list of accomplishments. "Sorry for the ink blots but I didn't have any Tippex."

Johann scanned the crumpled page and looked up. "Your name is Emilia Thomas?"

She nodded.

"Very well, Emilia, there's a violin over there. Play something."

She stared at Johann defiantly. "You could say please."

He raised an eyebrow.

"Fucking hell, Emmy," whispered Alfie urgently. "Do what he says!"

"Please," said Johann in amusement.

She walked over to the chair and picked up the violin. It was a beautiful instrument, sleek with a deep bronze colour and, jolted, she realised it was a Stradivarius. She had never come close to such a precious instrument before. Positioning it under her chin, she tuned the strings with her eyes closed. Lifting the bow, she launched into the second movement of Mozart's Violin Concerto Number Three. Johann watched her intently until she had finished and then motioned for her to approach him. She sauntered over, her hips swinging, and stood with her head held high.

"Right." He smiled. "I would like you to join my team. I need someone to look at a trumpet concerto and edit it."

"What? Me?" she asked, stunned.

"Yes, you."

"What's the concerto for?"

"A new film I'm working on."

"What film?"

"It's a new film by Scorsese. Very hush hush."

"Oh." She swayed slightly. "Sorry, I didn't realise. I mean, before today, I'd never heard of you before."

"That's interesting."

"I mean, film is something I know nothing about."

"Right."

"But I've heard of Martin Scorsese."

"Of course."

Alfie watched this exchange with a worried look. "Is it just Emilia or is there anything for me?"

Johann didn't take his eyes off Emilia. "We'll find something," he said. "Just give your details to my secretary."

Alfie half-bowed as he backed out of the room. Emilia curtseyed mockingly and with a laugh, followed her friend. The door closed.

They hugged joyfully outside the building.

"This is brilliant!" said Alfie. "He's so famous, Emmy. We're on our way to the bigtime."

"He's kind of full of himself though, isn't he?" she said as they walked away.

"I think he's entitled to be. I mean, he's an Oscar winning composer."

They turned out the gate.

"Let's go and have a pint to celebrate," Alfie suggested.

She smiled. "I'd love that."

# CHAPTER THREE

What followed was the most exciting time of Emilia's life. She quit her job with Tony Donoghue who warned her that she was making a huge mistake. Then she met Johann in London and started editing the trumpet concerto as promised. He helped her in the beginning, advising her what to do and giving her tips. They often worked late and would grab a bite to eat afterwards. There he would regale her with stories of Hollywood and the various award ceremonies he'd attended. She found that he was interested in helping her along in her career and told Alfie exactly that when he asked why she was spending so much time with the boss.

"He fancies you, Em," Alfie warned. "Anyone can see it."

"No way," she argued. "He's almost twenty years older than me for a start. My God, Alfie, maybe he just wants to help me in my career?"

Then one night, Johann insisted that she stay late in the recording studio to look at the over-dub of a flute solo. Two heads bent over the music, they added in changes in pencil and argued over tempo. He took off his glasses and tilted her chin upwards. "Kiss me," he commanded.

Shocked, she moved backwards, but he pulled her to him and kissed her passionately. She pressed herself against him eagerly. She was in love and she couldn't stop it.

Alfie guessed straight away.

"You slept with him."

Emilia blushed. "No, I did not."

"Yes, you did." He frowned. "You know he's married to Cassandra Rosso, right? The opera singer?"

"They're not close."

"Says you." He shook his head. "They've two kids, Emmy."

"It's a marriage of convenience," she said definitely. "Cassandra travels all the time. He never sees her. The kids have a nanny."

"Emmy, listen to yourself. It's the classic story." Alfie put on a moaning voice.

*"My wife doesn't understand me. I'm locked in a loveless marriage."* He pushed her gently. "Pull yourself together."

"Leave me alone." She scowled. "Can't I be happy for once?"

What followed was a long affair. Johann's family home was in Hertfordshire, a 18th century sprawling estate which was home to his wife and children, their nanny, Gertrude, and his two dogs, Shelley and Byron. Emilia saw pictures of the impressive red-brick building, but was never brought there. His family home was just for family. He liked to keep her separate from all of that.

So they met at his flat near Primrose Hill in London as often as possible. After a night of lovemaking, he would surprise her in the morning with fresh croissants from the bakery down the street. She knew it was wrong, sleeping with a married man, but she couldn't help herself. The twenty years between them didn't seem to exist. He was sophisticated and sexy. He was the one.

They also spent time in his apartment in Prague where he would go to write music. He disliked being disturbed when he worked, so he would go a week before, get some work done and then send a first-class plane ticket for her to come out and join him. Together they would walk the streets and bridges of the famous city, taking in an opera and holding hands. On St Charles' Bridge, she rubbed the brass of St John's statue, vowing she'd come back to Prague, but also wishing more than anything that Johann would stay with her forever.

In the beginning, Johann tried to buy her things but she flatly refused. There was no way she wanted to be a kept woman. She'd had a frugal upbringing and didn't need fancy things. However, when she met him for lunch in the Ritz in Paris wearing a multi-coloured Peruvian jumper, he insisted that she buy some 'decent clothes' as he called them, and promptly took her to Chanel. Hours later she emerged onto Rue Cambon wearing a simple black trouser suit, brown leather pumps and a brown handbag with the famous logo.

"Do I look the part?" she asked in a posh accent.

Johann kissed her nose. "It's definitely better."

One weekend, he drove them to Birmingham in his Aston Martin to have tea with her parents. Emilia was slightly embarrassed when his car pulled up outside the red bricked terraced house, but she shook herself. This was her home and she was proud of it. Her parents' eyes were on stalks when they first encountered the older man in his expensive clothes. However, after a cup of tea and some Marietta biscuits, Johann went on to charm her mother with his stories of the rich and famous. He then took her father outside to inspect the Aston Martin.

As Emilia washed the cups at the kitchen sink, her mother poked her waist.

"Is he married?" she hissed. "He's no spring chicken."

Emilia paused and then nodded. "Yes. He is."

"Kiddies?"

She nodded again, turning an ugly shade of red.

"Now, Emmy. You know what to do." Her mother looked stern.

She twisted the tea towel in her hands. She purposely didn't think about it. It was a marriage of convenience. That's what he said. A farce. She debated whether to argue but decided against it. Her mother would react just like Alfie did. She would rubbish it.

Johann's London flat had a studio where he kept the majority of his instruments. It was there he allowed her to play his Stradivarius violin which she relished. No other instrument produced a sound like it. It had a guttural sound: a gorgeous timbre and tone that had no equal.

"Where did you get this?" she asked, placing it carefully in its case.

"Word of mouth. My father's best friend was a composer and, when he died, his wife decided to sell a lot of his assets."

"Was it expensive?"

He nodded. "Yes, it was. More money than most people dream of. There are only about six hundred and fifty of these violins in the world today and most people don't want sell. They loan them out to musicians instead. I was lucky when Marguerite agreed to sell it to me."

"How rich are you?" she asked in wonder.

He laughed. "I'm doing okay."

On their second Christmas Eve together, he produced a large box, wrapped in gold paper.

"Happy Christmas," he whispered, kissing her nose. "My wonderful Emilia."

She pulled at the shiny paper enthusiastically, revealing a wooden rectangular box. Opening the lid, she saw an antiquated violin case. Her eyes widened. Unfastening the clasp, she opened the cover and gasped.

"Your Strad! I couldn't possibly!"

He laughed. "You can and you will." He pushed a lock of auburn hair from her cheek. "No one I know plays violin like you, Emmy. I want you to have it."

"But it's priceless."

"Piano is my instrument." He trailed his finger down her cheek. "In one week, we will be on the cusp of a new millennium. Imagine that? It will be the beginning of great things."

She picked up the violin and tuned it automatically. Then she played an arpeggio, her eyes closed in wonder.

"Should you keep this for your children? I mean, won't they be angry that you gave it away?"

"Stefan is not interested in music." His expression darkened. "Incredible, I know."

"And Rosa?"

"She has talent, but lacks ambition." He put his hand on her arm. "Forget the children. Accept my gift. It's yours."

She kissed him hard on the lips. "I will keep it by my side constantly."

News of his divorce hit the tabloids three years later. Johann had warned her that there might be repercussions. His wife was a fiery Italian diva called Cassandra Rosso. Even though she'd had a lover in Milan for years, she played the victim with the media. Determined to get her just desserts, spoke openly to the press about Johann's infidelity and this was printed all over the world. Emilia's name was mentioned as were others. In horror, Emilia read about an American clarinet player and German cellist. She confronted Johann immediately.

"Why is my name on a long list? I didn't realise I was sharing you with half the Philharmonic Orchestra."

"Emmy, darling. It's Cassandra. She's out to ruin me. It's just bitterness."

In her gut she knew he was lying.

"So, what's next for us then?"

He paused. "Well, I have to fly to LA for a week but we can meet in London when I get back."

"When will you be back?"

"Soon." He rubbed his temple. "I need to lie low for a while until this divorce business passes. I hope you understand."

Her eyes filled with tears.

He kissed her forehead. "Go and live your life, little Emmy. Have some fun. I'll see you soon."

It was a month later when he finally returned to England. Sullen and hurt, Emilia refused to see him. She ignored his calls and sent the bouquets of roses back. Eventually he called to her house and stood on the threshold until she opened the door.

"I'm sorry." He stared at her searchingly. "I was working the whole time. I stopped in New York and …"

"Why didn't you call?"

"Cassandra is looking for full custody of the children. I was stressed." He looked tired. "Full custody! From a woman who's never there. She's unbelievable."

"Will she win?" she asked, softening slightly.

He pointed to his car. "Not if I can help it."

Emilia looked at his Mercedes and saw two faces staring out at her.

"I think it's time you met Stefan and Rosa."

He gestured for the children to come to him. The car door slammed and Stefan, eleven, glared at Emilia. Rosa, eight, followed suit. Both of them looked like their Italian mother with dark brown hair and large brown eyes.

"This is Emilia," said Johann. "My girlfriend."

Emilia blushed in confusion. "Your girlfriend?"

"Yes." He took her face in his large hands. "Let's be together. For real this time. Move in with me."

"Really?" Her heart soared.

"Yes. Not the apartment – my house in the country."

Emilia gasped. How she'd dreamed of this moment.

Rosa stared at them. "Will you be our new mummy?" she asked. "You'd definitely be better than Gertrude. She's our nanny and she makes me eat my vegetables. Will you make me eat vegetables?"

Stefan glowered at them. "She's not our mummy, Rosa. Shut up."

Emilia looked at Johann helplessly. He nodded encouragingly.

She cleared her throat. "No, I'm not your mother nor do I want to be," she said eventually. "Let's just be friends."

"Will you make me eat my vegetables?" demanded Rosa.

"Not if you don't want to."

"Good." She beamed at her. "I'm definitely your friend then."

Stefan elbowed her. "Shut up, Rosa!"

"Shut up yourself!" She shoved him sideways. "I'm just sick of cabbage. It's all Gertrude makes. *Ich hasse Gemuse essen!*"

*"Rosa, sich beruhigen,"* said Johann, taking her small hand. "Speak in English. Emilia doesn't speak German."

"You don't?" Rosa looked shocked. "I can speak Italian, French and German."

"That's amazing." Emilia smiled. "I can only speak Brummy English."

"Brummy?" she repeated confused. "What's that?"

Emilia laughed. Johann laughed too. "Now, enough of languages. Who wants to get some pizza?"

Stefan scowled.

"Come on, Stefan. You can have anything you want."

The boy got back into the car and slammed the door.

Emilia's heart ached for him. She understood why he was angry. Of course he viewed her as a usurper.

"Get into the car, Rosa," said Johann. He turned to Emilia. "Would you like to join us?"

She felt her head spin. "Of course. Let me get my coat."

# CHAPTER FOUR

In the end, custody was settled out of court and an agreement was made. Due to Cassandra's hectic touring schedule, Johann kept the children during term-time. Holidays and Christmas would be spent in Florence with their mother. She had moved there permanently as she disliked the English weather. Johann kept on the nanny, Gertrude, to run the family home in Hertfordshire. Gertrude had arrived in England ten years before. Although strict, she was devoted to the Weber children. She wasn't paid to judge, but she wished both parents would put their children first. Cassandra got all the bad press as she lived in a different country entirely, but Gertrude felt that Johann was equally to blame. He spent weeks in London, working on a score. He travelled the world and even when he did come home to Hertfordshire, he rarely spent time with the children.

Of the two, Rosa was her pet. When Cassandra had left for a tour of Australia when Rosa was six months old, it was Gertrude who had stepped in. She believed in hard work and discipline, and refused to spoil Rosa in any way. However it was impossible to resist the charms of the beautiful, doe eyed child, and soon she was crooning German lullabies to the bundle in her arms.

Johann started working on a big score for a new film and was consumed with his music. When he was busy like that, everything and everyone was pushed to one side. Emilia, left on her own in the big house most days, started to spend more time with the children. Johann was quite clear that he needed space to work. Locked away in his studio, he barely stopped to eat.

Stefan was initially sullen and cold. Then, one day, she asked if he would show her how to play his PlayStation. He spent hours on it and she was eager to learn.

Reluctantly, he handed her the controls and within an hour they were laughing uproariously as she ranked last in everything.

"Maybe I should give up," she said, throwing her hands up in the air.

"I was the same when I started,' he said kindly. "Practice makes perfect."

Rosa was a different story. She took to Emilia straight away. Naturally musical, she was curious when Emilia played any instrument, and asked if she could teach her.

"I hate my music teacher at school," she explained. "Can you be my teacher?"

Emilia let her try all the instruments in the room. Rosa soaked up everything she said, effortlessly emulating her.

"You could be very good," said Emilia. "You need to practise."

"Practising is boring," said Rosa haughtily. "Who cares about scales? I want to learn Girls Aloud songs."

It was on Johann's cello that the little girl really shone. The instrument was too large for her small arms but she made the best of it.

"I love this sound!" she exclaimed, moving the bow up and down.

Emilia smiled. "You remind me of my best friend, Alfie. He plays the cello."

"Will he teach me? I hate my..."

"Music teacher. I know."

Rosa smiled, showing a large gap where her front tooth fell out. Emilia gazed at her fondly.

"You're such a pretty little thing," she said.

"Oh, I know." Rosa propped the cello against the wall. "*Bella piccolina.* That's what Mamma calls me."

"You look like her."

"Why wouldn't I?" Rosa gave Emilia a funny look. "She's my mother, silly." She ran over the Emilia and hugged her spontaneously around the waist. "Let's go get some ice cream in the village."

"Again? We got some yesterday!"

"Yes. I want to try the caramel one today."

"It's no wonder that you're losing all your teeth."

Cassandra decided to visit, unannounced, six months later. She pretended that she wanted to attend Rosa's Christmas music recital but, in fact, she wanted to see this Emilia who had replaced her. She arrived on a cold December day, top to toe in fur, with a bag full of gifts.

Rosa was just back from a ride on her pony, Pegasus, when the Mercedes pulled up and her mother emerged.

"Rosa, *bella,*" she crooned, smothering her daughter in kisses and expensive French perfume. "Your mamma is here to see your concert."

"You are?" Rosa looked shocked.

Emilia, who was helping Stefan to clean the stables, appeared in dirty clothes and muddy wellington boots, her face red from exertion.

"You must be Emilia," said Cassandra with a smug smile.

"Hello." Emilia cursed silently.

"Mamma!' Stefan dropped his yard brush and ran to his mother. "I can't believe it. I thought I wouldn't see you for another few weeks!" He looked genuinely thrilled.

Johann appeared around the corner of the house and stopped dead.

"Cassandra!"

"Johann." She flicked her long dark hair.

"Why are you here? The children are due to fly out on the 20th."

"Well, I wanted to see my Rosa play her cello."

"That'd be a first." Johann's eyes were cold.

"Now, now. Don't be like that." She laughed. "I presume I can stay here?"

Emilia pulled herself together. "Of course."

"*Grazie.*" Cassandra bowed her head. "You are too kind." She turned to Rosa. "Now, *carina.* Tell me all about school." She took her daughter's hand in hers and they walked towards the house.

Just as they reached the front steps, Rosa wrenched her arm away.

"Why are you here?" she demanded.

Cassandra's eyes widened. "What do you mean?"

"Why did you come here? We were going to see you soon anyway."

"To hear you play."

"That's not true. You've never bothered before."

"Rosa, *bella*..."

"Don't call me *bella.* Did you ask me about school? Do you know that I won a singing competition last week or that I passed my swimming grade?"

"Rosa! Stop this."

"No. I won't. Emilia was there. Emilia came to my concert and helped me practise for my recital tonight. You're never here. You don't care."

Cassandra looked thunderstruck as Rosa rushed into the house. Johann walked up to her, his eyes flashing.

"I think that's your cue to leave, Cass. I emailed their flight details. Make sure someone picks them up on time."

Cassandra's large eyes filled with tears. "Don't say that."

Emilia pulled at Johann's shirt. "Johann! That's a terrible thing to say."

"It's not, Emmy. She's a disgrace. She abandoned us years ago. My children have had a hard time, growing up without a mother. Now, she swans in here, expecting to be welcomed with open arms..."

Cassandra gasped. "I'm trying to be a good mother!"

"We're fine without you."

Cassandra spotted a tear-stained Rosa looking out the bay window. "Rosa!" she called. "Come to your mamma!"

Rosa stared at her and then turned away.

"It's you! You have turned her against me." Cassandra turned on Johann furiously. "You have poisoned her!" She started to curse in Italian.

"I did nothing of the sort."

"You're not a great father. You're selfish and weak." She stamped her foot. "I cannot understand why I'm being blamed."

"I'm a damn sight better than you."

Cassandra laughed sardonically. "Don't be ridiculous. You've slept with every whore in Europe."

"Stop it!" Stefan put his hands over his ears. "Stop fighting."

"Leave, Cassandra." Johann looked at her coldly. "The children will spend the holidays with you. That was the agreement."

Emilia put her arm around Stefan's shaking shoulders.

"You cannot stop me from seeing my children," Cassandra spat.

"Leave." Johann turned his back on them all and went into the house.

Later that night, after a bottle of Amarone, Emilia asked Johann about Cassandra.

"I met her in the early eighties," he began, swirling his wine around his glass. "She was playing Aida in Covent Garden. She had this dark beauty and this thrilling voice. I was entranced."

Emilia tried not to feel jealous.

"She's Italian, as you know. I'm of German descent. We were opposites from the beginning. She was so tactile and passionate. I was more reserved." He shook his head ruefully. "The fights we'd have. She'd throw things at my head. Then we'd make up and…" He smiled.

Emilia wished she hadn't asked.

"Our marriage started well. She retired from the stage and we bought this place almost straight away. She liked the big house and the grand furniture. She enjoyed giving large dinner parties and entertaining her guests with arias from famous operas."

Emilia looked around the grand room. She could see a younger Cassandra standing by the marble fireplace, singing her heart out to mesmerised guests.

"Stefan came along, and then Rosa. I was working a lot. She grew bored." His face darkened.

"Bored? How could a full-time mother be bored?"

"The pull of the limelight became too much. London called and soon she was back at rehearsals, playing Mimi one night and Violetta the next."

"So what happened the children?"

"We hired Gertrude. She was strict from the start. I liked that as I had a similar nanny when I was a boy." He smiled. "She's German – it's all about discipline and hard work."

"Stefan and Rosa are devoted to her, despite her insistence on eating vegetables."

"I'm not surprised." He placed his glass on the table. "It was Gertrude who taught them to cycle and tie their shoelaces. She was there on their first day of school. She nurses them when they're sick. Cassandra missed a lot."

"It must have been hard for them. Not having a mother around."

"Rosa coped better than Stefan. He had a picture of Cass by his bed. Oh, when she deigned to come home, it was like Christmas. Chocolates from Vienna, dolls from Prague, lace from Venice. She would concentrate wholly on them, reading them bedtime stories and taking them for fish and chips or to the cinema."

Emilia said nothing.

"Then she'd leave and Gertrude would have to pick up the pieces." He looked up. "That's why I was so hard on her today. She's so selfish. Turning up without warning. Upsetting them." He sighed. "I must admit I haven't been the best father in the world. She was right about that. I can't blame her totally."

"You are," said Emilia loyally, taking his hand. "Don't beat yourself up. You're here now." She blushed. "I think you're amazing."

His gaze met hers. "You really do, don't you." It was a statement rather than a question.

She looked away first.

"Now, I must go and work on the final movement of my score. Time is ticking by."

"Oh, I thought we'd go to bed." She sat back in dismay.

"My little Emmy, someday you'll understand the feeling, the urge to create. It takes over one's life. I will not rest until I crack it."

# CHAPTER FIVE

When Johann's submission was rejected and binned, Emilia was on hand to support him. The invited audience, who watched a pre-screening of the film with his score, didn't like it, and the overall consensus was that it had to be replaced. Johann took it very badly and Emilia found it almost impossible to cheer him up.

He spent more and more time in London, working on a mini-series for the BBC. She offered to help, but he refused. He didn't like to be crowded. Plus, Rosa needed someone to take her to the dentist and Stefan had an important rugby match coming up.

Then she heard stories of another woman. A young Japanese viola player who had joined the London Symphony Orchestra was seen leaving his London flat. She confronted him and he denied it. A huge row followed where she demanded that they spend more time together. He suggested that Emilia move to Los Angeles and work on film scores.

"You're locked away in the country. You haven't produced anything in months. It's time you started making a name for yourself."

"What about Stefan and Rosa?" She felt the ground give away beneath her. "They need me. I can't just leave."

"They're off to Florence for the summer. You know that. It's time you got back in the game." He scribbled down some numbers on a piece of paper. "This is the number of my great friend, Raphael Baptiste. He's trying to make it as a director. Our families have been friends for generations."

"Raphael who?"

"He's Rosa's godfather. Make friends with him. He's around your age and will be very successful, I believe."

"What are you saying?" she whispered.

"I'm saying that you need to work. You need to use your talent. You're wasting away here, Emilia. Get out and make a name for yourself." He walked out of the room.

Shocked, she couldn't argue. He was right. She was almost thirty and she had forsaken her career to play Mary Poppins to his abandoned kids. Alfie was emailing her constantly about jobs and opportunities but she had ignored them. She looked at the number Johann had written down. The country code was 0033.

*France.*

She put it in her pocket. Numbly she went upstairs and sat on the bed. Johann's bed. It no longer felt like hers. Bursting into tears, she fell on the pillow.

Johann made a few calls and accompanied her out to LA. They stayed with another composer called Philip Krantz, sharing a bed in his mansion in the Hollywood Hills. Even though Johann slept by her side, she could feel him slipping away. Together they attended lots of parties and he introduced her to lots of people. She met directors, producers, actors and musicians. Everyone was friendly and welcoming and soon she was freelancing as an orchestrator. This took up a lot of time and they saw less and less of one another.

Then, one Tuesday morning, Johann broke it off with her over brunch.

Two days later he flew back to London, leaving her alone. Philip Krantz kindly offered to let her stay on until she found an apartment. After a week, she sourced a small one bedroomed condo in Pasadena. The tiny kitchen and living area felt like a cage. The bed was uncomfortable and she yearned for some proper English tea. Her mother used a overseas telephone card to call her up and she lived for those conversations. Her familiar accent calmed her and she kept up to date with what the neighbours were up to and how she got lovely pears at the Bullring. After a long day at the studio, she would come home to an empty flat and obsess over where Johann was and what he was doing. She had given so much of herself to him, she felt like she didn't know who she was anymore.

After her break up with Johann, she went crazy, trying to fill the void with meaningless affairs and substance abuse. By day, she was an orchestrator and by night, she was a party animal. Hollywood was the perfect place to forget. Night after night of cocktails, cocaine to lift you up and then weed to calm you down, followed by skinny dipping in pools by moonlight. She kept pushing it and pushing it until Johann himself called her up and asked to meet. He was in town for a meeting with MGM and had heard of her debauchery. She steeled herself not to fall for his charms but, within two hours, they were back in bed. Nestled in his arms, she never felt happier. Then he told her that he was moving to Prague for a year to work on his new score.

Sitting up straight, she felt like someone had punched her in the gut. He would never be hers. He would never commit solely to one person.

Pulling the sheet up around her breasts, she asked him to leave. Heartbroken, she moved back to London.

She threw herself into her work, becoming a full-time orchestrator for film studios. A few flings with various directors and producers followed, but no one ever came close to replacing Johann in her heart. Banishing him from her mind, she focused on becoming the best female composer of her generation. In the early noughties, she wrote the score for a film called *Mary,* a spooky gothic tale chronicling the period when Mary Shelley wrote her famous novel *Frankenstein.* Starring an up and coming actress called Mia Sutherland, it was a huge success, earning them both numerous awards. Emilia Thomas became a leading female powerhouse in the world of film, writing scores for successful movies.

Then the French director Raphael Baptiste burst onto the film scene when he wrote and directed a film based on Cocteau's *Orphée.* Just as Johann had predicted, Raphael became an overnight success. Young, gorgeous and brooding, he was like a French Jim Morrison. His lead actor and friend, the Oscar winning actor Bertie Wells, introduced Emilia to Raphael at one of his famous parties and they hit it off immediately. After a brief affair that fizzled out almost as quickly as it had begun, she composed the score for his next film. It went on to win awards and soon their union became synonymous with success. He was Hitchcock to her Hermann. She loved working with Raphael. Despite his reputation as an arrogant tyrant on set, she knew that he was a genius. She also knew that whatever they worked on would be top class. In the years that followed, her career went from strength to strength.

Sometimes she found it hard not to regret decisions she had made, but then she looked at her beautiful home and her illustrious career, and chided herself for being so selfish. Her biggest regret was losing Johann, but then she realised that he was never hers to lose. She contented herself with growing vegetables in a glasshouse and feeding the ducks on a Sunday at the village green. She played violin at Alfie's wedding to Miranda, and was godmother to his twins, Ava and Arabella. The slow pace of life suited her. She had had enough drama to last a lifetime.

***

Two days later, Emilia's phone rang. She was just watering her favourite yucca plant when she saw the French director, Raphael Baptiste's, name flashing on the screen. She guessed he was calling about his latest film, *Josephine.* She had composed the score for this biopic on the life of the Empress Josephine Bonaparte, but its release had been delayed due to the pandemic.

"Hi, Raphael. How are you?" She plucked a dead leaf off the stem.

"Not good. Not good."

She dropped the leaf. "What's wrong?"

"*Putain!* They've delayed *Josephine* again! Until September. Can you believe it?"

"Well, we are just out of a global pandemic. I can see the logic."

"I feel it will never be on screen."

"Why don't you release it online? Let people stream it? Everyone is doing that."

"My film? *Online?*"

She closed her eyes and waited.

"This masterpiece will not be seen on the screen of an iPhone or a laptop! I'll forget you said that."

She said nothing. Raphael was notoriously arrogant and dramatic. That's why they didn't mesh well as a romantic couple. She was quiet by nature and disliked scenes. She knew that underneath his haughtiness, he was kind and loyal. She also knew that he was a workaholic and that quarantine had not suited him.

"How's Isabelle?" she asked, referring to his wife.

"She's well."

"And the baby? Anouk?"

"She's walking."

"That's nice. You must send me a picture."

"Yes, yes." He sounded tired. "Tell me this film will première. I'm losing hope, Emmy."

"It will première. Now, use this time to write something new. I'm almost finished Carey's film so I'll be idle. Give me something to work on."

"I have a great script but it's unfinished." He groaned. "It's impossible to work with Anouk. She cries so much."

"She's a baby, Raph. That's what they do."

"And I love my wife – I do. But no marriage can last without a break from one another."

Emilia laughed. "What's the new script about?"

"Yeats and Maud Gonne."

"Wow. That's interesting."

"It has taken over two years of research of cultural and political history. If I could just finish it, I would pitch it."

"Finish it, pitch it and call me. Bye, Raph." She hung up the phone and tipped the last drop of water into the plant pot. Her leaves looked quite droopy and she winced. What was it about house plants? She inevitably killed them.

She placed the empty jug on the tiled floor.

After dinner, she ambled into her sitting room and picked up the framed picture of Raphael and her at the BAFTAs seven years before. He looked handsome in his tuxedo, with his arm slung loosely around her shoulder. His collar length dark hair fell over one eye and he looked his usual haughty self.

Raphael had been through a lot over the years. After his initial success, troubles had followed– his much-publicised battle with addiction and his subsequent fall from grace in Hollywood. Years of self-doubt. Depression and isolation.

Then he'd turned his life around. His glorious comeback and his recent marriage to the supermodel, Isabelle Flynn. His new daughter, Anouk. Worldwide success with his films. He was the ultimate comeback story. The world was at his feet.

Then the story broke of Raphael's love child. A child he never knew existed until a tabloid newspaper printed the scandalous scoop. The result of a one-night stand when he was a student, the baby had been adopted by a childless couple and had grown up in England. What really added to the story was the fact that this child was Caspian Cole, the lead singer of a popular band called Doctor Eckleburg. Tall, arrogant and remarkably similar in looks to his famous biological father, there was no doubt that the story was true. Psychologists mused over the likelihood of both men seeking and finding fame, unaware of their connection. It brought up the Nature/Nurture debate once more, some believing that it proved beyond doubt that nature laid down the blueprint for personality development.

Emilia replaced the photo on its shelf and sighed. One thing she was learning as she grew older was that life could throw anything at you at any given moment. Just when you thought you had it all figured out.

# CHAPTER SIX

Over in London, Caspian Cole was having a bad day. The pandemic had stopped the arts in its tracks. Concerts had been cancelled, tours postponed. Doctor Eckleburg had been in the middle of an American tour when coronavirus had struck. Now there was a backlog of bands, dates and venues, all gloriously colliding in the biggest traffic jam the music world had ever seen. His manager, Jax Mastrano, had called four times that morning, full of plans for future arena gigs, listing out venues all over America. Caspian had put a stop to it right away. He was in the middle of a new album. It was unthinkable to go on tour now. He and Jax had argued heatedly and in the end, he'd hung up. It was all about money to people like Jax. Never about the art.

Caspian closed the lid of his piano with a bang. On one hand, he welcomed the return of live music. He was sick of online events, a blend of live and pre-taped moments. Over the course of the pandemic, he and the rest of the band had pre-recorded various performances for the Grammys and the Brits, and it was like singing into a vacuum: he missed the screams of the audience as they stamped their feet in time to the music. He had felt caged and yearned for the adrenaline, the lights, the roar of the crowd. Playing music virtually was not the same thing.

On the other hand, he had no intention of playing gigs with an unfinished album. He had no interest in playing his old music on stage, not when his head was filled with new melodies. He had penned eight songs to date about his birth mother whom he'd never met. All he had were photographs, a few personal belongings and a fuzzy VHS video of her singing at a concert. Haunted by the fact that she lost her life so young, and desperate to connect with her, he threw himself into writing music for the woman who had given him life, but who had also given him up. Was he angry about that? Not at all. Mary's background had been humble, he understood that she had put him up for adoption to give him the life she could not provide.

He shivered when he thought of her untimely death, killed instantly when a car struck a wall at speed. How would the public react to this album when it was finally released? Maybe his fans wouldn't get it. Maybe they'd scorn at his attempt to immortalise his mother. That gut-wrenching fear was intrinsic to his career, but it never got easier.

Caspian stood up and stretched. Blonde and tall, he was remarkably similar in looks to his recently revealed biological father, Raphael Baptiste. Fans adored him as not only was he handsome, he was an incredible musician. His songs were intelligent, soulful and brilliantly written. Even though the other members contributed the odd song, it was Caspian who wrote the most. According to Rolling Stone magazine, Doctor Eckleburg was ranked as one of the most influential bands in the world. The other three band members - Ethan Hackett, the lead guitarist, Alex Ryder, the bassist and Fionn O'Connor, the drummer - all lived relatively normal lives, despite Dr. Eckleburg's phenomenal success.

He had taken to getting up early so as to have some time alone to write music. His famous fiancée, Madison Ryan, was one of the biggest selling female artists of all time and tended to take over their apartment with her stylists, publicists and personal trainers. He glanced at the framed cover of Rolling Stone on the wall. Madison's face stared back at him, her blonde hair falling over her beautiful face. Underneath was written:

***Madison Ryan: Ireland's Pop Princess and Global Superstar.***

Caspian rolled his eyes.

*She was all that.*

It was in a small club in Soho, that Madison had laid eyes on Caspian for the first time and knew she had to have him. Even though Doctor Eckleburg were undiscovered, Caspian carried himself like a star. His arrogance and stage presence had attracted Madison immediately.

What followed was a passionate affair. Together they became paparazzi gold, being followed constantly and written about in celebrity magazines. Critics argued that Doctor Eckleburg owed their rapid success to Madison. Her high profile had instantaneously catapulted them onto the world stage. Caspian vehemently denied this. It was their art, their music, that did that. However, the other members of the band privately agreed. They'd been nobodies with about a thousand followers on Instagram before Caspian and Madison got together. Now they had close to ten million. Whether true or not, her fame definitely helped them along and Doctor Eckleburg became well-known across the world. Their second album went platinum in days and they had two Brit awards and a Grammy. When Caspian walked to the local shop for some milk, he was followed. He was asked for selfies constantly. His face was perpetually splashed across TikTok. He was everywhere.

In late 2019, Madison was selected to sing the theme tune of Raphael Baptiste's new film, *Josephine.* She met the famous director and couldn't pinpoint why he seemed familiar. His gestures, his bone structure, his manner. Then came the bombshell – Caspian was Raphael's lovechild. Raised with love by his adoptive parents George and Prudence Cole, Caspian had been completely unaware of his famous heritage. His biological mother was dead, killed in a car crash when he was a baby. Madison stood by him through the adoption scandal and they got engaged. Madison's kindness and support surprised Caspian during the tabloid storm when his birth story was revealed. The giant diamond on her finger was a symbol of their commitment to one another and she flashed it at every opportunity.

However, thrown together for months during lockdown put pressure on their relationship. Caspian, who took song-writing very seriously, needed space to create. He disliked being interrupted when he was in the zone and could stay up until dawn if the mood was right. Head bent in concentration, he'd play the notes over and over again, adjusting the key, adding in some sharps and flats, testing it out. Then Madison would turn on a pumping playlist at full blast to accompany her online workout with her personal trainer, Boris.

"Why can't you use your airpods?" shouted Caspian in frustration.

"Why don't you go to your bloody studio?" she shouted. "It's sitting there, empty, while you're here driving me mad."

Doctor Eckleburg had purchased a disused warehouse in North London and converted it into a makeshift studio. They named it The Forge as it was historically a foundry where blacksmiths worked. The large atrium had wooden floors and a high ceiling, with an upright piano, a drum kit and amps. It was where the band went to practise new songs or to cooperatively write some music before Covid shut everything down. Caspian only frequented this place to rehearse with the others. He never had the space to write when he was there as it was noisy and chaotic. Plus, his Steinway was at home as he needed it by his side at all times in case inspiration struck.

"My band is scattered across Europe, in case you haven't noticed. My piano is here. Why would I go halfway across London during a global pandemic to write music when I should be able to do so in my own home?"

Madison stalked off and slammed the bedroom door.

Ross Curtis, Madison's manager, organised a virtual appearance on *The Jimmy Kimmel Show* which aired from the comfort of her own sitting room. At one point, Caspian brought her a glass of juice, waved to the camera and then disappeared again. Twitter nearly broke down from the deluge of tweets. People were obsessed with the golden couple of the music world.

No one knew that Caspian's casual interruption had been planned. Bethany, Madison's publicist, had orchestrated the whole thing. Madison looked relaxed in her Juicy Couture tracksuit and Ugg boots. However, her chill out look had taken two hours to create. Mona, her stylist, had artfully painted her eyes and mussed up her hair so as to look laid-back and unconcerned.

Then, they had joined other famous musicians for the One World: Together concert. Along with Elton John, The Rolling Stones and Taylor Swift, Caspian played piano while Madison sang, giving fans a glimpse of their apartment. It went viral in minutes. Then, the other members of Doctor Eckleburg appeared, all playing from their sitting rooms. The band played their big hit, *Charisma*, and Madison joined in, harmonising with Caspian, her arm slung around his shoulders.

To the outside world, they had it all. Fans couldn't get enough of this gorgeous young couple. They didn't see the reality: the fights, the competition, the clash of egos that erupted time and time again. Madison liked to be the centre of the universe and hated anyone stealing her limelight. Caspian, who had inherited Raphael's haughty arrogance, felt that he was the epicentre of his world also. What followed were arguments of cataclysmic proportions.

Caspian switched on the coffee machine and glanced at the clock. It was close to half six. Madison would be up soon, ready for her morning workout. She was like clockwork: an invigorating session with her personal trainer, Boris, fresh fruit for breakfast and some voice training exercises. When they first met, they had separate apartments and spent the majority of their time on the road. She could be in Berlin while he was in Tokyo. When they did meet, it was only for a weekend or a week in Barbados.

Now, she was busy again. Ross Curtis, her manager, had lined up a big summer schedule of concerts and television appearances. A change of image was in the pipeline and a new style of music was being explored. She was going home to Dublin later that day to see her parents. She had pleaded with Caspian to come with her, but he'd declined. The thought of an empty apartment was too tempting: peace and quiet where he could work uninterrupted.

He sipped his coffee and ambled over to the window. The dawn was beginning to break over the London skyline.

*"Caspian?"* came a familiar voice from the bedroom.

*"Yeah?"*

The door burst open and Madison walked in, dressed in one of his t-shirts and fluffy socks. Her long blonde hair was tousled.

"I just got a text from Ross."

"Oh?"

"He wants us to appear on *The Graham Norton Show* together." She poured a glass of water.

"Again?" He groaned. "We were on it recently."

"Months ago!" She shook her head.

"And talk about what exactly? There's nothing going on."

She banged the glass on the kitchen counter. "There will be loads going on. My new album, my world tour after it's released. It would be the perfect time to sing *Possess Me* before the release of *Josephine*."

"If it's ever actually released," he added.

"Don't be so negative. Raphael called last night and said it will be September."

"I'll believe it when I see it."

"It's not his fault Covid has delayed everything!" She glared at him. "You could talk about the new album you're working on."

"It's too soon to talk about that." His face hardened. "It's not ready."

"We could always talk about our wedding." She waited for a reaction. "I mean, we've been engaged for ages and still no plans."

Caspian closed his eyes. "We're just coming out of a global pandemic, Mads. Come on."

"We could still chat about it," she said obstinately. "Our fans are chomping at the bit." She faced him. "*I'm* chomping at the bit. I can't wait to get a dress and start planning."

"Soon," he promised. "Just let the world settle down a bit first. There are more important things to think about right now."

Her face remained mutinous for a moment before breaking into a big smile. "I guess you're right." She walked towards him and wrapped her arms around his neck. "I've ten minutes before my Zoom call with Boris. Want to start my work out early? As you're not coming home to Dublin with me and all." She kissed his lips softly.

Caspian picked her up easily. "I can't go to Dublin, Mads. I'm trying to write music. You know that."

"I know." She kissed him softly. "You need some space."

"Exactly that." He kicked open the bedroom door.

*

A few hours later, Madison zipped up her Louis Vuitton holdall. "There! Finished." She frowned. "I think I might have packed too much."

Caspian, who was lying on their bed, looked up from the book he was reading about Lord Byron.

"You always pack too much," he said with a shrug.

She flopped on the bed. "I wish you were coming with me," she said petulantly. "We are engaged, you know."

"We talked about this, Mads. I need to write. I must go home and touch base with Mum; she's so insecure since the adoption thing. I want her to see that nothing has changed."

Madison bit her lip. "Fine." She traced her finger up and down his bare arm. "It's just it's been so long since we've all been together. You, me, Cliona and Fionn."

"We met during the summer."

"That's ages ago. When's the last time you actually saw Fionn face to face? He's your drummer, for God's sake."

"I'm not ready to perform…"

"I know, I know. But the world is getting back on track. You can't stay under the radar forever. You have that American tour to honour. Fans paid money for those tickets."

He leant down and kissed her nose. "I'll be ready soon."

Madison sighed. "Well, I'd better get going. My flight is in a couple of hours."

He put his book down and pulled her into his arms. "I love you, Maddy."

She inhaled his skin. "I know."

# CHAPTER SEVEN

Fionn O'Connor, the drummer of Doctor Eckleburg, still enjoyed relative anonymity and this suited him just fine. He could go to the supermarket without being mobbed or ride the tube without anyone noticing. The odd time a fan would ask for a selfie, but that was rare. Tall, with brown hair and blue eyes, Fionn had that unmistakable Irish charm that made him irresistible to the opposite sex. Born in Dublin to Aonghus and Constance O'Connor, a writer and a lifestyle guru respectively, Fionn's childhood had been slightly chaotic. Aonghus wrote books and Constance, a retired actress, wrote lifestyle blogs. Even though Aonghus was a successful author, they never seemed to have much money, spending it recklessly whenever they had any in their bank account. Constance loved going on foreign holidays, drinking fine wines and eating out in expensive restaurants.

"When God made us, he matched us," Constance would say. "We're hopeless with money. Just hopeless. We could have a thousand euros left to our name and we'd end up going on a minibreak to Paris and blowing the lot."

Constance seemed to live in a colourful silk robe, her brown curls pinned back with a coral comb, and yesterday's makeup giving her panda eyes.

"I'm a disgrace," she'd say laughing. "I should get dressed, but it's far nicer to prance around in comfort."

Their family home on the exclusive Sorrento Terrace, inherited by Constance, was Victorian and virtually impossible to heat properly. Fionn gave them money to replace the windows when he received his first royalty cheque.

"It's just so dull to spend one's money on windows," Constance complained.

It wasn't just the windows. The walls were damp and the roof leaked, and the boiler didn't work at all. When Doctor Eckleburg started to make real money, Fionn transferred thirty thousand euros to his mother's account to replace the roof. Instead, she bought a hot tub and booked a cruise around Japan for herself and Aonghus.

"Sorry, darling," she told a shocked Fionn when he saw that the roof was still in the same state. "It's just the hot water is a godsend for Daddy's arthritis and the cruise tickets were a steal."

Fionn's little sister, Cliona, who was barely a year younger than him, also lived in London. Small and quiet, she had straight brown hair and glasses. She and Fionn were extremely close. They took it in turns to go home for a weekend to check up on their wayward parents. Cliona, who was sensible, found that she had to monitor her parents and advise them. She spent her weekend running after them, trying to clean up the mess they left behind, organising the bills, and putting on loads of washing. She'd return to London, exhausted, and complain to Fionn how Constance let the cat walk all over the newly mopped floor.

Having studied film at college, Cliona was now a trainee filmmaker. Through Fionn, she met her long-term boyfriend, Alex Ryder, who was the bassist in Doctor Eckleburg. Inseparable, they shared an apartment in Chelsea. Cliona had been hired to direct the band's next music video so she attended some rehearsals to channel her vision. Fionn teased her about the blatant nepotism calling her a 'nepobaby', but she brushed it off. This was her big chance to make her mark and she wasn't going to mess it up.

"I'd say a proposal is imminent," Constance told Fionn on the phone. "They're made for one another. Alex is such a lovely boy. If only you'd find someone special, my love. I'd die happy then."

Fionn, refusing to be pressured, was an expert at deflecting his mother's advice about his love life. He was doing just fine and had no plans to settle down just yet.

When the pandemic swept the world, everything came to a standstill. All productions were halted and the band were encouraged to stay at home. Their manager, Jax Mastrano, sent a memo about being good role-models for their fans. Alex and Cliona stayed at their flat in London, quite happy to batten down the hatches. Ethan Hackett, the lead guitarist of Doctor Eckleburg, flew to Poland with his girlfriend, Stella, who hailed from Gdansk. Caspian Cole also stayed in London, writing music.

Fionn, who had just broken up with a Ukrainian model called Mariska, decided to go home to Dublin for lockdown. He boarded the plane, ordered a beer, and read The Irish Times from front to back. Caspian would never be able to do that. He was recognised everywhere he went.

Fionn's return rendered lockdown a glorious experience for Constance. She had never had her son at home for such a long period of time to fuss over and spoil. She made sumptuous dinners in his honour, getting deliveries of food from the various local businesses. Determined to feed him up, she pored over old recipe books and spent hours making sourdough from scratch. At night, they listened to music or watched old movies. Greymalkin and Paddock, the family cats, slept on Fionn's lap next to a roaring log fire as the moonlight illuminated Dalkey Bay.

Fionn found being back at home strange in the beginning. His old bedroom seemed to be stuck in a time warp. Old Nirvana posters still hung on the walls and the stack of records had an inch of dust on top. Every morning he'd don his runners and head out along the coast road for a run. The dark winter sky was often misty with rain, but he didn't care. There was nothing like the Irish sea air to fill your lungs.

His old drum kit still stood in the attic room at the top of the house. Every afternoon, he'd set up a Zoom call and connect with the rest of the band to practise. The resulting music would be ever so slightly out of sync, mainly due to the O'Connor's bad Wi-Fi connection, and this drove Caspian crazy.

"How can we work like this?" he yelled, slamming the lid of his piano shut.

Despite the inconvenience, Doctor Eckleburg managed to write two new songs. An upbeat track written by Ethan, who wanted to experiment with livelier rhythms, and a ballad by Caspian, all about having lost his identity.

"I understand that Caspian needs to come to terms with his past," Fionn told Constance over a plate of homemade ravioli, "but my God, it's depressing. I'm not sure our fans will go for it."

"He'll come around, my love," she consoled him. "It's his way of expressing his grief. It's cathartic."

"Fair enough, but there are four people in this band." Fionn grated some parmesan over his pasta. "An album of soulful songs about tragedy and loss is not the direction we want to take."

"It's just a phase." Constance squeezed his hand. "Mark my words, by this time next year, he'll be back to normal."

Fionn's birthday fell on the 23rd March and Constance relished the occasion, decorating the sitting room with bunting and baking an enormous chocolate cake with Maltesers on top. Cliona flew home from London for the party.

"Hey, little sis," said Fionn, pulling her into a bearhug. "How's my little Steven Spielberg?"

"Ha, ha." She made a face. "I'm not quite on that level yet but I'm getting there."

"How was the shoot last month?" asked Constance, referring to the crime drama that Cliona had worked on. "I followed that director on Instagram and he posted some great photos."

"Oh, fine. A few setbacks with the actors getting Covid, but all in all, it went smoothly." Cliona punched Fionn playfully in the arm. "How's life as a gentleman, Fionn? When was the last time you did an honest day's work? 2020?"

He punched her back gently. "Hey, I'm ready to get back on stage. Even back in the studio. It's Caspian who won't commit. He's obsessed with the new album he's working on."

"Oh, yeah. The one about his birth mother." Cliona sighed. "He must be traumatised."

"Well, traumatised or not, he's losing us lots of revenue. Jax is on the verge of a breakdown."

"Why don't you come back to London?"

"I'm between apartments." Fionn leant in and whispered, "It's also because of Mum. She loves having me around."

"She'll be okay." Cliona rolled her eyes. "You're no youngster anymore, Fionn. You'd want to think about settling down."

"Whoa! Stop that right now." He held up his hands. "I'm enjoying my freedom."

# CHAPTER EIGHT

Madison Ryan flew home to Dublin for the week with her ex-Navy Seal bodyguard, Todd, by her side. A private Bentley was waiting at the airport. Wearing huge glasses and a beanie hat hiding her famous blonde hair, she jumped into the back of the car, concealed behind the tinted windows. The car sped down the M50 towards the south of the city.

Madison had grown up on Vico Road, an exclusive part of Dublin by the sea. Her house was an impressive stone building that stood behind huge walls which afforded it complete privacy. It had a stunning sea view, a panoramic vista of the Dalkey Bay. Her mother, Louise, had inherited the property and it had been in her maternal family for generations.

Louise was doing yoga online when Madison walked into the sitting room.

"Hiya, Mum." She waved.

Louise Ryan was in her early sixties but worked hard on looking much younger. Her coiffured hair was dyed brown, her body looked supple and lean, and her teeth were pearly white.

"Hello, darling," she said, arching her back. "Daddy's in the den. Go and say hello."

Madison's father, Kevin Ryan, was a renowned indie film maker who made it big in the nineties with his film on the Famine. During the pandemic, Kevin was forced to work from his study as film sets had been closed down and foreign travel was not advised. Madison couldn't remember the last time he'd spent longer than a week there.

"Hi, Dad." She waved at Kevin who was watching CNN.

"Hi, Maddy." He motioned for her to take a seat. "Did you watch the coverage of the French presidential election?"

"Not really." She yawned. Politics didn't interest her. In fact, nothing really interested her unless it was about Madison Ryan.

"Is Caspian with you?" Kevin pressed 'pause' on the TV.

Her face hardened. "No. Did Mum not tell you?"

"No, she didn't." He eyed her speculatively.

"He's writing and he also wants to spend time with Prue and George."

"Well, that's understandable."

"Hmmm."

"Mother has booked us into The Merrion for dinner."

Madison sighed. They never dined at home. Never once did Louise roast a chicken on a Sunday. They always went out to posh restaurants and dined on fancy food she could barely pronounce. She thought of her best friend Cliona's house which was the opposite. Her parents always cooked everything from scratch. The house was warm and cluttered, and no one cared when beef stew was overcooked and the meat was dry.

When Madison was younger, she used to call to Cliona's house most days. She liked the mess and the bustle. She would often walk into the sitting room to find the contents of last night's cheeseboard congealing on the grand piano, surrounded by empty wine glasses.

Madison sighed and forced a smile. Her house has never been like that and it never would be.

"The Merrion sounds great. Thanks, Dad."

***

The next day, Madison returned from a 10km run with Todd by her side. Her father was reading *The Irish Times* in the conservatory, sipping an espresso.

"Much activity on the road?" he asked, without looking up.

"Very little, thank God. I hate when people bother me on a run."

Kevin raised an eyebrow. "I would've thought you'd be left alone around here. All your neighbours have known you since you were a child."

"Oh, you'd get the odd fan asking for a selfie." She stretched her leg outwards and winced. "I think I've sprained my calf." She looked up at her bodyguard. "Remember, Todd? When I nearly fell in that pothole?"

"I do indeed, ma'am," said Todd in his American twang.

Louise appeared with a cup of tea. "Morning, sweetheart," she said to Madison. "What are your plans for the day?"

"I have an online workout with Boris in a minute. Then a Zoom meeting with my publicist and my daily FaceTime with Caspian."

"How is he?"

"Working incessantly." She bent down and touched her toes. "He's writing songs about his birth mother. I'm not sure the rest of the band will go for it."

"Speaking of the rest of the band, I saw Fionn O' Connor walking on the beach yesterday," said Louise. "He came home to quarantine and then just stayed on."

Madison looked disdainful. "Of course he did. Waited on hand and foot by his adoring mother."

"Fionn's a lovely boy," reflected Louise. "Always so polite."

"To you, maybe." Madison scowled. "He's such a pain, always teasing me." She rubbed her neck. "I'm calling over there later for dinner."

"To see Fionn?" said Kevin innocently.

"Ha, ha." She made a face. "No, to see my best friend, Cliona, who unfortunately for me is related to Fionn."

"That'll be nice." Louise smiled. "The old gang back together."

"Well, I'm not sure about the old gang. Cliona's the only member of *my* gang. Fionn is just her annoying older brother."

Louise looked wistful. "You know, I always thought you and he would end up together. You were so close as children."

"Fionn?" Madison laughed loudly. "Are you for real? He drives me mad! All he does is make a fool of me. Even now."

"It's nice that he hasn't changed then," said Kevin. "People often act differently around you when you're famous."

"Fionn's famous too. He's the drummer of one of the biggest bands on the planet."

"Biggest bands?" Kevin snorted. "Doctor Eckleburg have a long way to go before they're in the same league as The Stones or Led Zeppelin."

"Oh, what do you know. Your musical taste is stuck in the seventies." Madison flicked her blonde hair. "I'm off for my workout."

"Enjoy, darling." Louise waved from the wicker chair as Kevin buried his nose in the newspaper.

***

Later that evening, Todd knocked on the old oak door of the O'Connor's house. The sound reverberated through the hallway. Madison stood behind him, her face concealed with a hood. Constance opened the door and held out her arms.

"Maddy, darling! Come in!"

Todd scanned the hallway and the sitting room. "It's okay to enter, ma'am."

Madison followed Constance down the hall, through the kitchen and out into the back garden. Aonghus was lighting the barbecue and six chairs were laid out around a circular table.

Cliona appeared with a bowl of salad. "Hey, Mads. Glad you could make it."

"Hi, Clio. Hi, Aonghus." Madison shivered. "It's not really barbecue weather, is it?"

"Constance wants to use our new garden furniture. We can move inside if it becomes unbearable," said Aonghus. "I'm sure Cliona has a spare jumper or something."

"I'm okay." Madison sat down. "So, any news?"

Cliona tossed the leaves with two giant forks. "Nothing really. You?"

Madison sighed. "Caspian is working constantly. He won't fly over because he wants to spend time with Prue and George. He thinks they're insecure. I mean, fine, whatever. They're feeling a bit left out now he knows the truth about Raphael, but what about me? I'm insecure too!"

Cliona let her rabbit on. The subject matter moved to her weight and hair, to Caspian's reluctance to set a date for the wedding, and then on to Mustique as a possible destination for her honeymoon. She nodded at the right times, dutifully letting her friend talk.

"Why didn't Alex come home with you?" asked Madison, referring to Cliona's boyfriend.

Cliona poured some wine. "He wanted to spend time with his parents." She looked up. "Like Caspian, I guess."

Fionn appeared, back from the local supermarket, two bags in his hands. He deposited them on the grass.

"Hello, Maddy. I heard you might be joining us." He grinned, his dark hair flopping over his eyes.

"Hi, Fionn." She barely looked at him and turned back to Cliona. "So, you can see why I'm depressed."

"What's wrong, Mads?" said Fionn with mock concern, opening a can of beer. "Did you break a nail? Did you put on two ounces?"

Madison threw him a look. "At least I look good, unlike other people."

"I'm a catch."

"Right."

Constance walked out the door holding two more bottles of wine. "Did you get the chicken wings, sweetheart?"

Fionn nodded. """The last pack."

"Wonderful. Are the coals ready to go, Aonghus?"

"Not quite."

"Great. We've time for an apéritif. Clio, run inside and bring out some glasses. I have some gorgeous crème de menthe."

They dined on steak, wings, salad and potatoes. The conversation was dominated by the pandemic and the effect it had on life in general.

"It's eerie," said Constance. "One hundred years ago, Spanish Flu ravaged the world. What followed was a decade of recklessness and partying: the Roaring Twenties. Those who survived the Great War and the pandemic, that 'lost generation', lived life to the max. There was huge inflation and massive social change." She sipped her wine. "Maybe history will repeat itself. I, for one, will be making up for lost time."

"Me too," said Madison. "I mean, my tour was cancelled."

"As was ours," said Fionn.

"Raphael's film was postponed," went on Madison dolefully.

"Oh yes, *Josephine,*" said Constance. "Any news on a release date? I'm dying to see it."

"September, apparently. My song will be everywhere for the next few months as we want it to climb the charts again."

"It was a lovely tune." Constance hummed *Possess Me* and turning around, she gestured at Todd to sit. "Please have some steak, Todd. There's plenty left over."

'No, thank you, ma'am." Todd crossed his massive arms and continued to stand sentinel by the kitchen door. "It's not protocol to eat with my employer."

"Oh for God's sake, that's nonsense," said Constance. "Sit down and have some food."

Todd glanced at Madison who nodded. "Eat. It's fine."

"Clio, fill a plate for Todd," said Constance, refilling her glass with some Bordeaux.

"Fionn is just as able," Cliona objected. "I've been running and racing all over the place."

"Poor Fionn walked to the shop earlier."

Cliona rolled her eyes and got up. She put some food on a plate and handed it to Todd.

"I'll eat this in the kitchen, ma'am," he said gruffly. "Thank you."

"If you want." Constance beamed at him. "A man of your size needs to keep up his strength."

Todd went into the kitchen and closed the door.

"Mads! You might get abducted while he's in the kitchen!" said Fionn looking alarmed.

"Shut up."

"Seriously, you're at risk! I think I saw a suspicious looking squirrel over there giving you the side eye."

"Can you just stop?" She glared at him. "I need Todd with me constantly. You're only a drummer. You don't understand what it's like to be followed and obsessed about."

"The main person obsessing about you is yourself," he said scornfully.

Later that night, as she snuggled under her duvet, Madison thought about her wedding. Oh, how she dreamed of that day. She could see her dress already. Kevin leading her up the aisle. Caspian looking handsome in his suit, his blonde hair slicked back. Cliona would be bridesmaid, of course. She wondered who Caspian would ask to be his best man.

*Fionn?*

She made a face.

*Hopefully not.*

She smiled as she envisioned the gazebo erected in her garden at home, the blue sea of the Dalkey Sound in the background. The champagne glasses in perfect rows on the white clothed tables. The waiting staff in uniform, handing out delectable canapés. Famous faces mingling with childhood friends.

*A select few of childhood friends.*

The speeches. Her father talking about what a blessing she was so late in their lives. Would Raphael speak? He'd definitely be more interesting than George Cole.

She drifted off to sleep, her mind filled with white dresses, lace veils and a seven-tiered cake decorated with white fondant treble clefs.

# CHAPTER NINE

Caspian spent the first few days without Madison working incessantly, writing the bare bones of two songs during her absence. Even though he'd never known his biological mother, he felt connected to her. He pored over an old videotape of her singing at a concert when she was a teenager, trying to get a sense of what she was like. With her blonde hair swinging in a ponytail and her pretty face, she looked so vibrant on the stage. It made the hairs stand up on his neck. How in one instant, a life could be extinguished. Without mercy.

The songs he'd written were poignant and heart-breaking, mostly slow in tempo, filled with rhetorical questions and regret. He knew it would be hard to get them over the line with the rest of the band as they were so intensely personal, but he was determined. He'd release a solo album if necessary. Picasso had had a blue period – he would have his also.

His mother, Prudence, called and asked him to come home on the Thursday night so as to make it a long weekend. She had a leg of lamb ready to roast for Easter Sunday. He apologised and said he'd be there on Friday evening as he couldn't leave his piano as he was in the zone. How could he leave his apartment now and watch soaps each evening on the television before being tucked up in his childhood bed?

The other band members were happily taking a break from music. He heard about Fionn the most as Madison saw him daily. The way Caspian saw it, she spent most of her time at the O'Connor's house. He didn't blame her as her family home was like a museum. When she rang, she'd tell him how Constance needed to get a grip, worshipping Fionn like a demi-god, and, how truth be told, Fionn was the most annoying guy on the planet. He also heard about Cliona and her boring dress sense. And, of course, Madison Ryan's daily routine, how she'd completed a 10K run that morning. The phone calls would inevitably end with her asking him to fly to Dublin and join her, but he couldn't face it. He needed space to write. He also couldn't let Prue down. He had promised he'd go home.

The weekend in his childhood home in Banbury came and went. His father, George, showed him the garden, pointing out the tulips he'd planted the December before. Prue made 'proper' dinners as she called them, piling Caspian's plate with roast potatoes and cauliflower cheese. A few fans waited outside the house for a glimpse of their idol, but when it started to rain, they gave up. Caspian had installed security cameras when Doctor Eckleburg had made the bigtime. Fans had frightened his parents, approaching George when he was taking out the bins and Prudence at the supermarket. Things were particularly bad when the adoption scandal hit the press. Journalists waited like predators for his poor parents to emerge so that they could grill them about his past.

Now, his childhood home was like Fort Knox.

His father drove him back to London in his Volvo. Prudence had given him a box of flapjacks and a loaf of brown bread to bring home. They barely spoke on the journey as Caspian's brain was full of melodies and ideas. George recognised this mood and stayed quiet, listening to BBC Radio 4 as they drove along the M40.

They pulled up outside the apartment building on Young Street.

"See you soon, son." He shook Caspian's hand. "Your mother loved having you."

Caspian leaned over and hugged him briefly. "Bye, Dad. I'll see you both soon."

Minutes later, he was sitting at his Steinway playing the song that had formed in his head the day before. It was like scratching an itch, such was the relief. Dawn was breaking over the horizon when he finally went to bed.

Madison arrived back to London a few days later. She showered Caspian with kisses and produced an enormous bottle of his favourite aftershave, a Toblerone and some black pudding. They went straight to bed and made love for the afternoon.

"I missed you," she murmured into his shoulder as they lay naked in their bed.

He nodded sleepily.

"I mean, if we were married, you'd have to come home with me."

He kissed her forehead and kept his eyes closed.

"We should start making plans. The world needs something to look forward to. I actually dreamt about it the other night."

Caspian kissed her hair. "We will."

Madison sat up, her blonde hair flying.

"We will? *We will?* What kind of answer is that? God, you're such a typical guy! Do you realise how much work goes into organising a wedding?"

"We're rich. We can hire people to do that."

"My wedding will be my vision. Not some stranger's."

Caspian sighed loudly. He couldn't focus. The world was still in turmoil. People were dying, economies were crashing. It simply wasn't the time.

Caspian's phone started to ring.

She nudged his shoulder. "Who is it?" she whispered.

"Fionn," mouthed Caspian. Madison made a face, got out of bed and walked away, slamming her bathroom door behind her.

"So, is the ball and chain back?" said Fionn cheerfully.

Caspian nodded. "Yep."

"Tell her I miss her already."

Caspian grinned. "I bet you do."

"I'm thinking of coming back to London soon," said Fionn. "I called the others and they're on board. We need to get back to work. We could rehearse at The Forge, get back in the game. Jax wants to book Abbey Road so we can record some new songs."

"I'm not quite ready to record anything."

"There's also the American tour we abandoned…"

"I'm not going on the road right now."

"Caspian, we've got to honour our fans. Otherwise, they'll have to be refunded and Jax won't agree to that."

"I don't care. It's unthinkable to leave my work and stand on multiple stages singing old music that doesn't excite me."

"That's our job, Casp."

"Not until we're ready," he said obstinately. "I've so much I want to show you. I have the bare bones of a new album."

"Yeah, Mads said you've been insufferable, working all day and night. Why don't you go to The Forge to write? It's lying there empty most of the time."

"I like my own piano. The one at The Forge is below standard. I like waking up at 3am and writing music. I can't be restricted by time and place. Creativity can strike suddenly."

"God, sorry I asked."

"I got a lot done when she was in Ireland."

"I can imagine."

"I'm glad she's back though. I missed her, as noisy as she is."

"Yeah, she's not that bad." Fionn laughed. "Although, she still can't take a joke. I told her that I won twenty pounds on a seahorse race and she believed me."

"She doesn't really focus on the outside world," said Caspian loyally.

"Yeah, just on herself. See you in a few weeks."

Later that morning, Caspian sat at his piano and groaned. Madison was even noisier than usual. The workouts, the chatter, the blaring TV as she picked at her cubed watermelon and bitched about Ariana Grande. Even though to the outside world Madison and Ariana were friends, Caspian knew she was intimidated by the pretty American. Now, Madison was doing star jumps to *Shake It Off.*

"Maddy!" he said in frustration. "Can you please turn down the iPod? I'm trying to work."

"Are you for real?" She put her hands on her hips. "You've been on that bloody piano all morning. Can you take a break? I live here too, you know."

Caspian got up, grabbed his coat and walked out the front door.

Working from home was too difficult. He should never have given up his own apartment when they got engaged. Maybe Fionn had a point. Maybe he should move his Steinway to The Forge. The band's road crew or roadies had been out of work since Covid as live performances had dwindled down to nothing. Yet they still hung out at The Forge sometimes as Jax had told them that a new tour was imminent. He imagined his precious instrument in the middle of the main room, with coffee cup rings and crumbs strewn over the lid, a beer can used as a lid prop.

He shuddered.

He couldn't work like that.

Fate mercifully intervened the next day. Raphael emailed him and asked him to visit.

Caspian debated what to say. His fingers hovered over the keyboard for a moment. Then he replied saying that he was trying to work on a new album which was behind schedule due to the full apartment. He thanked Raphael and said he'd definitely visit sometime soon.

Five minutes after he pressed 'send', his phone pinged in reply.

It was Raphael again, offering him a room in the big house of his estate in Amiens.

"This is where I get my inspiration," he wrote. "You should come and avail of it."

Caspian had been to the Baptiste family home once. It had been a fleeting visit, more of a 'tick the box' exercise than anything else. It was just after his half-sister Anouk's birth two years before. He and Madison has called with a present and had had lunch with Isabelle, Raphael's wife, and Raphael himself. The tiny baby had slept through the whole thing. They hadn't met since. Raphael's hectic schedule, and indeed Doctor Eckleburg's, made it almost impossible to meet up properly. Then, when the world locked down, travel was for essential reasons only.

Caspian thought of the gardens and the golden fields of wheat that stretched as far as the eye could see. He imagined himself seated at Louis Baptiste's Steinway, music flowing from his fingertips. Then he thought of Madison and the noise and he made his decision. He rang his manager.

"Jax?"

'Hey, Caspian. What's up?"

"I'm going to France."

"What? I wanted to talk to you about Detroit. I think we should stick to the original tour schedule and pick up where we left off."

"There will be no gigs until I'm ready."

"Look, Caspian. This hiatus is going on a bit, if you get what I mean. You must finish what you started, okay? Just eight venues. Then we can discuss the world tour."

"I'm going to France, Jax. I'm going to finish the music I've started. Forget that tour. It's in the past." He hung up the phone.

Madison looked at him in shock. "You're going to France without me?"

Caspian zipped up his bag. "It's only for a week."

"Why can't I come?"

"Mads, I love you, but I need to work. If you come, Todd comes. No offence, but a circus follows you everywhere."

"Caspian!"

"It's true. Plus you have that concert coming up in LA." He rubbed her cheek. "Just give me some time. I need to get to know Raphael a bit better. I think I need to do that alone."

"Fine. But I'm going the next time, okay? I did sing the song for his new film, after all."

"Great." He smiled. "I'll call you every day."

He rang his mother from the safety of his private jet as he felt that it was important to tell her. Prudence was naturally upset. The revelation of Caspian's birth had rocked their family and she was terrified that Raphael, with his glamorous lifestyle and exciting life, would steal her only son away.

"Don't worry, Mum," Caspian assured her. "I'll come and stay again when I get back."

An air steward placed a cup of coffee on the table next to his seat.

"Buckle your seatbelt, please."

Caspian nodded. "Sure."

Later, as the car sped towards Amiens, he reflected on why he had agreed to come. Maybe it was because he was curious. Maybe he wanted to get to know the man whom he resembled so much.

# CHAPTER TEN

The Mercedes pulled up outside large gates an hour later. They opened to show a long tree-lined avenue with a huge house with two turrets at the end. The Baptiste mansion near Amiens in Picardy. Once home to the world famous photographer, Louis Baptiste. Now, home to Louis' great-grandson, Raphael.

*His real father.*

He gazed at that the willow trees trailing along the surface of a small stream as the car approached the big house. The stone walls were covered with ivy and the manicured lawn boasted a fountain with statues of cherubs. A black lurcher bounded up and barked loudly at the car.

Caspian got out and the dog immediately jumped up on him, sniffing his coat.

"Hey, doggy, hey." He pushed him sideways gently.

The front door opened to reveal a tall man with shoulder length brown hair.

"Caspian! Welcome," he said in perfect English.

"Hello, Raphael, good to see you."

The dog barked loudly and jumped on Caspian again.

"*Zola! Arrête!*" said Raphael in a commanding tone.

The dog ignored him, his tail wagging.

"*Zola!*"

Caspian patted his head. "Down, boy."

"*Zola! Reste- là!*" shouted Raphael and Zola reluctantly obeyed.

The two men paused.

"I don't remember a dog the last time I was here."

"We got him during lockdown."

"Oh."

Raphael opened the door wide. "Come, come. Isabelle is waiting."

Isabelle, Raphael's American wife, was sitting on the sofa in a large drawing room. A retired model, she had given it all up to live in France with her famous husband. With her long red hair and pale skin, she was strikingly beautiful. In her arms was a dark-haired little girl of about two.

"Caspian! Good to see you." She beamed up at him. Despite living in France for close to three years, she hadn't lost her American accent.

Caspian gave a little wave.

Isabelle got to her feet and held the baby on her hip.

"Say hi, Anouk!" she said, smiling.

Caspian held out his hand and Anouk grasped his finger.

"Hello, little one."

Anouk smiled. Her dark hair and eyes were exactly like Raphael. His half-sister.

There was a knock on the door.

"*Monsieur Baptiste?*" said a small lady apologetically.

*"Oui, Coralie?"*

*"Téléphone."*

Raphael left the room. Minutes later they heard shouting.

"He's like a caged lion," said Isabelle. "He was desperately trying to work on a new screenplay, but he feels stifled."

Caspian said nothing.

"Anyway, the best thing to do is to take no notice," she said smiling. "He's just mad at everyone and everything." She gestured for him to follow her out into the courtyard. "Let's have a drink," she said. "It's cold, but bearable. Have you got a sweater?"

"I'm okay." He took a seat on a rattan seat.

"Would you like some lemonade? I made it myself." She pointed to the jug on the table.

He nodded. "Okay."

She poured two glasses.

"I made so much of this when I was kid. I tried to sell it outside my house to make enough money to go to Disneyland."

"Did you succeed?"

"I made three dollars and fifty five cents." She laughed. "I was so goddamn proud. I showed it to my dad and demanded that he book the tickets right away."

Caspian grinned. "I'm guessing you didn't go then. I mean, three dollars is impressive but…"

"Oh, I did." She sat down. "Daddy could never refuse me anything. Not his little girl."

"Madison sends her love."

"How is she?"

'She's fine." He shrugged. "Her schedule is jam packed already."

A soft breeze blew some leaves off the lawn. The tree-lined garden was immaculate, beautifully kept by Raphael's gardener, Michel. He had been with the Baptiste family for generations.

Raphael appeared. "I will kill Massimo one day. *Putain!*"

"Raph! You'll have a heart attack if you don't calm down. Now, forget about work. Talk to Caspian. He's come all this way." Isabelle gave him a pointed look.

*"Pardon,"* said Raphael.

Caspian reddened, unsure of what to do. Raphael was fascinating to him yet he intimidated him too.

"Lemonade?" offered Isabelle, making conversation.

"*Non.*" Raphael made a face. "I love you, but that stuff is awful."

"Hey, mister!" Isabelle's pale skin went red. "Take that back!"

"I'd like a coffee." He called Coralie, the housekeeper. "*Coralie! Un café, s'il vous plaît!*"

Caspian swirled his lemonade around and around.

"How's Madison?" asked Raphael, taking out a cigarette and lighting it.

"Madison is Madison," said Caspian. "It got a bit intense being locked down together."

"Tell me about it," said Isabelle, glaring at her husband.

"Her days are planned out and she sticks to the schedule religiously. I'm the opposite." Caspian shrugged. "It's hard to work at our place."

"I'm furious about her song. It was such a smash hit and now it's wasted." Raphael scowled. "It was such bad luck to release it when we did."

"She's disappointed too."

"It happened Billie Eilish with that James Bond movie," said Isabelle. "No one could've known that the world would come to a standstill."

"Yes, but now it's imperfect," said Raphael mutinously. "You know I hate when things are flawed."

Coralie appeared with a tray. She put a cup of coffee on the glass table and a bowl of sugar cubes wrapped in white paper.

"*Merci,*" said Raphael without looking up. Coralie scurried away.

"So, Anouk has a new tooth!" Isabelle beamed at Caspian. "I noticed it yesterday. You know she got her first tooth when she was four months old? That's crazy young."

"I think I was about the same age when I got my first tooth," said Caspian. "I remember Mum talking about it."

There was an awkward pause.

"It must be a Baptiste trait then," said Isabelle eventually.

Raphael stirred his coffee. Caspian gulped his lemonade.

Thankfully, Anouk started to cry.

Raphael showed Caspian to Louis Baptiste's suite in the east wing.

"This was my great-grandfather's room," he said gruffly. "It can be your space from now on."

Caspian gazed at the large bedroom and adjoining bathroom and dressing room. There was even a sitting room to the right, with a view of the courtyard and gardens.

"Thank you," he said meaningfully.

He unpacked his bag and lay down on the bed. He liked the décor as it was minimalist, and, of course, the photographs on the wall were awe-inspiring. One was a portrait Louis had taken of Che Guevara in a Cuban bar, a large cigar in his hand and his long hair over one eye. Another was a full-length shot of Marilyn Monroe, wearing a silk robe and looking over her shoulder with a sad expression.

Suddenly his phone started to ring. It was Madison.

"How was your trip?" she asked.

"Fine. How was your day?"

"Good. Ross rang and said that Savannah agreed to help me write my new album. She was so slow to commit, but now it's really happening."

"I'm so happy for you, Mads. She's a genius. What a coup to get Savannah Morris on board."

"I know! It's a dream come true. She has seven Grammys."

"I thought she'd retired."

"Well, she's making an exception."

"She must like you."

"Yeah, I think she does actually. We bonded that time I stayed on her farm. In fairness, she's the best in the business." She paused. "How's your work going?"

Caspian ran his fingers through his hair. "I just arrived, Maddy."

"So, when will you be home?"

"Soon."

Madison sighed. "I wish I was there with you."

Caspian's expression softened. "Next time, baby. I promise."

An hour later, Caspian entered the large dining room awkwardly. He still felt like a stranger: a guest. Isabelle was feeding Anouk, making funny faces at her daughter as she spooned some green goo into her mouth.

"Take a seat," she said with a smile. "I hope you like veal. It's ethically sourced."

"I eat everything," he said simply. "Maddy's the picky one."

Isabelle scraped the bowl. "Is she releasing new music?"

"Savannah Morris has agreed to help her to write her new album."

"That's exciting."

He smiled. "She's never written a song by herself before. She's on a high."

Raphael appeared, running his hand through his dark hair. "Apologies," he said, nodding. "I had to take a call."

Isabelle handed him the bread basket. "Dinner is on the way."

"Good. I'm hungry." He sat down, took some baguette and tore it apart.

"Caspian was just telling me that Madison is collaborating with Savannah Morris on her next album," said Isabelle. "She's changing direction."

"That's good." He took a bite of bread.

Caspian smoothed his napkin on his lap. "She's never been involved in the process before and Savannah is such a tour de force in the industry."

"It's strange," said Raphael thoughtfully. "I would never have put Savannah and Madison together. They are like frost and fire."

"Opposites attract, right?" Isabelle beamed at Coralie as she entered the dining room with three plates. "Dinner's here, you guys. Bon appétit."

After dinner, Raphael suggested that he and Caspian go for a walk.

"I want to show you the land," he said curtly, his hands in his pockets.

"Okay." Caspian put on a hoodie and followed him outside. They walked for five minutes or so, through a small orchard and over a fence. Zola bounded ahead of them, sniffing tree stumps and barking at flies. Raphael pointed out a small dwelling in the distance and told him it belonged to Michel the gardener.

"His family have been tenants of my family for years," he explained. "His father was gardener here before him."

Caspian stared at the expanse of fields and large oak trees that dotted the landscape. He breathed in the fresh air and closed his eyes, the only sound the babbling brook on his right.

"I can see why you love this place," he said softly. He opened his eyes to find Raphael staring at him.

"Let's sit," he said, positioning himself on a fallen trunk of a beech tree.

Caspian sat opposite him on a mound of grass.

"I want to talk to you about your mother." Raphael looked up. "I want to talk to you about Mary."

Caspian took a deep breath.

"I met her when I was very young. It was a one-night stand. I never expected her to become pregnant."

Caspian said nothing.

"I told her to have an abortion because it seemed the right thing to do. We were both so young and we didn't know each other." He looked up. "I was at university in Paris and she was in Ireland. I didn't want to be tied down."

Caspian's expression darkened. "So, you left her alone to cope with it all."

"She gave me the impression that she was terminating the whole thing. I didn't know you had been born." He ran his fingers through his hair. "You've had one-night stands, have you not? What would you have done? Married her?"

Caspian paused for a second. Images of various groupies flashed through his mind.

"No," he answered truthfully.

"I'm sorry for what happened to Mary. I'm sorry that she had to go through all that pain."

Caspian's eyes filled with tears. "I just wish I could've helped her. She had such a hard life. She only had her dad and they had no money. Then she was killed in that crash. It's all so unfair."

Raphael got up and patted his back. "I cannot imagine how you feel. Cheated, I think. Angry. I'm sorry for that."

"Stop apologising." Caspian wiped his nose with his sleeve. "You couldn't have stopped that accident."

"I know, but I wish it had been different."

Caspian stood up. "The past is the past. We can't change it."

"*Non*, we cannot." Raphael's dark eyes were filled with compassion.

Caspian straightened his shoulders. "Let's go back. I want to show you something."

Caspian entered the music room and took a seat at the Steinway. His fingers hovered over the keys and he pressed a few random notes to get the feel of the piano. Then he started to play a haunting tune, his fingers moving like lightning across the keyboard. Clearing his throat, he began to sing.

*The void is deep,*
*The emptiness is real,*
*On flames I leap,*
*Desperate to feel.*
*I wish I'd known*
*The sound of your voice,*
*The touch of your skin,*
*I'll never win,*
*I'll never win.*

Raphael stood on the threshold, his dark eyes enigmatic. Caspian resembled his great-grandfather, Louis, so much. Now, watching him sitting at the same piano, he got a rush of *déjà vu*.

In truth, he barely remembered Louis. He had died when he was a small boy. Ironically, Caspian owed his life to Louis. Raphael had gone to Cork to open an exhibition of Louis' work and it was there that Mary had crossed his path. Fate had led him there and now their child was sitting in front of him. He shivered.

He had denied it initially: Caspian was an imposter. A wannabe with an agenda, trying to cash in on the Baptiste name. But then his own mother, Agathe Baptiste, had seen it straight away. It was she who had urged Raphael to make contact with Caspian in the beginning. He still remembered her words. "He is a Baptiste. I'm sure of it."

*How right she'd been.*

The song came to an end.

"I have more," said Caspian in a choked voice. "They're all about her."

Raphael walked over to the piano and pulled Caspian to his feet. Without a word, he hugged him close, slapping his back awkwardly. Caspian, unsure of how to respond, patted his shoulder hesitantly.

"Come," said Raphael with shining eyes. "I must tell you about your family."

Raphael disappeared and came back with a big leather-bound book.

"This was my great-grandfather's portfolio," he said, tracing the surface with his index finger. "It's priceless."

Caspian gazed at it. He had googled Louis Baptiste and read about his illustrious career as a photographer. He knew that some of his portraits hung in famous galleries around the world.

Raphael opened the book and laid it on the table in front of them. On the top page was a signature and a date: Louis Baptiste, 1935.

"He filmed so many," said Raphael proudly. "Picasso was his favourite. He would invite him over to watch him in his natural habitat, painting a huge canvas or sketching something. Often without his shirt. Louis would take impromptu shots." He turned a page and there was Pablo Picasso, his brush in his hand, staring contemplatively at a half-finished painting.

"This ended up as *Le Rêve*," said Raphael. "Imagine that. Louis saw this great work in the early stages."

"Amazing," said Caspian in awe.

"Look at this," said Raphael, flicking onwards. "This is Ernest Hemingway. He was a great friend of Louis'. They spent a lot of time together in Paris."

Caspian looked at the photograph on the page. It was dated 1924 and it was Hemingway holding a baby.

"That's his son, John," said Raphael, pointing to the child.

Caspian flicked on through, seeing images ranging from James Joyce to Jackie Kennedy.

"Louis played piano too," said Raphael. "That piano was his, in fact."

"Did he live here all his life?" asked Caspian.

"Yes. He travelled a lot, but his home was here."

"When did he die?"

"1979. He was eighty-eight years old. I hope I live as long."

"So, he was my great-great-grandfather."

"Yes. My mother thinks you resemble him." Raphael smiled and Caspian blushed.

"You must meet *Maman* again. The last time was so rushed." Raphael paused. "We plan to have a christening for Anouk in June. Maybe you and your band could come and play some music?"

"I'd like that." Caspian really meant it.

# CHAPTER ELEVEN

Rosa Weber was beautiful and talented. She had been told that all her life. How could she be anything but? Her father was Johann Weber, the award-winning composer. Her mother was the Italian diva, Cassandra Rosso. She had excelled at the Conservatoire de Paris, aced her audition for the London Symphony Orchestra, and played the cello like a dream. Then, in true Rosa style, she'd ruined the whole thing. Too many late nights and missed rehearsals resulted in warnings and eventually her notice. She was now a member of the Southbank Philharmonic, only because her father had pulled strings.

All her life she had been bombarded with infidelity, mainly thanks to her father. Her mother was never around so she craved attention. Her brother, Stefan, had dealt with their difficult childhood differently. Reserved, he had married young and worked in finance. He got all the stability he needed from his wife and child.

*If only she were that simple.*

Instead, Rosa Weber spent her time breaking hearts and leaving a trail of destruction. She got so caught up in the game, she forgot the rules.

Rosa and Stefan were in Florence the summer Emilia left Hertfordshire for America, and so were unaware that she had gone. Cassandra, on a break between operas, uncharacteristically took a week off to spend time with her children at her luxurious apartment which was a short walk from the Santa Maria del Fiore cathedral. Stefan cast aside his Nintendo and beamed. Rosa got to try on her mother's make up and high heels. Cassandra  liked the novelty of showing her children the beautiful city with its winding river and ancient bridges. Together they walked the streets, looking at churches and statues, chattering in Italian. Cassandra pointed to the Basilico near her home.

"It looks so plain," she said, pointing to its simple façade. "But inside, you will be mesmerised!"

They walked into the church and the children gasped.

"Baroque," said Cassandra, pointing to the ornate décor, "and in that little room over there, there is a crucifix by Michelangelo."

"We're learning about him a school," said Stefan in wonder.

"Never judge something by its outward appearance," Cassandra whispered, bowing her head reverently in the dark church. "Look deep inside. It is there that you will find true beauty."

Every morning was exciting as the day held endless possibilities. Rosa followed Cassandra like a puppy, played her cello with passion so as to impress her, and drew countless pictures of them together under a bright sun.

Together, they walked around the city streets, Cassandra pointing out statues and works of art for them to appreciate. One day they stopped by a white statue a few yards from the Piazza della Signoria. "Look, children. This is Fortuna, the Goddess of Chance," said Cassandra in her rich voice. "She was the daughter of Venus and Jupiter."

"She's beautiful," said a wide-eyed Rosa.

"She is very powerful, *bella.* She decides your fate."

"What's fate?"

"Your destiny." Cassandra rubbed her cheek. "You must try to be a good person and Fortuna will smile on you."

"What's the wheel for?" asked Stefan, pointing to a disc shape by the statue's side.

"It is the Wheel of Fortune," said Cassandra gravely. "When it spins, it can bring happiness or sadness. Luck is by nature unpredictable."

Rosa gazed at the statue.

"*Fortuna Imperatrix Mundi,*" went on Cassandra, 'Fortuna, the Empress of the World. Our destiny is guided by her whims. I believe that if you make good choices, she will be good to you."

"Fortuna," echoed Rosa.

Later that night, Rosa lay in bed and thought about Fortuna. What had her mother said? Good people receive good luck? She tried to be good, she really did. Well, most of the time. Gertrude would chide her for not eating her vegetables and her father got angry when her school reports were below par, but she was generally well-behaved.

She often wondered if her mamma was a good person. She was always too busy. All of her friends lived with their mothers, why couldn't Cassandra give up singing and come home to England? She could make her pancakes in the morning, just like Emilia did, and sing her to sleep. She could tell her more stories about gods and goddesses and come to her recitals. Rosa didn't see a problem with them all living together: Johann, Emilia and Cassandra. The house in Hertfordshire was huge and could accommodate lots of people. They could be a family.

One night, after a delicious bowl of tagliatelle, Rosa broached the subject.

"Why don't you come home and live with Daddy? Stefan wants you to come home. I want you to come home."

"I must go and make music,' Cassandra answered in her thrilling voice. "It is my duty, *bella*. Why I was put on this earth."

"You must meet Pegasus properly!" Rosa looked tearful.

"I will see Pegasus in here,' Cassandra answered, closing her eyes and placing a hand on her breast. "I will see you riding him through the fields."

"But Mamma…"

"Rosa, you know it's not possible…"

"Why?"

Cassandra sighed. "I cannot be tied down, *bella*. I belong to the world."

"I hate you!' Rosa stood up violently, knocking her chair backwards. "It doesn't matter if I'm good or bad, Fortuna has cursed me forever having a mother like you."

Stefan and Rosa arrived back from Florence in late September. Johann was waiting at the Arrivals gate at Heathrow, and when Rosa looked for Emilia, her father told them bluntly that Emilia had gone to America. Stefan, although upset, shut down emotionally. He had learned to suppress his feelings and get on with things.

Rosa cried her eyes out all the way home. She rushed into Gertrude's arms and asked her nanny if all adults were the same? Did they all leave? Gertrude didn't answer. She was used to picking up the pieces, but it broke her heart to see her little *Englechen* so lost.

Later that night, as Rosa lay in bed, she clutched her teddy and fought back the tears. She had expected things to be the same: Emilia was the one who helped her to prepare for school, making sure her pencil case was filled with pencils and a proper ruler. Emilia made pancakes on a Sunday morning, allowing the children to pour over as much syrup as they wanted. Emilia helped her play her violin and knew Britney Spears' songs by heart.

She vowed to be good. She would no longer stick her tongue out at her Music teacher when the old lady wasn't looking. She would stop stealing coins from her father's pockets and she certainly wouldn't hide Stefan's PlayStation controllers anymore. If she was the best-behaved child in England, surely Fortuna would help?

The years flew by and Rosa forgot about Emilia. After completing her A-Levels, she moved to Paris to begin her studies at the Conservatoire de Paris. Rosa played piano and violin beautifully, but cello was her passion. She spent four years learning with Pierre Monteux and passed her Masters Diploma with the highest distinction. Her best friend at school, Bianca Carmichael, also moved to Paris as she wanted to be a conductor one day. Her instrument was violin, another string instrument, so their little apartment by Rue de l'Université was habitually filled with music as they practised well into the night.

Bianca and Rosa had a lot in common. Both girls were interested in symphonic repertoire and subsequently moved to Berlin to be part of the Berlin Radio Symphony Orchestra for one year. Bianca continued her studies and started a second Masters at the Hanns Eisler Musikhochschule while Rosa availed of the lively Berlin nightlife.

During the summer, Rosa was invited to play in different ensembles and travelled to festivals all over the world. Bianca, driven and ambitious, decided to move to Moscow to train under the famous Russian conductor, Piotr Khruskev. The girls met in late July when Rosa spent a week in St. Petersburg playing Baroque music with some of her old classmates from Paris. She had black shadows under her eyes from too many late nights and Bianca chided her gently.

"You look like something the cat dragged in," she said, shaking her head. "Do you ever sleep?"

Rosa laughed. "I'll sleep when I'm dead."

That autumn, Bianca moved to France to play in the Orchestre de Paris and Rosa joined the London Symphony Orchestra. Johann, using his contacts and influence, organised the audition. Rosa played like a dream and was hired on the spot. She liked playing with the other cellists, many of whom were Professors of Music with years of experience. Johann, although proud of his daughter, was also wary. He had heard rumours about Rosa: how she liked to play around with married men, how she enjoyed socialising a little too much. He made the mistake of calling her up after her first week at the LSO and warning her to behave herself.

"Good God, but that's hypocritical," she said bitterly. "Sorry, Dad, but I learned from the best."

The first few months went well. She became firm friends with a Czech viola player called Radoslav Rehák who was two years older. He had been playing with the orchestra for six months longer and was a frightful gossip. He regaled her with stories about different musicians, embellishing his tales for shock value. However, soon Rosa herself became the subject matter of these stories. She was photographed leaving the house of a well-known art dealer, Pablo Fernández, in the early hours of the morning. Pablo, a fifty year old billionaire, had just married his fourth wife, a Serbian woman named Nikolina. He denied all accusations of an affair, but unbeknownst to him, his new wife had hired a private detective to follow him. What followed were pictures of Rosa in his arms, kissing him in a taxi and sunbathing topless on his yacht off the south coast of France. Johann called her up, furious at her behaviour, but she hung up on him.

Eventually, her time at the orchestra came to a natural end. She was hopeless at arriving on time and had used every excuse in the book. Too many late nights and subsequent no shows got her written warnings which culminated in dismissal.

It was two years later when Rosa met Bianca again. Rosa, who had made ends meet by playing chamber music at weddings, auditioned for the new all-female Southbank Philharmonic. Johann had made a few calls to the Board and found out that Bianca was the new talent that had been recruited for this pioneering project from the Arts Council.

"Your friend, Bianca Something, the girl at the Conservatoire, she's the Maestro!"

Rosa went to the audition and gave it everything she had.

"You're in," said Bianca joyfully. "Thank God you're so good. I was dreading saying no to an old friend."

The girls moved in together a few months later. They rented a three-bedroomed flat near Richmond where they used the master bedroom as a make-shift studio. Sheet music covered the carpet. Both worked unpredictable hours and spent hours playing music together, often well into the night.

Bianca, determined to succeed, spent most of her time poring over scores, tapping out rhythms and listening to various renditions of famous musical pieces. The deep, timbre sound reverberated through the apartment as her arm moved up and down.

One weekend, Bianca invited Rosa to her father's house in Buckinghamshire. He had moved back to England from Hong Kong and was anxious to reconnect with his daughter. Rosa's curiosity was piqued immediately. Bianca told her that her parents had separated when she was thirteen. Her father had been having an affair, her mother had found out and all hell had broken loose. The resulting divorce had been acrimonious and bitter. Bianca, an only child, had remained living with her mother. Her father, David, power-hungry and driven, was a workaholic and, as a result, Bianca rarely saw him.

"Your father? Really?" Rosa raised an eyebrow. "I thought you two weren't close?"

Bianca nodded. "Yes. I'm as surprised as you are." She pursed her lips.

Later, Rosa googled David Carmichael and saw that he was an entrepreneur who owned a tech company in London. He had moved to China seven years before, settling in Hong Kong, but was now coming home to British soil. Tall, handsome and haughty, he looked every inch the millionaire that he was.

She hid the phone when Bianca asked what she was doing.

"Nothing! Are we ready to go?"

# CHAPTER TWELVE

David Carmichael lived in a huge house in Buckinghamshire. When Bianca's Golf pulled up outside the house, he emerged from an impressive looking doorway.

"Bianca! Good to see you, darling." He hugged her briefly. "It's been too long."

"Hi, Dad." Bianca looked awkward. "Um, this is Rosa." She stepped aside and Rosa smiled.

She had worn her favourite green dress – it was fitted at the waist with a full skirt and a sweetheart neckline. Her long dark hair was loose, falling over her shoulders. Her full lips were painted a dark red and her brown eyes sparkled.

David stared at her for a moment and then smiled. "Rosa," he said, bowing his head.

She held out her hand. "David," she mocked and he laughed. "Or would you prefer Mr Carmichael?" she continued playfully. "I don't mean to be familiar."

"David is fine."

Bianca cleared her throat. "So, shall we go inside? It's chilly."

"Of course." David walked inside and guided them through a huge hall with black and white tiles into a large drawing room.

"Drink?" he asked, gesturing to a cabinet.

"A non-alcoholic beer, please." Bianca took a seat on the couch. "I'm driving."

"A white wine," said Rosa with a smile. "I'm not."

David got the drinks and Rosa gazed around the room. "I like the art," she said, noticing a Turner and a Stubbs.

"Thanks. I like to collect paintings." He smiled. "So, you play in Bianca's orchestra, I hear? Predictable, I suppose."

"Yes, I suppose." She laughed. "Genetically I'm predisposed."

"What's your instrument?"

"I play piano and violin quite well, but cello is my favourite."

"Like Jacqueline Dupré."

"Sort of. I'm more of a Yo-Yo Ma fan."

Bianca cleared her throat. "Any hope of that beer, Dad?"

David nodded. "Of course. Sorry. Back in a sec."

When the door closed, Rosa turned to Bianca. "He's so nice!"

Bianca didn't reply.

"I mean, he's being very friendly."

"Hmmm."

"Give him a chance. He's trying hard."

David appeared again with a bottle of 0% Tiger beer. "Will this be okay?"

Bianca nodded. "I'd like a glass if you have one."

"Of course." He disappeared again and came back with a tall glass which he handed to Bianca. He deliberately brushed his fingers against Rosa's as he handed her a glass of wine, and faced his daughter. "How's it at the helm? You must feel like you've lots to prove."

"Tiring, but I'm learning a lot."

"And you, Rosa." David turned back to her. "How do you find her as a boss?"

"She's great," said Rosa genuinely. "She's so patient. I'd never be able to lead like that."

"So, you're a leader." David smiled at Bianca.

"I suppose."

"I'm proud of you."

"Right." Bianca took a gulp of beer.

They dined on shellfish that David had prepared himself.

"This lobster is to die for," said Rosa, closing her eyes in pleasure. "So soft."

"I like to cook," said David, taking a sip of wine.

"Well, that's one thing Bianca did not inherit from you," said Rosa with a giggle. "Her only meal is Spaghetti Bolognese."

"You've never complained before," said Bianca icily.

"Oh, I'm not complaining," she said hurriedly. "Stop being so sensitive."

David refilled her glass. Rosa felt her stomach swirl. She'd already had more than enough to drink.

"So, what are your plans for the future?" asked David. "Are you happy playing cello?"

Rosa paused. "I don't know. I was thinking of becoming a composer like my father, but I'm not sure yet."

"For films?"

"Maybe. My godfather is a famous director so I could pull some strings." She winked.

"Oh? Who's that?"

"Raphael Baptiste."

David looked impressed.

"I haven't seen him in ages," she continued. "He has a baby girl now and I've yet to meet her."

"He married that model, didn't he? Isabelle Flynn?"

She nodded. "They're blissfully happy by all accounts. My father said it would never last, what with the big age difference and all."

"There's nothing wrong with age difference," said David, gazing at her.

"So, how have you been?" Bianca cleared her throat loudly. "How's work?"

David tore his eyes away. "Very well. That Chinese merger went through so all's good."

"And how's Yvonne? I thought she'd be here this evening."

David patted his mouth with his napkin. "We broke up."

"Oh?" Bianca looked surprised. "I thought I saw you in Tatler recently."

"It didn't work out."

"Right." Bianca put her knife and fork together on the plate. "Why?"

David shrugged. "We fell out of love. It happens."

"Oh, I know." Bianca tried to mask the bitterness in her voice.

Rosa's eyes travelled from father to daughter. "This meal is delicious, David," she said in an effort to change the subject. "Thank you."

"My pleasure," he said, his eyes connecting with hers.

"Anyone new on the scene?" Bianca took a sip of water.

"New?" David raised an eyebrow. "No, as it happens."

Rosa took a huge gulp of wine. The tension was palpable.

"So, Dad," Bianca stood up, "we need to get back. I've an early start in the morning."

"But I have some pud."

"No need." Bianca made eyes at Rosa to move.

She nodded and placed her napkin on the table. "Yes, we should go. Thank you again for a lovely evening."

"Bianca, this is crazy! It's so early."

"Sorry." She put on her coat and Rosa did the same.

David walked them out.

"So, we should meet again soon."

"Oh?" Bianca pressed her fob to open the car.

"Yes." David put his hands in his pockets. "For a drink or whatever."

"Sure, why not?" Bianca forced a smile. "Well, see you soon then." She got into the car.

Rosa smiled and waved. "Nice to meet you!" she said, smiling.

David stared at her for a moment and smiled back. "The pleasure was all mine."

Bianca didn't speak for most of the journey. Rosa could tell that she was upset, her knuckles were white from gripping the steering wheel.

They pulled up outside the apartment and she switched off the ignition. "I'm sorry for leaving like that."

"It's fine."

"He's just so smug. I want to punch him sometimes."

"Don't worry." She rubbed her arm.

"He's so arrogant. Can you imagine cheating on my mum like that?"

"Ssssh. Don't think about it." She unbuckled her seatbelt. "I thought he was charming."

"You don't know him like I do."

"Look, let's go inside. The box has been ticked. You don't have to meet him again if you don't want to."

A week later Rosa was walking home from Sainsbury's when a black BMW pulled up on the kerb in front of her. A window opened and she inhaled sharply. David Carmichael was behind the wheel.

"Hello, Rosa," he said.

"Hello," she said, caught off guard.

"Do you want a lift?"

She paused. It was raining and she didn't have a jacket.

"Okay, if you're sure." She jumped into the passenger seat and put her cloth bag on the floor. The interior of the car gleamed. It was a walnut finish with black leather seats. David was dressed in a striped shirt and navy pants. His gold Rolex gleamed on his powerful wrist.

"Is Bianca at home?" he asked, indicating out onto the road.

"I'm not sure," she answered. "She had a meeting with the Board this morning." She raised an eyebrow. "Have you not contacted her?"

David said nothing. He just kept driving.

"I can call her?" She picked up her cloth bag and rummaged around for her phone.

"Don't."

Her head shot up. "Don't?"

David pulled in and faced her. "Let me take you for lunch. I know a nice pub down the road from here."

"Lunch?" She looked confused.

"Yes. And a drink." He smiled. "I won't bite."

"But what about Bianca?"

"I'll call her later. She can join us."

Rosa felt her heartrate increase.

"Would you like to join me?" he asked again, staring at her.

"Yes." Her chest heaved. "Yes, I will."

The affair lasted four months. They met in hotels, at the house in Buckinghamshire, in charming guesthouses in the Lake District. He spoiled her, bringing her gifts and flowers. He was domineering and arrogant and she loved it. When they'd eat in a restaurant, he'd order for her, deeming her too young to know enough about good food. Besotted, she let him take control, pretending to enjoy the foie gras he insisted she have.

Bianca conveniently started going out with her personal trainer. Caught up in the rush of a new relationship, there were some weekends when she didn't come home at all. Rosa would call David and ask him over, but he refused to sleep at her apartment. Instead, he would pick her up in his BMW and book them into somewhere luxurious.

One such weekend, they stayed at a five-star hotel in Berkshire. David, who was obsessive about his weight, rose at five to go to the gym. Then, he ate only fruit at breakfast and wrinkled his nose up at Rosa when she scoffed two croissants in row.

They spent the day in bed, ordering room service of champagne and strawberries, which Rosa had mostly to herself. That evening, they went to the restaurant and David's phone rang as they sat at the bar drinking an aperitif.

"Back in a sec," he said, walking outside into the foyer.

Rosa took this opportunity to go to the bathroom. She fixed her hair so it fell becomingly around her face, and applied some red lipstick to make her lips fuller. She arrived back to the bar to find David's seat empty. Walking out into the foyer, there was no sign. She gestured at a young waiter who had served them half an hour before.

"I'm looking for my..." She paused, unsure of what to call him. Boyfriend seemed so juvenile.

"Your dad?" said the young waiter helpfully.

Rosa reddened. "Oh, he's not my father."

The waiter blushed an ugly red. "I'm so sorry, Miss. I didn't realise."

"Don't worry!" She laughed.

"Well, I haven't seen him." He scurried away, mortified.

When David returned ten minutes later, she made the mistake of telling him what happened.

"The poor guy," she said with a laugh. "He was so embarrassed."

David didn't laugh.

"What's wrong?" she asked, noticing his angry look.

"He should be fired. What an impertinent thing to say."

"No! He made a mistake. It's fine."

David scowled. "Well, I don't think it's funny."

# CHAPTER THIRTEEN

That was the beginning of the end.

She saw him less often. There was always some business meeting or a Zoom call he couldn't miss. She found herself alone most weekends as Bianca spent all of her free time with Adam at his place. Rosa was relieved about that. She felt duplicitous and fake when she defected inquiries about her love life. Professionally, things were fine. It was all about the music. They worked well together and were preparing for an outdoor concert at Warwick Castle in the summer. Rosa had wanted to tell Bianca the truth for months, but David had forbidden it. He said that no one was to know. His relationship with his daughter was tenuous enough already. Rosa argued that he was a free agent and that after the initial shock, she would be happy that they had found one another. David was adamant. Bianca was not to know.

Then David told her that he'd met someone else.

Just like that.

He called her on a Tuesday evening and ended the relationship.

She couldn't believe it. Was she not exciting enough? What was wrong with her? No one ever wanted to stick around.

She called him over and over, but he didn't pick up. Eventually he texted her and asked her to delete his number from her phone. It was nothing personal, he said. He wished her the best and said a final goodbye.

The weeks that followed were a blur. Broken-hearted, Rosa closed herself off from everyone. Each night, she paced her bedroom floor, willing her brain to shut down and sleep.

It was as if the whole world had disappeared from under her feet. She couldn't believe that she'd let a man in like that. She was Rosa Weber. She played with people's hearts. It was not the other way around.

Yet, David had penetrated her shield. She had grown used to having him around. She liked how he took control and looked after her.

She yearned to talk to someone about it, but Bianca wasn't an option. Her mother wouldn't understand. Stefan would berate her for messing around with someone twice her age.

Emilia flashed though her mind. Lovely, kind Emilia. She had fallen in love with an older man. She had known what it was like to lose him. She reflected on the last time she'd seen her. They had gone for ice cream in the village. Then, she and Stefan had been shipped off to Florence for the summer to live with Cassandra. When they arrived back for the new school term, all traces of Emilia had disappeared from the family home.

She sighed. Emilia was long gone, confined to the past.

A few days later, Bianca put her hands on her hips. "What is wrong with you, Rosa? You're like a zombie lately."

"Nothing."

"Nothing? It doesn't look like nothing. Man trouble?"

Rosa reddened. "Something like that." She lit a cigarette with a shaking hand.

"What happened?"

"Nothing I can't handle. Just leave it okay?" She inhaled deeply and closed her eyes.

"You look like you haven't slept in weeks." Bianca waved the smoke away from her face.

"I'm fine."

"You're not fine. You nearly fell asleep during Elgar yesterday." Bianca sat down on the couch next to her friend. "Sorry I haven't been around so much. Things are great with Adam, but I shouldn't abandon you either."

"Gosh, not at all." Rosa plastered a smile on her face. "I'm happy for you, Bi. It's all fine."

"I'm keeping an eye on you, okay?"

"Okay."

"And try not to smoke indoors. I'll let it go this time, but please go outside."

"Noted."

The next week, after Rosa slept through her alarm and missed her third consecutive rehearsal, Bianca forced her to go to her doctor.

"Get some meds to help you sleep," she urged. "You look wretched. Plus you can't miss any more days. It's getting awkward with the Board."

Rosa knew she was right. Yet she couldn't shake herself out of it.

After a while, she stopped going into work altogether. She couldn't face it. After a night of drinking, she found it hard to motivate herself to move out of bed. Bianca came home one afternoon and found Rosa curled up on the couch, wrapped in a woollen blanket, smoking a cigarette. Bianca opened the curtains immediately and waved the smoke away.

"I'm calling your dad," she warned. "Seriously, Rosa. You've got to pull yourself out of it. I'm down a cellist all week."

"Don't call him," she pleaded, stubbing out the cigarette in an overflowing ashtray. "He'll just berate me."

"Well, what else am I supposed to do?" Bianca walked over to the kitchen and picked up a tub of tranquillisers. "How many of these are you taking? You were only supposed to have a few to help you sleep."

"Not many," Rosa lied.

"Good. That's the last thing you need." She frowned. "Look, Adam will have to take a back seat. I'm coming home for good."

"To keep an eye on me?"

"Yes. Why not?"

Rosa laughed. "I'm fine, Bianca. You need to calm down. I had a stomach bug all week. I'll be back tomorrow."

"Last week it was the flu. The week before it was period pains." Bianca looked sceptical. "Come on, Rosa. I can't keep covering for you like this."

"I have a doctor's cert," she argued. "The Board can content themselves with that."

"It's not just the Board, okay? Everyone is talking about you. You need to pull yourself together." Bianca's face softened. "I know it's a man. I can tell. Why won't you talk to me?"

Rosa's eyes filled with tears.

"I'm fine," she repeated. "Please, just drop it."

She returned to work the Monday after. The strings section broke into a round of applause when she entered the auditorium.

"Good to see you again," shouted Katarina, the lead violinist. Rosa forced a smile and took her position to the right of Bianca. The sheets of music swam before her eyes. She watched Bianca tap the baton on the music stand in front of her.

"Right, everyone," she said loudly. "Let's go Bach to Bach." She smiled. "Sorry for that disastrous joke, but we do need to brush up on the Baroque part."

Rosa held up her bow and waited for her cue.

That night, after a few gin and tonics, she googled David Carmichael. His handsome impassive face stared back a her. How dare he treat her this way? They were so happy. He had been so attentive and then, out of the blue, he cut all ties. Why? He had never told her why. She was sick of people casting her aside, like she wasn't important enough. Her parents had done it all her life.

She exited out of the article she was reading and googled trains to Buckinghamshire.

She deserved to know. She would make her way to his house and ask him out straight.

The next Saturday she took the train as planned. The train pulled into the station at around five, just as the sky was darkening. She pulled out her Google Maps. It was about a mile to his mansion. There were no taxis so she started to walk. Her head was buzzing with possible scenarios and conversations. She arrived at the gate and took a deep breath. Taking a bottle of gin out of her bag, she took a large swig. His BMW was parked outside the front door. She trailed her finger along its sleek body and remembered the many times they'd made love in the back.

The lights were on in the sitting room. Even though the curtains were closed, she could see a silhouette walking past.

Taking a deep breath, she rang the giant doorbell. Then she rang it again.

Her hand trembled as she waited. How would he react? She was on his turf. It could go either way.

The door opened and a smiling David appeared. His face changed immediately.

"What are you doing here?" He looked over his shoulder.

"I want to talk to you," she said tremulously.

"It's not a good time," he hissed. "Please leave."

"Why? Is my replacement here?"

"Rosa! This is entirely inappropriate, calling to my home like this." He walked out onto the flagstones and put the door on the latch.

"What's inappropriate is how you used me and then cast me aside without a second thought!" Her eyes filled with tears.

"It had come to a natural end."

"What? A few days before, we were here. In your bed."

"Stop behaving like a child." He grabbed her shoulders gently. "It was nice, you and me. But it's over."

"What about Bianca?"

"What?" He let go of her abruptly. "What did you tell her?"

"Nothing," she said bitterly. "Nothing about you."

"Good. I don't want it known." He stepped back. "Ever."

"Oh, I know."

"Look, Rosa. You'd better leave."

"I can't. I walked from the station. The last train is in half an hour and I won't make it."

He put his hand in his pocket and pulled out his car keys.

"Come on, I'll drop you there."

She rubbed away her tears. "You will?"

"Yes." He looked impatient.

"Should you let your guest know?"

"Just leave it."

"Won't she be worried?"

"Rosa, I said leave it." He jangled the keys in his fingers. "Now, come on. We need to get going. Have you got your ticket?"

"I only bought a single fare." She looked despondent.

He reached out and rubbed her shoulder. "You'll have to forget me. Forget us. It was never going to be anything."

She closed her eyes.

"You're a beautiful girl. Never think otherwise."

"Beautiful?"

He nodded. He was standing so close, she could smell his skin. That musky familiar smell. Automatically she felt herself sway towards him, resting her head on his chest.

"Have you been drinking?" he asked, pulling back.

She didn't answer. Gin, happy pills, you name it.

"Rosa, I…"

She lunged forward and kissed him hard on the lips. He pulled back in surprise but she wound her arms around his neck and didn't let go. For a moment, he reciprocated.

It felt so good. Even her fuzzy brain could feel the endorphins racing through her body. He desired her. He just didn't know what he wanted.

Then he pulled back violently and held up his hands. "Stop! It's over."

Her chest heaved as she regained her balance. "Really?" she said, her eyes glittering.

"Yes." He ushered her down the steps. "Get into the car, Rosa."

She howled and shoved him backwards. Caught by surprise, he dropped his car keys and fell through the door.

"Jesus, Rosa, what the fuck are you doing? That could've hurt me." He straightened up.

"Good!" she screamed, springing at him and hitting his broad chest with her fists. "You let me think that we had a future. You let me believe that you loved me."

"It wasn't that simple…" He held her wrists and pushed her backwards.

"Oh? Really? How so?"

"It had run its course. I've met someone else. I'm only human, Rosa."

She felt something snap. With a vicious shove, she pushed him backwards onto black and white tiles. Then she bent down, grabbed his car keys and slammed the heavy front door.

*"Rosa!"*

She could hear him shout but she didn't care.

The car was parked outside. She pressed the unlock button and jumped in. The engine roared to life and she accelerated, just as he appeared on the flagstones.

"Rosa!' he roared. "Don't drive. *Rosa!"*

He found the car half a mile down the road, stuck in a ditch. His heart in his mouth, he raced towards the driver's door. Rosa's eyes were closed, her head resting on the airbag.

"Thank God," he muttered. He opened the door and smoothed her hair back off her face.

Rosa's eyes opened and darted around wildly.

"Sssh," he said soothingly. "You're fine. Everything is okay."

"What happened?" she said in a strangled voice.

"You had a small accident. It's all fine."

"My neck hurts."

"How much did you drink?"

"I don't know. Half a bottle of gin?"

"Anything else?"

"Some Valium."

David looked grave. "We could go to the hospital, but you'll have to explain all of this."

She rubbed her neck. "Would I go to jail?"

David shrugged. "Driving under the influence. Probably."

Rosa's brown eyes looked fearful. "The papers. It would be in the papers."

David nodded. "Exactly."

He had been thinking same thing. How the hell would he explain her presence at his home? Driving his car?

He waited.

"What about your car?" she said in a small voice. "Is it badly damaged?"

"I'll make a few calls. It's fine."

"I'm sorry." Her eyes filled with tears. "I want to go home."

"Don't worry." He forced a smile. "Let's just get you out of here."

# CHAPTER FOURTEEN

He drove her back to London himself in his Range Rover.

The car came to a halt outside her apartment building.

"Rosa," he began.

"Don't say it." She started to wring her hands.

"You must never contact me again." He put his hand on her knee. "Promise? We had a lucky escape tonight."

She nodded miserably.

"Get on with your life."

"Why did you break up with me?" Her brown eyes glistened. "Why?"

David shrugged. "Nothing lasts forever."

"You truly believe that?"

He nodded. "Familiarity breeds contempt. You're a sweet girl, but it's a big world out there. I'm not a long-term relationship man."

Rosa picked up her bag. "Goodbye, David." She took a deep shuddering breath. "I hope you find happiness one day."

He reached out and stroked her cheek. "You too, Rosa. You too."

She opened the door and got out of the car. David revved the engine and drove away. Rosa watched his Range Rover indicate right and disappear from sight. Then she turned around to find a horrified Bianca standing at the door of the building, her key in her hand.

"What the hell were you doing with my dad?" she said hoarsely.

Rosa stared at her for a moment. "We've just broken up." She raised her head.

"Say again?"

"David and I, we had a relationship. Now it's over."

Bianca held on to the door knob for support. "I don't believe this."

Rosa stepped forward. "I'm sorry."

"Sorry?" She held up her hands. "How dare you? How dare you, Rosa? Why him? Of all the men out there, why him? Just because you don't have a functional relationship with your own father, you have to steal mine?"

"I didn't steal him. He's not mine."

"How could you?" Bianca turned around and ran down the street.

"Bianca!" Rosa called after her.
"Just fuck off!"
"I'm sorry!" Tears began to stream down Rosa's cheeks.

Rosa woke the next day. Her neck ached from the force of impact. Her right arm was sprained and her ribs were bruised. She struggled to remember what happened. Then she saw the road. She felt her stomach flip. The blurry lights, the noise of the traffic, the steering wheel turning to jelly in her hands. How everything was in slow motion as the car roared and careered into a tree. She remembered feeling totally calm, accepting. Then, nothing.

She felt like a different person. Wracked with guilt. What if she'd killed someone?

Then she remembered Bianca's face. The horror, the disgust.

She had to leave London. She couldn't pretend anymore. Bianca didn't deserve a friend like her. She was the lowest of the low. She needed a fresh start.

"Ow!" she said with a grimace as she sat up. She needed to see a doctor. Her neck felt like it was about to snap.

Rosa held the phone away from her ear as Johann yelled at her from thousands of miles away.

"What did you do now?" he shouted. "I lined that job up for you and you've thrown it all away?" He started to curse in German.

"There must be other jobs," said Rosa dolefully. "Is there anything going on in LA? A change of scenery might be a good thing."

"What is it this time?" he asked angrily. "Who were you carrying on with?"

"No one," she lied.

"Rosa!"

"No! I'm not like you, you know."

"Don't be disrespectful."

"Look, Dad, I need to leave London for a while. Can you help me or not?"

There was a pause.

"No, Rosa. I can't."

"Are you serious?"

"Yes. You've got to face this on your own. Learn from it."

"Daddy!"

"Call me when you come up with a plan."

Johann hung up.

Later that evening, she sat out on the balcony of her apartment, listening to the sounds of the city. The skyline was illuminated with orange and the clouds concealed a half moon. Sirens wailed, voices were carried along by the breeze. She opened the camera on her phone, switching the perspective so she could see her own reflection. Her dark eyes looked huge in the dusky light and her lips glistened with pink gloss. Her long hair was piled on top of her head, with tendrils escaping down her neck. .

Her neck brace was the only thing that marred her appearance. It was big and cumbersome. She touched it gingerly and winced.

Whiplash was the least of her worries.

She lit a cigarette and inhaled, blowing smoke rings with perfectly round lips.

Bianca had texted, saying that she was at Adam's place and that she no longer wanted to share a flat with her. She finished the curt message with:

*I never want to see you again.*

Rosa understood completely. The inference was that she wasn't welcome at the orchestra any longer. Bianca knew she couldn't fire her for sleeping with her dad, but she was counting on Rosa to do the right thing.

She debated whether she should call Stefan, but then decided against it. He was so judgemental and his wife, Claudia, didn't like her. There were seven missed calls from her landlord on her phone. Her rent was late.

Bianca had bailed her out the last few times, but that was no longer an option.

Her earnings were paltry to say the least, and her mother refused to bankroll her any longer. Cassandra had always been an easy target. Rosa knew that her mother was guilty about never being around. So, she never refused when she asked her for money.

Then, last summer, she had travelled to Florence for a few weeks to play at the Terre di Arezzo music festival. There, she met Viktor, Cassandra's younger Russian lover. It didn't take long to charm him. She was a younger, prettier version of her mother after all. Cassandra wasn't impressed when she arrived home unexpectedly to find a naked Rosa wrapped in Viktor's arms.

She lit a cigarette and sighed. She owed money everywhere. Her credit card bill was huge, she was behind on her rent, she needed to pay Gertrude back. The list was endless.

Now, she was unemployed to boot.

She picked up her phone and opened Google. She typed in 'Get rich quick' but before she pressed 'search' she noticed a headline about Raphael Baptiste below the search bar.

She had forgotten about him. Her godfather. She rarely saw him as he and Johann were estranged. Johann never spoke of it, but she remembered how Johann had composed a score for one of Raphael's films and it has been rejected. Incensed, he had cut all ties with Raphael and refused to work with him ever again. Her whole family had been invited to his wedding to Isabelle Flynn but, in the end, she was the only one who had attended. That was the last time they'd met and he'd barely had time to speak to her that day.

She clicked on the link and read it quickly. It was about Raphael's new film and how it was finally due for release in September.

She threw her cigarette on the ground and stubbed it.

A few weeks in the French countryside was just what she needed. Johann would be angry, but what did she care?

London held too many bad memories for her now.

# CHAPTER FIFTEEN

Emilia walked down Hollywood Boulevard, her giant sunglasses shielding her eyes from the glare of the sun. She'd just had a pleasant lunch with the director, Corey McGrath, who was delighted with the score she had written for his new film, *Mayflower*. The test audience at the pre-screening had reacted favourably so it was confirmed. It was a relief when things worked out. She had struggled with the love theme for so long and then it had just clicked.

She paused to cross the road and glanced sideways. A man was standing with his back to her, with broad shoulders and dark hair. Her stomach leapt.

It couldn't be.

It couldn't be him.

A limousine pulled up beside the man and he opened the door. She tried to call out, but her throat was dry. Yanking off her glasses, she lunged forward, reaching out to grab his sleeve. Instead, she fell forwards and they both collided with the car door.

"What the fuck!" he said, turning around abruptly.

She inhaled sharply. The angry face looking down at her was not Johann. Not even close. On retrospect, she should have known. This man had dark hair, not grey, and was around the same age he was when he left her. Immortalised in her memory.

"I'm very sorry," she said, red-faced. "I thought you were someone else."

He turned away and got into the car, slamming the door behind him.

Emilia put on her glasses and straightened up.

She had to pull herself together. How many years had it been? Too long. Too long to still care.

A week later, she arrived back in England. She texted Alfie to say that she'd landed and when the taxi pulled up outside her house, the lights were on.

"Thank you," she said to the driver, handing him the fare.

He helped her carry her suitcase to the door and then drove off back to the city. She inserted the key into the lock and opened the heavy oak door. Blinding Lights by The Weeknd was blaring from the kitchen.

Alfie.

She left her suitcase by the foot of the stairs and dropped her keys on the hall table.

Sure enough, Alfie was in by the Aga, stirring a pot of ragù and singing along to the music. There were packets of dried fusilli on the countertop and two frozen garlic breads on a baking sheet, ready to be put in the oven.

"Alfie?" She couldn't help but smile. "What are you doing?"

He dropped the wooden spoon with a clatter and spun around. "Emmy! You frightened me."

"Well, this is my house."

He laughed. "Fair point." He was wearing an apron with 'Mr Good Lookin' is Cookin' on it. "Miranda and the girls are on the way over. Our oven broke last week and the new one hasn't been delivered yet. I thought we could all eat my fabulous pasta together. We're sick of Deliveroo."

"As long as you wash up too."

"As per usual." He rolled his eyes as he popped the bread in the oven. "We won't stay long. I know you're probably jet-lagged."

She went to the fridge and poured a glass of water. "Carey says hi. He's delighted with the score. It's confirmed."

"That's great."

"I'm always so nervous. I remember years ago, Johann was working on a score for a film and it was binned."

Alfie raised an eyebrow. "I haven't heard that name in a while."

Emilia smiled sadly. "I thought I saw him. I actually walked up to this random man, thinking it was Johann."

"It's because you were in LA, that's all. You were expecting it."

"Maybe I'll never get over him."

"You are over him." Alfie frowned. "You're in love with a ghost: a fantasy. I don't think you ever saw him for what he really was."

"What do you mean?"

"Arrogant, selfish. I hated you two together."

"You were jealous."

"Yes, I was. But I could also see that he would never have allowed you to become who you are today if you'd remained a couple. There's only room for one star in his head: himself."

The back door opened and a smiling Miranda appeared, followed by the twins.

"Something smells good," she said, kissing Alfie. "Emmy! I hope you mind our joining you. Did Alfie tell you about our oven?"

"No problem." Emilia smiled. "Good to see you all."

"How was America?" asked Arabella, who had blonde hair like her mother. "Did you see anyone famous?"

"Well, I had dinner with Jerry Bruckheimer."

"Who?" asked Ava quizzically. "Is he an actor?"

"Not exactly." Emilia laughed. "However, I think that Robert Pattinson was across the room."

"OMG, did you speak to him?" demanded Arabella. "He's so cool in The Batman."

"No, I didn't."

"Oh, that's disappointing." Ava sighed. "I definitely would've asked him for a selfie or something."

Emilia ruffled her hair and sat down. Miranda rooted around in her bag and produced a wedge of parmesan and a grater.

"How did you know that I didn't have a grater?" asked Emilia in surprise.

Alfie heaved the pot of pasta off the hob and brought it to the table. "You have many talents, Emmy, but cooking is not one of them. I would be surprised to find a breadknife in this place, if I'm honest."

Emilia made a face. "Ha, ha."

"Come on, grab a bowl and a fork," said Alfie with a wink. "Let's eat the best ragù I've ever created."

"Oh, Daddy, you always say that," said Arabella, rolling her eyes.

# CHAPTER SIXTEEN

"*Madame? Madame?*"

Rosa opened her eyes and blinked, feeling disorientated. The taxi driver was looking at her impatiently. For a moment, she had no idea where she was.

"*Pardon.*" She stretched and winced. She must have fallen asleep just outside Paris. Her back felt cramped from being slouched in the passenger seat. Her fuzzy brain clicked into gear as she peered out at the large black gates.

"*Attendez,*" she said, opening the car door, getting up and pressing the buzzer.

"*Allo?*" came a female voice.

"*C'est moi. Rosa.*" The security camera moved slightly and pointed at her.

The gates opened slowly and jumped back into the taxi. Large trees lined the road leading up to a huge mansion with turrets. The home of Raphael Baptiste: her godfather.

She craved a cigarette but she was all out. She had smoked the last one outside Charles de Gaulle before she hailed the taxi.

She fiddled with her gold bracelet. Her whiplash had subsided and she had left the neck brace back in London. She had only seen Bianca once since that fateful night. She and Adam had come to the flat to box up the last of her possessions. On her way out, Bianca stopped and turned to face Rosa.

"I hope you find happiness someday," she said with shining eyes. "I'd hate to be as fucked up as you." Then she had left, slamming the door behind her.

Johann refused to take her calls even though she'd left countless voice messages. Cassandra was on tour and couldn't be reached. Rosa sighed bitterly. The messages she'd sent her mother had been read; the blue ticks mocked her every time she checked her WhatsApp. Cassandra just hadn't bothered to reply.

She thanked God that Raphael had been so obliging. When she'd called and asked to visit, he'd been delighted.

"I'm so glad," he said enthusiastically. "This silliness with your father has gone on too long. You will also be good company for Isabelle. She gets so lonely sometimes."

The taxi pulled up outside the main door of the old house. Rosa watched the driver heave her huge suitcase out of the boot. She took her cello case herself. She had booked two seats on the flight over: one for herself and one for her cello. She winced as she thought of her credit card bill.

"*Merci,*" she said with her winning smile.

He stood back expectantly, waiting for payment. Rosa held up her hand and said, "*Attendez*," before bounding up the steps and knocking loudly.

The front door opened and Zola, Raphael's lurcher shot out. His jumped on her, his tail wagging, and barked loudly.

"Hello," she said, rubbing his head. "Hello, boy."

"*Arrête!*" Raphael pulled Zola back, who resisted and tried to break free. He turned to Rosa and smiled. "Welcome! Excuse my crazy dog."

"What's his name?"

"Zola."

"Great name." She hugged him and kissed his cheek. "It's good to see you. It's been so long."

"You look well," he said, appraising her. "So like your mother."

"God, don't say that." She bit her lip. "Would you have any cash on you?" She gestured at the driver who was tapping his foot impatiently. "I maxed my credit card to get here."

He shook his head. "I never carry money." He took out his phone. "*Sans contact?*" he asked the driver.

He nodded and jumped behind the steering wheel to activate the card machine.

"I'm so sorry," said Rosa, blushing. "There's about ten pounds in my bank account."

Raphael waved her away. "It's fine."

The driver held the card machine out the window of the car and Raphael tapped the screen.

As soon as the payment was approved, the taxi drove off at top speed. Zola followed it down the driveway, barking madly.

Raphael kissed her on both cheeks. "How are you? Did you receive your birthday card?"

"Yes," she answered mechanically. "Thank you."

"It was Isabelle." He blushed. "She's much better at remembering dates than I. I'm afraid I haven't been the best godfather to you. I forget things."

She smiled. Nine times out of ten he had forgotten her birthday, but then he'd make up for it unexpectedly. Like the time he picked her up from school and brought her to his film set to meet her idol, Colin Farrell.

"It's fine." She patted his arm. "You've taken me in now and I'll be forever grateful."

"Is your father still giving you the frozen shoulder?"

"Cold shoulder,' she corrected, "and yes, he is. He's so angry."

"He'll get over it. He is still giving me that shoulder too." Raphael shrugged. "You are young and beautiful. Drama will follow you. It's not your fault."

Rosa wasn't so sure. She had been feeling the wrath of karma for some time now. Maybe she should take it as a signal to turn over a new leaf.

"Lunch is ready. Come, Isabelle and Anouk are already seated."

Isabelle was tying Anouk into a wooden highchair, her head bent in concentration.

"Goddamn!" she said with gritted teeth as the clasp refused to close.

"Zsa Zsa," said Raphael, using her pet name. "Rosa has arrived."

"Rosa!" Isabelle pushed a lock of red hair back from her face. "So good to see you." She turned to Raphael. "Can you close this? It just won't work for me."

Raphael walked up to the highchair and calmly clicked the clasp into its place.

"Aw, come on!" Isabelle rolled her eyes. "I've been at that for ten minutes."

"You're too hot-headed," he said, kissing her nose.

"Me? Hot-headed?" She laughed. "That's pretty ironic, babe." She gestured to an empty chair. "Please sit, Rosa. We're having salad. I hope that's okay."

"Sounds great." Rosa smiled and sat down. Anouk giggled and banged the side of her highchair with a plastic spoon.

"Hi," said in her high little voice.

"Hello!" Rosa smiled at the dark haired little girl. "She's so cute. I love her curls."

"Anoo cute." She threw her spoon on the ground and laughed. Zola made a move to eat it, but Isabelle was too quick. She picked up the spoon, wiped it with a napkin, and gave it back to her daughter. "You've never met each other, right?"

Rosa shook her head. "The last time I was here was for your wedding."

Raphael took the seat at the head of the table. "Has it been that long?"

"No one really travelled during the pandemic." Rosa shrugged. "Well, except my mother."

"How is Cassandra?"

Rosa sipped her water. "Good, as far as I know. She's not the best at keeping in touch." The blue ticks flashed through her brain and her expression darkened.

"How was your trip?" asked Raphael as a small woman brought in a tray of plates.

"I slept for most of it," said Rosa. "That's all I seem to do lately."

Raphael's phone started to ring.

"Excuse me," he said, leaving the room.

Isabelle regarded Rosa thoughtfully. "I'm so glad you decided to come here," she said softly. "It gets pretty lonely here sometimes."

"Oh?"

"Raph will be working day and night from now on. His new film finally has a release date so he'll be travelling a lot. He's also got another script almost ready to go. We can hang out."

Rosa felt her eyes fill with tears. No one had been nice to her in so long. Isabelle reached out and clasped her hand. "Hey, it doesn't take a genius to work out that you're running from something."

"What have you heard?"

"Just bits." Isabelle's green eyes were kind. "Just forget it and move on. This is a new beginning."

Rosa inhaled shakily.

"I was in rehab a few years ago," Isabelle continued. "I didn't think I'd ever be happy again. Life throws things at us all the time. What's important is how we pick ourselves up."

Rosa nodded.

"Now, eat." Isabelle picked up her knife and fork. "Raphael could be a long while. Thank God we're having salad. At least it can't get cold."

After lunch, Isabelle showed Rosa her bedroom. It was a large space overlooking the courtyard at the back of the house. Beyond that were fields of wheat and an orchard.

"Raphael thought you'd like the view," she explained. "He says it's quite like your place back in England."

Rosa nodded. "It's similar."

Isabelle opened the old window. "Make yourself at home. We have the house to ourselves for a week. Raph has to go to New York. Use this holiday as a new start. Have you ever changed a diaper?"

Rosa shook her head.

"Great. I'm going to teach you some new skills."

"Oh, I don't know about that…" Rosa wrinkled her nose. "I'm not used to children."

"You'll love it." Isabelle smiled. "One thing, Raph mentioned that you smoke, right?"

Rosa nodded. "Not as much as I did. To be honest, I'm trying to stop."

"Raphael is the same," said Isabelle. "He does so well and then he gets stressed and he's back to square one."

"Same."

"If you want to smoke, please do it outside. I don't want smoke around Anouk."

"Of course."

"Awesome. See you when you're settled."

# CHAPTER SEVENTEEN

The next morning Raphael left at eight to catch his flight to America. At the front door, he kissed Isabelle and ruffled Anouk's hair.

"I hate to leave you."

Isabelle pushed a lock of his brown hair behind his ear. "It's only a week. We'll be fine now that Rosa is here. Bring me back some Twinkies."

Rosa came down stairs just as the black Range Rover drove off.

"Morning,' she said with a yawn.

"Hey, you." Isabelle smiled warmly. "Did you sleep well?"

"Surprisingly, yes."

"Breakfast?"

"Just a coffee, please."

"Go on out to the veranda."

Rosa walked out onto a large wooden deck overlooking a green expanse of lawn. Flowers lined the edges, brilliant colours highlighted by the morning sun. The air was balmy for April, so she discarded her robe and took a seat on a wicker chair. She took a cigarette from the packet in her pocket and lit it, breathing in deeply. The nicotine calmed her, satisfying the craving she'd felt since her eyes opened that morning. The warning signs on the packets, shocking information designed to dissuade people from smoking, meant nothing to her. She just didn't care.

Isabelle reappeared with Anouk and Rosa stubbed out her cigarette hurriedly, remembering the warning about smoke around the little girl. She waved the air around her, willing the smoke to blow away.

Isabelle placed Rosa in a highchair.

"*Non*," she said, wriggling, "*non, Maman.*"

"You stay in there and give your momma a break," said Isabelle, rolling her eyes at Rosa. "She's a nightmare lately, climbing up on everything."

Rosa smiled at the little girl. A woman appeared with a pot of fresh coffee, two cups, milk and sugar on a tray.

"Thanks, Coralie," said Isabelle. "We'll manage from here." She poured two cups and sat down opposite Rosa. Anouk banged the table of her high chair and gave the odd shout.

"So, we couldn't christen Anouk because of Covid. I was so disappointed. My parents haven't seen her properly in ages."

"Where do they live?"

"Philadelphia. They didn't leave the house during Corona. It was handled so badly over there. I wanted to fly them over here, but my dad wouldn't come. He likes his own space and hates French food."

"Have you rescheduled the christening?"

"Yeah. It's in a month's time." She beamed. "It's going to be incredible. All of our family and friends are coming. Caspian and his band Doctor Eckleburg are playing."

"I saw him on TV for that charity concert online," said Rosa thoughtfully. "He's awfully like Raphael, isn't he?"

"Yeah, a blonde version."

"Are they close?"

Isabelle paused. "Kind of. He stayed here a while back but it was a little awkward, you know? I guess they're too alike." She laughed. "It's crazy that I'm his stepmother and there's about three years between us."

Coralie placed a tray of viennoiserie on the table. Isabelle reached out and took a mini pain au chocolat.

"You know he's engaged to Madison Ryan, right?" said Isabelle, feeding Anouk a piece of her pastry.

Rosa nodded. "I had all her albums when I was a teenager." She sang the chorus of *Text Me Back,* one of Madison's early songs.

"Well, Madison sang the theme song from Raphael's new film, *Josephine.*"

"Yeah, I remember it. It was out ages ago. " Rosa hummed the tune. "It was a good song."

"When it was released, the film itself was meant to follow soon after. Then everything was postponed indefinitely. Raphael was so mad. The song went to number one in tons of countries, but then just faded away. Such bad timing."

"They should re-release it."

"They're about to, I think." Isabelle took another pain au chocolat. "Thank God I'm not modelling anymore," she said, taking a bite and closing her eyes in pleasure.

Rosa finished her coffee. "Does Raphael still keep horses?"

Isabelle nodded. "Yes, we have four. Do you ride?"

"Yes, I love it." Her eyes lit up. "That feeling when you're on a horse's back at top speed and you feel like you're flying."

"Wow, you sound like a pro. I'm only a novice. I used to go on vacation to Montana and do some trails. Nice and slow."

"I'm not a pro." Rosa blushed. "Not really."

"Well, take a look. Luna is my horse but I never get a chance to ride her now. Rajah belongs to Raphael. He's the big black stallion. Don't even go there. He won't let anyone ride him except his master."

"Luna sounds great." Rosa beamed at her.

"Jean is the head groom. He's really nice. Ask him to tack Luna up for you."

"I will, thanks."

"Please stay for the christening." Isabelle's green eyes beseeched her. "Stay here, practise your French and keep me company."

Rosa wandered out to the stables that afternoon. Rajah was just as Isabelle described: a black Arabian stallion who towered over the others. Along with Isabelle's mare, Luna, there was an old piebald pony named Alouette, and a colt called Odi, which the stable hand told her was short for Odysseus.

Rosa approached Rajah and tentatively reached out to rub him. He was truly a beauty with his elegant sleek body. As she stroked his mane, she couldn't help but marvel at his finely chiselled head. Alouette nudged her arm from the right, looking for treats.

*"Je n'en ai rien,"* said Rosa apologetically, holding up empty hands. "I've nothing."

She ambled over to Luna who was a chestnut brown colour with a white patch on her forehead.

"Oh, but you're beautiful," said Rosa, rubbing her flank. "You remind me of Pegasus."

Something clutched her heart when she thought of her old friend. How simple life had been back then. She would spend hours riding through the meadows, her face tilted to the sun, without any of the worries she now harboured. A tear rolled down her cheek. Who was she fooling? The past could not be glorified like that. Worries had always been a constant in her life.

She wiped her eyes with her sleeve and walked out into the sunshine.

"*Bonjour*," came a deep voice behind her and she turned around. A man of about fifty was standing at the entrance to the stables, a bucket in his hand.

"*Bonjour,*" she said with a smile.

"Can I help you?" he asked in heavily accented English.

"I'm Rosa, you must be Jean."

He nodded. "Yes."

"I would like to ride Luna sometime if that's okay."

He nodded. "You tell me when."

"Thank you," she said smiling. "*Bonne journée!* Thank you!"

Later that afternoon, Rosa and Isabelle took a car into the medieval Saint Leu district in Amiens. Situated at the foot of the famous Gothic cathedral, it was comprised of pretty little houses along the banks of the canal. Isabelle put Anouk into her buggy and together they strolled along the small streets, visiting antique shops and stopping for a coffee in one of the bars. Isabelle did most of the talking, telling Rosa about Raphael's new film and his unpredictable lifestyle.

"Some nights I wake up and he's working on that script at four a.m. He gets obsessed."

She talked about America and how she missed it. How living in a strange country with a dubious grasp of the native tongue was challenging.

"I miss Philly. It's so different here."

Rosa added a cube of sugar to her coffee and stirred. "Why don't you go back to modelling?"

"Back to modelling? Are you crazy?"

"Why not? You look as good as ever. Plus you're modelling royalty."

"People have forgotten who I am."

"No they haven't. Not at all."

"Gabby does keep asking me to come out of retirement but I always refuse. I'm past it."

"Gabriella? The designer? I love her work. She's a good friend of yours, isn't she?"

"Yeah, she's my best friend. We studied together at Parson's in New York. She designing Anouk's christening dress actually. The ancient Baptiste one is way too small at this late stage. Babies are normally christened within weeks here."

"Wow, lucky Anouk."

"I know, right? She'll be so chic."

"So, take Gabriella up on her offer! Go back to the catwalk."

"Not with Anouk." Isabelle shook her head.

"Part-time. Special occasions. It would do you good to get out."

Isabelle shook her head. "No. That ship has sailed."

Rosa said nothing. She suspected that Isabelle was insecure. Models were scrutinised and held up as paragons of beauty. It was understandable that she was hesitant.

Anouk, who was sleeping in her buggy, sighed loudly.

"This little lady has the life," said Isabelle fondly. "No worries except where her next bottle of milk is coming from."

"Do you think she'll be a model like you?"

"No way. She's Raphael through and through. I can't see her being bossed around by anyone."

# CHAPTER EIGHTEEN

Later that night, Raphael phoned from New York. Isabelle took the call in the drawing room, leaving Rosa alone with Anouk. The little girl was changed for bed and looked adorable in a velour pink suit with bows.

Rosa wondered what kind of baby she and David would have had. Brown-eyed like her or blue-eyed like him? She pushed the thought away. Every time she thought of him she felt her heart lurch. She asked herself over and over why he did it. Why he had stamped on her heart so callously.

Anouk grabbed her finger and squeezed it, murmuring "Osa" which was Anouk's version of Rosa.

Rosa's expression softened. She felt a small glimmer of hope. One day this would be her life: her reality. Just because David had dumped her didn't mean she would never find happiness again. In little Anouk, she saw possibilities. If she changed her wayward ways now, she would be eligible to be someone's mother. A good mother, a present mother. Not like Cassandra. David and the crash and the whole disastrous affair was the wakeup call she needed. She was going to be a good person. She would change for real this time. Maybe if she were a better person, good fortune would follow.

She picked Anouk up and hugged her, kissing her soft head.

"You and I are going to be great friends," she said softly. Anouk clapped her hands.

"Osa!"

A week passed quickly. Rosa's days were filled with helping with Anouk, a morning ride on Luna, walks around the estate and coffees in town with Isabelle. She found that she liked using her French again. It had been so long. A short conversation at the pâtisserie led to a longer chat with a waitress in a bar. Her brain clicked into gear and soon she was gabbling away at tremendous speed.

"You're so lucky to speak all those languages," said Isabelle enviously. "Raph hired a tutor for me but I just can't get the accent."

"I can help you," offered Rosa. "The best way to learn a language is through every day use in authentic situations. Not from a book."

"You were so lucky to have an Italian mom talking to you all the time."

Rosa's expression darkened. "She wasn't around a lot."

Isabelle stirred her coffee. "Where is she now?"

"Milan." Rosa looked up. "She's just back from a tour."

"Artists are hard work. Raphael drives me crazy most days and I always feel second-best."

"Second-best. That's exactly it." She looked up. "You and Anouk? I love your relationship. How you put her first. How you spend all your time caring for her."

"She'll probably be a rebellious teenager," said Isabelle, "having been smothered as a child."

Rosa shook her head. "She's lucky."

The waiter put the bill under the ashtray.

"So, I'm your new tutor." Rosa smiled. "What's that?" She pointed to the cup.

"A *tasse*?" Isabelle shrugged. "Don't ask me if its male or female. I don't get that gender bit at all."

"Hey, that's pretty good. *Une tasse.*"

"*Une,*" repeated Isabelle.

Anouk clapped her hands together. "*Bon, Maman.*"

"You see, she's proud of you." Rosa laughed.

"It's depressing that my kid speaks more French than I do," said Isabelle drily.

***

At the end of the second week, Rosa opened her cello case. Up to then she simply didn't have the time to practise. It was propped against the wall in the old music room that Louis Baptiste had used when he was alive. It was a sizable room at the back of the house with books lining the walls and a musty feel. A grand piano stood by the windows, complete with a velvet upholstered stool. There was a violin stand to the right, yellowing sheet music of Czardas on display. Framed pictures of music degrees and accolades covered the gable wall. Louis Baptiste himself was pictured directly over the piano, similar to Raphael in height and stature.

Coralie sourced a wooden chair for Rosa to use and she spent an hour every morning playing again, losing herself in the music. The D string was her favourite for its soulful sound and she would play beautiful, lyrical cantilenas. Her preference was Bach and with eyes closed, she would tackle his cello suites with deep sonorous elegance. One morning she played the *Game of Thrones* theme tune and Isabelle popped her head in the door.

"Hey, I loved that show! You're awesome."

Isabelle taught her how to change a nappy, make batches of purée dinners and treat nappy rash.

"Sudocrem is the best," she said, closing the nappy. "You're going to be a pro when you have your own kids."

It took a while for Rosa to learn. The first nappy she changed fell off. The second was fastened the wrong way around. She overheated the milk and burned her wrist when she tested it. The worst was when Anouk managed to take a battery out of a remote control and put it in her mouth while Rosa was watching TikTok on her phone. In the nick of time, Coralie walked in and figured out what had happened. She reprimanded a horrified Rosa in French, shaking her head in disapproval.

However, Rosa gradually became used to caring for the little girl. Soon, she was making formula with one hand and holding Anouk on her hip with the other. She urged Isabelle to go into Amiens for a spa day.

"You might as well take advantage," she said. "I'll take Anouk for a walk around the grounds."

Rosa enjoyed playing with the baby, reading her stories and singing her songs. She felt peaceful when Anouk was in her arms. Everything else just melted away. The smell of baby powder was comforting and as she cuddled the small body, she didn't feel as raw.

At night, she and Isabelle would watch romantic films.

"Raphael hates when I make him watch stuff like this," said Isabelle, selecting *Bridget Jones' Diary.*

Rosa settled into the cushions, comfortable in her pyjamas, and sipped her hot chocolate. She had definitely made the right decision. A change of scenery was exactly what she needed.

Half way through the film she reflected on why she hadn't seen that David was a Daniel Cleaver type rather than a Mark Darcy. When the end credits appeared she felt slightly hopeful. Not all men were complete bastards after all. Isabelle put her hand on her chest.

"Colin Firth is so handsome. We must watch *Mamma Mia* tomorrow night before Raph comes back."

# CHAPTER NINETEEN

Raphael stopped off in London on his way home to see his old friend, Bertie Wells. An Oscar-winning actor, Bertie was one of Raphael's oldest and best friends. Adored by his contemporaries, Bertie knew everyone who was anyone. He had a starring role in Raphael's new venture, *Josephine*, playing the empress' first husband, Alexandre de Beauharnais. Dressed in his habitual shirt and colourful cravat, his grey hair swept off his forehead, he opened the door of his Belgravia mansion.

"Raph, old chap, you look as dashing as ever!" Bertie smiled broadly. "How was New York?"

"Stressful,' said Raphael, walking past him and removing his jacket. "You know how I hate cities." He shook out his dark hair and rubbed his eyes. "Did you arrange lunch with Emilia?"

Bertie nodded. "Tomorrow at The Westbury. She's looking forward to seeing you."

"Good."

"That score she wrote is sublime! I listen to it constantly. I think it will be nominated for all sorts of awards."

"Perhaps."

They walked into the conservatory where there were two places set for lunch.

"I just feel like this film is cursed." Raphael took a seat and rubbed his temple. "Do you know how hard I had to fight with the studio not to stream it online? A film by Raphael Baptiste will be shown in the cinema. Not on a laptop or phone."

"Films on-demand was the only option for many," said Bertie fairly. "The pandemic saw to that. Lots were forced to skip the cinema entirely."

"Yes, but not mine!" Raphael glared at him. "It will be premièred in the old-fashioned way or I will throw it in the bin. Tom insisted that the same happen with the new Top Gun film. He, like me, understands cinema."

"They gave you a date, have they not?"

"Yes. September."

"Wonderful! It'll give me time to look good for the red carpet."

"It feels like everything has peaked prematurely," continued Raphael, ignoring him. "Ridley just wrapped a film about Napoleon. Can you believe it? He got Joaquin Phoenix as his lead. *Josephine* could be overshadowed by that."

Bertie slapped him on the back. "Buck up, old friend. Yes, it was unfortunate. Yes, the timing was terrible, but we will use this to our advantage. It will be the most anticipated film of 2022. The hype will be stupendous!"

"I'm not sure…"

"Raphael! I insist that you shirk this mood! Your last film grossed £600 million worldwide. *Josephine* will be a triumph, I don't doubt it! Let Ridley Scott make a hundred films about Napoleon. Yours will be released first and will be in time for the Oscars. Nothing to worry about."

Emilia stood on the threshold of her house, waiting or Alfie to arrive. She didn't own a car so he had offered to drop her to the station. The train ride into the city took about an hour.

"I can call a taxi," she protested, but he wouldn't hear of it. The sun shone in the blue sky and for a moment she closed her eyes and let it shine on her face. She loved when spring turned into summer. There was always a feeling that anything was possible with the long days and balmy evenings.

Alfie's old Mercedes appeared around the corner, music blaring. The car came to a halt in front of her and Alfie jumped out.

"I didn't know you were a fan of pop music," she said in amusement.

"I was forced to play it," he said, gesturing to the back seat. Emilia bent down and saw Ava and Arabella sitting in the back seat.

"Hi, girls!" sha said, waving.

"Hi, Emmy," they chorused.

Emilia got into the car and tied her seatbelt. Sheets of music, tennis balls and empty juice cartons littered the floor. Alfie resumed his seat behind the steering wheel and revved the engine.

"*Oh, no, no, no,*" he sang, grinning, jamming the gear into first. The old Merc spluttered as it sprang into action.

Later, as she sat on the train, Emilia smiled when she thought of her friend.

Darling Alfie. He looked after her no matter what. He made sure she ate properly and paid her bills on time. He listened to her insecure rants about her compositions and patiently put up with her moods. When he had married Miranda ten years before, Emilia had been happy for him but also worried that he would slip away. However, they were as a close as ever, and she and Miranda were great friends.

The twins, Ava and Arabella, were eight years old and keen musicians. They could already play violin and had just started the cello.

The green fields whizzed past, interspersed with small villages nestled in the woodland. A woman with a small baby sat in the seat opposite her. Emilia smiled at the sleeping bundle as the woman kissed the baby's head.

Funny how children had never really crossed her mind. Sure, she had had fantasies of having Johann's babies, but that all disappeared when she lost him. Then it was just work, work, work. Now, she was almost forty-five, so being a mother seemed unlikely.

Her phone buzzed and she saw a message from Bertie. He and Raphael would be at The Westbury by half one. The table was booked under his name.

Emilia smiled. She was looking forward to seeing them both.

Bertie's driver drove down Conduit Street in his Bentley, coming to a halt outside the impressive front door of The Westbury Hotel. The flags flapped in the breeze as he and Raphael exited the car. Vladimir, Bertie's personal bodyguard, ushered them inside and they headed straight for the dining room.

Emilia was already seated at the table. She stood up as they approached. Her auburn hair was now blonde, and fell just below her ears.

"Raph!" she said, opening her arms to embrace him. They kissed each other's cheeks.

"And Bertie," she said, kissing him too. "Good to see you both."

"Good to see you too," said Raphael.

"How's the lovely Isabelle?" she asked.

"She's well," said Raphael, taking a seat. "She sends her love."

Bertie took a seat too and beamed at them both. "It's not often I'm in the company of such genius." He waved at a passing waiter. "May we have the wine list, my good man?"

The waiter nodded and scurried away.

"It was shame about Madison Ryan's song," said Emilia, buttering a slice of bread. "Bad timing with Covid and all that."

"Yes, unfortunate." Raphael scowled. "How were we to know the world would come to a halt?"

"It will climb the charts again," she went on. "If Madison makes a few live appearances and promotes it, people will download it. I'm sure of it."

Bertie held up his hands. "You could release a post-pandemic remix of it. A banging tune that could grace the nightclubs of Ibiza."

"*Non!*" Raphael glared at him. "That would be preposterous."

"Music is one of the most powerful codes, Raph," said Bertie. "Look at Céline

Dion on the prow of that ship? That soundtrack sold millions because of that song."

Emilia nodded. "Remember Bryan Adams and that song he recorded for a Robin Hood film? It's one of the bestselling singles of all time." She smiled. "In fact, I remember snogging boys to that song at the disco in Solihull back in the day."

Raphael scowled.

"My point is, Michael Kamen wrote the score, but it was Adams' song that catapulted the film into the limelight."

"Quite right," agreed Bertie.

Raphael took a seeded bread roll from the basket and tore it apart viciously.

"I think we should release a TikTok with the song to remind people," said Bertie. "I spend hours at night scrolling through those videos. It really is the biggest platform in the world right now. It would definitely help box office sales."

"This film does not need any help,' said Raphael icily. "It's a masterpiece already."

"Of course it is." Bertie grinned. "Now, change the subject. You look so tortured, I can't cope with the drama."

Raphael put on his glasses to read the menu. "My eyes get worse by the day," he said crossly.

"Me too," said Emilia. "The curse of old age."

"Tell us about this christening," interrupted Bertie. "I, for one, can't wait. This pandemic has curbed my socialising no end."

"It will be family and close friends only. You two, of course, and a few others." Raphael cleared his throat. "Caspian and his band will play a few songs." He cast his eyes down.

"That's wonderful!" said Bertie in delight. "You two are really progressing."

"Not really..."

Emilia put her hand on Raphael's and squeezed it. "I'm looking forward to meeting him. He's very talented, like his dad."

Raphael said nothing.

Bertie waved at the waiter. "Here's that wonderful young man with the wine list. Emilia, darling, shall we opt for white or red?"

Straight after the main course, Raphael went outside to smoke and take a phone call.

Bertie refilled their glasses. "So, any action in your love life? I heard that it fizzled out with that Italian flautist."

"Yes, he was far too dramatic and he wanted me to move to Florence."

"What's wrong with that? *Firenze* is magnificent!"

"I like England. I like my house. I adore the lavender fields nearby. I don't like oppressive heat."

"Okay."

She leaned in closer and lowered her voice to a whisper. "The real reason was that he was terrible in bed."

Bertie laughed out loud. "Now, we know the truth."

She laughed too.

"I do love the score, Emmy. It suits the film perfectly."

"Yes, I'm pleased with it," she agreed. "Raph and I, well, we just click. I can't explain it, but I seem to know exactly what he wants. When he sent me the temp track, I was inspired immediately."

"Is he still as bossy as ever?"

She laughed. "Yes, without a doubt. When I started, the composer pulled rank and didn't put up with any interference. Now the director is the boss. Luckily Raph treats me with respect."

"Quite."

Raphael arrived back, zipping up his jacket. "I must catch my flight to Paris," he said, kissing Bertie and Emilia on both cheeks. "Sorry to leave so abruptly."

"Duty calls," said Bertie with a wink. "It must be hard on poor Isabelle, all alone with the baby."

"She has help at the moment, in fact. Rosa is there."

"Rosa?" repeated Bertie.

"My goddaughter. Rosa Weber."

"Johann's daughter?" asked Bertie in surprise. "I thought you and Johann were estranged over that silly score years ago?"

"Yes, he's still bitter about that film, but that doesn't affect my relationship with Rosa." Raphael ran his fingers through his hair. "She and Johann had a falling out and she needed somewhere to stay."

Neither of the men noticed that Emilia's face had turned white.

"So, I'll see you both at the christening. *A bientôt!*"

Everyone stopped to look as he walked out of the dining room.

"He's still dishy even though he's middle-aged," said Bertie, tilting his head sideways for a better look.

Emilia took a sip of water, her head swimming.

A waiter appeared.

"Dessert?" he asked with a big smile.

"Why not?" said Bertie, taking the menu from him. He scanned the list. "Shall we share a crumble?"

Emilia took a deep breath. She couldn't believe how winded she felt. "Sure," she said mechanically.

"Blackberry crumble with crème anglaise, my good man!" Bertie snapped the menu shut. "Two spoons." He focused in on her face. "Are you all right, my dear? You look so pale."

She twisted her napkin around and around. "I just got a shock when he mentioned Rosa. I haven't heard about her in years."

Bertie put his hand over his mouth. "Oh, but of course! You and Johann had a thing. How could I have forgotten that?"

"It was a long time ago."

"You obviously still have feelings."

"No, no. Not at all."

Bertie put his hand on hers. "It's okay to have feelings, Emilia. We're humans after all."

She shook her head. "Johann was a lifetime ago. It's all fine."

"Hmmm."

"Do you think he'll be at the christening too?" She looked like she was about to faint.

Bertie shook his head. "Not at all. He cut Raphael off that time when his score was rejected. A bad loser is what he is. Frightful behaviour."

"I just…"

"No need to explain. You heard what he said: it will only be close friends and family. Rosa is an unexpected addition." He nudged her playfully. "Now, let me tell me more about that flautist and his short-comings."

Later that night, Emilia took her beloved Strad from its case and stroked the sleek body. She remembered the night she received it: she had been so young and sure of herself then. Over the years she had toyed with selling the violin, cutting ties with the past, but she never did. Not only was it a superb instrument, it was also proof that Johann had loved her, no matter how briefly. It was a symbol of their passion and every time she played it, she was young, carefree Emilia again.

Hearing about Rosa had been a shock, but what did she expect? Of course Raphael's goddaughter would be at a family gathering. Rosa was only nine or ten when the relationship had ended. Why would she remember a Brummy ex-girlfriend who made her pancakes and plaited her hair?

Emilia replaced the violin in its case and closed the lid.

# CHAPTER TWENTY

Raphael's return changed the dynamic in the house. Gone were the cosy nights watching romantic films on the large screen in the sitting room. His very presence was dominating, and Rosa often heard him on the phone long into the early hours of the morning. He had a short-temper and snapped at everyone, but his staff were devoted to him and ignored his volatile manner. Sometimes he joined them for meals, other times he remained in his study, working on his new script, drinking lots of coffee.

One morning, Rosa was heading out to the stable for her morning ride, when Raphael appeared in long boots. "I will join you today," he stated.

"On Rajah?"

He nodded.

Jean was waiting in the courtyard with both Luna and Rajah, all tacked up and ready to go.

"Is it true that Rajah won't let anyone else ride him except you?" asked Rosa.

Raphael took the reins from Jean and expertly mounted the horse. "It's true. Rajah comes from a long line of stallions. My father's horse was Rajah's sire. No one but Papa could ride him."

"So, it's a Baptiste tradition."

"Yes."

Rosa swung her leg over Luna and pulled on the reins. "Where do you want to go?"

"Follow me." Raphael yanked Rajah to the right and spurred the animal to move. Rosa followed and they were soon galloping through the large field to the south of the house. The sun was rising in the sky, its yellow rays lighting up the dew that remained on the grass. Rosa kept her head down as the wind cut her face. Raphael didn't look back once to see if she was keeping up. He just thundered on at great speed.

When they reached a large ditch, Raphael pulled on the reins and Rajah halted. Rosa did the same and Luna stopped too. Rosa's cheeks were pink from the cool morning air and the exertion.

"You ride well," said Raphael approvingly, pulling the reins.

"Thanks, so do you."
"Johann had horses, had he not?"
"Yes, I had a pony when I was young. Pegasus."
"Ah, yes. I think I remember."
"She died." Rosa's face fell.
"I'm sorry."
"It's life." She shrugged. "Nothing lasts forever."
Raphael regarded her speculatively. "Is that why you won't let anyone close to you?"
"Excuse me?" Rosa's head shot up.
"You are a hard one to read, Rosa. You come here to escape, but what if you're trying to escape yourself?"
"You're talking riddles."
"I see your life. No stability, no structure. You play around and move on. It's typical."
"Typical?" Her voice was dangerously low.
"You don't take things seriously because you feel that no one ever took you seriously. Anyone you've ever loved has left you or treated you as second-best."
Rosa looked at him in horror. "Stop talking."
"Pegasus, this man you were carrying on with, your parents."
Rosa's eyes filled with tears. "Just stop."
"You need to be with people who won't let you down. Real friends. Dependable ones. Look at me and Bertie. He stuck with me all those years. Anyone else would not have been so loyal."
Rosa stared at him, her eyes shining.
"You don't have a best friend, do you?"
She thought of Bianca and her stomach sank.
"You fell in love and he hurt you."
*David.*
"Your father is never there. Your mother is jealous of your youth and beauty."
Rosa bit her trembling lip.
"So, you must listen to your godfather. Find someone you can trust who will not let you down. Do not rush into things. Find a friend or a lover who will respect you. Then, maybe you'll learn to respect yourself."
With that, Raphael spurred Rajah on and galloped off.
Rosa stayed immobile for a minute, her ears ringing. Every word he had said was true. Every single word.

She went straight upstairs after she had handed Luna back to Jean. She didn't want to face Raphael again for a while. She couldn't argue with what he'd said, but every fibre in her body resented being lectured. He was on the other side so it was easy for him to be judgmental. His life had turned spectacularly around. A lovely wife, a beautiful daughter, a long lost son. His career had emerged from the ashes and he was now one of the leading directors in cinema. He had made it through the hard times. She was stuck in the middle.

She took off her clothes and threw them on the ground. Switching on the shower, she stepped under the hot spray, letting it massage her aching muscles.

Isabelle's parents, Patrick and Elaine, flew in from the States three days before the christening. Rosa, Isabelle and Anouk were out in the garden, sitting on a rug on the grass. Zola was splayed out next to them, soaking up the heat.

"Look who's here!" said Patrick, appearing around the corner with Elaine.

Isabelle gasped, got up and catapulted herself on her father. Then she hugged her mother, and promptly started to cry.

"Oh, guys, I've missed you so."

Zola, roused by the commotion, jumped up and barked.

Elaine disentangled herself and made a beeline for Anouk who was sitting on a rug on the ground. "Come here, sweetheart. Give me a kiss." She picked up the little girl and hugged her tightly, inhaling her. Zola growled at Elaine.

"Back off, doggy. I'm her grandma," said Elaine mildly.

Rosa watched this exchange silently. Elaine looked similar to her daughter, except with dark hair. Isabelle had mentioned that her mother was a retired model too. Patrick had a warm, open face and a booming voice.

Raphael appeared and Zola jumped on his master joyfully.

"*Zola, dégage!*" said Raphael, pushing the dog down. He strode over and shook hands with Patrick. Then he embraced Elaine.

"Welcome," he said with a smile. "I hope you're not too tired from the journey."

"We're okay. I got some sleep." Patrick smiled. "How was your trip to New York?"

"Busy. Sorry I couldn't visit you, but I had no spare time."

Elaine spotted Rosa. "Oh, do you have a new nanny? You never said."

Isabelle shook her head. "No, this is Rosa. She's Raphael's goddaughter. She's been staying with us."

"How do you do?" Elaine held out her hand and Rosa shook it warmly.

"I'm well, thank you."

"Although, she's so good with Anouk, I wish she'd stay forever." Isabelle sighed. "I don't know what I'm going to do when she's gone."

"I'm not that proficient." Rosa blushed.

"You're amazing at changing diapers." Isabelle winked. "And she's teaching me French. I'm one hundred times better already."

Rosa held up her hands. "It's nothing really."

Elaine kissed Anouk's forehead. "Well, it sounds like you're a good person to have around. I know Isabelle gets lonely here sometimes." She glared at Raphael. "It's hard living with a workaholic."

Raphael didn't notice as he was showing Patrick the trailer for *Josephine* on his phone.

"Come on," said Isabelle. "Lunch is ready. Let's go and sit."

After lunch, Anouk went for a nap. Elaine and Isabelle took a walk around the garden, followed by Zola, opting to stay under the shade of the trees to avoid the sun. Both women had pale skin that burned easily. When they reached an old stone bench by a pond, Isabelle sat down. She patted the space next to her and Elaine followed suit. Zola lay down by Isabelle's feet and sighed.

"Anouk loves that willow tree over there," said Isabelle, pointing to a graceful tree with long trailing branches. "She runs under it and pulls the leaves."

"How have you been, honey? Really?" asked Elaine, changing the subject. "You never say much in your messages."

Isabelle paused to pick a twig off her skirt. "I'm good, Mom. Honestly. Quarantine was a godsend. Raph couldn't travel and he really bonded with Anouk. Yeah, he drove me insane at times, but it was nice to just be, you know?"

"I met Gabby a few weeks ago in New York. She said she asked you to model at her London show."

"I said no."

"Why?"

"I'm done with that life."

"That's crazy, you were so good at it. You're too young to disappear like this." Elaine took her daughter's hand in hers. "You will regret it, Zsa Zsa. In another ten years you will look back on this and wish you'd done more."

"You gave up the catwalk when I was born."

"Yes, but I lived in Philly and was surrounded by my family and friends. I joined baby groups and made playdates. I volunteered at local charities. You're completely isolated over here. You don't speak French…"

"Whoa, stop right there. I'm much better…"

"You don't have friends your own age. I'm worried about you, baby." Elaine frowned. "Raphael works and thrives on it. He's constantly creating and pushing himself. You need the same stimulation. Anouk needs to see her Mom do things for herself, not for others."

"I'm past it."

"Isabelle…"

"No, Mom. I'm not going back. Not for Gabby, not for anyone."

Rosa made her excuses after dinner and went upstairs to her room. She tried to ring her father, but it went straight to voicemail. He was really punishing her this time.

She looked out the window at the charming courtyard and the leafy trees. She had grown used to the view, delighting in the colours of the dawn and the twilight as shadows danced on the cobblestones. She would miss the smell of the honeysuckle and the poppies dancing in the breeze. She sighed. She couldn't stay here forever. Reality beckoned. Her overdue credit card bill played on her mind. She couldn't hide forever.

Isabelle had mentioned that Caspian and Madison were flying in the night before the ceremony. She was curious to meet them in the flesh. When she was a teenager, she had Madison Ryan's albums on her iPod, liking the easy beats and repetitive refrains. She remembered tying her hair in bunches and learning the dance routine to 'You and Me', an early hit of Madison's back in the day.

Then she'd outgrown her music and lost track of her career. She googled her and hundreds of images popped up. Madison looking beautiful in a red gown at the Met Gala at the start of May. Madison in a bikini on the deck of a yacht. Madison arm in arm with Caspian Cole, both blonde, both gorgeous, decked out in designer clothes. She clicked on Madison's Wikipedia page.

A privileged upbringing in south Dublin. A career that exploded. Tales of spoilt tantrums and diva-like behaviour. Her much-publicised relationship with Cal Scott, the lead singer of the boyband, The Southsiders. His betrayal; her heartbreak. Her collaboration with legend Savannah Morris for the *Josephine* movie and new-found respect in the industry. Her loyalty to Caspian during the adoption revelations. Her engagement ring which resembled the Hope Diamond.

She typed 'Caspian and Madison wedding' into the search engine and lots of tabloid links popped up.

***Sad Mads – still no date for the golden couple***

***Why won't you maddy me?***

Rosa frowned as she scanned the articles, all of which asked the same question: when would they set a date? 'Insiders' reported that it was Caspian who didn't want to rush things. Others said that it was rumoured that Madison had a world tour coming up in 2023 and they would be separated for months on end. Rosa stared at Caspian's image. He was so similar to Raphael with his beautiful bone structure and haughty demeanour. She clicked on his Wikipedia page.

*Born: Caspian George Cole 23rd May 1996 (age 26) Cork, Ireland*

Alma Mater: Guildhall School of Music

*Occupation: singer, songwriter, musician and lead singer of band Doctor Eckleburg*

*(see **Alexander Ryder, Ethan Hackett, Fionn O'Connor**)*

*Spouse (s): 0*

*(see **Madison Ryan**)*

*Children: 0*

*Instruments: piano, vocals, guitar*

*Years active: 2018 – present*

*Website: doctoreckleburg.com*

Rosa scrolled down and clicked on 'Personal Life'.

*Cole is a supporter of Liverpool F.C. According to an article released by Quartz in 2020, Cole has an estimated wealth of £35 million.*

*Cole and Irish singer **Madison Ryan** got engaged on New Year's Eve 2019.*

*In September 2019, it was revealed that Cole was adopted at birth by George and Prudence Cole. The family moved to Liverpool before settling in Banbury. Cole is the biological son of director **Raphael Baptiste** and Mary Kennedy (deceased).*

*Cole has a half-sister, **Anouk Baptiste**, daughter of **Raphael Baptiste** and model **Isabelle Flynn** (see **Gabriella Alvarez; Oberon**)*

*In 2019, **Bronwyn Jones** claimed that Cole had sex with her on three separate occasions. More accusations followed, totalling in seven different women who alleged they had intercourse with the singer while he was in a relationship with **Madison Ryan.** Pictures were printed in newspapers and online. Cole refused to comment.*

Rosa exited the article immediately and threw her phone to one side. Was there such a thing as true love? Why wasn't one person enough? Madison was pretty, successful, famous. Why then did he look for someone else?

She lay her head on the soft pillow.

She rarely saw a functional relationship. Raphael and Isabelle aside, she didn't know any other couple who were faithful. She had been instrumental in making many relationships dysfunctional, carrying on with married men. Was it a safety net? Pursuing men she knew would never commit? How could they hurt her if she had no expectations in the first place? Her thoughts drifted to David. He had been different. She had really seen a future with him. Then, he has cast her aside like a used plaything. She prayed that Isabelle and Raphael would make it. She didn't want Anouk growing up like she did.

# CHAPTER TWENTY-ONE

Later that evening, Emilia got a text from Bertie.

***A car will pick you up in the morning. B x***

She typed a thumbs up emoji and sent it. Bertie had invited her to travel with him to Paris on his private jet. Both Raphael and Isabelle didn't drink, so Bertie booked two hotel rooms at Hôtel Marotte for them both.

"We might need to avail of the residents' bar, my darling," he said when he called her the night before. "I can't see the christening being too wild."

She neatly folded a cashmere cardigan and placed it in her suitcase. She had packed light, like she always did. A white suit for the ceremony, her cotton nightdress, some underwear and comfortable clothes for the flight home. She had googled Rosa and was bowled over by her beauty. She looked like her mother, Cassandra, but she had a look of Johann too. She scanned the various articles about her and could see that she was still finding her place. She never seemed to settle anywhere and was linked to a string of different men. Emilia was no psychologist, but she wasn't surprised at all. Rosa had always been the needier child. She had relied on her far more than Stefan. She didn't like to think about how the little girl reacted when she found out that she'd left for America.

Emilia sighed. Would Rosa even remember her? It was so long ago. She couldn't predict how their reunion would go. The one thing she did know was that it would stir up lots of old memories: memories that she wanted to keep buried.

"Caspian? Did you see my Gucci bag?" Madison threw the cushions off the couch and searched. "I had it last week for that after-party."

Caspian wrote some notes on a sheet. Then he played some notes on the piano. Frowning, he crossed out what he'd written and started again.

"Caspian? Did you hear me?"

He rolled his eyes. "Can't you see I'm working?"

She walked up and snatched the music from the piano. "We're leaving in a few hours. You've nothing packed. I can't find my bag. This is a disaster. And there you are, writing a stupid song?"

He scowled and relieved her hand of the sheet music. "To answer your question, no. I didn't see your bag." He turned back to the keys and played a flurry of minor notes.

"Ugh, you drive me crazy!" She stalked off and slammed their bedroom door.

Caspian scowled. Why couldn't she see that he was desperately trying to finish a song that had popped into his head the day before. He couldn't control inspiration – it struck when he least expected it - and then he couldn't think of anything else. Madison was driving him crazy, looking for a Gucci bag indeed, and he couldn't concentrate. He knew she was in awe of his famous father – she became uncharacteristically shy and tongue-tied around Raphael – so packing the right clothes for this weekend away was her main objective. He, however, wanted to finish the song.

"Caspian!" Madison yelled from their bedroom. "Forget that piano, okay? You need to get ready!"

He threw down his pencil in disgust. He was slowly learning that it was easier to give in.

Rosa made faces at Anouk as she ate her porridge. The little girl giggled and flicked her spoon resulting in white goo all over the floor.

Isabelle crossing names off a list, her brow furrowed.

"Can you believe those Italian cousins bailed on us? Raph didn't even want to invite them, but his mom insisted. Now, at the last minute, they've cancelled."

"Some people!" said Elaine, reading her book at the kitchen table.

"So, how many guests are actually coming?" asked Rosa.

"About thirty," said Isabelle. "We've got producers, some of Raph's crew. Bertie, of course, and Emilia. Caspian and Madison, his band…"

"Emilia?"

"Emilia Thomas. Do you know her? She writes most of Raph's scores for his films."

"Yeah, I know her." Rosa bit her lip. "I mean, I knew her. She lived with us for a few years. She and my father, well, they were together."

Isabelle's eyes widened. "Really?"

"Gosh, it was ages ago, but she was the closest thing I had to a mother." Rosa looked up. "She used to make pancakes and take me to school."

"How come you haven't seen her in so long?" asked Elaine curiously.

"One summer, Stefan and I went to Florence to stay with Mamma, and when we got back home, Emilia was gone. Just like that."

"That's awful!" Isabelle looked shocked. "So, she didn't say goodbye?"

Rosa shook her head. "Nothing."

"I've met her a few times and she seems so gentle," said Isabelle. "I can't believe she just left, I've got to say."

"Who knows what happened," said Elaine fairly. "Break ups are complicated. Maybe she felt it was the best thing to do."

"So, she's coming?" asked Rosa. "Definitely?"

Isabelle nodded. "Yeah, she RSVPed. She's flying over with Bertie."

Rosa smiled. "I'm glad. I'd like to see her again."

Fionn heaved his kick drum into the van.

"I can't believe we're shifting our own gear again," he said, shoving it into the right hand corner. "Talk about regressing."

Ethan Hackett, the led guitarist of Doctor Eckleburg, inhaled his cigarette. "I don't mind it actually. It takes me back to the good old days when we made our own choices."

"We still make our own choices," said Fionn. "I just wish we had our team to lug this stuff around."

Alex Ryder, the bassist of the band, appeared with his guitar, a rucksack and a speaker. "What did I miss?" he asked cheerfully.

"Nothing," said Fionn. " We're almost ready to go. Did you say goodbye to my little sister?"

Alex nodded. "She was suitably devastated at our forced separation, but she'll be fine."

"Last I heard she was planning a girls' night out in Soho."

"Oh, and that." Alex smiled.

Ethan closed the back of the van. "Caspian is flying with Maddy and they're staying at the Baptiste mansion, he said."

"I bet Madison is delighted with that," said Fionn. "She loves being important."

"He said he's pretty nervous."

"Understandably," said Alex. "Things must be so weird between him and Raphael. They're both so intense. I mean, I can't see them discussing the rugby or the weather."

"I'm sure Maddy will rabbit on and on about her hair and her weight, so there's nothing to worry about," said Fionn with a grin.

"Why are you so hard on her?" laughed Alex. "You really are awful."

"Because I've known her forever and see beyond the glitz. She's just Maddy Ryan from down the road to me. My sister's annoying BFF."

"Look, she has actually saved us," said Alex practically. "We don't have enough room in the van for four and Caspian would've bored us to tears talking about the new album."

"True." Fionn twirled his drum stick. "I'm shocked he agreed to this gig. Playing our old songs. You know what he's like when he's writing. Tunnel vision."

"Well, Raphael asked him so he couldn't refuse."

Rosa grabbed her coat and bag.

"Are you sure you don't mind being our tour guide?" asked Elaine. "I feel bad asking you to accompany us old-timers."

"I don't mind at all." Rosa smiled. "We'll walk around Amiens and then get a bite to eat."

Patrick scrolled through a Lonely Planet article on his phone. "We've just got to see the cathedral, honey. It looks awesome."

"We'll see that and Tour Perret, and even a Jules Verne museum."

"Hey, I read *20,000 Leagues Under the Sea* when I was a kid." Patrick looked delighted.

Rosa smiled. "Don't wait up, Zsa Zsa. We'll be late."

Isabelle gave her a grateful look. Caspian and Madison were due around five and she had so much to organise for the christening. When Rosa suggested that she take her parents on a city tour, it gave her much needed space.

"Are you sure you don't want us to take Anouk?" said Rosa on the threshold.

Isabelle shook her head. "Mom and Dad are enough for anybody. Plus, she's due a nap soon. You guys go ahead and have fun. Coralie is here to help if I need it."

"See you later!" Elaine blew her daughter a kiss. "We'll send you photos on WhatsApp."

Caspian and Madison arrived in Amiens at that evening. The Sikorsky S-76 helicopter landed on the field by the main house, the main rotor whizzing around and around.

Madison had insisted that her bodyguard, Todd, and her driver, John, accompany them.

"You know Raphael won't like a circus," said Caspian, drumming his fingers on his thigh. That song still plagued him and he imagined the keyboard on his leg. He was almost there. There was just one riff that needed work. Just one riff…

"I already cleared it with Isabelle," Madison retorted. "You know I can't be left vulnerable. The house doesn't have proper security. I need John and Todd to protect me."

The doors of the cockpit opened and Todd got out to check the premises. Caspian made a move to follow, but Madison stopped him.

"Wait until we have the all-clear." She checked her appearance in a pocket mirror.

"Christ," said Caspian, rolling his eyes.

Todd re-appeared five minutes later. "All seems okay, ma'am. However, when I tried to check the interior of the building, Mr. Baptiste told me to get out."

Caspian suppressed a smile.

"That's okay, Todd." Madison elbowed Caspian. "I'm sure it's safe."

"Still and all, I'm not comfortable, ma'am. One slip up is all it takes."

"I'm going in." Caspian got out.

Isabelle sipped her elderflower cordial and bounced Anouk on her knee. Raphael had just arrived back into the room in a rage, saying that he'd met one of Madison's heavies in the kitchen and how she needed a reality check.

Rosa had texted to say that they had stumbled upon an open air jazz concert and not to wait up. Elaine had sent on dozens of photos and it looked like they were having a wonderful time. Patrick and Elaine posing in front of the impressive Gothic cathedral. A plate of steak tartare and frites. A short clip of the jazz band.

The door opened and Madison walked in. Her blonde hair was tied up, she was dressed casually in jeans and a white shirt, and gold bracelets jangled on her wrists. Zola sprung up and barked madly.

"Raphael! Isabelle! How are you?" She embraced them fondly, ignoring the dog, and Isabelle got a whiff of Dior. "Thank you for having us."

Caspian walked in at that moment, his blonde hair concealed under a beanie hat, his hands in his pockets. Zola wagged his tail and rubbed against his thigh.

"Hey, boy. Hey." Caspian scratched behind his ear. Straightening up, he looked guardedly at Raphael.

"Hi," he said gruffly.

"Caspian, good to see you." Raphael walked over and thumped his back awkwardly. "You look well."

"So do you."

"Great to see you, Caspian!" Isabelle got up and hugged him. "Thanks again for agreeing to play at the party. Anouk is delighted."

Caspian looked down at his half-sister, who was on Isabelle's hip. "Hey, little one," he said softly, taking her plump little hand in his. "Look, Mads, she's smiling."

Madison smiled briefly at Anouk and then sat down on an upholstered armchair. "So, when's Bertie coming? I can't wait to see him again. It's been ages."

"Tomorrow. He's staying at the Marotte with Emilia."

"So, we're the only guests actually staying at the house?" Madison smiled smugly.

"Well, my parents are here too. They just went into Amiens for a look around," said Isabelle. "Are the rest of the band coming tomorrow, Caspian?"

"Yes." Caspian ran his fingers through his hair. He looked distracted and kept walking around.

Madison crossed her legs elegantly.

Raphael approached Caspian. "Do you need something? I sense that you're uneasy."

Caspian raised an eyebrow in surprise. "Well, I could do with using a piano for a while."

"Then, go. You know where the music room is." Raphael waved him away.

"Thanks." Caspian smiled gratefully and walked out the door.

Madison stopped mid-sentence. "Where's he gone?" she asked sharply.

"He needs to work," said Raphael simply. "I recognised the look on his face. It is similar to me when I'm prohibited from creating."

"Oh, for God's sake!"

Isabelle patted her arm. "Welcome to my world."

# CHAPTER TWENTY-TWO

Dinner was a pork stew with sauté potatoes and green salad. Madison picked at her meal and opted for sparkling water instead of wine. Isabelle looked at her full plate in concern.

"Did you not like the pork? I can get something else for you."

Madison shook her head. "Not at all. It was delicious. I just don't eat very much."

"That's awful," said Isabelle. "Even when I was modelling, I still ate lots of cheese. I was lucky as it didn't affect me, but even if it had, I don't think I'd have given it up."

"You say that," said Madison, "but like you said, it didn't affect you. Did you ever get trolled for looking below par? For having a spot on your chin or a pot belly? It's the worst."

"Not really."

"Well, I have. I've grown up in the spotlight and it can be hell." She shrugged. "So, I follow a strict diet." She smiled. "It's not so bad. A small price to pay for being envied and adored."

"God, I don't know about that." Isabelle looked dubious. "Does it really matter what you look like? At the end of the day? Surely it's about your music."

"Of course it matters what I look like." Madison looked shocked. "People look up to me as a paragon of perfection. They buy magazines with me on the cover because I symbolise a dream life, one where I look amazing all the time. Come on, Isabelle. You must have felt like that at the height of your career."

"I don't remember being scrutinised as much as that."

"Well, no offense, but modelling is one dimensional. You walk down a catwalk, pose for a shoot. My work is modelling, singing, performing, acting, all in one. I have my fans, but I also have Caspian's fans. I'm constantly watched."

"I guess."

"Anyway, who's coming tomorrow?"

"Well, Agathe is coming up from Paris."

"Caspian's granny." Madison inhaled sharply. She sensed that she had to make a good impression there.

“There will be some cousins. A few close friends. My best friend, Gabriella, the godmother. Her husband, Hugo. Bertie, of course. Emilia Thomas.”

“Oh, Emilia! I met her briefly when Savannah and I recorded *Possess Me.* She called to the studio on the last day.”

“She’s sweet,” said Isabelle.

“May Todd see the guest list? He’d like to do some background checks.”

Isabelle’s eyes widened. “Are you serious?”

“I’m deadly serious.” Madison looked surprised. “One slip up is all it takes. That’s what Todd says all the time.”

“I’ll give you the list, but don’t tell Raphael.”

Madison raised an eyebrow. “Why not?”

“Just trust me.”

Bertie met Emilia in the hotel bar for a drink, his bodyguard, Vladimir, lurking in the background. People pointed and stared, but no one approached him. He liked France for that reason. People weren’t so accommodating in the States or even London for that matter.

“What gift did you get for Anouk?” he asked, sliding the olive off the cocktail stick in his martini and swallowing it.

Emilia sipped her wine. “A bracelet with her name engraved on it. It’s cute.”

“I started a trust fund. I am the godfather after all.”

“Lucky Anouk.”

“So, have you met Caspian before?” Bertie sipped his drink innocently.

“No! Do tell. Is it terribly awkward?”

Bertie shrugged. “I can’t really say. I’ve never seen them together. It’s quite the scandal.”

“Things must be better between them if he’s performing at the party,” said Emilia practically.

“Apparently so.”

“I’m happy for Raphael,” said Emilia, thoughtfully. “It must have been a terrible shock to find out you had a child after twenty odd years.”

“Yes, a huge shock. Still, he’s lucky only one such child has turned up so far. He was quite the Lothario in the old days.”

“Bertie!”

He nodded at the barman to bring more drinks. “You know, I remember when you two were a thing. That brief affair, both so young and talented.”

“Brief being the operative word.” Emilia shook her head. “He was difficult in those days. All the drugs. I couldn’t cope.”

“Yes, he was,” agreed Bertie sagely. “Still, he’s out the other side. I’ve never seen such devotion to a woman. He adores Isabelle and it seems to work despite the age difference."

"She can't be much older than Caspian."

Bertie leaned in. "There was a big development a few months ago. Caspian came over on a solo trip and there was a bit of father-son bonding. They're destined to be close. I just know it."

Emilia popped some crisps in her mouth and munched.

"Madison will be there tomorrow too." Bertie nodded at the barman to replenish the drinks. "She's a force of nature, that girl. She sort of sucks the energy out of a room as she's so dynamic."

"Yes, she's quite something."

"Do you know her well?"

Emilia shook her head. "Not at all. I collaborated mainly with Savannah on that track. I popped into the studio on the last day to put my spoke in. We wanted to include a sample of the theme tune, about ten seconds or so. We had to chop it and arrange it to fit right after the chorus."

"I love that part!" said Bertie.

"Anyway, she surprised me. Madison, that is. She has a much better voice than I gave her credit for."

Michel Sardou played in the background.

"So, what's your next project?" Bertie bit the olive off the stick.

"I'm not sure. Raphael mentioned a film about Yeats."

"You're busy."

"Yep."

"I'm going to try for that new Marvel movie. I fancy being a superhero."

"You'd be great, Bertie."

"What would your superpower be? If you could pick any?"

"I'd like to be able to tell the future. Like Cassandra."

Bertie sipped his drink. "Speaking of Cassandra," he began and Emilia stiffened, "are you nervous about meeting Rosa tomorrow?"

"Not at all." She cast her eyes down.

"Good. Poor Rosa is having a bad time." Bertie leaned closer. "I'm an awful gossip, but what can I do? I have a face that invites people to tell me everything."

"Go on." Emilia's interest was piqued.

"Rosa's a bit of a wild child. She's outrageously talented of course, but won't commit to anything or anyone. She was kicked off the LSO and now she's been fired from the Southbank Philharmonic. Johann is at the end of his tether, darling. She's constantly in trouble."

"Oh no! That's awful."

"Awful," Bertie agreed. "She's been *in flagrante* with scores, pun intended, of young musicians, married or not. Let's just say this hiatus to France was needed. She had to leave London for a while. Her latest was her best friend's father. Some property tycoon."

Emilia's hand flew to her mouth. "I feel so bad for her. It just seems so inevitable. She never had a chance. Not with that upbringing."

"She had been drinking a lot and taking prescription drugs. Another one of my moles told me that. Anyway, she came to stay with Raph and Isabelle a few weeks ago, she's off the booze, and has turned over a new leaf, so to speak. Apparently the French air suits her. I wanted to give you the low down before you meet her tomorrow."

"Thanks. I'll keep it in mind." Emilia sipped her drink. "She may not even remember me."

"Oh, she will." Bertie patted her arm. "Sounds like you were the closest thing she had to a mother."

# CHAPTER TWENTY-THREE

Rosa woke the next morning as the sun was rising in the east. The house was quiet so she slipped on her jodhpurs and boots and stole downstairs to the stables.

Living in London, she only got to ride when the opportunity arose yet here, it was a daily pleasure. She adored racing along the fields, immersed in nature, jumping over fences and streams.

She saddled up Luna herself as Jean didn't start work until seven. The horse whinnied as she tied the buckles and secured the reins. She loved going for a ride at sunrise. There was something special about seeing the day before the rest of the world.

She glanced at the helmets hanging on the rack. Gertrude warned her over and over again to wear one, but she disliked it. It made her head sweaty. She much preferred the feeling of the wind streaming through her long hair as she raced along through the fields. This thrill made her feel alive. She knew it was wrong, but she did it anyway. The quintessential folly of humans.

The clip clop of Luna's hooves reverberated around the courtyard as they trotted out to the gate. Minutes later, they were out in the fields of the Baptiste estate. Her legs squeezed the horse as they galloped along at speed as she tilted her face up to the emerging sun.

Agathe Baptiste, Raphael's mother, arrived in her chauffeur-driven car. Elegant in Chanel, she entered the house in which she'd spent most of her married life. Tall, with coiffured grey hair and impeccable posture, she stood in the huge entrance hall and removed her stole.

"*Maman!*" Raphael, handsome in a dark grey suit, walked towards her with open arms. They embraced and he kissed both her cheeks. Isabelle followed, Anouk in her usual position on her hip.

"Hey, Agathe. Good to see you." She also kissed the lady's cheeks. "Look, Anouk, it's your grandma." She held the baby upwards.

*"Coucou, ma petite,"* said Agathe fondly. She stroked Anouk's soft hair. "She has grown."

"She's pretty tall, I guess," agreed Isabelle.

"*Mamie!*" said Anouk, reaching out for Agathe. The old lady stroked her cheek.

"You look well today, *chérie*," said Agathe in approval, looking at Isabelle's pale pink dress which clashed gloriously with her red hair. "A brave choice of colour, but it works."

"My best friend Gabriella designed it. She's coming later."

"Ah, yes. I read about this Gabriella. She's become quite the couturière."

"Rosa has been here for the past few weeks," said Raphael. "She has been a great help to Isabelle."

"I've heard of her antics," said Agathe with a frown. "She needs to settle down."

"She will, *Maman.*"

"Where is Johann in all of this? I'm not surprised that Cassandra is of no use, but Johann should have intervened."

"He and I, well, we're still not on speaking terms."

Agathe looked disdainful. "Pride is the cause of such silliness."

"Rosa's much better since she got here," said Isabelle enthusiastically. "She can change diapers now and everything."

"Come, let's have some refreshments before the guests arrive," suggested Raphael. "Père Bernard is outside."

"Wonderful!" said Agathe. "I would love to see him; it's been so long." She followed her son through the hall towards the patio. When they reached the door, she pulled at his sleeve.

"Is Caspian here?" she whispered.

Raphael nodded. "He's upstairs with his girlfriend. He should be down soon."

Agathe nodded. "Good. I want to get to know my grandson."

# CHAPTER TWENTY-FOUR

Madison wiped her eyes viciously with a wet wipe.

"I need Mona here right now!" she said angrily, referring to her makeup artist. "This is the third time I've tried to put on this stupid eyeshadow!"

Caspian wasn't listening. Instead he was peering out the window into the garden. Despite a relatively early night, he felt like he hadn't slept at all. Today was always going to be hard as he would be meeting some family members for the first time. It felt like he was on display, on show for others to watch and judge.

"Caspian, have I time to start my eyes again?" Madison brushed some shadow on her eyelid.

"I suppose. There's nothing much going on. Just Agathe speaking to the priest."

"Agathe? Your granny?"

He nodded and kept his eyes trained on the garden. He watched Raphael walk into the garden and gesticulate to Agathe and Père Bernard.

"So, how do I look?" Madison stood up and waited for him to turn around.

"Hmmm?"

"Caspian! How do I look? This is important!"

He looked around. Madison looked sensational in a figure-hugging red dress and black high heels. Her long blonde hair was curled and cascading down her back.

"You look nice," he said vaguely, turning back to the window.

"Nice?" Her voice was dangerously low.

"Yes, nice."

"This dress cost more than most people earn in a month."

"So?"

"So, it's not just nice. It's amazing!" She picked up her clutch bag. "God, you drive me crazy sometimes." She disappeared into the bathroom.

Caspian looked in the mirror and straightened his collar. His blonde hair was slicked back, showing off his beautiful bone structure. Suddenly he heard the loud clip clop of hooves on the cobbled stones. He walked over to the open window at the opposite side of the room that looked out on the courtyard. A horse appeared around the corner at speed with a young girl on its back. Her long brown hair fell loose and her cheeks were pink from the breeze. She pulled hard on the reins and the horse stopped. She patted its neck and expertly threw her leg over to dismount.

Caspian gazed at her as she took the reins and led the horse towards the stables.

Fionn pulled the razor down his jaw and shook the foam into the sink.

Alex was already dressed and sipping a coffee on the small balcony of their hotel room.

"We're late," he called, checking his watch.

"I'm almost ready," said Fionn, wiping his face with a wet towel.

"Ethan texted, he's down at the van."

Fionn walked out of the bathroom and threw his towel at Alex. "You're worse than my mother. I'll be ready in five."

He opened his suitcase and pulled out a blue shirt and a grey pants. They had become slightly wrinkled so he gave them a shake.

"What time is the ceremony again?"

"Noon."

Fionn checked his phone. "It's 11.30. Plenty of time."

"I googled where Baptiste's house is and it's going to take us twenty minutes."

Fionn threw a sock at him. "Pressure is for tyres. I bet you ten thousand euros Madison is still curling her hair. There's no way she'll be on time so there's zero need to panic, okay?"

Agathe sipped her iced tea. The garden looked well, almost as good as when she when she was in charge of it herself. The gladioli near the fountain were new. She made a note to tell Michel how pretty they were when she saw him. Now that she lived in Paris, she only had a small garden to nurture: a small patch of grass in the middle of a courtyard, surrounded by potted plants and ferns.

She looked up. Caspian walked towards her, flicking back his shoulder-length blonde hair. For a moment she could see Louis. It was uncanny, the resemblance.

Caspian halted, his hands in his pockets.

"Hello," said Agathe warmly. "It has been so long." She held out her cheek for him to kiss.

"Hello," he said, pressing his lips to her soft skin. She smelled of roses.

"I hope this is not too strange for you," she said softly. "After all these years, to find out something like this. I hope we can move forward."

Caspian nodded. "Me too."

"I've seen you play piano. Raphael sent me clips. You're very good."

Caspian blushed. "Thank you."

"Louis used to play. I remember it. You are so similar to him."

They stared at each other.

"Life never ceases to surprise me." Agathe grasped his hand. "*Mais la famille avant tout.* Family comes first. Always."

Madison arrived outside at that moment. "You must be Agathe!" she said, holding out her hand. "I'm Madison, your grandson's fiancée. So delighted to meet you."

"Hello," said Agathe formally.

"Is the rest of the band here yet?" Madison asked, turning to Caspian. "They're cutting it a bit fine."

Caspian nodded. "They're on the way."

"I will leave you," said Agathe, bowing her head. "Perhaps we will speak later," she added to Caspian. She walked off with Père Bernard, speaking in rapid French.

"Madison!" Caspian turned on her angrily. "We were having a private conversation."

"Ugh, it's all drama with you. If it's not Raphael, it's his mother. It's no big deal, Caspian. Just relax. Stop taking life so seriously."

Caspian walked off.

Rosa had a shower and scrubbed the mud off her hands. Her morning ride had taken longer than anticipated and she felt guilty for leaving Isabelle alone for so long on such a busy day.

She put on a white cotton dress with a square neckline which accentuated her tanned skin. A small bit of eyeliner and mascara and she was ready. She didn't bother tying up her dark hair, instead, she left it loose down her back. White strappy sandals completed the look.

There was a knock at the door.

"Rosa? Can I leave Anouk with you for a little while? There's a problem with the caterers."

She opened the door to see Isabelle in a pink dress with squirming Anouk in her arms.

"No problem at all."

"You look pretty," said Isabelle, handing her the baby. "I'll be about twenty minutes, okay?"

"Take your time." She smiled at Anouk and kissed her small nose. "I've missed you, *amore mio*." She started to sing a lullaby in Italian and closed the door.

Emilia smiled at Vladimir as he opened the door of Bertie's car for her.

"Thank you," she said, taking a seat in the back of the hired Mercedes. Bertie was already sitting on the other side.

"You look enchanting, my darling," he said, observing her white suit. "So simple yet gorgeous."

"You look pretty dapper yourself."

The car pulled out onto the street and headed south.

"Today should be good fun," said Bertie, twisting the gold signet ring on his pinkie. "Firstly, I'll be the main man at the baptismal font, being the godfather and all."

"True," said Emilia with a smile.

"We'll get to see Caspian and Raphael interact which will be fascinating."

Emilia raised an eyebrow at this.

"And of course, you and Rosa will be reunited."

Emilia's stomach flipped at this.

When Johann had disappeared from her life, she had tried to banish all memories of him. The house in Hertfordshire, the apartment in London, the trips abroad, his children. She had to exorcise him and his memory as much as possible to survive. However, the film composing world was small and she heard of his successes and failures every now and then.

The night she won her Oscar, she could feel his presence. Like, he was watching her on the screen. Maybe it was silly but she had felt something. As she avoided social media, it was easier to escape news and updates about him and his family. If Cassandra's voice came on the radio, she switched the channel. If any of her senses were aroused by any remanent of their life together, she pushed it away.

Now, she was about to meet the little girl with whom she had bonded all those years ago. The little girl who was now a woman.

*Rosa.*

She inhaled deeply.

Anouk fell asleep the minute Rosa put her down on the soft pillow. Grabbing some cushions, she made a makeshift border around the little girl, to prevent her from falling off the bed should she wake. Picking up her phone, she opened Twitter and started to scroll. There was just news about Brexit and the French presidential election. She clicked to see that was trending and saw Prince Harry, Piers Morgan and Madison Ryan. Her interest piqued, she clicked on Madison's hashtag. There were various tweets about the re-release of the song she'd recorded for Raphael's film. Then, a photo of Madison and Caspian in London the day before, hand in hand, surrounded by bodyguards. She zoomed in on Caspian's face. He looked sombre, a green beanie hat covering his blonde hair.

She had yet to meet the famous couple. They had gone to bed by the time she had returned from Amiens the night before.

She was also looking forward to seeing Emilia again. Even though her memories of their time together had faded slightly, she made her feel safe. The time Emilia had lived with them was one of the happiest of her life. She thought of what Raphael had said that day on the meadow. How she needed to surround herself with good people, people who would look out for her. Emilia seemed like a good place to start.

Tip-toeing over to her bedroom window, she drank in the activity below. There was a big gazebo on the lawn and inside it were three round tables and chairs, all covered in white cloth. A small table stood at the top, waiting for the christening cake: a *croquembouche*, a tower of choux buns filled with crème patissière. Traditionally served at French weddings, this cake was ideal for a party. Guests would take a profiterole and pop it in their mouths, to balance their meal with something sweet. As it was far too hot to have the cake on display, it was waiting in the cool cellar to be brought out.

The head table was rectangular and at a right angle to the others. It was set for nine places. Raphael and Isabelle in the middle, Agathe on Raphael's right, Patrick and Elaine on Isabelle's left, and then places for Caspian and Madison. Rosa was to sit at the other end with Anouk's baby chair right next to her. She had offered to feed her and look after her during the meal. Isabelle seemed stressed so it was the least she could do. Her time in France had been a godsend and she would be forever grateful.

Anouk moved in her sleep and gave a little cry. Rosa went to her immediately and kissed her soft head.

# CHAPTER TWENTY-FIVE

Doctor Eckleburg's van pulled up to the Baptiste mansion. Ethan whistled.

"This is some house," he said in awe. "Look at the gardens."

"It's pretty impressive," agreed Alex.

A valet waved them to the right and gestured for them to park their vehicle next to a silver Porsche.

Fionn laughed. "Would you look! There are two Porsches, three Bentleys and a bloody Ferrari. Can anyone see a Fiesta or a Polo? Thought not."

"We'll really lower the tone," said Ethan with a grin, backing the van into the instructed space.

Fionn walked straight up to Caspian and shook his hand. "Good to see you," he said. "Sorry we're a bit late."

"That's fine." Caspian seemed distracted.

Alex shook Caspian's hand too. "This is a nice house. The garden is incredible."

Caspian shrugged. "They have a full-time gardener."

"Mum would adore one of those. She's always giving Dad grief for the amount of time he spends tending to the flowers and the vegetables." Alex gazed at the rows of brightly coloured tulips which acted as a border around the green grass.

Ethan, who was trailing behind smoking a cigarette, waved. "Hey Casp, sorry we're late," he called.

"It's fine!" Caspian gave him a thumbs up.

"How are things going?" asked Fionn in an undertone. "How's Raphael?"

"Good, good." Caspian tried to smile. "I mean, he's busy with the ceremony and all."

"So, you're holding up okay?"

"I'm fine."

Alex made eyes at Fionn. Caspian looked far from fine. He was fidgeting and kept glancing around.

"Where's Maddy?" asked Fionn, changing the subject.

"She's talking to Agathe." Caspian pointed to a glamorous old woman sitting on a wicker chair next to a gesticulating Madison.

"Agathe?" Alex looked confused.

"My..." he paused, "my...grandmother." He swallowed as he said it.

Alex made an 'oh' sound.

"In fact, I'd better rescue her. Agathe, I mean." He attempted to smile.

Fionn laughed. "Rescue her is right. She's probably getting a blow by blow account of Madison's exfoliation regime."

"So, I'll see you later." Caspian walked away.

"He seems weird," said Ethan matter-of-factly. "Like he's on another planet."

"To be fair, he must feel like an outsider," said Fionn. "He has no set identity. People don't know how to treat him and he knows it."

"Time will heal all of that," said Alex. "Now, come on. I could murder a coffee. Let's find someone who can help."

As Caspian approached he could hear Madison say 'wedding'. He groaned inwardly.

"Hello, you two," he said loudly, stopping her in mid-sentence.

"Oh, hi!" She beamed up at him. "I was just telling Agathe about how you proposed. Although it's so long ago, it's hard to remember. She really wants to know when the big day is, but I still can't say." Her blue eyes challenged him.

"Soon," he said blandly. "We'd better go. The ceremony is about to start."

Agathe watched them silently.

"I've got to check my hair," said Madison, standing up. "Come on, let's go inside." She held out her hand.

Caspian paused. "I was going to accompany Agathe to the chapel."

Agathe smiled. "There is no need. Raphael will do so. I will see you later."

Caspian reluctantly followed Madison into the house.

"Why are you being so moody?" she hissed as they climbed the steps.

"I'm not moody."

"Come on, Caspian. You've a dour expression. Cheer up. I can't see why you're letting all of this affect you."

"Maddy, I..."

"What?" She turned to face him on the threshold of the house. "Your mum died. That sucks. But you never actually knew her, Caspian. You've got to let it go."

He stared at her in disbelief.

"I love you, but it's hard to love you right now. It's all doom and gloom. Rather than focusing on the negatives, look at the positives. You've a new family. A powerful family. You're engaged to me. Smile, for God's sake!"

His muddled brain barely registered what she was saying. All he knew was that he didn't want a scene.

"Just go and fix your hair," he said, forcing a smile. "I'll wait down here."

"Fine. See you in a sec." She kissed him briefly on the lips and disappeared up the stairs.

Caspian lounged against the bannister in the hallway.

An Italian man walked by and nodded formally. Caspian nodded back, trying to remember if he was a cousin or a producer that Raphael worked with in the past. He was hopeless at remembering names and he had been introduced to legions of people in the space of an hour.

He felt uncomfortable. He was here, on the Baptiste estate, yet he felt like he didn't belong. Everyone knew who he was, it was impossible not to. He looked more and more like Raphael every day. Some addressed it straight out, others feigned politeness and stuck to small talk. In truth, he was exhausted from the whole thing.

A door closed at the summit of the staircase and he looked up. The girl he had seen riding the horse that morning was descending the stairs with Anouk in her arms. Her long dark hair fell in waves around her slim shoulders and her brown eyes regarded him curiously as she approached.

"Hello," she said with a smile. "I'm Rosa."

Caspian recognised the name, he was sure Raphael had mentioned a Rosa, but couldn't quite place her. She had a British accent, but with a slight tweak. His musical ear picked up on it straight away. With her dark looks, she looked Spanish or Italian. Perhaps she was originally from there.

"Hello," he said, holding out his hand. "I'm Caspian."

"I know." She smiled, showing white teeth. "I've been anxious to meet you."

"Like everyone else," he said with a pained look. "I'm quite the talking point."

Their eyes locked for a moment. Anouk shouted 'Maman' and started to wiggle.

"I'd better keep moving," said Rosa, apologetically. "They're waiting for this little one in the chapel. It's her day after all."

"See you later," he said, giving a little awkward wave.

"See you." She disappeared through the door of the living room en route to the garden.

Madison wasn't long after her. 'Why were you talking to the nanny?" she demanded.

He shrugged.

"Is my lipstick straight?" she asked, tilting her head upwards.

He nodded.

She took Caspian's arm. "Let's go and get a good seat. We should be up the top with the rest of the immediate family."

"Gabby!" Isabelle squealed in delight. "Gabriella Ruiz Alvarez, you get over here right now!"

Isabelle ran towards her best friend, the fashion designer, Gabriella. Both American, they had studied together at Parson's School of Design in New York. Isabelle had gone on to become a successful model, and Gabriella trained under the fashion giant, Oberon. They had remained close friends over the years. Gabriella looked the same: dark eyes and hair from her Puerto Rican heritage and a warm smile. Her self-made maxi dress artfully concealed her swelling stomach as she was six months pregnant with their first child. When Isabelle had asked Gabriella to be Anouk's godmother, Gabriella had booked flights to Paris straight away. Hugo du Maurier, Gabriella's husband, stood by her side, dressed in a navy suit.

"I can't believe we're finally meeting in person! It's been so long." Gabriella hugged Isabelle tightly.

"It's so good to see you." Isabelle's eyes filled with tears. "I've missed America so much. Being with you now makes me think we're back in our little apartment on Commerce, drinking chardonnay."

"I know, right?" Gabriella wiped the tears from her cheeks. "Covid really sucked."

Hugo waited dutifully in the background.

"Hugo! Hey!' Isabelle beamed at him. "Come here and give me a hug. Congratulations on the baby. I'm so excited for you guys." She held both of their hands in delight.

Bertie held Emilia's hand as they walked up the garden path.

"We'd make a gorgeous couple," he said, nudging her. "Especially since I got my Botox refill."

"I don't know how you put needles in your forehead."

"Oh, it's fine. The end result is worth it." He laughed. "I don't look a day over forty."

Raphael spotted them straight away. "Emmy! Bertie! Welcome." He kissed Emilia on both cheeks. "You look so elegant."

"Ahem!" Bertie looked affronted.

"Of course, you look elegant too." Raphael laughed. "Come, Isabelle is anxious to see you." He led them to the gazebo to his wife who was chatting to her parents. Gabriella and Hugo had gone upstairs to freshen up.

"Hey, you guys!' Isabelle went straight to Bertie and hugged him fiercely. Then she hugged Emilia. "So glad you could make it."

"It's lovely to see you," said Emilia, really meaning it.

Bertie looked around. "Where is Anouk, my darling goddaughter? I am her moral guide from now on."

"God help us," said Emilia, winking at Isabelle.

"Ah, she's coming now," said Raphael. "In the arms of *my* goddaughter as it happens."

Emilia froze. Turning slowly, she watched Rosa walk towards her with Anouk in her arms.

"Emmy?" she said in a tremulous voice. She looked like a little girl for a moment.

Emilia nodded. "Hello, Rosa."

"I'm so glad to see you."

Emilia felt something clutch her heart. "I'm so glad to see you too."

Rosa handed Anouk to Isabelle and ran into Emilia's arms. They hugged tightly for a moment.

"You've grown up so much," said Emilia, wiping away a tear.

"Your hair is blonde."

"I decided to lighten it to combat the grey."

"You're so successful now. An Oscar!"

"It's nothing."

"I can't believe that you're here. Remember your pancakes? Gertrude tried to learn but she never made them like you."

"God help us." Emilia laughed. "I'm not the best chef."

Rosa laughed too.

"How's Stefan?" asked Emilia.

"Married to a witch called Claudia." Rosa made a face. "She doesn't really like me."

"I'm sure that's not true."

Rosa grinned. "Oh, it is. I go out of my way to make it so." She hugged Emilia again. "Oh, Emmy. We must catch up. I've so much to tell you." Rosa clung to her.

Bertie blew his nose on a paisley silk handkerchief. "This is like one of those real-life dramas where families are reunited after the war. Beautiful."

Père Bernard appeared, wearing his cassock. "Raphael!" he called.

"We must go to the chapel," said Raphael. "It is time."

"We'll talk later," Emilia promised, squeezing Rosa's hand.

# CHAPTER TWENTY-SIX

Anouk Agathe Elaine Baptiste was christened in chapel on the estate, just like her ancestors before her.

Caspian watched Père Bernard pour the sacred water over her small head and wondered what his life would have been like had he been born a traditional Baptiste. Then he pushed that thought away. He was drowning in 'what ifs' and needed to pull himself out of it.

Bertie insisted on standing to the right of the font as that was his good side. Gabriella stood on the left and got to hold Anouk for the big moment when Père Bernard baptised her.

After the final blessing, the congregation stood up and clapped. Isabelle, holding Anouk, stood next to Raphael as they posed for photos on the altar. The baptismal gown trailed down the skirt of Isabelle's pink dress, the white lace glinting in the sunlight. Gabriella and Bertie stood on either side of the Baptistes, smiling as cameras clicked and flashed.

"If anyone puts anything on social media, they will be guillotined in the old fashioned way," said Raphael cheerfully.

Madison nudged Caspian. "We should be up there," she whispered loudly. "We're family after all."

"Shhhh," said Caspian pointedly.

Raphael strode down to the front pew where Agathe was sitting. He took his mother's hand and led her up onto the altar. Agathe pulled Raphael's sleeve and whispered something in his ear. Raphael nodded and gestured for Caspian to join them.

"Come," he commanded.

Caspian reddened slightly, and shuffled in his seat.

"Come," repeated Raphael.

"Get up, for God's sake," whispered Madison loudly. "They're waiting."

Caspian got up awkwardly. Madison made a move to follow, but Raphael held up his hand. "In a moment," he explained. "Just Baptistes in this shot."

Caspian's head shot up to see Raphael's brown eyes staring meaningfully at him.

"You are my son. You are a Baptiste. Stand with us."

Caspian stared at his father. Raphael had said it loud enough for the whole congregation to hear. There were muffled 'ooohs' and 'ahhhs' followed by Bertie clapping loudly.

"How touching!" he said, wiping a tear from his eye. "Come, Caspian. Stand in my spot."

Caspian walked towards the altar, feeling strange. Isabelle smiled encouragingly and Agathe nodded in approval. Raphael resumed his position next to his wife and the four of them stood up straight. Isabelle holding Anouk, Raphael by her side. Agathe stood regally next to her son with Caspian on her right.

Cameras flashed incessantly for about twenty seconds. Bertie, who was back in his seat next to Emilia, took photo after photo on his phone. "What I would do to sell these," he said in an undertone. "I could retire comfortably. Imagine what the media would do with a shot like this? The father, the matriarch, the lovechild, the model, and the heiress."

Emilia couldn't disagree. Raphael and Caspian stood on either side of Agathe, both tall with the same haughty expression.

"Now, Madison, join us." Raphael gestured for her to come forward.

Madison scowled and toyed with telling him to go and jump in a lake, but then thought better of it. She walked up to Caspian and nudged his arm viciously. "This is all your fault," she said in an undertone. "If you'd get it together and actually set a date for our wedding, I'd be just as much a Baptiste as Isabelle."

"You're here now," he said with a shrug.

Anouk, fed up of the noise and the attention, started to cry loudly. Bertie made a big show of covering his ears.

"You're awful!" said Emilia with a grin. "She's only a child."

Rosa, who had been watching everything from the second row, jumped up. "I'll take her back to the house," she said to Isabelle. "She must be hungry."

"Thank you so much," said Isabelle gratefully. "I've got to thank the priest."

"Not at all." Rosa kissed Anouk's red cheek.

Caspian walked over and let Anouk grasp his finger. Then his eyes travelled upwards and connected with Rosa's. They both smiled at the same time.

Anouk arched her back and reached out for Caspian to take her, trying to break free from Rosa's grasp.

"I think she's getting a tooth or something," said Rosa, gathering the long christening gown upwards so as not to trip over it. "Her cheeks are so red."

"She's had a big day," said Caspian. They gazed at one another. Suddenly Anouk let out a shriek.

"Okay, okay, Mademoiselle Anouk, I get the message. Let's go." Rosa walked down the aisle, stealing a furtive glance back at Caspian before she exited the chapel.

"Thank God the baby's gone," said Madison, appearing from behind with Fionn in tow. "No offense, as she's your sister and all, but I hate the sound of wailing. There's nothing worse."

"It's a big day for her," said Caspian fairly.

"Hmmm."

"This chapel is amazing," said Fionn, craning his neck upwards to admire the painted ceiling.

Caspian nodded. "It's pretty impressive."

Madison tapped her foot. "Let's go and have some champagne. I'm allowing myself three flutes today. I did half an hour extra in the gym yesterday morning to compensate."

"Mads, the world will not end because you overdo it on the calorie front," said Fionn dismissively.

"Gabriella looks amazing even though she's pregnant," went on Madison, ignoring him. "Her dress is so flattering. I might ask her about her bridal couture as she's here."

"Not this again." Caspian sighed.

"What?" she said angrily. "Time waits for no man, Caspian. Look at Bertie's face! Do you want me to have to resort to fillers before we walk down the aisle? Because it's starting to look that way." She covered Fionn's mouth with her hand, prohibiting him from speaking. "Don't say one word, okay? I know you were about to interject."

Fionn pulled her hand away. "Aw, Maddy. You think so little of me. All I was going to say was that I like your crow's feet. They give you character."

"Oh, piss off!" She clutched her fists.

Fionn laughed, but this only served to infuriate her even more.

"Raphael pretty much christened you a Baptiste today," said Madison hotly to Caspian. "What about me? I want definition too."

Caspian kissed her nose. "We'll talk about this later."

She scowled and walked off, her bodyguard, Todd, by her side.

"Jeez, you're a saint to put up with her," said Fionn, shaking his head.

"She's a saint to put up with me," said Caspian loyally.

"Really?"

"I'm just not ready to marry her yet."

"That's understandable."

"I mean, I'm working on it. There's just a lot going on in my head at the moment."

Fionn said nothing.

"Let's go and set up." Caspian walked away.

Emilia followed Rosa out of the chapel.

"Rosa!" she called. "May I come with you?"

Rosa smiled warmly. "Of course. I'm just going to give Anouk a bottle. Walk with me."

Emilia fell into step beside her. "So, how's life? I heard you went Paris. Did you enjoy it?"

Rosa nodded. "I loved it." She paused. "I thought of going to Oxford. I remember you talking about your student days, but, in the end, Daddy thought the Conservatoire would be better suited."

Emilia flushed with pleasure. "Really? Do you remember me telling you about Oxford?"

"Of course. Your friend, Alfie, and the choir, and the time you fell into the river when you were punting."

"Yes, I did have fun there."

"I must admit, I've never tried punting. It's on my bucket list."

"Bertie mentioned the LSO," said Emilia gently.

Rosa frowned. "Well, he must also have mentioned that it didn't last very long. Daddy was so angry with me. Then, I moved onto another orchestra and that went wrong too." She stroked Anouk's curls.

"Don't worry, sweetheart." Emilia rubbed her shoulder. "Everything will be okay."

Rosa's eyes filled with tears. "It's so good to see you. I really mean that."

"I feel the same."

"Have you seen Daddy lately?"

Emilia's face tightened. "Not for years."

"He should never have let you go."

"That's all past now. It feels like a dream."

Rosa smiled sadly.

"Maybe when we get back to England, you can come and visit." Emilia's eyes crinkled at the corners. "I'll make some pancakes for you."

"They'd better measure up."

"Yes, it will be a lot of pressure." She laughed.

They entered the house by the kitchens. There were silver platters lined up, filled with delicious canapés in rows. Rabbit terrine crostini with mini cornichons, mini quiches with crab and dill, rare beef on puff pastry with mushroom duxelles. Rosa smiled at the chef, took a baby bottle from the cupboard, poured some milk into it and gestured for them to go to the nursery.

After Rosa had laid Anouk down on a soft blanket with her blue teddy by her head, she turned to Emilia.

"I'm not a saint, Emmy. I've messed up." Her eyes cast down. "A lot."

"Haven't we all?"

"Yes, but now I'm unemployed. Daddy won't answer my calls. I owe rent and my credit card bill is enormous. My best friend hates me and I can't seem to hold a man. I escaped over here to breathe and now I don't want to go back."

"Stay here then. Raphael won't mind. It's good company for Isabelle."

"Yes, but I'm running away. Things aren't going to get better if I disappear." Her brown eyes filled with tears. "I need to settle down and make a career for myself. Like you, I fell in love with a much older man and he stamped on my heart. Like you, I ran away."

Emilia's face froze. "Rosa, I…"

"You don't need to explain. I understand. It was easier to disappear and hope that we'd forget about you." She laughed bitterly. "But we didn't. You were the closest thing we had to a mother."

"I'm sorry."

"It's fine. What's done is done."

Anouk, who had no intention of going to sleep, kicked off the blanket. "Osa, up!" she ordered.

"This past month has given me a chance to reflect," continued Rosa. "I'm going to change. I'm going to find a job on my own, without my dad's connections. I'm going to find a suitable boyfriend and try not to scare him away."

Emilia fingered the lacy trim on Anouk's blanket. "How is your father?"

Rosa shrugged. "In America. I haven't seen him in person in almost two years. He's working on a new score and it's all consuming. He's also not talking to me at the moment."

"Were you close before that?"

"Well, he's been more supportive than Mamma, if that's what you're asking." She glanced down at Anouk. "She's not tired at all! I suppose she did nap earlier."

Anouk threw the empty bottle out of the cot.

"I'd better bring her back down with us."

Emilia held out her hand and Rosa grasped it. "I'm so glad we've found each other again."

Rosa smiled. "Me too," she said, meaning it.

# CHAPTER TWENTY-SEVEN

After the main course had been cleared, Raphael got to his feet and clinked his glass with his pastry fork. The crowd quietened down and looked up at him.

"Just a few words," he said smiling. "I find speeches boring."

"Hear! Hear!" shouted Bertie, raising his wineglass.

"Thank you to Isabelle for making me so happy." He raised his glass. "To family!"

Caspian blushed a dark red. Agathe noticed and nudged her son. Raphael cleared his throat.

"Of course, I cannot mention family without including Caspian. I'm very glad that he is here today."

Caspian kept his eyes cast down.

"Thank you to *Maman* and Elaine and Patrick: all wonderful grandparents." He raised his glass.

"To Gabriella, for being a wonderful godmother."

The crowd cheered.

"And of course, my old friend, Bertie: the godfather."

"Delighted to be in the official family photos for posterity!" said Bertie with a wink. "I'm not against Photoshop or airbrushing. Just putting it out there."

"And finally, to my daughter, Anouk." Raphael turned to the little girl in the highchair. "*Mon ange. Félicitations, ma petite.*"

The tables were cleared and the chairs lined up for Doctor Eckleburg's performance. Ethan and Alex propped their guitars against an amp and went for a beer near the fountain. Caspian disappeared to Louis Baptiste's music room to warm up his voice. Fionn, at a loose end, walked over to Emilia who was standing by the entrance to the gazebo.

He grinned at her and held out his hand. "Hello."

"Hello," said Emilia with a polite smile.

"I saw you in the chapel."

"Oh?"

They looked at each other.

"My name is Fionn. I'm the drummer in the band."

"Emilia."

"How do you know Raphael and Isabelle?"

"I work in film. You?"

"I don't really know them at all. I was invited because of Caspian."

"Right."

"Are you a fan of Doctor Eckleburg?" he asked playfully.

"I don't know much about contemporary music, I'm afraid. I'm a composer. Mainly classical pieces."

"Whoa!' Fionn looked impressed. "That's pretty cool. You're the real deal."

"Yes, I suppose." She looked amused.

"Well, I play drums."

"*Whoa!*" she mimicked and he laughed.

"You have an Irish accent," she observed.

"Yep, I'm from Dublin. Best place in the world."

"So I hear."

"Have you been?"

"Just once. I was a guest conductor for the Wexford Opera Festival. I flew in to Dublin Airport."

"Ah, so you haven't really been to Dublin."

"No, I guess not."

"We should remedy that, Emilia. You need to walk the streets with a local, drink a pint of the black stuff and see Trinity College Library."

"Really?"

"And who better to show you around than a drummer?" he teased.

"Who indeed?"

"Let's go and get a drink," he suggested.

Emilia raised an eyebrow. "Are you flirting with me?"

"Maybe."

She bit her lip.

"Would it be so terrible if I was flirting with you? I mean, you're pretty gorgeous."

"You seem so young."

"I'm twenty-eight."

"I'm almost forty-five."

"So?"

"I could be your mother."

Fionn laughed. "Hardly." He took her hand and kissed it gently. "Come on, let's get a drink and chat. I'm not so bad when you get to know me."

Anouk started to wiggle and whinge loudly in her buggy. It was Elaine who had suggested wheeling her around the garden in the hope that she'd fall asleep. The noise proved too much and the little girl was over-stimulated and exhausted.

"I think it's time for bed." Rosa kissed her forehead. "I'll just ask your *maman.*"

She spotted Isabelle talking to Madison over by the fountain.

"So, I said to Savannah there's no way I was changing the bridge, you know? I mean, she may be a multi-Grammy winning artist, but I know what's what."

Anouk focused in on Isabelle, reached out for her, and started to cry. "*Maman, Maman,*" she wailed, arching her back. Rosa made a face at Isabelle. "Sorry," she mouthed.

Isabelle smiled apologetically at Madison. "Sorry to interrupt, but I've got to put Anouk to bed."

Madison glanced at Rosa. "Just get your nanny to do it. That's what you're paying her for."

Before Isabelle could correct Madison, Ethan tapped the microphone, causing it to screech.

"Testing, one, two," he said in his deep voice.

Madison turned towards the stage area. "Ah, Doctor Eckleburg are about to play. You should wait a minute and let Anouk hear her song."

"I guess." Isabelle lifted her out of the buggy and cradled her close. "Let's see how it goes."

Caspian walked onto the stage area and accepted the microphone off Ethan.

"Good evening or *bonsoir*," he said shyly. His shirt was open at the neck and his long blonde hair was tucked behind his ears. The crowd cheered.

"We're going to play a few songs if that's okay."

Bertie, who had had nearly a bottle of champagne to himself, whooped.

Fionn tapped his drumsticks together and stretched his arms. Ethan tuned his guitar slightly as Alex made funny faces at Anouk.

"This is a song I wrote about my little sister." Caspian kept his eyes down.

Raphael raised his glass.

"In honour of her special day. It's called *Belle.*"

He took a seat at the keyboard and inhaled. Playing the right hand only, he played a melody and started to sing.

*Bella baby, baby belle.*
*Blessed are you,*
*May you live to tell,*
*The world's great secrets,*
*Deep in our hearts,*

*May we never be apart,*
*Bella baby, baby belle.*

Emilia watched Fionn as he beat out the rhythm on the percussion drum. He caught her looking at him and winked. She blushed and averted her eyes.

It was a mellow tune, almost like a lullaby. Rosa watched Caspian play, his blonde hair falling down over his eyes as he bent his head over the keyboard. His voice was even better live.

The song came to an end and the guests clapped loudly.

"Bravo!" shouted Raphael, "Anouk loves it."

Anouk started to scream at the top of her lungs.

Caspian laughed. "I can see that."

He looked younger when he smiled, Rosa observed. His face lost its intensity.

Isabelle waved apologetically at the band. "I'll just put Anouk to bed. See you soon," she promised.

Fionn waved his drumstick. "Hope we don't keep her awake with the noise."

After Doctor Eckleburg had played seven songs, Caspian announced that they would be taking a short break. He took a swig of water from a bottle and saw Agathe walk into the conservatory.

He followed her inside. She was sitting in a large rattan chair with blue cushions with her head tilted backwards and her eyes closed.

Caspian coughed politely and her eyes opened.

"Ah, Caspian. Your music is wonderful."

"Thank you," he said, blushing.

"Sit down. I was wondering when we would get a chance to speak alone."

"It's been a busy day."

"Yes, it has. Anouk is blessed to have so many people who love her." She gestured at the chair opposite her own. Caspian obeyed, stretching his long legs out in front of him.

She regarded him. "Tell me about yourself," she said softly. "I want to know you. We've lost a lot of time, but we must not dwell on that. Let's start from now."

Caspian shifted in his seat. "There's not much to tell," he said simply. "I had a wonderful childhood. My parents gave me everything I needed."

"Raphael said you studied music."

"Yes." He nodded. "I always loved singing and playing piano." He laughed softly. "My dad, I mean, George, didn't approve at first. He thought it was no career for a young man."

"Look at you now. So successful. You are driven, like my Raphael." Agathe regarded him thoughtfully. "I always think of Louis when I look at you. You remind me so much of him."

"Raphael showed me his pictures. He certainly had an interesting life."

"He was wonderful. When I married Pierre, he welcomed me into the family like a daughter. Of course, he died soon afterwards, but I'll never forget the time we spent together." She paused, then leaned forward and grasped Caspian's hand. "Come and visit me in Paris, *mon petit.* We need to get to know one another properly."

Caspian squeezed her hand. "I'd really like that."

"Just you," she added. "Madison is enchanting, but she speaks a lot."

He smiled. "I understand."

"Don't delay."

He nodded.

# CHAPTER TWENTY-EIGHT

Madison was alone by the rose bush when Caspian returned.

"Where did you get to?" she demanded. "I've been stuck here on my own for ages."

"I went to speak to Agathe. She wants me to visit her in Paris."

"Oh, let me guess," she said bitterly. "On your own."

"Yes." He looked uncomfortable.

"Just Baptistes then, is it?"

"Maddy!"

She turned away.

"Maddy, you've got to relax."

"You're shutting me out!"

"I'm not. Truly." He pulled her into his arms. "It's just been a difficult day."

"I'm tired of things being difficult," she said in a muffled tone. "It would be nice for you to remember that I exist too."

He smiled. "How could I forget?" he said, kissing her hard on the mouth. She resisted initially, but then succumbed. He moulded her to him, his fingers in her hair.

"I love you but you've got to let me deal with this myself," he murmured into her neck as he left a trail of kisses.

Bertie appeared with a bottle of champagne and three glasses. "Care to join me, you two?"

Madison shook her head. "I've gone over my quota for today."

A door banged and Raphael appeared from the house, pulling Rosa by the hand. She seemed to be resisting, trying to break free from his grasp.

"What's Raphael doing with the nanny?" asked Madison in confusion.

"The what?" Bertie didn't follow.

Raphael leapt onto the stage and tapped the microphone. "I know Doctor Eckleburg are on a break, but to fill the void, I would like to ask Rosa to play something."

"Raphael!" Rosa put her red face in her hands. "Please stop."

Michel the gardener walked up to the stage area carrying Rosa's cello. Coralie placed a small chair next to her.

"*Merci*," said Raphael with a nod. He turned to Rosa. "Just one tune. Please! Do it for Anouk. *Maman* would love it."

"No! This is so embarrassing." Rosa scanned the crowd, her cheeks flushed.

"Look, *Maman* has come outside especially." Raphael pointed at Agathe who was standing at the door of the conservatory, leaning on her walking stick.

Emilia waved at Rosa and gave her a thumbs up. "I'd love to see you play," she called.

Rosa bit her lip. "Fine! But only because it's you."

"*Génial.*" Raphael gave her his heart-breaking smile. "Talent should not be wasted."

Rosa took the cello from Michel and plucked the strings. Taking a seat on the stool, she placed the instrument between her legs and fiddled with the pegs. Raphael angled the microphone downwards to catch the music. Her bow poised, Rosa closed her eyes and launched into Bach's *Suite pour violoncelle seul.*

Madison nearly dropped her champagne. "What the hell? A multi-tasking nanny. Now I've seen it all."

"Nanny?" said Bertie in confusion.

"Yes, nanny. Childminder. Babysitter." Madison gave him a strange look.

Rosa's not a nanny." Bertie started to laugh. "That's Rosa Weber, Maddy darling."

"Rosa who?" she said rudely.

"Rosa Weber. Daughter of Johann Weber and Cassandra Rosso."

"Still not familiar."

Caspian tore his eyes away from Rosa. "Cassandra Rosso the opera singer?"

Bertie nodded. "The very one. Rosa there attended the Consérvatoire de Paris. She has played in great orchestras."

"Why is she here looking after Anouk then?" demanded Madison.

Bertie sipped his champagne. "She had some trouble with herself. She needed to get away. So, she took time out at her godfather's place."

"Raphael is her godfather?" Madison looked gobsmacked.

Caspian held up his hand for silence. His eyes watched Rosa's every move as her arm moved like lightning, arching the bow and angling it to produce that deep, mellow sound. Her long hair fell over her shoulder as she played, her slender arm changing position perfectly.

"She's taking some time out to re-evaluate things," Bertie whispered. "It's been great for Isabelle, you know, having company while Raphael travels. She gets so lonely."

Madison tried not to feel jealous. This Rosa had gone completely under her radar. She thought she was a glorified au pair. Now, she was something different: she was competition.

Rosa played the final note and hung her head, her eyes still fastened shut. The crowd erupted, clapping madly. Agathe held her arms up as she applauded.

"*Bravo, ma belle!*" she called.

Madison placed her glass on a nearby table and scowled. She liked to be the only star around the place. Cliona always chided her on this unattractive trait, but she couldn't help it. Maybe it was insecurity. How she wished she could play an instrument like that.

Bertie pulled at her arm. "Cheer up, my love. The limelight will soon be focused on your dashing boyfriend again. Rosa has left the stage."

"I'm not bothered at all, Bertie." She forced a smile. "Fair play to her. That was a nice tune."

"Yes, it was." He regarded her thoughtfully. "Go and make friends with her, Maddy dear. She's nice."

"Maybe later." Madison had no notion of it. "Come on, Caspian…" She turned to find him gone. "Where's Caspian?"

Bertie pointed up the stage. "Making friends."

Madison narrowed her eyes.

"You should do the same." Bertie patted her shoulder.

"You played beautifully." Caspian ran his fingers through his hair. "I had no idea. I mean, you were incredible…"

"Thank you." Rosa smiled at him.

"I saw your mother perform in London when I was twenty or so," he said. "My mother, Prue, and I went to Covent Garden. I was studying music at Guildhall and your mum was starring in *Tosca.*"

Rosa's expression changed. "I'd better take this back inside." She placed the cello in its case and closed the clasp. She didn't want to hear about Cassandra.

"I've always wanted to learn cello," he continued enthusiastically. "I mean, I can play a little violin, but it's obviously not the same thing."

"Not really." She looked at him in amusement. "Good luck with the rest of your gig. I enjoyed the first part."

She heaved the case on her shoulder and walked away.

Madison walked up and poked his back. "What were you two talking about?"

Caspian could see that she was rattled. "Music. Cellos. Nothing."

"Right." Madison frowned.

Caspian kissed her nose. "Go and have another drink. We have a few more songs left to play."

After the gig, Fionn sought out Emilia immediately. He found her talking to an Italian producer, laughing as he told her a story.

"Hey!" He smiled. She looked guarded for a moment, but then reciprocated. The producer, sensing something, made his excuses and left.

"Your gig was great," she said.

"The drumming was especially brilliant," he said with a grin.

"Oh, terrific."

The stared at each other.

"I'm going to get a beer and maybe we could go for a walk in the garden?" Fionn waited for her to refuse.

"Okay, I'd like that." She held up her empty glass. "Please get me a refill of champagne too."

"Coming right up."

Caspian made sure that Madison was happily seated next to Isabelle before he made his way to the music room. Watching Rosa play the cello had ignited something in him. He felt inspired and wanted to express it through music. He opened the door and entered the dark room. The garden lights, draped over the trees, illuminated Louis' grand piano. He switched on the light and strode up to the keyboard. After a few bass notes, he stopped. Nothing could reproduce that deep sound. Looking to his right, he spotted Rosa's cello, propped against the wall. He debated what to do. Surely, she wouldn't mind if he had a look.

He opened the case to reveal the sleek instrument. Taking the neck carefully, he extracted it from the velvet interior and lightly tapped the strings. Emulating what he'd seen Rosa do, he placed it between his legs, pressed on the fingerboard and drew the bow across the strings. The resulting sound was cacophonous and he winced. Using his instinct, he tried to produce a melody, moving his fingers up and down the neck, teasing out the notes. So engrossed was he in his task, that he didn't notice the door opening and a wide-eyed Rosa coming in.

"What the hell…"

He opened his eyes and dropped the bow with a clatter. "Oh, I'm terribly sorry." He stood up awkwardly. "I couldn't resist. I came to play piano but when I saw the cello, I…"

"Did you manage to play something?" she asked.

He shook his head. "No. Not at all, in fact." He smiled sheepishly. "I made a horrendous attempt at a melody."

She laughed. "Getting the right note is all about practice. You say you can play the violin?"

"Well, I wouldn't say I'm proficient…"

"There are no frets on a cello either. Do you want me to show you a basic scale?"

"Yes." He looked surprised. "If you're sure?"

"It's fine. I was actually on my way to bed, but I can show you quickly."

"Bed? Already?"

"Yes." She took the cello from him and sat down on the stool. "I was up early this morning."

"Oh yes," he said distractedly. "You went for a ride."

Her head shot up. "How did you know that?"

"I saw you come back. Our bedroom looks over the stables."

"Oh."

"From what I saw, you're pretty good on horseback."

"Well, I ride most mornings, just before sunrise. It's so beautiful here." She pressed down on the neck of the cello. "Anyway, look closely. This is a basic scale."

She played it slowly, emphasising where her fingers were on the strings and lifting the bow deliberately so he could see the angle. "I'll do it again and then you can try."

She played it again, faster this time. He watched her intently.

"Now, let's swap over."

He took a seat and accepted the cello form her outstretched arms.

"Now, put your finger here." She reached out and took his hand, placing his forefinger in a specific spot. Then she did the same with his other fingers. "So, hold up the bow. Put your fingers back in the same position." Caspian obeyed. "Now, do this." She took his arm and helped him moved the bow across the strings.

"That's a C major!" He smiled in delight.

"Yes," she said. "Exactly."

Again, she noticed the difference when he smiled. His face lost all of the drama, the intensity.

"Show me again," he said hurriedly. "Show me all the notes."

"Whoa, calm down." She laughed.

"Please." His brow furrowed, he played C major again perfectly. "I'm a fast learner."

"Oh, okay." She played A minor. "I'll give you a few scales to practise and then I'm off to bed."

# CHAPTER TWENTY-NINE

Fionn caressed Emilia's hand. They hadn't stopped talking for hours. She was singularly the most interesting woman he had ever met. He didn't hear the loud music nor did he notice his empty glass. He couldn't stop looking at her.

"So, tell me about your childhood," she said. "All I've done is talk about myself."

"There's not much to tell." His brown hair flopped over his eyes. "I had a great time. My mother adores me. That's about it."

She smiled. "I can see why."

"Why what?"

"She adores you."

He blushed and then groaned. "Look at the effect you're having on me. I'm all red in the face."

"It's quite sweet actually."

"Stop. I feel like a teenager."

Her face changed. "Well, you are much younger than me."

He put his fingers to his lips. "Ssssh. Don't be ageist." He held out his hand. "I'll just get more champagne. Don't move, okay? I'm afraid that you're going to disappear if I let you out of my sight."

"Where's Caspian?" Madison looked around. "Did he mention going to bed?"

Bertie tried to focus on the remaining guests. "No idea, Maddy. To be honest, I've had far too much Dom Perignon and I can't see anything, not to mind your gorgeous beau."

Isabelle put the baby monitor up to her ear. "Did you hear that? I think Anouk's awake."

"I'll go and check on her, honey," offered Elaine. "What are grandmas for?"

Raphael, who had been saying goodbye to Agathe, walked up to the table. "Have you seen Caspian? Maman wanted to say goodbye personally."

"You're looking for him too?" Madison stood up. "He's been gone for over and hour. I'll check our bedroom."

She walked into the house and straight up the stairs. The catering staff were boxing up empty glasses. She opened the bedroom door to find their bed empty, the sheets unslept in.

She met Raphael on the stairs. "He's not in bed anyway," she said crossly. "There's only one other place he could be." She marched past him in the direction of the music room.

The heavy oak door was closed when she got there. She could see light streaming out from under the door sill.

*Bingo,* she thought.

She pushed open the door to find Caspian playing a cello, his eyes closed in concentration. He kept playing the same scale over and over again.

"Caspian?" she said in surprise. "What are you doing? We've been looking for you."

He opened his eyes and smiled. "Check this out." He played the A minor scale perfectly. "Doesn't it sound amazing?"

"Raphael was searching for you. Your granny wanted to say goodbye."

"Oh, no." He looked genuinely upset. "I just got lost in the music."

"For a change." She smiled slightly. "I didn't know that you played cello."

"I don't. That girl Rosa showed me some scales."

"Rosa?" Madison's eyes narrowed. "Oh, she did, did she?" She put her hand son her hips.

He nodded. "She left about ten minutes ago and went to bed."

"Right."

"She said I'm pretty good for a novice."

Madison scowled. "Put that thing back in its case and come back to the party. It's rude. You can play cello all you want tomorrow."

He stared at her for a moment. Reluctantly, he placed the instrument back in its case.

"I'll meet you outside, okay?" She banged the door after her.

Emilia trailed her finger in the pond. She was sitting on the stone wall with Fionn by her side. The surface water was mostly covered with lily pads so she sought out clear water to immerse her hand in.

"So, how did you end up in Hollywood?" asked Fionn, gazing at her.

"I shagged a film composer," she answered simply.

He raised an eyebrow. "Fair enough."

"How did you become a famous drummer?" she asked.

"Well, I didn't shag anyone important, if that's what you're asking."

"I wouldn't judge you if you had."

"No, Caspian did that for me. The minute he got together with Madison, things started to happen for us. He tries to ignore it, but it's a fact."

"He must hate that."

"Yep, he sure does." Fionn looked thoughtful. "You know, sometimes I think that she's too strong for him. They just don't seem to fit. Two enormous egos clashing all the time. It must be exhausting."

"You're very wise," said Emilia. "For such a young lad," she added with a grin.

"I'm an old man. Look at my wrinkles?" He leaned in and kissed her lips softly. "But I'm not as worldly as I'd like to be with women. Maybe you could teach me that?"

"I'm not that worldly either."

"Hey, you shagged a film composer. That's more than I have."

Emilia's expression changed and he noticed immediately. "Sorry, did I say something wrong?"

"No, not at all."

He traced his finger down her cheek. "You loved him, right?"

She nodded.

"But he broke your heart."

She nodded again.

He took her hand. "Come on, let's get out of here and you can tell me all about Hollywood."

"What? Leave the party?"

"Yes. I want you all to myself without this crowd and the noise."

Her heart fought with her head. In the end, her heart won. "I'm at the Marotte."

"Sounds great. Beats sharing a hotel room with Alex any day."

Emilia opened the door of her hotel room. Fionn followed her inside and took off his jacket.

She released her hair from the pins that held it up and shook it free. "Shall we have a drink?"

"Sounds good."

Emilia suddenly felt nervous. She rarely did this kind of thing. She felt naïve and gauche, unsure of how to behave. Fionn noticed immediately.

"Let's have that drink, will we?" His eyes were warm.

"Yes," she said gratefully. "Whiskey?"

"That sounds nice."

"Irish or Scotch?"

"Need you ask?"

"I'll ring for room service."

She picked up the phone and asked for a bottle of Jameson and two glasses. Fionn took a seat on the bed.

There was a knock on the door. Emilia answered and accepted the tray from the waiter. She poured two drinks and a glass to Fionn. Then she took a seat beside him. They clinked glasses, her bangles jingling.

"To us," he said, taking a sip.

"Us?"

"Yep." He turned sideways and tilted her head upwards. "I've always been cynical about that bolt of lightning, you know, that love at first sight business."

"Oh?"

"But now I'm not so sure."

"Fionn, I…"

"Ssssh, don't speak." He took her glass and placed it on the bedside table with his own. "Don't think." He pushed her back gently onto the soft pillows. Then he started to unbutton her top, slowly exposing a lacy bra. Emilia closed her eyes and let him do it. He nibbled on her earlobe and then moved down her neck until he reached the pulse at the base.

"You're so beautiful," he whispered.

She pulled at his shirt and a button popped. "Hey!" he protested. "I can't sew those back on, you know."

She laughed and pushed the shirt off his shoulders, revealing a smooth torso. He yanked at her bra and released her breasts, cupping them with his hand. Then he kissed her, deeply and passionately.

"So smooth," he murmured, running his hand down her leg.

"I waxed just before I came here," she said breathlessly, as he pressed his hips against her.

He tugged at the suit. "Can you help me out here?"

She lifted her hips and shimmied out of it. Fionn threw it on the ground.

"Now, I think we'll leave the lacy bra," he said, his lips curved into a smile. "It's pretty sexy."

"Whatever you like." She fumbled with the buckle of his belt. "However, I prefer my men naked, so if you don't mind, give me a hand."

Emilia woke at dawn and stretched. Suddenly, she noticed the body in the bed next to her.

Her hand flew to her mouth and she sat up straight, holding the sheet close to her breasts. Fionn woke up and yawned, flexing his arms.

"Hey, you," he said huskily.

She regarded him warily.

"What's up?" He sat up, the sheet falling down to his navel.

Emilia averted her eyes. "I had a lot to drink last night," she began.

"Oh, please." He nudged her playfully. "Don't be so predictable. Let me guess, it was a big mistake and it should never have happened."

She raised an eyebrow. "Well, you have a point."

"Why, Emilia? Are you being ageist again?"

"No," she lied.

"Was I terrible in bed?" He grinned.

"No," she said blushing.

He grabbed her and pulled her down on to the pillows. "So, get over your insecurity and kiss me. Last night was *go hiontach* which is Irish for very good altogether."

She tried to look stern, but failed. "I just feel uncomfortable…"

"Why? Because you're socialised to think that we should be the same age? Nonsense." He nibbled on her ear. "You're not getting rid of me that easily."

She gazed up at him. "I'm not, am I?"

"Nope." He kissed her hard on the mouth.

# CHAPTER THIRTY

Madison was sipping some orange juice on the terrace when Raphael appeared, yawning.

"Good morning," he said with a smile. "Where's Caspian?"

"Still asleep. He needs his full eight hours." Her blonde hair was tied in a pony tail and she was still in her workout gear.

"Did you run around the estate?"

She nodded. "Todd and I ran ten kilometres."

Coralie brought out some coffee without having been asked.

"*Merci,*" said Raphael with a nod.

"So, Ross rang and he's organised another appearance on SNL at the start of July."

"SNL?"

"Saturday Night Live?" She looked at him strangely. "You've heard of that, right?"

Raphael shrugged. "Yes, but I've never watched it."

"Anyway, they've written a sketch about the song and how it went nowhere. I'm going to disappear into a black hole on stage." She giggled. "I mean, it's pretty accurate."

Raphael didn't smile. "I don't like that image. My film will not disappear into obscurity."

"It's about the song, not the film," she said hurriedly, "and it's a only a joke."

He sipped his coffee. "I, too, have appointments. The studio want to push the film as much as possible. Ridley's film will be out in 2023 so it gives us time."

"Yeah, I read about that."

"My film was made in 2019 and Josephine's story is a different angle. It will be fine." He didn't sound convinced. "I'm flying to LA next week to meet with the producer ahead of the release."

"I can't wait!" She beamed at him. "It's been so long since we've had any excitement. Soon we'll have the première. It's going to be so much fun."

He raised an eyebrow. "Then we are very different. I hate that side of it."

"You're just like Caspian," she said. "Whereas I live for it. I can't wait to dress up and get my hair done."

Raphael hid a smile. "Have you any other plans?"

"How do you mean?" she said guardedly.

"With your music?" he said.

She relaxed. "Phew, I thought you were going to mention the other 'M' word and I'm so frustrated."

"M?"

"Marriage."

"Ah!"

"Caspian won't set a date. He keeps putting it off. I want to start planning. I want to search for a dress and…"

He cut her off. "Don't worry about this. It will happen when it's meant to happen." He added some more sugar to his coffee. "Isabelle mentioned that you are to work with Savannah again. Is that true?"

"I'm meeting her in a few days. We're going to write a new album together."

"I can't believe that she agreed to work with you."

Madison snorted. "She's lucky to work with me."

"She's truly one of the greatest songwriters of her generation."

"Well, we bonded when we wrote *Possess Me.*"

"How have you, as you say, bonded?"

"When I stay at her place and she lectures me on how shallow I am." Madison grinned. "She's scary. We didn't like each other at all at first, she was so bossy and mean, but now we're great pals. She's a genius and I want to be respected in the industry. She says that I'll be more involved in the process this time which is exciting."

"That is exciting."

"Then, an album and a world tour, I suppose. The usual."

"I'm happy for you."

"Thanks, Raphael." She blushed slightly. "That means a lot."

Rosa found Caspian in the music room, playing the C Major scale over and over.

She twirled a lock of her long hair around her finger and stood on the threshold.

"Did you get any sleep last night?" she asked when he'd finished.

He grinned. "Sssh! Madison thinks I'm asleep. She hates when I get obsessed like this."

Rosa watched him play. "You're much better," she said, marvelling at how quickly he'd mastered the scale.

"I won't stop until it's perfect." He played it again, his blonde hair falling over his eyes.

"So, you and the band are heading back to London today, right?" She edged closer.

He finished the notes before he answered. "Yes. Maddy and I fly back this afternoon. The other members of the band are taking the tunnel."

She trailed her finger along the curve of the grand piano. "I need to go back to London."

"Oh?"

"I need to find a job."

"That shouldn't be a problem. You play so well."

"You'd be surprised."

He regarded her seriously. "You could give lessons. I'd pay you for starters. I've never heard a sound like this." He played another scale with gusto.

She laughed. "You couldn't afford me."

"Oh?" He put down the bow. "Name your price."

Rosa thought of her credit card bill and rent arrears. "Five hundred pounds a lesson."

"Done."

"What?" She laughed again. " Tell me you're joking."

Caspian shook his head. "Not at all."

"That's a fortune."

"I can afford it."

She eyed him warily. "I've nowhere to live."

"With that hourly rate, you should find a nice flat easily."

"I've debts to clear first."

"How about Bertie? Or Emilia? They live alone in large houses."

"I couldn't possibly…"

"Think about it." He smiled and his whole face lit up. She felt something clutch her heart. He really was gorgeous when he smiled.

"I'll think about it." She backed out of the room and then popped her head around the door. "Keep practising those scales."

Gabriella and Hugo left after lunch.

Isabelle blew a kiss at her friend as she sat into the back seat. "Good luck with the sonogram next week," she shouted.

"Bye!" Gabriella waved.

The car drove off down the drive.

Raphael put his arm around her waist and they walked back into the house.

"Come to LA with me next week," he said, kissing her bare neck lightly.

"America?" She halted. "God, I don't know."

"I have some dinners and meetings. You know I hate doing that alone."

"What about Anouk?"

"Bring her too."

Isabelle looked dubious. "It's a long way…"

Raphael's expression darkened. "If I didn't know any better, I would say that you have become a recluse. Do you want to stay in Amiens forever?" He ran his fingers through his hair in exasperation.

"Raph!"

"I want my Isabelle back. Adventurous, fun loving Zsa Zsa. Where is she?"

Isabelle looked hurt. "She's right here."

"Prove it." His brown eyes challenged her.

"Fine. I'll come to LA. Happy?" She turned on her heel and stalked off.

# CHAPTER THIRTY-ONE

Doctor Eckleburg arrived back in London that evening. When all of their gear had been emptied and put back in the studio, Fionn called a cab.

"Cliona and I are going to grab some pizza and a few drinks. Do you want to join?" asked Alex.

"I'm okay," said Fionn. 'I'm actually pretty tired so I'll see you next week for rehearsal."

Alex looked at him strangely. "Are you sure you're okay? You've been acting weird since you didn't come home last night."

Ethan laughed. "We're still waiting for the gossip."

"There's zero gossip," Fionn said cheerfully. "Nothing interesting to relate at all."

"Liar." Ethan waved. "Stay safe, guys." He hopped in the van and drove away.

"You're positive you don't want to come?" Alex put his bag over his shoulder.

Fionn shook his head. "I'm exhausted from doing nothing remotely scandalous. I need to sleep."

"Fair enough." Alex took out his phone. "I'm just going to call a cab. Although, I could share yours?"

Fionn shook his head. "I'm going in the opposite direction."

"But you live down the road from us."

Fionn rolled his eyes. "Stop fishing for info. I'm not telling. Now, go home to my little sister and forget all about me."

"It wasn't that middle-aged woman I saw you with last night, was it?"

Fionn frowned. "Sorry?"

"The tall woman. Emilia something."

"No."

"I mean, she's a good twenty years older than you."

"So?" Fionn's habitual good mood vanished.

Alex, sensing that he'd said something wrong, changed the subject. "See you next week, mate."

"See you."

An Uber arrived. The driver opened the window. "O'Connor?"

"That's me." Fionn got into the back.

Using Google Maps, the taxi finally pulled up outside Emilia's house.

"This is a nice spot," said the driver, gazing at the garden and the nearby lavender fields.

Emilia was writing some notes on sheet music when her doorbell rang. She walked barefoot out into the tiled hall and opened the heavy oak front door. Her hair was wet from the shower, curling in tendrils around her neck.

"You didn't waste much time," she said, unsure of what to do.

Fionn dropped his bag and pulled her to him. Falling slightly sideways, he propelled her into the hallway, kissing her face and her neck.

"Wow," she said, breathless. "Hello to you too."

"I missed you," he murmured into her hair. "You smell nice."

"That's my shampoo."

He kissed her hard on the lips. "I hope you don't mind my being here."

Her face softened. "I don't mind."

He looked relieved.

"Come on." She took his hand.

They walked into the drawing room. It had high ceilings and French windows leading out to a big garden. There was a long sofa adorned with silk pillows, a Persian rug and a walnut coffee table. A grand piano stood near the marble fireplace with a harp next to it. Her beloved violin was in its case by a music stand and sheets of music lay scattered all over the floor.

"Sorry about the mess," she said, blushing. "When I'm working I tend to use the whole room. The benefits of living alone, I guess."

"Hey, it's no bother." Fionn grinned. "You should meet my mother. She doesn't know the meaning of tidy." He walked up to a painting of a ballerina in first position. "Is this a Degas?" he asked.

She laughed. "I wish. No, my friend Alfie painted it."

"Friend?"

"Yes, friend."

"Good."

A few hours later, they lay on the rug, their legs intertwined with each other.

"Emilia," he said softly.

"Yeah?" Her head lay on his chest.

"Will you play something for me?"

She groaned. "I don't think I can move. You've used all my energy."

"Please?"

She stretched. "Okay, okay." Sitting up, she reached for her clothes.

"No, don't get dressed." He stroked her thigh. "Just play as you are."

"Okay," she repeated. Walking over to the piano, she picked up her violin which was lying on top. Opening the case carefully, she removed the velvet cloth. The bronzed instrument stared up at her, a reminder of Johann. She always felt sad when she saw it as it was a symbol of their time together and her loss. Yet as she took it out and placed it under her jaw, she didn't feel the usual rush of pain. Automatically she tuned it, twisting the pegs until she was satisfied. Then she launched into *Méditation*, her head moving with the strokes of her bow.

Fionn watched her as she played. The dawn light gave a glow, causing shadows to dance on the wall behind her. She seemed perfectly happy to play without clothes on, confident in her own skin.

She was different to the other women he'd slept with. She didn't worry about silly things like fake tan or how many followers she had on Instagram. She was comfortable with herself, mature and worldly. As he watched her angling the bow and producing exquisite sound, he felt mesmerised.

"Who wrote that?' he asked when she had finished.

"Jules Massenet. It's from the opera Thaïs. It began its life as an intermezzo between scenes." She looked up shyly. "I'm not a linguist but I heard this before and I think it's lovely." She cleared her throat. "*Rien de telle que la Méditation de Thaïs pour s'évader un instant de ce monde*, or, loosely translated, there's nothing like this song to allow us to escape from the world, if only for a moment."

Fionn stood up and grabbed her by the waist. "Speak French again," he growled, kissing her neck.

'Stop," she said with a laugh. "It's French with a Brummy accent and not at all good."

"It's sexy." He pulled her down onto the rug once more.

Fionn left the next morning.

"We have a band meeting at twelve. Our manager is worried about Caspian's procrastination."

Emilia kissed his nose. "Always remember that you're working for the man. It's hard to be creative and true to yourself when millions of pounds are involved."

"Well, Caspian does his own thing anyway," said Fionn, "but he should well remember that we are a band and a democracy."

"Make sure you get this across at the meeting."

"I will." He pushed a lock of her hair behind her ear. "Can I come back tomorrow?"

She shook her head. "I'm working."

"When then?"

"I'll ring you."

Fionn frowned. "If you don't, I'll just arrive. I feel like if I'm not around, you'll get all self-righteous and break up with me."

Emilia said nothing.

"Ring me," he said, kissing her hard on the lips. "Don't forget."

Fionn arrived at the Odyssey Management building on Camden Street to find Ethan and Alex waiting.

"Is Caspian with you?" asked Alex.

Fionn shook his head. "I haven't seen him since France."

They entered the building and took the lift up to the second storey.

Jax Mastrano, the band's manager, was sitting at his desk when they walked into his office. He was dressed in an expensive suit and a gold ring gleamed on his pinkie.

"Where's Cole?" he asked, wiggling the computer mouse and activating the screen. "I said twelve."

Ethan called Caspian for the second time. "He's not answering."

Jax pushed his chair back angrily. "I'm sick of this, boys. I'm not going to lie." He stood up and started to pace. "We have lost millions in revenue since Covid and we need new music. We need some hits to remind the world that we exist."

"We're working on it."

"He refuses to play your old stuff and then I hear that you played a private gig in France?"

"It was his sister's christening," said Fionn fairly.

"I couldn't care less. My point is, why can't he do that for the public until this new album is completed?"

"He's nearly ready," said Alex.

"He's been saying that for months. Have you heard any of this new album?"

Fionn shook his head. "He's very private about it."

"So he could be writing complete shit and we don't know?"

"Maddy says it's good," said Fionn. "She hears the odd song."

"Fucking hell." Jax ran his fingers through his hair. "We need to get into the studio. We need to start touring. Doctor Eckleburg are not established enough for a prolonged hiatus. You've got to play the game." He turned to Ethan. "Try him again."

Ethan pressed Caspian's number but it rang out.

"Nothing."

"Try Madison."

"She rarely answers her phone. It's Bethany who takes care of that."

"Well, ring Bethany then! For fuck's sake."

Ethan stood up and put his phone pointedly in his pocket. "You'd want to watch your tone, Jax."

Jax held up his hands. "Sorry, sorry. I'm just stressed. People are on my back and I'm in the dark."

"I'll pop over to Caspian's place on my way home and see where he is." Fionn stood up. "We'll be in touch."

Todd answered the door.

"Arms up, sir."

Fionn raised his arms and let Todd frisk him gently.

"Todd, how long have we known one another?"

"It's Miss Madison, sir. She insists that I'm thorough."

Todd stood back when he'd finished.

"I'm looking for Caspian. Is he here?"

Todd shook his head. "I haven't seen him."

"I'll ask Maddy." Fionn followed Todd down the hall and into the huge white kitchen where Madison was eating blueberries from a bowl. She was dressed in workout gear with her hair in a ponytail.

"Hey Maddy," said Fionn and she jumped.

"Fionn! What are you doing here?"

"Looking for Caspian. He didn't show up today and Jax is on the verge of a cardiac arrest." He grabbed a fistful of blueberries and threw them up into the air, one after the other, catching each one in his mouth as they fell back down.

"I haven't seen him since this morning," she answered. "He was going on about meeting his mum for lunch so maybe that's where he went."

Fionn noticed two large suitcases standing by the window. "Are you off somewhere?"

Madison nodded. "I'm off to write some music. Savannah Morris is going to help me."

"You? Write music? Is this the Twilight Zone?"

"Shut up," she said mildly. "I've loads of ideas."

"About what? An ode to Maybelline?"

"I said shut up!" She threw a blueberry at his head and missed. "I'm hoping to co-write most of my new album."

"When's that being released?"

"Next year."

Fionn groaned. "If only Caspian was as ambitious as you are."

"He's nearly finished," she said loyally. "I heard him say it to Prue on the phone. She's all paranoid about it. It's inspired by his birth mother." She stood up and stretched. "I'll pass on the message when I see him.

"Which is?"

"Caspian, focus!"

Fionn laughed. "Fair enough." His phone started to ring in his pocket. Taking it out, he saw 'Emilia' flashing on the screen. His cheeks reddened slightly and Madison noticed.

"Who's calling you?" Like lightning, she bolted over behind him and looked over his shoulder. "Emilia? Who's that?"

Fionn put his phone back in his pocket. "No one."

Madison gasped. "Not Emilia Thomas. She's ancient!"

"I'll just be going."

"Fionn! She's old enough to be your granny. That's just gross."

"Shut up!" he said angrily. "Jesus Christ, what does it matter?"

Madison didn't flinch. "Of course it matters. She's way too old for you."

"Maddy!"

"Okay, maybe not your granny, but she's definitely old enough to be your mother. You could do a lot better. She's wrinkly."

"You're so shallow, do you know that? Maybe, just maybe, I like her because she's interesting and talented. Maybe I don't worry so much about looks."

"Judging by your track record, it's obvious that you've low standards." Madison laughed. "Remember Martina Croston when we were kids? She had rabbit teeth and pimples. What were you thinking?"

"Martina was sound. She was funny and sweet."

"Funny looking more like." Madison made a face.

"I remember when you had spots," said Fionn thoughtfully. "I recall a particularly large one on your nose."

"You do not," she scoffed.

"Oh, I do. Around the time I put chewing gum in your hair."

Madison shoved him sideways. "I'll never forgive you for that."

Fionn laughed. "Your face when you realised what I'd done. One of my cherished memories."

"Ugh, I'd forgotten how annoying you were."

"Beauty is in the eye of the beholder, Maddy. You'd do well to remember that."

"I don't even know what that means." She grinned. "All I know is that I work hard to look like I do. Others should do the same." She pointed to the door. "I'll tell Caspian that you called."

Fionn laughed. "Tell him that Jax is on the warpath and if he doesn't produce something recordable soon, we're done for."

"I just had a thought! If you marry this Emilia, then she'll be your old lady. Literally." Madison burst out laughing.

Fionn clapped his hands. "Your wit is beyond compare. Brendan Behan eat your heart out."

"Who?"

Fionn walked off, closing the door with a bang.

Caspian arrived home an hour later. His mother, Prue, was in London for the day so they met for a quick lunch in a café in St John's Wood. When he mentioned his new album, she looked stricken.

"It's just I feel like you're slipping away," she said with a sob.

The rest of the visit was Caspian trying to reassure his mother that she was still his number one.

"Writing about Mary is therapeutic," he explained. "I need to connect with her. Only through art. You're my true mother." He kissed her cheek. "*True Prue*." He smiled.

"It's just Raphael is so famous and George feels like a pale reflection." She blew her nose with a hanky.

"Dad is anything but," said Caspian firmly. "He taught me to ride a bike and how to shave. He was there for me. I'll never forget that."

They parted ways after that and he promised to visit soon.

"Madison?" said Caspian loudly. The kitchen was deserted. "Maddy?"

He walked into the bedroom and heard the shower. The bathroom door was slightly ajar so he pushed it open and a cloud of steam engulfed his face. Madison was singing 'Edge of Seventeen' at the top of her voice, scrubbing her scalp with fragrant shampoo.

Caspian pulled off his t-shirt and dropped his jeans and boxers. He pulled the glass shower door open and stepped in behind Madison, making her jump.

"Caspian!" She rubbed the suds out of her eyes. He kissed her deeply, pulling her body close. The hot water beat down on them as he lifted her slightly, opening her legs and slipping inside her. Madison gasped and threw her head back. He kissed her neck and started to move, pushing her back against the tiled wall.

"Fionn called over," she said later as she dried her hair with a towel. "You missed some meeting today with Jax."

"Oh yeah." Caspian pulled on a pair of boxers.

"Jax is angry that you're stalling. I think the band are a bit worried."

"There's nothing to worry about. I'm almost there."

"I told Fionn that you'd call him."

"I'll do it later."

Madison threw the wet towel at his head. "You've got to hurry on. People are running out of patience. Get it finished when I'm up at Savannah's place."

Caspian pulled on a t-shirt and refused to feel any pressure. He would not be rushed. Greatness took time.

# CHAPTER THIRTY-TWO

Madison left for Norfolk two days later leaving Caspian alone in the apartment. The silence was exactly what he needed. At Fionn's insistence, he had spoken to Jax and assured him that he was on the verge of completion.

He spent a few hours transposing one of the songs to a more suitable key, but couldn't stop thinking about the cello. It was like a drug: he had to play again. Grabbing his coat, he called his driver to take him to Stringers of London. He would buy one and practise his scales. Yes, he had an album to finish, but he couldn't concentrate.

Two hours later, he arrived back to the apartment empty-handed. Confronted with student, symphony, solo, and superior models, he couldn't decide what to purchase. He didn't know enough about it. A mini Jax appeared, wagging his finger at him, forbidding him to deviate from the task at hand.

With a sigh, Caspian pushed the cello from his mind and set about finishing the last track of the album.

Madison watched the green trees sway in the wind as her Mercedes wound up the country lane. It had been a few years since her last visit to Savannah's place in Norfolk yet nothing had changed. The lazy cows still regarded her sleepily from the fields; the wildflowers still adorned the hedgerows, multicoloured varieties Madison couldn't name. She'd hated Nature Studies in primary school. Who cared which leaf came from which tree?

Then, Savannah's house came into view.

*Savannah Morris.*

Singer-songwriter and producer.

Winner of seven Grammy Awards for her work as a solo artist, songwriter and collaborator. When she was at the peak of her fame, she had sensationally given it all up to live with her artist husband, Andreas Sharman. After five glorious years together, Andreas had died. Heartbroken, Savannah hid herself away on the small farm she and Andreas had bought when they were first married. Now in her sixties, she was content living simply on their small holding. There she grew her own vegetables, had a small orchard, had four chickens who provided her with free range eggs, and two bee boxes which yielded some pots of honey each year.

In her day, she was known as one of the most difficult artists to work with and Savannah's reputation as a virago was entirely justified. She didn't suffer fools and if she didn't like you, you knew about it. Feared by most, there was huge surprise in the industry when she agreed to write the theme song for Raphael Baptiste's new film about the Empress Josephine. Such was her talent and iconic position, it was seen as a huge coup. She was, in fact, cajoled by the charismatic French director, and eventually gave in to his requests. She wrote two songs, one of which would be chosen as the main theme song for general release. Madison Ryan, with her worldwide appeal and powerful voice, was commissioned to sing the song and so the two women met for the first time at Savannah's farm in early 2019.

After a tempestuous start, mainly due to Madison's refusal to live simply without her entourage, they became firm friends. Madison realised that there was a soft side to the diva that was Savannah Morris. Madison also found that she didn't mind donning wellington boots and sloshing around in the mud.

They worked together on the song, recorded it in London, and then parted ways. When the song was released, it went to number one in twenty countries and critics praised Madison for her beautiful voice. Savannah, who had grown fond of her protégée, encouraged Madison to change her style and be true to her music. "Let go of your pop princess persona," she said seriously. "You could be so much more." Madison, through Savannah, realised that she wanted to be taken seriously as an artist.

When she asked Savannah to work with her and help her write some songs, Savannah had refused point blank. She was finished with that part of her life. She had no interest in creating music anymore.

Madison persisted and after a few weeks, Savannah agreed to help out with the proviso that Madison write the music too.

"You've got to be involved in the process," she told her. "Come and visit after the christening and we'll have a look."

The Mercedes pulled up outside an old whitewashed house and Madison smiled. Everything looked the same. Even the rusty old plough was still propped against the barn door. Her driver, John, took her bag out of the boot, and her bodyguard, Todd, vacated the car immediately to run a security check. Savannah Morris stood at her front door, her kaftan blowing in the wind.

"What are you doing?" she asked Todd, glaring at him.

"Just checking the environs," he answered in his American accent.

"I assure you that it's quite safe," she snapped. "Unless you count my chickens as would-be assassins."

"Just doing my job, ma'am." He strode over to the car and opened the back door. "All's clear."

Madison swung her legs out and stood up, shaking her blonde hair behind her.

"Hi, Savannah!" she called. "It's so good to see you."

"Get rid of those two," said Savannah authoritatively. "You know the rules. Just you." She turned on her heel and went inside.

Madison turned to Todd. "Don't take any notice of her. She's grumpy most of the time."

"It's fine, ma'am."

"Keep your phone on at all times. I'll call you when I need you to come for me."

"I don't like leaving you here unchaperoned." Todd crossed his huge arms.

"You can't argue with Savannah," said Madison with a shrug. "She's scary."

John honked the horn. "Come on, Todd. We'll stay in the pub in the village."

Todd reluctantly got into the car and it sped off.

Madison followed Savannah into the old house. She found her stirring soup in a pot on her old Aga. The air smelled of basil and freshly baked spelt bread was on a board by the window.

"Why do you insist on dragging those buffoons around with you?" Savannah added some salt to the pot and stirred it again.

"I need to feel safe."

"Rubbish. There's no need for twenty-four hour security like that."

"It's fine for you. You live in the back end of nowhere. I'm always in the public eye."

"You choose that life."

"Oh, Savannah. Let's not fight two minutes in. Just forget about Todd and John."

Savannah placed the spoon down on the countertop. "Raphael called. The song is climbing the charts nicely again."

"Yes, like Kate Bush and *Running Up That Hill.* Our song has been reborn. I've some promo gigs coming up."

"In America?"

"Yeah."

"Tea?"

Madison shook her head. "Just water for me."

Savannah went to a cupboard and retrieved a glass. She filled it directly from the Belfast sink and handed it to Madison.

"In case you're worried, the water comes directly from my well."

"It's fine," Madison lied. It was just like Savannah had read her thoughts. She never drank water from a tap, just expensive Italian water in glass bottles that she imported especially.

"How's your man getting on?"

"Caspian? Oh, he's great. He's desperately finishing his new album at the moment."

"Have he and Raphael become close?"

Madison shrugged. "They've bonded a little. It's still awkward though."

Savannah said nothing.

"We got engaged, did you hear?" Madison held up her diamond on her left hand.

Savannah screwed up her nose in distaste. "What a dreadful ring!"

"What?" Madison stared at her in shock.

"I mean, I'm not surprised at your choice."

"Hey! I love this ring."

"Yes, I see that."

"Did Andreas buy you one?"

Savannah held up her hand and showed Madison a simple gold band. "One ring was enough."

"But he was mega rich! He could've bought a huge diamond."

"Oh, Madison." Savannah shook her head. "You've so much to learn about value."

"I know about value. I love my rock and I've no regrets about it."

The two women stared at each other for a moment until Savannah chuckled. "This experiment will be interesting."

Madison nodded. "You can say that again."

Madison dropped her bag in the guest bedroom. It was basic in design: a narrow single bed with cotton sheets, a small bedside table, a small mirror on the wall and a ceramic sink in the corner. The first time she'd seen this room, she'd been horrified.

"No full-length mirror! No en suite bathroom!" she'd wailed. Savannah had scowled and told her in no uncertain terms to get over herself. After a few days, Madison had grown used to the simplicity of her little bedroom. The pitch darkness of the countryside at night meant that she slept soundly in her little bed. As she was required to help Savannah on the farm, she didn't need the full-length mirror to check her outfit. Her habitual attire in Norfolk was jeans and a t-shirt.

This time around, she knew the score. She had to change the sheets on her bed herself and help with the chores. Savannah did the cooking as she was accomplished in the kitchen, but she expected Madison to feed the chickens and water the vegetable patch.

Three days passed quickly. In the morning she accompanied Savannah on her daily rounds. The chickens got some meal, eggs were carefully extracted and placed in a wicker basket. The tulips got a good watering and any ripe fruit or vegetables were picked. The only thing Madison was not permitted to do was help with the bees. Savannah had a beekeeper outfit and explained to Madison that she was never to approach the hive without protection.

In the evenings, after a delicious meal sourced from the farm, Savannah would sit at her piano and play music. She played around with various melodies and encouraged Madison to contribute. Songs began to take shape, albeit slowly, and Madison gained confidence. She learned to speak up if she didn't like a riff or the direction the tune was going. Savannah listened respectfully and took her opinion on board. By the end of the week, they had written the bare bones of three songs.

"Thank you," said Madison, her eyes shining. "I've such a good feeling about this."

Dinner was mostly from the garden. Beetroot salad, the leaves and beet all home grown, with feta, walnuts, mint, and balsamic dressing. Savannah had made some focaccia bread and added sea salt flakes, sprigs of rosemary and olives, finished with a drizzle of extra virgin olive oil from Puglia. She baked it in the Aga and when cool enough to handle, sliced it into long fingers.

Madison loved the food. It was so different to her usual diet which was predominantly fruit and fish. She found that the pace of life on the farm was relaxing. She didn't feel so pressurised as there was barely any phone service and no wi-fi at all. Maybe that was the secret to it all. Living a simple life, immersed in nature.

They had walked to town the day before to get some milk and pick up the Sunday papers. Madison had used that opportunity to ring Caspian to tell him that she would be another week at least. Ross wanted her back in London to promote the song, but she didn't want to break the spell. She and Savannah were in sync and some of the music they created made her feel genuinely excited. Her publicist, Bethany, was busy posting about the film and re-sharing old performances of the song. She also made a few TikToks with samples of the chorus and *Possess Me* was now on the 'Recommended' list. She was due to appear on Jimmy Kimmel with Aurora Sinclair, the star of the film. Things were heading in the right direction.

# CHAPTER THIRTY-THREE

Rosa kissed Luna's nose.

"*Schnucki*," she crooned to the horse, brushing its mane with a stable brush. She bit her lip and rested her head against Luna's flank. She was feeling restless. All she knew was that she couldn't hide in France forever. Maybe she should take Caspian's advice and give lessons. She could charge a fortune. All she needed was a place to live.

Her father was a lost cause. He had bailed her out too many times. She toyed with calling her mother. Cassandra blew hot and cold, but might deign to help her out. She took her phone out of her pocket and accessed WhatsApp. The last three messages she had sent her mother remained unanswered, the blue ticks mocking her. Typing quickly, she asked Cassandra to call her.

After a quick shower, she dressed in a light linen dress and went downstairs. She entered the drawing room to find Isabelle and Anouk making a jigsaw on the coffee table.

"How was your ride?" Isabelle helped Anouk as she struggled with joining two pieces together.

"Wonderful." Rosa closed her eyes. "It's truly my favourite part of the day."

"Raphael wants me to go to LA with him on Monday," said Isabelle, handing another piece to her daughter. "He's tired of travelling alone."

"That sounds great! Go and have fun."

"I don't want to bring Anouk half way across the world." Isabelle continued. "Raph thinks I've become a recluse and that I'm making excuses, but that's not it. He has no idea what it's like travelling with a two year old."

"I can look after her,' said Rosa simply. "It would do you two good to get away."

"Oh, no. I couldn't possibly. It'll be for a whole week." Isabelle shook her head. "That's a long time."

"Coralie is here," pressed Rosa. "You should go with your husband. You need to live your life. Go shopping, eat out, have a spa day."

Isabelle looked unsure.

"I'd be happy to help." Rosa smiled. "I'd enjoy it."

Isabelle's face brightened. "You know, I haven't been to America in years. What with coronavirus and all."

"Then it's settled." Rosa was firm. "I'll look after Anouk as thanks for taking me in."

"You're always welcome here."

"I know, but it's still really kind of you to let me stay indefinitely."

Isabelle placed the final piece of the jigsaw in position and waited for Anouk to slot it into place. After a few tries, the picture was complete.

"Bravo, baby," said Isabelle, kissing Anouk on the head. "You're a genius."

Anouk picked up the completed puzzle and broke it apart.

"Again," she said in her high voice. "*Encore, Maman.*"

Rosa giggled. "She made me do the exact same puzzle yesterday."

"This is the fourth time," said Isabelle drily. "I could do it blindfolded." She arranged the pieces once more and prompted Anouk to begin.

"I've been thinking about getting a job."

"You're leaving?" Isabelle looked up, alarmed.

"Soon." Rosa sighed. "I need to get a job and pay back some money. I texted my mother for advice. She must know someone I can stay with."

"Have you looked for work?"

"There's nothing at the moment. Caspian suggested that I give lessons."

"Cello lessons?"

Rose nodded. "I could charge a lot of money for that." She laughed. "I told him that I'd charge him five hundred pounds an hour and he agreed. Imagine that."

"You'd give Caspian lessons? I didn't know that he wanted to be a cellist."

"He took to it really quickly."

"Oh, he did." Isabelle raised an eyebrow.

"If he's willing to pay me that much money, I'm not going to refuse."

Cassandra rang later that evening. Rosa jumped when she saw her name flashing on the screen.

"Hello?"

Cassandra started to babble in Italian, but the line was bad so Rosa missed most of it.

"Mamma, slow down," she said in English. "I can't hear you."

She pressed her other ear with her finger so as to drown out all other noise.

"Your papa has an apartment in London, *angioletto.* It's where he brought his whores all those years."

Rosa flinched.

"Ask him can you stay there. He's in America all of the time now."

"He's not really talking to me."

"Call him. He won't refuse you."

"I've no job or money."

"You'll figure it out."

"How are you?" Rosa bit her lip.

"I'm in Moscow. Then, it's Vienna to record a new album."

"Maybe we can meet sometime?"

"Yes, why not? I'll call you when I'm back in Europe. Ciao."

The line went dead.

Rosa waited for the familiar hurt feeling, but it didn't come. She no longer felt rejected; Cassandra's lack of interest was a *fait accompli*. She couldn't miss what she never had.

She debated whether to ring her father but decided to wait. She needed to have a plan first. He would be more likely to hand over the keys to his place if he thought that she was working. The cello lessons idea wasn't really a viable option. She knew Caspian had been carried away in the moment and could she really teach novices how to play an instrument like that? She was a lot of things, but she wasn't a teacher. Her father would berate her for wasting her fine training. She should be playing in great orchestras, not giving lessons to pop stars.

***

Fionn kissed Emilia thoroughly. "I have to get back home," he murmured.

"Of course." She pulled her robe tightly around her naked body. "I should get some work done too."

"It's so hard to leave." He played with her hair, twisting it around his thumb. "You've put a spell on me, Emmy. I can't get enough."

She said nothing. Instead, she stroked his cheek. "You need to go. We can't live like this forever."

"Why not?" He pulled her into his arms. "We could never get dressed. You could play violin and we'd be so happy."

She smiled ruefully. "That sounds like a dream."

"So let's live the dream."

"No." She tried to be firm.

"Will you call me?" Suddenly he looked very young and she felt a pang. Was she out of her mind? She had enjoyed their brief interlude but there was no way it could be anything more.

Pulling back, she wrapped her arms around herself protectively. "You should go," she said quietly.

"Emilia?"

"Fionn, this will never work..." Her eyes met his.

"Of course it will."

"No! I'm too old." She stood up.

He grabbed her by the waist and pulled her onto his lap. "Enough of this ageist crap," he murmured into her hair. "I'm not letting this go. Don't even try and convince me otherwise."

"I have grey hairs peeking through."

"So? I like grey hair."

She closed her eyes. "Please don't waste your time with me."

He pushed her back onto the couch and sucked her nipple until she gasped. "Stop over thinking," he ordered. "Just go with it."

Isabelle clung to Anouk and kissed her repeatedly on the cheeks and forehead.

"I can't leave her," she said, inhaling her hair. "We've never been apart."

"Get into the fucking car," roared Raphael.

"If she wakes up during the night, bring her into your bed and stay with her until she drops off. That's what I do." Isabelle kissed Anouk's forehead.

Rosa smiled. "Don't worry. She's in good hands."

Isabelle sighed sadly. "I love you, baby."

Raphael reached out and yanked his wife into the car. "Bye," he said, closing the door. The car sped off leaving a trail of dust.

Rosa giggled and put Anouk down on the ground. Taking her small hand, she led her into the garden. She pointed out some starlings feeding their babies in a nest. To her delight, a ladybird flew off a green leaf, right in front of them.

"*Coccinelle!*" she said in French and Anouk beamed.

"Occinelle," she repeated in her high little voice.

After a thorough exploration of the garden, Rosa led the little girl inside. Coralie was waiting with Anouk's lunch so Rosa lifted her into her highchair.

"What will we do for a whole week?" Rosa thought aloud. "Watch Encanto?"

Anouk clapped her hands. "Bruno!' she said in delight.

Rosa laughed. "Bruno it is."

# CHAPTER THIRTY-FOUR

Caspian closed the lid of his piano with a loud bang. The building opposite his and Madison's Kensington apartment was undergoing a facelift and the sound of drills was driving him crazy.

He stalked over to the window and opened it wide. "Shut up!" he howled but no one could hear. The men in hard hats didn't even acknowledge him, continuing with their work unfazed. Jax had called, demanding a date for the album, reminding him of the strings he would have to pull to get Abbey Road, and he had two missed calls from Fionn who wanted to start rehearsals. Now, with all the noise and disruption, his work was at a standstill.

He fastened the window shut tightly and kicked a book of sheet music across the room.

He thought of Louis' Steinway in Amiens with longing. It was so quiet and peaceful there, the room facing west and so capturing the golden rays of the sunset each evening. Picking up his phone, he called Raphael who answered on the fifth ring.

'Caspian," he stated.

"Hi, Raphael." He swallowed. "Um, I was wondering if I could come and stay for a few days. I can't work in London at the moment. I'm under a bit of pressure to finish this album."

"Of course, but I'm not at home."

"Oh." He tried to mask the disappointment in his voice. "Oh well, not to worry."

"No, no, you should go to Amiens. Rosa is there with Anouk."

"Rosa?" He brightened again.

"Yes. She might like the company."

"I'd hate to intrude…"

"The house is big. You won't impose at all," insisted Raphael. "She's family and so are you. Make friends with her."

"Friends?"

"*Oui*, friends."

"Why?"

Raphael paused. "Let's just say she needs good people in her life."

Caspian blushed.

"You're welcome in Amiens anytime. Please believe that."

The next day, a black Range Rover pulled up outside the Baptiste mansion.

Rosa was lying by the pool in a red bikini availing of Anouk's naptime to relax. She was listening to Doctor Eckleburg with her airpods, humming along to *Mosaic*, their big hit from a few years back. Her eyes closed, she was unaware of a figure walking towards her.

"*All the pieces come together,*" she sang loudly, "*like a Mosaic.*"

Suddenly she felt a cool hand on her arm, shaking her gently. She jumped and sat up in surprise, her phone falling onto the patio with a clatter.

An amused Caspian was towering over her.

"You!' she gasped.

"Hello," he said with a grin.

Rosa blushed and pulled her airpods from her ears. "You gave me a fright."

"Sorry about that." He looked summery in a green t-shirt and khaki mid-length shorts.

"Raphael and Isabelle are gone to LA." She pulled on her silk robe hurriedly. "Did you not call him?"

"Of course I called him. Did he not tell you that I was coming?"

Rosa shook her head, feeling flushed.

"Christ." Caspian ran his fingers through his hair. "He said he'd tell you. I'm sorry for just turning up like this. I had to leave London. I need to work."

Rosa bit her lip. "It's fine."

"Are you sure you don't mind?"

"Mind?" Her voice came out as a squeak. "Why would I mind?"

He smiled. "Great."

Rosa looked around warily. "Where's Madison?"

"In Norfolk working on her own music." He sighed. "Everyone is on my back, Rosa. Jax, my manager, the band, the fans. We need to record this album as soon as possible and I'm just not ready. I can't work at home as they're renovating the place across the street. Music consumes me and I can't think of anything else."

Rosa relaxed slightly. "I get that. My father is the same. When he's in the zone, nothing can distract him."

"I can help you with Anouk. She's my sister after all."

"Have you much experience with babies?" she asked sceptically.

"None," he said cheerfully.

Rosa laughed. "Well, that's helpful."

Madison phoned as Caspian was unpacking his clothes. He was in his usual bedroom: Louis' suite in the east wing.

"So, we've almost four songs." She sounded exuberant. "Four songs that I helped to write. I get why you're such a pain now when you're in the zone. It's addictive."

"That's great, Maddy." He walked to the window. Rosa was outside in the garden, her long dark hair flying in the breeze as she chased Anouk around the gladiolas. He gazed at her as she grabbed Anouk and kissed her repeatedly, her face glowing.

"I should be back on Saturday, all going well. I need to get fitted for my dress for Jimmy Kimmel. Remember? The promotion interview for the film."

"When's that again?" He smiled as Anouk fell over and Rosa copied her, causing the little girl to squeal in delight.

"Two weeks. You're coming, aren't you? I have to look amazing. Aurora is so pretty. I like her and all, but I have to look better."

"Right."

Rosa looked up at that moment and saw him watching her. She hesitated, but then smiled and waved. He nodded and turned away.

"What are you up to? Did you water the plants?" Madison's voice jolted him back to reality.

"Yeah, all done," he lied. "I'm just working on a new song."

"A new one? Jesus, Caspian, why don't you finish the others and keep Jax happy?"

"I am," he said hotly. "It's just I got inspired and I had to write it down."

"Fionn told Clio that they're going to record the album with or without you."

"I get it." He closed his eyes.

"Just finish it, okay? Then we can focus on other things."

He groaned inwardly and prayed she wouldn't mention the wedding.

Thankfully, Savannah called Madison to lunch.

"Oh, I've got to go. I'll call you tomorrow," she said, hanging up.

A little white lie was necessary in this situation. Notoriously fiery, Madison would have had a fit if she'd heard that he was in France unchaperoned with Rosa. He would tell her when they were both back in London. No point in creating drama when she was clearly so happy.

He threw his phone on the bed and left the room. He needed to work and he didn't want any distractions. He passed Coralie on the stairs and smiled hesitantly. She nodded in response, still unsure as to how to behave around him. He was a Baptiste by blood, but not in name. Even though he strongly resembled the men in the portraits that hung in the gallery downstairs, he was still an outsider.

Minutes later, he was seated at the piano, playing the bridge of his new song. It had an upbeat rhythm, unlike the others, and his fingers moved rapidly along the keyboard. This particular song was about Mary's childhood. He imagined that her childhood was happy, a time when she would sing and smile and hang out with her friends. With her blonde hair and cheeky smile, he could feel that she was the type of person who would light up the room. After all, she had attracted the attention of Raphael Baptiste all those years ago.

Humming along, he banged out the tune, lost in the music.

Another few days should do it. Then he would be ready to unleash his deeply personal work into the world.

It was after eight when he finished. He emerged out onto the terrace to find a singular place set at the rattan table. Coralie appeared from the shadows with a basket of bread.

*"Voulez-vous dîner?"* she asked politely.

Caspian looked embarrassed. "Were you waiting for me? Gosh, sorry. I lost track of time."

*"Pas de problème."* She gestured for him to sit.

"Where's Rosa?" he asked, looking around.

*"Elle a déjà mangé,"* explained Coralie. "She already eat." She pretended to put something in her mouth and chewed theatrically.

"Oh, okay." He smiled. "Yes, I would love to eat." He made the same gesture, patting his stomach.

Coralie nodded and disappeared into the house.

Caspian eyes drifted around the terrace with its exotic plants and spotless paved stones. He could see why the family preferred to use this space in the summer. The silence was all encompassing; all he could hear were the rustle of the trees as a soft summer breeze blew through the leaves. Coming to France was the best decision he'd made in a while. For some reason, he felt at ease, despite the awkward moments. It's was almost like the ghost of Louis Baptiste welcomed him home and he felt like he belonged.

Forty minutes later, after Caspian had eaten a goat's cheese and honey salad with crusty baguette and a pichet of cold rosé, Rosa appeared. Her dark hair was tousled and her eyes sleepy, as she had to lie on her bed with Anouk and sing her lullabies until she eventually dropped off. Zola was behind her, his nose twitching as he smelt the leftover cheese on Caspian's discarded plate.

Caspian was drinking a second glass of wine, his long legs stretched out in front of him. He regarded Rosa in amusement.

"She knows Isabelle and Raphael are away," said Rosa with a groan. "Every time I tried to get up and leave, she'd wake and say 'Osa' in her little voice."

"She calls me Yan Yan." Caspian sipped his wine. "It's pretty full on with her, isn't it?"

Rosa nodded and sat down. "Zola doesn't help either. He insists on sleeping on the bed with us, but never stays still." She leant down and scratched Zola's head as he lay at her feet.

Caspian stood up. "I'll get another glass from Coralie. It will relax you."

"Please, don't." She looked down. "I don't drink anymore."

"Why?" He looked surprised. "I mean, sorry. It's none of my business, you don't have to tell me."

"No, no. It's fine." She forced a smile. "I had a bit of trouble with alcohol a while back. Things got a bit out of control."

"It can be a curse." Caspian frowned and resumed his seat. "So many people I know have given it up. Look at Raphael and Isabelle. Both tee-totallers."

"And happier for it." Rosa poured a glass of water. "Did you get much work done?" she asked, changing the subject.

"Yes, I did. That piano is heaven to play. Plus there were no distractions. No construction sites, no Maddy singing at the top of her voice, no iPods blaring."

She smiled. "You two are so different. I mean, that's not a bad thing, but she's such a celebrity and you're so introverted."

"Yin and yang." He laughed. "As Anouk would say, Yan Yan."

Rosa giggled.

Zola barked suddenly as a bird flew out of a bush nearby.

"*Zola! Silence!*" said Rosa in a panic. "If you wake Anouk, I swear…"

Caspian clicked his tongue and Zola reluctantly lay down again.

"Good boy," he said approvingly. "Stay quiet."

"Zola means calm in Zulu." Rosa shook her head. "Quite ironic really."

"I presume he's called after Émile Zola?"

"Oh, I'm sure. Raphael has a first edition of *Les Rougon-Macquart* in the library."

"Really?" Caspian's eyes widened.

Rosa nodded. "I had a Zola poster on my wall when I lived in Paris. *La passion est encore ce qui aide le mieux à vivre*. I loved that."

"What does it mean?"

"Passion is what helps us to live better lives."

Their eyes met for a moment before she looked away.

"So, what are your plans now? Are you going back to the UK?" Caspian traced the rim of his wineglass with his finger.

Rosa sighed. "I need to go back. It's just so hard to take the plunge. I'm on the black list with almost every orchestra I know. My dad won't answer my calls. I owe so much money." She looked up. "It's easier to live here. I feel protected."

"But why are you running away? Really? All of those are reasons, but not reason enough."

Her cheeks coloured. "What do you mean?"

He held up his hands. "Hey, I don't want to pry."

"Well, you are." She sat back and crossed her arms.

"Sorry."

Rosa bit her lip. "No, I'm sorry. I'm overreacting."

He said nothing.

"There was a man," she said, her eyes averted. "David." She took a sharp breath. "I was in love with him and he dumped me."

Caspian's brown eyes were filled with compassion. "You don't have to tell me."

Rosa inhaled shakily. "No, I want to tell you." She straightened her shoulders. "He was everything to me and then he got bored. Dropped me." Her eyes filled with tears. "He was much older than me. In fact, he was my best friend's dad."

Caspian's eyes widened.

"I know, right? I'm such an awful person."

"No, not at all." He shook his head.

"Bianca went ballistic when she heard about it. They had a fraught relationship anyway, and then I came along and made it worse."

"And this David, why was he so special?"

Rosa looked out at the swaying willow tree. "I don't know. He was rich, powerful, sure of himself. He would almost tell me what to wear or what to eat. I liked that. I liked being looked after."

"Sounds like he controlled you."

"No, it wasn't like that." She reddened again. "I was in control too."

Caspian looked dubious and sipped his drink.

"Maybe it's because I didn't really have a good relationship with my own dad growing up," she said eventually. "Maybe David, in a weird way, was a replacement."

Caspian shrugged. "Daddy issues."

Rosa stared at him for a moment. "You could be right." She shivered slightly. "The evenings here get quite cold, don't they?"

He took his hoodie off the back of his chair. "Wear this," he offered. "I don't need it."

"I can run upstairs…"

"I insist."

She put on the hoodie which was fleece-lined and sighed. "This is so warm. Thank you."

He smiled.

"Did you make much progress today?"

Caspian nodded. "Surprisingly, yes. It's such a relief as I was about to be cancelled by everyone. Now, I'm saved. A couple of more days should do it."

"Congratulations," she said warmly. "I remember Daddy when he finished a score he was working on. He'd always celebrate and take us out for pizza." She sighed. "If he was home at the time. He wasn't at home very often."

"It's hard to live with a creative person." Caspian mused. "Isabelle will tell you. Maddy will tell you. Art can be all-consuming." He poured another glass of wine.

"So, let's get back to those lessons. You can teach me when you're back in London. I'll pay you a fortune to clear your debts."

"If I go back to London," she said. "I'm thinking of cutting my losses and heading Stateside. Or maybe back to Moscow."

"Really?"

"There's nothing to keep me in Europe at the moment."

"What about your mother?"

"Italy? I'm not going there." She shook her head. "Far too hot and I sort of burnt my bridges there too."

"How so?"

"Mamma had a much younger boyfriend and…" She blushed.

Caspian stared at her in fascination.

"But I've changed. I'm a different person now. I'm not going back to being *that* Rosa."

"I'd like to have met her," Caspian admitted.

"You wouldn't have stood a chance." She smiled. "No offence, but I wouldn't like to cross your fiancée."

Caspian laughed. "And you'd be right."

A soft breeze ruffled her hair so she pulled his hoodie tightly around her. "Are you superstitious?"

Caspian shrugged. "Not particularly."

"My mamma told me about a Roman goddess once: Fortuna." Rosa shivered. "When I was little, I made a pact with myself to be a good person. I believed that if I ate my broccoli and practised my cello, then good things would happen."

"Did it work?"

"Well, my good behaviour didn't last long enough to find out." She laughed. "Gertrude, my nanny, worked hard to keep me in line, but I spent my days trying to outwit her."

Caspian grinned.

"But I've had some terrible luck lately," she went on. "So I'm going to change my ways and hopefully my luck will change too."

Caspian looked thoughtful. "I'm not sure it works that way."

"Oh, it does. My mamma told me that if I'm a good person, Fortuna will bless me."

Caspian said nothing. If only things were that simple. His own mother had given him up so that he'd have a better life. She made the ultimate sacrifice. Her good deed did not bring luck, quite the opposite, in fact.

Rosa stood up and took off the hoodie. "I'm off to bed. Thanks for the extra clothes."

She placed it on the table.

Caspian smiled warmly. "No problem. Sleep well."

# CHAPTER THIRTY-FIVE

Four days passed in Amiens. Caspian met Rosa at mealtimes and spent the remainder of the day working. Madison called at the same time each night, filling him in on her day and the progress of the songs she was penning with Savannah.

"I can't wait to see you," she'd say before hanging up.

"Me too," he'd reply.

In truth, he couldn't think beyond his music. He had sent a demo of three songs to the rest of the band and the feedback had been positive. This had given him the confidence to record three more songs which he planned to send on after dinner. He knew that Alex was anxious about the album being too depressing. That fans wouldn't go for songs about death and loss, one after the other. But Alex didn't get it. No one did.

He stretched his arms. This would be his greatest work. He could feel it in his bones. Mary was guiding him, leading him to the elixir of his talent.

When he went to the dining room an hour later, the table had been cleared. Rosa was nowhere to be seen. Coralie had left a note saying that she was gone to the cinema in town and that there were leftovers in the fridge.

Caspian sighed. Being an artist was a lonely existence. He grabbed a banana and went back to the piano.

At 4.30am, Caspian closed the lid. He rested his head on the piano for a moment and savoured the moment.

It was finally ready. Picking up his phone, he was about to text the band but stopped. It was the middle of the night.

He walked to the kitchen which was spotlessly clean and spied a baguette on the counter. Picking it up, he pressed it between his fingers. It was past its best, but still edible. He opened the huge fridge and scanned its contents. He took out some saucisson and brie with cherry tomatoes.

"Midnight snack?" came a voice from behind him and he jumped. Rosa stood in the doorway wearing an oversized t-shirt, Zola by her side.

"Something like that." He smiled. "How come you're up?"

Rosa yawned. "Anouk started to cry and by the time I got her back to sleep, I was wide awake." She walked to the cupboard and took out a glass. "And really thirsty. Why are you still up?" She took a bottle of Acqua Panna from the fridge and filled her glass.

Caspian ran his fingers through his hair. "I think I just completed my new album. I think I'm ready to share it with the band."

"That's great," she said, really meaning it.

"They think it's going to be sombre and sad, but there are some upbeat tracks in there. Fifteen in total."

"That's impressive."

Caspian looked pensive. "It never gets easier, you know. Making music. You're only as good as your last song. I get so nervous."

"This is from the heart. I'm sure it will be wonderful."

"It goes deeper than that."

"What happened to your mother?" she asked, putting the empty glass on the countertop. "I mean, I read stories about you, but it was mostly about Raphael."

Caspian inhaled deeply. "She was young, still in school. She met Raphael one night in a club. He was a student in university, over to open an exhibition in Cork."

"An exhibition?"

Caspian nodded. "Of Louis' work. There must have been an immediate attraction. She ended up pregnant with me, he went back to France, and she had to do it all alone." His face darkened.

"But Raphael didn't know about you, right?"

Caspian shrugged. "He says he thought she had an abortion."

"But she didn't."

"No. She gave me away, put me up for adoption. She didn't have much money, the nuns told her it was the right thing to do." He tore the bread in his fingers apart. "Then she was killed in a car crash a couple of years later."

"I'm so sorry."

"All I have is a box of her things. Albums, books, jewellery. There's a video tape of her singing at a school concert." He face softened. "She was so pretty. So full of life."

"Do you have a photo of her?"

He pulled his phone out of his pocket. "Just a couple." He frowned as he searched his photo library. "This is her when she was fifteen."

Rosa gazed at the young blonde girl wearing a blue top and jeans. She was smiling, with her face tilted up towards the sun. "Oh, Caspian. She was beautiful."

"I know." He sighed. "It's like a part of me has been lost forever. I never got a chance to speak to her or hug her or ask her why. I'm not sure that I'll ever get over that."

"Your music will help." Rosa rubbed his arm gently. "This album will be cathartic."

"May I play a song for you?" His brown eyes met hers intently.

"Really?"

"I'd like to share it with you."

He walked out of the door and she followed. The lights were still on in the music room, the curtains drawn. Zola bounded in the door, just before Rosa closed it.

"No barking," she said, wagging her finger. "You've got to be quiet." Zola curled up by the piano, his brown eyes staring up at her sheepishly.

Caspian took a seat at the piano and squared his shoulders. "This is called *Another Life*."

The intro was slow, a series of notes in a minor key. Caspian had his eyes closed, playing from memory. He hummed the melody before he started to sing, his voice husky.

*Imagine you and me*
*Together and free*
*In another life*

*What would you say?*
*If we had one day*
*In another life*

*Some say you can't lose*
*What you never had*
*But you're in my blood*
*Forever loved*
*And I'm glad, not sad*

*That we found each other*
*Worlds keep us apart*
*But you're in my heart*
*And we'll meet again*
*In another life*

Rosa felt tears well up in her eyes. She thought of her own mother who was given every chance and threw it away. When she was a child, she'd pretend that her *mamma* was a princess locked away in an enchanted tower who could only escape now and then to see her family. Her heart hardened at the memory. Even then she couldn't face the truth. That her mother was selfish and didn't want her.

She walked over to her cello and picked it up. Caspian didn't notice as he thundered on the piano keys, his head down as he played the complicated instrumental part of the song before the final bridge. She closed her eyes and waited for him to play the familiar melody of the chorus. Lifting her bow, she joined him, adding the deep bass sound of the cello, transforming the song. Caspian jumped and turned around. She smiled at him.

"Keep playing," she mouthed.

He nodded and started from the beginning. Rosa stumbled a few times, playing the wrong note, but soon they were in sync, and music filled the room like never before. Caspian projected his voice above the chords, harmonising in places with the cello.

The song ended and no one spoke.

Rosa rested her head against the neck, her bow lifeless in her other hand.

Caspian swung around on the piano stool and stared at her.

"That was incredible."

She nodded. "It really was."

"Here, try and accompany me on this one." He played the intro to another track, stumbling slightly on the complicated riff. "I need to practise," he murmured.

Rosa watched the notes and lifted her bow. Her brow furrowed, she played a few notes, blending in with his melody haphazardly at first.

"Sorry," she said laughing. "Your fingers move so quickly."

"Let's start again," he said with a nod. There was a feeling in the pit of his stomach: one he hadn't felt in years. The cello gave the music a whole new dimension. He could barely breathe, such was the anticipation. He played the intro, sang the lyrics, and when he reached the bridge, Rosa was ready. Lifting her arm, she drew the bow across the strings, with her left hand pressing down on the fingerboard. Caspian closed his eyes. This took it all to a whole new level.

"Will you play on the album?" he asked when they had jammed for four songs.

Rosa laughed. "I'm not part of the band. Anyway, popular music isn't really my thing."

"It's not pop," he said haughtily.

"Sorry. What I mean is, I'm classically trained. I'm used to playing in an orchestra. I'm not sure I'd be a good fit."

"Why not? You could play as a session musician. Look at *Eleanor Rigby* and *Something in the Way*. All with session cellists."

Rosa blushed. "I suppose. Sorry, I must seem like such a snob."

"Please consider it." He got up and fell to his knees in front of her. "What you did there was amazing. I will never hear those songs in the same way again. I need you on the album."

"You're crazy," she said, going even redder.

"No, I'm not." He took her free hand in his. "Please. I'll say it to the band tomorrow."

Rosa stared at his earnest face. "I'll think about it."

"You could stay at ours. We've lots of space."

"I'm not sure that Madison would like that."

"She'd be fine."

"It's okay, my dad has an apartment in London that he rarely uses. I just need to work up the courage to call him."

"Say you've got to come back to London to record an album with one of the greatest bands on the planet. Surely he can't refuse you." Caspian smiled.

Rosa wasn't so sure. Could she go back to London? Caspian made it all sound so easy. She bit her lip.

"Here, take my number." Caspian scribbled it on a piece of manuscript. "I don't do social media, I'm afraid."

She stared at the numbers on the page.

"You can get me on WhatsApp. Come back to London. Play with us. You won't regret it."

# CHAPTER THIRTY-SIX

The next morning, Rosa pulled on her riding boots and zipped them up. Caspian made it all sound so easy. She needed some space and where better to clear your head than on the back of a horse? She had pleaded with Coralie to take Anouk for a walk in the buggy so she could have an hour free. She needed to think. Was she ready to go back? Playing on Doctor Eckleburg's new album sounded like a dream come true, but she knew what would follow. Late nights, parties, sex, drugs.

She met Caspian coming up the stairs.

"Hey," she said.

"Hey," he repeated, leaning against the bannister. "I hope you're not too tired after all that jamming last night."

"I'm okay."

"So, I spoke with the band. They're quite excited about a possible collaboration. It's early days, but it looks like it could be a definite." He looked down at her boots and jodhpurs. "You off somewhere?"

"I'm going for a ride," she said. "Coralie is watching Anouk."

"Can I come?"

She bit her lip. "For a ride?"

"Yes."

"Now?"

"Yes. I'm not going home until tomorrow."

"You don't have a horse."

"Surely there's one I could borrow."

"But you must be busy with your music."

"I could do with a break."

"Oh, you could."

"I could."

"I'll ask Jean if he has a suitable horse for you then."

"Thanks. I'll just get a jacket." He nodded and walked on up the stairs towards his room. Rosa marched purposefully down the hallway to the back door which opened out into the courtyard. Jean was just walking out of the stables when she appeared.

*"Bonjour, Jean!"* She smiled at him and he reciprocated.

*"Bonjour, Mademoiselle."* He pointed to the ancient building. *"Luna est là."*

*"Merci."* She walked in to find her beloved horse waiting for her.

She stroked her head and whispered endearments in Italian. Jean had saddled her up and she was all set.

Suddenly she heard low voices talking. She peered out the door to see Caspian gesticulating to Jean.

"*Cheval,*" he said, pointing to the stables. "*Pour moi.*"

Rosa walked out into the sunshine. In rapid French, she explained to Jean that Caspian wanted to join her on a horse. Jean laughed and pointed to Caspian's clothes: jeans, a sweatshirt, a denim jacket, and Converse low tops.

Rosa gave Jean a meaningful stare.

"Okay, okay, I get one." Jean's English was sparse. He led Caspian inside. "Alouette!" he said, pointing to the old piebald pony in the far left stall.

"I'm not riding that," said Caspian rudely. "She's ancient."

Rosa wagged her finger at him. "Don't be mean. Alouette is a sweetheart."

"I want to ride him," went on Caspian, pointing to Rajah.

Jean laughed. "No, no, Rajah no for you. Only Monsieur Baptiste." He turned to Rosa. "Explain, Mademoiselle."

"Rajah doesn't allow anyone else but Raphael to ride him," she explained to Caspian. "So, you'll have to make do with Alouette."

Caspian ignored her and walked up to the beautiful black horse. Reaching out, he stroked his mane. The horse pulled his magnificent head back, but Caspian persisted, stroking the strong neck rhythmically.

"Rajah," he said softly. "Like a king. You wouldn't mind my riding you, would you?"

Rajah's eye rolled slightly, but he allowed Caspian to rub him.

Jean shook his head. "*Non.* This is not okay." He turned to Rosa. "It is dangerous."

Rosa watched Caspian. He kept murmuring things to the horse who seemed to be quite at ease in his presence.

"Maybe it'll be okay," she said.

"It will not." Jean was defiant. "Rajah is only for Monsieur Baptiste. No one else."

"Saddle him up, Jean," said Caspian authoritatively.

Jean looked torn.

Rosa's eyes met Caspian's. He looked so like Raphael, standing next to Rajah like that. Somehow she trusted his judgement.

She repeated the instruction in French to Jean.

"*Mademoiselle!*" Jean threw up his arms in protest.

"Please." She smiled. "Let Caspian try. All that can happen is that he gets thrown."

Jean started to curse under his breath, but did as he was asked.

Caspian stood back and watched as Jean brushed the underside of a dark blue pad with the Baptiste emblem on it. He placed it on Rajah's back, followed by a black saddle, before tightening the girth. He handed the stirrups to Caspian.

"Good luck," he said, shaking his head in bemusement.

Rosa started to lead Luna out into the courtyard. "Come on, Cowboy," she said with a laugh. "Let's see how long Rajah puts up with you."

Caspian accepted a helmet from Jean, put it over his blonde hair, and tightened it. His heart was thumping in his chest. He didn't particularly want to be thrown off a horse like this, but he couldn't back down now. Rosa put her foot in the stirrup and swung her other leg over Luna's saddle. She bent down and kissed her horse's head, stroking her mane. Jean straightened the saddle pad and patted the horse on the rear end.

Caspian stared up at her, drinking in her beauty. She made sitting on a horse look like the most natural thing in the world. Her back arched, she sat with perfect posture, one leg hanging loose down the flank of the horse. He could see the swell of her breast through her white t-shirt. The fullness of her lips.

*Rosa.*

"Come on," she called impatiently, yanking him from his reverie. "Coralie won't babysit forever."

Caspian pulled himself together. "Of course, right. Just let me get ready." He stroked Rajah's flank. "Come on now, boy. Don't let me down."

Jean stood to the side, ready to help when Caspian was inevitably dismounted. He knew Rajah's temperament.

Caspian put his foot in the stirrup and hoisted his other leg over. Rajah stiffened and lifted his front legs upwards in protest.

"Ssssh," Caspian whispered. "Ssssh, boy." He patted his head, calming him.

Jean watched closely. Rajah looked uncomfortable. Just a few more seconds and he would rear up on his hind legs, throwing this young man to the ground. He waited.

"Come on, Caspian," shouted Rosa, kicking Luna into gear.

Caspian stroked Rajah's head. "Come on, boy," he said. "Let's go."

Rajah lifted his magnificent head proudly and looked like he was about to rear up, but instead, he took off after Luna.

Jean's mouth dropped open. He had never seen anyone but Raphael ride Rajah like that. Never.

Caspian held on to the reins for dear life as the horse thundered through the fields at breakneck speed. He'd ridden horses back home, but he really hadn't had much practice since he moved to London. He'd certainly never controlled an animal like this. Rajah's enormous bulk, comprised of pure muscle, pounded the soft surface of the meadow, easily trundling through brambles and puddles. The wind cut into his face as they hurtled along. Rosa's hair streamed out behind her as she rode, her body agile as she controlled Luna's movements. She was still ahead of him, but only slightly, as Rajah was gaining on the mare.

Rosa looked back quickly, her face smiling, as they raced along.

They reached the wood at the far end of the estate and Rosa pulled on her reins to slow down. Caspian did the same and they came to a halt, just by a small brook. Rosa's cheeks were pink and her eyes were sparkling.

"Isn't it just the best feeling in the world?" she said joyfully, pushing her streaming hair from her face.

He pulled off his helmet and shook out his hair. "It's pretty good."

"The speed, the wind, the freedom." She swung her leg over Luna and dismounted. "It's heaven."

He followed suit and taking Rajah's reins, he led the horse to the brook to drink. Hie thighs ached from the ride as he was unused to such exercise. Luna was already drinking, her beautiful mane trailing down into the clear water.

Rosa sat on a rock and tilted her face up to the sun. "Imagine living here all of the time and getting to do this every day."

"Every day?" Caspian looked amused. "Surely you'd get fed up of it."

"Never." She shook her head defiantly.

Caspian took a seat on the grass next to her and put his helmet on the ground. "Why don't you wear one of these?" he asked, kicking the helmet gently with his foot.

"I just don't." She put a long tress of her hair behind her ear.

"You should."

"It takes the fun out of it. That's what my grandmother used to say."

"Your grandmother?"

"Yes, Granny Alexandra. She was a keen equestrian. She would say it's rather like wearing condoms, Rosa darling. Much safer, but not half as pleasurable."

Caspian raised an eyebrow. "Was she from the German or Italian side?"

"Neither. Alexandra was from Hertfordshire. Frightfully well got. She scandalised the family by running off to marry a German so soon after the war."

"So where is she now?"

"She died when I was twelve. I never saw much of her really. She lived in Berlin." Rosa's brown eyes looked sad. "I never really knew any of my grandparents. The Italian side were all dead before I turned eight. Alexandra outlived my grandfather.

His name was Johann too. Just like Daddy."

"So why is Raphael your godfather? Are you related?"

"Sort of. It goes back to Louis Baptiste. As you know, this was his estate." She waved her hand. "After his first wife died, Louis married again."

"By his first wife, do you mean, my great-great granny?"

"Yes. Hélène Baptiste." She nodded. "She died and Louis married again. His new wife was my great-grandmother who was also a widow. They had a wonderful marriage."

"What was her name?"

"Elise. Daddy remembers coming here when he was a boy. The families have been connected for decades. Agathe was delighted when Raphael was asked to be my godfather. She thought it would be a calming influence on him. It was unfortunate when they fell out."

"How so?"

"Daddy composed a score for one of Raphael's films. He spent months on it and was so sure it was in the bag, but it was rejected. Raphael swore it was nothing to do with him, but Daddy still blames him."

"So, how did your relationship survive? Is he a good godfather?"

She smiled. "In his own way. He forgets about me most of the time, but he's also there for me, you know? He never let that things with Daddy interfere with us and I'm grateful for that."

Caspian picked a blade of grass from beneath his feet and twisted it around his finger. Suddenly he looked up. "Hey, does this mean that we're related?"

Rosa nudged him playfully. "I suppose. Cousins or something."

"But not by blood," he said definitely.

"No, not by blood," she echoed softly. Rajah whinnied and they both jumped.

"We'd better get back," said Rosa jumping up. "Coralie said an hour. She needs to go to the market."

"Of course." Caspian got up and brushed the grass from his jeans.

"Don't forget your helmet," she teased, throwing it at him.

He placed it firmly on his head and closed the clasp. "You won't be laughing if you fall off."

"I never fall." She hoisted herself up onto Luna and adjusted the reins.

Coralie was feeding Anouk when they got back, her face disapproving.

Rosa apologised profusely and took the juice cup from her hand. "I'll take over," she said.

Coralie pursed her lips and pointed to the clock. Then she took her wicker basket and left.

"What's wrong with her?" asked Caspian. "We made it home in record time."

"She wanted to get to the market before the best produce is gone. It's probably too late."

"Why the fuss?"

"Raphael and Isabelle are due back tomorrow."

"Oh, I didn't realise. I'm leaving tomorrow."

"Yes, you're leaving." Rosa looked despondent for a second and turned away.

Caspian felt the same. The thought of going back to London made him gloomy. He liked being in France with Anouk and Rosa. He loved the serenity, the silence. The green fields and beautiful trees. He didn't want to return to a concrete jungle with traffic and noise and stress.

He forced himself to snap out of it. He had finished his album, done what he'd set out to do. Jax and the band were delighted with him. He was close to convincing Rosa to play cello on a couple of the tracks. Madison was due home too so he'd see her for the first time in over a week. He had nothing to be gloomy about.

Anouk threw her juice cup on the floor. "Yan Yan!" she called. "Up."

He reached down and picked up the cup.

"Big mistake," said Rosa, shaking her head. "She'll just throw it again and again."

Sure enough, Anouk threw the cup straight back down onto the tiled floor.

"Yan Yan get," she giggled.

Caspian ruffled her curls. "I'm not playing this game anymore, Anouk. You're on your own." He ignored the cup as it flew through the air. "Let's do something fun this evening. Let's go out. The three of us."

Rosa looked up. "I don't drive."

"Nor I. Let's ask Raphael's driver to drop us into Amiens."

"With Anouk?"

"Yeah, why not? We can bring her pushchair." He smiled. "I've never seen the cathedral."

Rosa's eyes brightened. "Oh, I love it. It overlooks the River Somme."

"I've seen pictures."

"Okay, let's go and see it. I'll ask Jean to organise a car."

# CHAPTER THIRTY-SEVEN

Madison pressed a few keys on the piano tentatively. Her musical ear picked up the notes and she played a scale. She didn't notice Savannah walking into the room.

"That's good, Madison. You should take lessons."

Madison jumped and turned around. "God, no. I've zero attention span. I'll leave the piano playing to my darling fiancé."

"How is he?"

"It's work, work, work with Caspian. He's obsessed with finishing his new album. Everyone is hassling him, but he doesn't care. He's always saying that genius can't be rushed."

"He may have a point." Savannah placed a cup of camomile tea on the coffee table. "Making music isn't all about making money."

"Try and tell Ross that," said Madison wryly. "My darling manager is a multi-millionaire because of my music."

"Well, stop working for the man, as they say. It's quite simple. Take a leaf out of Caspian's book."

"Why do you think I'm here?" Madison's blue eyes challenged her. "I mean, I've been without my entourage and proper wi-fi for nearly two weeks while we spend hours working on a song. I'm off the radar."

"And?"

Madison shrugged. "I suppose it isn't too bad."

"We have five songs on the go, three of which are almost ready. You've written some fantastic lyrics. I'm proud of you."

Madison blushed. "Oh, stop it. If you weren't here for the music part, we'd have nothing. I can't even play 'Do, Re, Mi' on this thing."

"The next step is to show Ross what we're working on. You're going into a new sphere, Madison. A new world. One where you'll be a song-writer, not just a performing puppet. Your entourage, as you call them, will have to be prepared. This will require an overhaul of your present image."

"I've always liked Stevie Nicks," said Madison thoughtfully. "Everyone thinks she's a queen. Harry loves her for one."

"Harry?"
"Styles."
"Oh."
"Anyway, I'm going to skip home early tomorrow morning and surprise Caspian. We need to reconnect."
"Remember my advice," warned Savannah.
"Yeah, yeah. Don't mention the wedding."

Raphael's Mercedes pulled up by Place Saint Michel. Martin, the driver, got out and opened the back doors. Rosa put on her glasses and exited the car, Anouk in her arms. Caspian followed suit, his blonde hair concealed with a beanie hat and large glasses covering half of his face.
Rosa handed him Anouk as she grappled with the buggy.
"Yan Yan, no," she said, pulling his hat off.
"Hey, stop that right now," he scolded. "I don't want to be recognised." He put on the hat again and Anouk pulled it off.
"Hey!" He tickled her and she giggled. "I'm trying to be incognito here."
When Anouk was strapped in safely, Rosa smiled at Martin and asked him to pick them up in this exact spot in two hours. He nodded, hopped into the car and drove away.
Caspian scrolled through his phone. "I found this great article on the cathedral. Did you know it's an UNESCO site?"
Rosa reached out and gently took his phone from his hand. "Instead of Wikipedia, maybe I could tell you about it?"
Caspian smiled. "Can I fact-check you?"
"If you like." She handed him back his phone.

Caspian pushed the buggy towards the majestic building. "Wow," he said, drinking in the sheer grandeur of its two towers and sculptures.
"It's one of the largest churches in France and was completed in less than a century which was pretty good going for those days," said Rosa, tilting her head back. "The spire is nearly 400 feet tall." They walked towards the central portal. "That's the Beau Dieu or Beautiful God," she explained, pointing to the figure of Christ surrounded by his apostles. "Beau Dieu is an expression of peace."
"It's incredible that it wasn't bombed to bits in the First World War," said Caspian in wonder.
"Yes, that was lucky."
"The people that built it, the architects and masons, were pretty ingenious."

Rosa sighed. "Unbelievable. Sometimes I feel so small in the presence of such works of art. How did they know so much without technology? Every part of this building is perfect and has endured for nearly a thousand years."

"It's pretty amazing," Caspian agreed.

"Have you ever been to Mont St Michel?"

Caspian shook his head.

"Oh, it's wonderful. There's an abbey on a rock off the coast of Normandy and it's an architectural wonder, over one thousand years old. I went there with my father when I was eight. We climbed up to the abbey and looked out at the view. They say that the Archangel Michael appeared in a dream and asked for the abbey to be built."

"I must go there."

"I love places of worship," went on Rosa. "There's something so calming about them. I love sitting in an empty church, listening to silence."

"Are you religious?" He looked surprised.

She shrugged. "I'm spiritual, I suppose. I don't go to Mass and I don't pray before meals, but I do think there's something higher. Something watching over us." She looked up at him and smiled. "Daddy is a non-practising Lutheran and Mamma is a Catholic, so there's always been conflict."

"Mine weren't bothered when I was growing up," he said.

"I don't think I've ever seen my dad in a church for anything but carol services when I was in the choir as a child. Maybe the odd wedding. Mamma is different; she goes to services every Sunday and always dragged us to various churches when we visited her in Florence." Her face darkened. "She had custody of us during school holidays. Every Christmas Eve, she would sing hymns to a huge crowd outside Santa Maria del Fiore. People love her, you know. It became a tradition. She'd take to the stage and sing The Lord's Prayer, things like that. Then she would be invited to a party and Stefan and I would be sent home with her driver to spend Christmas Eve alone."

Caspian reached out and rubbed her shoulder. "That's tough."

"That's life," she said bitterly. "I've learned the hard way never to rely on anyone, least of all, myself. Life is fickle, people are fickle. The moment you count on someone, they inevitably let you down."

"Rosa, that's just not true." He pulled her around to face him. "There's love everywhere."

Her brown eyes challenged him. "I don't know anyone who is faithful to anybody."

"What about Raphael and Isabelle? My parents, Prue and George? I know tons of people."

Rosa looked away. "Sorry, my crazy childhood has scarred me irrevocably," she said lightly. "Want to get some dinner or something?"

Caspian nodded. "I'd love to. But I'm paying."
Rosa laughed. "I'm not going to argue there. As you know, I'm heavily in debt."
"Until you play on the new album." He smiled. "That should be lucrative."
"I'll pay you back out of my first pay cheque."
They turned away from the church in the direction of the town centre.

They stopped at an Italian restaurant near the university. The owner, a small Sicilian man, cooed over Anouk and told Rosa in rapid Italian that they were a beautiful little family.

She laughed and said nothing. Anouk looked so like Caspian, it was the obvious assumption.

Anouk was placed in a small pine highchair, and proceeded to bang her cup on the side. Rosa gave her a packet of organic rice cakes and she beamed at her.

"After you," said Caspian, holding out a chair for her.

Rosa sat down at a small table set for two with a small candle in the middle. A basket of bread was placed on the edge with some balsamic vinegar and olive oil.

"I love dipping bread in balsamic," said Rosa approvingly. "And pasta is my dream food."

"Me too," said Caspian. "Madison never eats it. Too many carbs."

"My Italian blood demands that I eat some sort of pasta at least twice a week." Rosa patted her stomach. "It's worth it."

"You look perfect to me."

She blushed. "I wouldn't say perfect…"

"Perfect," he said firmly. "That David guy was a fool."

Rosa's head shot up, startled. "How do you remember that?"

"I listen." Caspian opened the menu. "Wow, they have arancini. We must have some."

Rosa stared at him for a moment before opening her own leather-bound menu. She hadn't thought of David in days. Not once.

"Do you mind if I have some wine?" Caspian opened a separate drinks menu. "I'd love a glass of red."

"Not at all."

Th waiter arrived and took their order rapidly. Rosa ordered a small bowl of penne with tomato sauce for Anouk.

"Why did I dress her in white?" she moaned. "Imagine how messy she'll be after dinner?"

"It will be a like a piece of art, I'd imagine. Something by Jackson Pollack."

Rosa giggled. "Coralie will be even more disapproving. She thinks I'm a second-rate babyminder at best."

"I think that you do a stellar job," said Caspian, taking some bread.

Rosa watched him tear it apart with his long fingers. "You were born to play piano," she said softly. "Look at those fingers."

"I know, my teacher at Guildhall said the same." He took a bite of bread and chewed. "Where did you go to university?"

"Oh, all over the world. I started in Paris, then Berlin and Moscow. I ended up in London but that went downhill pretty rapidly." She shrugged. "I could've had it all, Daddy says. But now it's too late. I don't practise enough, I don't commit." She looked up. "I'll end up as an old music teacher, living with my cats and watching primetime TV on a Saturday night."

"I seriously doubt that." Caspian smiled at the waiter as he deposited a huge goblet of Chianti on the table. "You're young, talented and beautiful. You'll undoubtedly make it big."

Rosa frowned. "You're always so complimentary. Almost too complimentary. Did someone put you up to it?"

Caspian shook his head. "Not in the slightest. I'm just being honest."

"So no one asked you to big me up, make me feel special?"

He reddened slightly.

"Ha, I knew it." She sat back triumphantly. "Raphael put you up to this."

"Not exactly."

"Oh, please. He told you to bolster me up because he thinks I'm depressed." She gasped. "Is that why you want me to play on the album?"

"No!" said Caspian angrily. "Yes, he did ask me to make friends with you because he's worried about you. But all the things I said, I really mean. I do think you're talented and I really believe you'll be a great cellist someday. Your contribution to my music will be amazing, that's why I need you." He reached out and took her hands in his. "And I do think that you're beautiful. In fact, you're probably one of the most beautiful women I've ever seen."

Rosa's eyes widened. "Caspian…"

"I mean it. You have to have more faith in yourself. Just because you've been treated badly in the past, doesn't mean it has to be your reality. Surround yourself with good people, nice people. People who will stick up for you and love you. Like Raphael and Isabelle." He released her hands. "Then that wheel you spoke of will spin and good things will happen."

"The wheel?"

"Fortuna's wheel?"

"Oh."

The plates of pasta arrived.

"Now, Anouk is about to create a masterpiece on her Benetton dress. Let's take a before and after photo for Coralie."

Rosa relaxed and smiled. "Okay."

"And ask that waiter for lots of parmesan. I'm a fiend for the stuff."

"Oh, you should visit Bologna," she said dreamily. "It's the food capital of Italy."

"Oh?"

"Yes, it's close to Modena." She pointed to the bottle of balsamic vinegar. "And to Parma, home to the famous prosciutto."

"Wow, I must visit." He kicked her gently. "Ask him."

"Jeez, okay." She smiled at the waiter. "*Posso avere del parmigiano, per favore? Grazie.*"

"*Prego.*" He nodded and scurried off.

"I envy you, you know," said Caspian, sipping his wine. "I'd love to speak lots of languages."

"And play cello."

"Yes, that too." He regarded her thoughtfully. "Maybe you could teach me Italian too."

"Why?"

"For my trip to Bologna where I plan to eat my body weight in cheese."

"There's Google Translate," she said, patting his arm. "Far easier."

"No, I mean it. I'd love to learn."

Rosa laughed. "You have an album to release. A wedding to plan. You won't have time to learn a new instrument and a whole new language."

"Oh, Maddy will plan all of that by herself," he said, accepting a bowl of grated parmesan from the waiter.

"Have you set a date?" she asked.

He shook his head. "Not yet. She's anxious to get the ball rolling, but I want to wait."

"That's hard." Rosa frowned. "For both of you."

"If Maddy has her way, there will be every celebrity on the planet invited, plus a magazine deal and a thirty-tiered cake."

"Caspian," said Rosa reprovingly.

"Look, we want different things. I'd love just the two of us on a beach somewhere. No crowds, no Instagram. Just us. Madison wants the full package." He looked up. "Is there a solution?"

Rosa shook her head. "I suppose you'll have to compromise."

"I'm not sure that she will."

"She will," said Rosa. "At the end of the day, it's about your love and commitment to one another. Not the publicity."

"How's your pasta?" he asked, changing the subject. "Mine is epic. These artichokes are a game changer."

"It's good," she said, twirling the linguine around on her fork.

Anouk threw a piece of bread at Caspian. "Yan Yan up. Anoo up!"

"You stay there until we're finished," he said firmly. "I'm sick of your bossy behaviour." He forked up the last of his pappardelle. "What time are Raphael and

Isabelle due back?"

"Not until noon."

"I leave at two." Their eyes met.

"This week was," she paused and blushed slightly, "nice."

"Nice?"

She smiled. "You're fun to be around."

"Thanks." He placed his fork on the plate at an angle. Anouk threw her bread at him.

"Up!" she shouted with a frown.

Caspian laughed. "Okay, okay. You win. Up you come."

# CHAPTER THIRTY-EIGHT

When they got home, Rosa took Anouk to bed, promising to come back down when the little girl was asleep.

"We could watch a film or something," she said shyly.

Caspian went to the music room to add some finishing touches to the last two songs he'd worked on. Zola took his usual position by the piano, his head resting on his paws. A pencil between his teeth, Caspian played the melodies over and over, changing the odd note on the sheet music and harmonising with his voice. After two hours, he closed the lid of the piano and walked down the hallway towards the living room. The grand clock in the main atrium read eleven and the house was in darkness. He peeked into the kitchen to see if there was anyone up, but there wasn't a sound. Rosa had obviously fallen asleep herself and failed to come back down.

He climbed the stairs and checked the nursery to find an empty cot. Sure enough, Rosa's bedroom door was open, and she and Anouk were fast asleep. He crept in and gently lifted Rosa's arm off the sleeping baby. Holding his breath, he lifted his little sister up into his arms and took her to her own room. There, he pulled the blanket up around her shoulders and kissed her forehead. She looked like her father, and so, like him too, with her beautiful bone structure. "Night, night," he whispered, closing the door quietly behind him.

He was about to turn left towards his own room when something drew him right. He stopped at Rosa's door and debated what to do. She was still in her clothes: a light summer dress that was crumpled from sleeping on it. Her long leg was draped over the blanket, and her long hair like a dark cloud on the white pillow.

Slowly, he extracted the blanket from under her body and pulled it up around her shoulders. She moaned slightly and turned on her other side, muttering something about Anouk. The moonlight filtered in through the crack in the curtains and illuminated her skin. For a moment, he wanted to reach out and touch her, but he stopped himself and exited the room.

It was about two a.m. when Anouk started to scream. Caspian had just fallen asleep after going through each song countless times in his head. He turned around and put a pillow over his head, but the screaming persisted.

Groggily, he sat up and checked the time on his phone.

Bloody hell, he thought in annoyance. Wearing nothing but his boxers, he walked down the corridor towards Anouk's room. She was standing up in her cot, her face red from bawling.

"Yan Yan," she said tearfully. "Yan Yan Anoo."

Caspian's expression softened when he heard his name. He scooped her up into his arms and kissed her head. "What's the matter?" he said softly. "Why are you crying?"

"Maman," said Anouk dolefully.

"Ahh, you miss your mother." He cuddled her close. "There's nothing I can do about that."

"Osa," she went on with a sob. "Osa Anoo."

"You want Rosa?" He picked up her teddy bear and smiled. "Well, I can help you there."

He hummed the Peppa Pig theme tune as they walked to Rosa's door. Tentatively, he knocked. After a minute, he knocked again. Anouk started to wail.

"Ah, don't cry," he said, jostling her up and down on his hip. Slowly, he opened the door. Rosa was sound asleep on the bed, her body in the exact same position as before.

"Osa!" said Anouk in delight.

Caspian switched on the light, walked to the bed, and gently shook Rosa's shoulder.

"Rosa!' he said in a loud whisper. "Rosa, wake up!"

Rosa's eyelids flickered and she turned her back to them both, pulling the blanket over her body.

Caspian rolled his eyes. "Rosa," he said, louder this time. "Wake up!"

Anouk reached out and pulled a long tress of Rosa's hair.

"Ow!" Rosa sat up straight. "What the hell?" She glared at Caspian and Anouk, completely disorientated. "Why did you do that?"

Caspian sat down on the edge of the bed. "Anouk has been screaming for ages. She asked for you so I brought her here. I didn't know what else to do."

Rosa focused in on the baby. "Screaming?" she repeated. "What's wrong?"

"I've no idea." He rubbed his eyes. "All I know is that I had just fallen asleep when she started to wail."

Rosa held out her arms and Anouk reached out for her. "Osa," she said happily, cuddling close to her chest.

"She just wants to sleep here," said Rosa wryly.

"She also asked for Isabelle so I suppose she's lonely."

Rosa glanced at Caspian's naked chest and averted her eyes immediately. He stood up awkwardly.

"Apologies for my lack of clothing. I always sleep like this."

"It's fine." Rosa purposefully turned away and placed Anouk on the pillow, pulling the blanket over them both.

"I'll get back to bed then." He backed away towards the door. "Night." Switching off the light, he walked out into the hallway. As he shut the door behind him, Anouk let out a yell. "Yan Yan! Yan Yan!"

He turned around immediately and opened the door. "Anouk?"

"Yan Yan!" She started to wail, pushing Rosa away from her as she tried to placate her.

Caspian ran his fingers through is hair in exasperation. "What's the matter with her now?"

Rosa sang a lullaby in Italian and stroked Anouk's hair, but to no avail.

"I don't know!" she said helplessly.

"Yan Yan!" Anouk repeated obstinately.

Caspian sat on the edge of the bed, reached out and took her little hand. "What do you want?" he asked softly.

"Yan Yan, Osa."

"She wants you to lie down." Rosa put her face in her hands.

Caspian tickled Anouk. "Lie down here? I have a big bed of my own, thanks."

Anouk's big brown eyes filled with tears. "Yan Yan Anoo."

"Oh, okay. Fine." Caspian lay down on edge of the bed, next to Anouk. "I'll stay until she drops off."

Rosa nodded. "Of course."

"It shouldn't take long. It's really late."

"Exactly." She held up the blanket. "Would you like to get under the covers? She tends to kick them off but it's worth a shot."

"I'm okay." He let his head sink into the soft pillow and closed his eyes. "Remind me never to have children."

Rosa giggled. "Me too."

Anouk laughed too, delighted to be sandwiched between them.

"Night," whispered Rosa.

"Night." Caspian stared at the moonlight on the ceiling, hyper aware of Rosa only a couple of feet away. If Madison saw him now. No amount of explaining would get him out of it.

He prayed that Anouk would fall asleep quickly so that he could go back to his own bed. He could smell Rosa's perfume, a sweet heady scent that had become so familiar over the past while. She left a fragrance trailing after her wherever she went.

He forced himself to think about the band and the new album. Then he thought of Jax and the hectic schedule that was being planned for the coming year. He closed his eyes. He hated the promotional side of things. He wanted to share his music with the world, but not night after night in huge impersonal stadia with thousands of people. It became a circus. He disliked mayhem. Madison would often say that performing live on stage in front of 80,000 people was her Shangri-la. She could die on stage like that, stomping around, singing her heart out to her screaming fans.

He moved slightly, angling his body off the bed, but Anouk started to whimper. "Yan Yan."

Caspian lay back and closed his eyes.

Sunlight was steaming through the window when Rosa woke up. For a moment, she didn't know where she was. Bleary eyed, she could see Anouk playing with a hairbrush over by the dressing table. The little girl had clearly been awake for ages. She could feel breath on her neck and, with a start, realised that Caspian was sound asleep in the bed beside her. His long body was spooning hers, and his large hand was cupping her right breast.

Rosa froze. Her body was moulded to his, and she could feel his heart beating. She put her hand over his and gently tried to remove it, but Caspian tightened his grip. Somnambulant, he kissed her neck lightly and sighed.

She felt the colour rise in her cheeks. He must think she was Madison.

"Anouk," she whispered hoarsely. "Come here."

Anouk giggled and shook her head. "Osa Anoo."

"Yes, Osa Anoo. Come here and wake Yan Yan."

The little girl ignored her completely and continued to brush her hair, singing a non-descript song.

Rosa shifted slightly, hoping that he'd turn away, but instead, he nuzzled her neck and pulled her even closer. Rosa closed her eyes. This was not a position she wanted to be in. She needed to extract herself without his knowing and pretend that nothing happened.

Mercifully, Anouk started to cry loudly when she got the hairbrush tangled in her dark hair. The noise woke Caspian from his slumber. It took him a few moments to process the situation, but Rosa could feel him stiffen when he realised how intimately they were positioned. His hand disappeared in an instant.

"I'm dreadfully sorry," he said, pulling back. "I don't know how this happened."

Rosa sat up, her long air dishevelled. "Me too. I thought you'd gone back to your own room."

"I must have fallen asleep." He pulled a pillow in front of his bare chest.

They stared at one another.

"Osa, Osa." Anouk toddled over the bed, the brush even more entrenched in her hair. "Ow."

Rosa swung her legs over the edge of the bed and knelt down. "Come here, *amore mio*." She started to gently tease the strands of hair from the bristles. "Stay still."

Caspian took this opportunity to walk to the doorway. "See you later," he said awkwardly.

"See you." Rosa flashed a brief smile before tackling the knots once more.

Rosa planned on staying in her room until Caspian left for his flight, but Anouk had other ideas. She had been awake for ages and was hungry.

"Okay, let's get you some breakfast," said Rosa, taking a deep breath. With any luck, Caspian would be at the piano, finishing off his work. Positioning Anouk on her hip, they walked down the stairs to find that the house was a hive of activity. Coralie was hoovering the hall and Michel was watering the plants. Even Jean had been called in to clean the windows. Raphael and Isabelle were due at noon so there wasn't much time.

The kitchen was empty and Rosa sighed with relief. She couldn't get Caspian out of her head. The warmth of his body as he lay close to her, the feeling if his breath on her neck. She shivered. What really played on her mind was how it all felt so right, so easy. Like he was the perfect fit.

She poured some cereal into a bowl and added some milk. Anouk banged her spoon on the table, anxious to start eating. Placing the bowl down next to the little girl, Rosa switched on the coffee machine and took her favourite cup from the cupboard. The coffee machine hissed as the dark brown liquid poured down. The aroma was comforting.

"Morning," came a deep voice from the doorway. Rosa whipped around to find Caspian lounging against the wooden frame. His blonde hair was wet from the shower and he was barefoot, dressed in jeans and a dark blue t-shirt.

"Hey," she said in a high voice, turning her back to him to add some sugar to her coffee, and then stirring it vigorously.

"Any sign of Raphael?" he asked, walking up behind her and reaching above her head for a cup. She could feel the heat from his body as he stood behind her so she abruptly moved to the right.

"Not yet," she answered curtly. "Soon."

"Well, I don't know about you, but I haven't slept that well in ages." He pressed the button the machine and turned to face her.

Rosa blushed deeply and Caspian raised an eyebrow. "Hey, you're not weird about that, are you? It was an honest mistake."

"Gosh, no." She took a gulp of coffee and it scalded her throat. She coughed. "We fell asleep," she said eventually, "it could have happened to anyone."

"It was just unfortunate, my position that is, when I woke up." His eyes were enigmatic.

"Sure, sure." She refused to meet his gaze.

"Madison never lets me spoon her like that. She's one of those independent sleepers. She has to have her own space."

Rosa looked up, confused. "Oh, I thought you thought that it was her. I mean, that I was her."

"No, I didn't." His eyes met hers intently. "I knew it was you. Subconsciously, that is. You smell like flowers. I think I was dreaming about you."

"Caspian," she began.

"What?"

"Look, let's talk about something else, okay?" She backed away. "I told you before, I've left that life behind. I can't be that person anymore. I want to be someone else."

Caspian held up his hands. "I'm not saying anything."

"What happened wasn't right," she went on.

"No, but it wasn't on purpose."

"I mean, imagine if something had happened."

"Imagine," he echoed softly.

She felt her stomach flip. When he looked at her like that, she couldn't think straight.

"Please, I want us to be friends," she said, her eyes huge. "Truly. I like hanging out with you. You make me laugh."

Caspian placed his cup on the countertop and held her shoulders, forcing her to look at him.

"We're friends, Rosa. Don't ever think otherwise."

Her heart was thumping so loudly she could barely hear his voice. She wanted to touch him so badly, her fingers ached. With supreme effort she kept her arms down by her sides. David had never made her feel like this. In fact, no one ever had. The old Rosa would have made a flippant joke to lighten the intense atmosphere, but she couldn't. She felt stunned.

"You're my godcousin after all." He released her and took a sip of his coffee. "Anouk prefers to throw cereal on the floor rather than eat it. Look at that mess."

Rosa pulled herself together and focused on the floor.

"Oh my God, Coralie will kill us! She's been vacuuming for ages."

# CHAPTER THIRTY-NINE

Isabelle bolted from the car as soon as it stopped outside the main entrance of the house.

"Anouk!" she yelled. "Anouk, baby!"

Rosa appeared from the living room with Anouk in a pretty yellow dress.

"Oh, look at you!" Isabelle swept her up into her arms and kissed her repeatedly. "Oh, I missed you so. You've grown in a week. Oh, Anouk."

Rosa stood back and watched their exchange. Never once had Cassandra kissed her like that.

Raphael followed his wife into the house, his phone in his hand.

"Rosa," he said with a nod. "All went well?"

She smiled. "We had a great time."

He kissed the top of Anouk's head. "Is Caspian still here?"

Rosa reddened slightly. "Yes, he's packing."

"Good, I want to see him before he goes." Raphael disappeared down the hallway.

"How was LA?" asked Rosa brightly, trying not to think about Caspian.

Isabelle inhaled Anouk's hair. "It was good, but I missed my baby."

"Did you meet many celebrities?"

"Not really. Just directors and producers."

Rosa paused and fiddled with Anouk's dress. "Isabelle?"

"Hmmm?"

"Caspian wants me to play cello on his new album. It means going back to London."

Isabelle clapped her hands together. "How cool!"

"We had a bit of a jam one night and he wants me to accompany the band on a few songs."

"That's so exciting. Have you told Raphael?"

Rosa shook her head. "Not yet."

"He'll be delighted for you." Isabelle grasped her hand. "*I'm* delighted for you."

"I'm delighted for myself. I might clear some of my debts." Rosa smiled.

Raphael entered the room to find Caspian sitting on the bed, staring into space. He jumped when Raphael said 'Hello'.

"You're back!" Caspian stood up. "How was America?"

"Good, good. Everything went to plan."

"That's great."

"Yes."

They stared at one another.

Eventually Raphael spoke. "Did you work well here?"

Caspian nodded profusely. "Like a dream."

"I'm glad." Raphael smiled. "It must be a big weight off your shoulders."

"Yes, huge. Thanks for letting me stay."

"You must think of this house as your home." Raphael raised his head and looked at Caspian directly in the eyes. "You may come when you want."

Caspian stared at his father. "I don't know what to say."

"Rosa tells me you're leaving today."

"My work is done. Madison will be home this weekend and she doesn't know I'm here for a start."

Raphael whistled. "That's brave."

They both laughed and it broke the ice.

"Rosa might play cello on the album. I'm hoping she'll come back to London to record some songs with us."

"That would be wonderful," said Raphael. "She needs direction."

Caspian's face grew animated as he related how she had joined in as he played one of his songs and the depth it had added to the sound.

"She's incredible," he finished.

Raphael shrugged. "Her gene pool is strong so I would expect nothing less. When is she planning to leave?"

"As soon as possible I hope. We're starting rehearsals next week. I can already think of at least four tracks she could work on with us."

"I'll miss her," admitted Raphael. "Isabelle too."

"She'll miss you as well. She's so happy here." Caspian smiled. "She loves going for a ride on Luna. That's her favourite thing in the world."

"Ah, yes. She's good with horses."

"I joined her. I hope you don't mind."

"Oh?"

"I rode Rajah."

Raphael looked startled. "My Rajah?"

Caspian nodded. "He's quite a horse. I felt like I was on a rocket."

"And he didn't throw you?"

Caspian shook his head.

Raphael said nothing, but a flurry of emotions coursed through him. He patted Caspian's back.

"Come, let's have some lunch before you leave."

When Coralie had cleared the plates away, Caspian got to his feet.

"Thank you for letting me stay," he said to Raphael and Isabelle.

"You're welcome," said Isabelle with a huge smile. "It's awesome that you finished your album under our roof."

Rosa fiddled with her napkin. She was afraid to look up.

Caspian kissed Anouk's forehead. "Bye, Trouble. I'll see you very soon."

"Yan Yan bye." She beamed up at him.

Raphael moved to get up, but Caspian held up his hand. "There's no need to walk me to the car. Martin has already loaded my bags."

"We'll see you in London?"

Caspian nodded. "Maddy hasn't stopped talking about the première. I'll be there, suited and booted." He smiled. "Rosa? Can you walk me out?"

She looked up in surprise.

"I want to make a plan for rehearsals."

"Oh, okay." She brushed crumbs from her shorts and followed him down the pathway towards the front of the house.

"We're starting next week. Ideally, I'd like you on board as early as possible."

She kicked a stone. "I have to call my father to ask about the apartment. I was putting it off if I'm honest."

He stopped when he reached the car. "You can stay at our place. I told you that."

She shook her head vehemently. "I could never intrude on someone's life like that." She could just see the look on Madison's face. "I need to call Daddy anyway so this is motivation."

"When can you be back?"

"I'll ring him today. Then, I'll text you." Their brown eyes met.

'Bye then." He leant down awkwardly and kissed her lightly on the cheek.

"Bye," she echoed.

The car drove off.

Madison left Norfolk straight after breakfast. She felt wonderful. She couldn't wait to show Caspian the sheet music. She imagined him playing his grand piano with her singing along. He might finally take her seriously.

Her phone started to ring as the car reached the outskirts of London. It was Bethany, her publicist.

"Hey Bethany, what's up?"

"Have you seen the pictures of Caspian?" she said bluntly.

"What pictures?"

Bethany paused. "It's probably nothing, but you need to see them."

"What pictures?" Madison sat up straight.

"Caspian in France with Rosa Weber."

"Who?"

"Rosa Weber. The cellist. Daughter of Johann Weber and Cassandra Rosso."

"The nanny?"

"Sorry?"

"Nothing. When were these pictures taken?"

"Yesterday. They were sightseeing in Amiens."

Madison felt faint. "But he's in London. Finishing his album. He watered the plants."

Bethany remained silent.

"Send on the pictures now."

"Okay."

The line went dead. Madison felt a ringing in her ears that almost deafened her. Why would he lie? Why would he go to Raphael's house without telling her?

She jumped when the WhatsApp notification came through. She opened the chat and four photos appeared. One of Caspian pushing a buggy, Rosa by his side. Another of them crossing the road by the cathedral. Another of them laughing. The last one was the three of them eating pasta. It was blurry as it had been taken through the window, but you got the gist.

Her heart constricted. She threw the phone to one side, feeling numb. She couldn't process it. Caspian wouldn't lie like that. Not now. Not after all they had gone through.

Bethany called once more, the shrill ringtone reverberating through the car.

"Yes?" Madison knew what was coming. It was what she paid Bethany for after all.

"We've got to contain this, Maddy. You two are trending. Old stories are resurfacing about Caspian. What time will you be home?"

"In an hour."

"I'll come over. We have to cover this and make sure the fans think that there's nothing wrong. He was babysitting his sister. That's all."

"That's all," echoed Madison.

Todd opened the door of the apartment and stood back to let Madison through. The place was spotless and silent. No one had been living there for a while, that much was clear.

Madison dropped her bag on the table and felt her eyes fill with tears. When Caspian was working, everything around him fell into chaos. Empty coffee mugs, half-eaten meals, sheets of music scattered around the floor. The apartment was gleaming, the lid of the Steinway shut.

She pulled her phone out of her pocket and googled Rosa Weber. Pictures appeared immediately. Rosa with her famous parents, Rosa as a child. Rosa in Moscow. Hundreds of images of a beautiful accomplished girl. There was a YouTube clip of a concert in Milan. Rosa dressed solo on stage, illuminated by a spotlight. Madison recognised the tune, but couldn't name it. Miserably, she exited out of the clip and thought of how proud she felt as she left Savannah's place. So proud of her achievements. How silly she felt now.

Bethany arrived twenty minutes later.

"I've done some digging. Caspian went to France to finish his album. Rosa has been living there for a few months." She looked up. "Raphael and Isabelle have been in LA this past week."

"So they were there alone?"

Bethany nodded.

"I see."

"Look, Madison. I'm not going to sugarcoat things, but there is no actual evidence of cheating. He was seen with her and his sister."

Madison said nothing.

"Maybe give him a call? The sooner you guys are seen out in public together, the better."

"Thanks, Bethany. That'll be all."

Bethany nodded. "Chat later."

Madison debated what to do. She had come home early to surprise him. He knew she was scheduled back the next day. Chances were he was on the way.

Two hours later, she was proved right. Caspian arrived with a bag over his shoulder. He stopped dead when he saw her.

"Maddy?" He ran his fingers through his hair. He always did that when he was jolted. She knew that.

"I came home early to surprise you." Her blue eyes were cold. "Except you weren't here."

He stared at her, trying to gauge how much she knew. Madison waited.

"I've been away," he said eventually. "In France."

"Oh?"

"I couldn't work here because of the construction work across the road." He loped over to the window and pointed to the building site. "It drove me crazy."

"So you went to stay with Raphael."

Caspian paused for a moment. "Yes."

"Except Raphael wasn't home, was he?"

"How do you mean?"

"He was in America with Isabelle." She walked towards him. "You spent the week with your little sister and her attractive nanny."

"Rosa's not a nanny."

"Oh, really? What else can you tell me about this Rosa?"

"Nothing. I don't know what you mean."

She held up her phone. "Then what the fuck is this?"

Caspian focused in on the photos of him and Rosa in Amiens.

"Cosy little family scene, isn't it?"

"We just went sightseeing and for some pasta."

"Right,' she said scornfully.

"We did! Nothing else happened. Nothing else is going on."

"Then why did you pretend to be here? I rang you every day. Every single day. You made out that you were here, at home. In our apartment. Yet all that time you were with her."

"I was working!"

"Oh, really."

"Yes! I finished the album. It's ready to share with the band."

"I'm sick of your album. I'm sick of you playing me for a fool. You have no interest in marrying me. Instead, you lie and spend the week with another woman in France."

"I went to Amiens to work. Can't you see that? Rosa being there was incidental."

"Yeah right."

"I do want to marry you." He grabbed her shoulders. "Of course I do. It's just I need time. Time to process all this emotional stuff."

"Then why didn't you tell me?" she asked wearily. "Why didn't you tell me that you were there?"

Caspian kissed her on the forehead. "It was easier not to. You're so fiery, Mads. I felt that you were better off not knowing. I knew how important your time with Savannah was and I didn't want to ruin it. If you'd known, you'd never have had the headspace to write music."

She let his voice soothe her. She willed herself to believe him. Life would be so much easier if she believed him.

"Trust me," he went on, "there's nothing to worry about." He kissed her nose. "Anyway, we're kind of related, Rosa and I. Her great-granny married Louis."

Madison looked away.

"And she is going to play some cello on the album."

Madison's head shot up. "She's what?"

"She's talented, Mads. It adds so much depth."

"I don't believe this…"

"What? Do you really think that if there was something going on that I'd invite her to work with us?"

"Fuck knows."

"It's professional, okay? Just professional. I swear to you." He forced her to look at him. "Rosa means nothing to me."

# CHAPTER FORTY

When Madison was gone for a shower, Caspian called the rest of the band members on Zoom. Alex had a bottle of champagne in his hands, ready to pop the cork. "We've waited so long for this, I thought it was worthy of celebration."

Caspian admitted Ethan who was smoking a cigarette on the balcony of his apartment.

He blew a large smoke ring and stared Caspian in the eye. "This is the end, yeah? We can get back to the studio?"

Caspian rolled his eyes. "Yes, bloody hell. I told you I'd get there."

"Well, this solo stuff isn't working." Ethan stubbed out his cigarette. "We're a band. It's not all about you."

Caspian held up his hands. "I'm not a dictator."

Fionn's name appeared in the waiting room and Caspian admitted him.

"Well, hallelujah, the album is finished." Fionn grinned.

"Almost," corrected Caspian. "I mean, the songs are in their infancy, but that's where you come in."

"So what's the plan? Do you have a demo?" asked Fionn.

"Yeah, I recorded most of the tracks. I've already shared it with you. Check your Dropbox."

"How about starting rehearsals at the studio next week?" said Alex. "Fionn, Clio and I are going to Dublin for the weekend but we'll be back by Tuesday."

"Dublin?" Caspian raised an eyebrow. "I was hoping we could meet up tomorrow and start working."

"It's Dad's birthday," said Fionn. "Mum's having a dinner party. We have to go."

"It's frustrating when you have to wait, isn't it?" Ethan lit another cigarette.

Caspian glared at him. "I've told you a million times, greatness..."

"Takes time," finished Ethan in a bored tone. "We know. Meanwhile, we're fading into obscurity as other bands resume touring and gigging."

"What the fuck, Ethan? It's never been about exposure or fame. You know that."

"Says you." Ethan glared at him. "You've got Madison. You're papped wherever you go. Not to mind a famous daddy. You needn't worry."

"How dare you!" Caspian looked thunderous.

"We all saw the pictures of you with that cellist. Nice work, man."

"What pictures?" asked Fionn sharply.

"Did you not hear?" Ethan raised an eyebrow. "Caspian was in France this past week keeping that hot cellist company."

"I was not!" Caspian banged his fist. "I went there to work. She was looking after Anouk. That's it."

"You could be banging her mother for all I care," went on Ethan, pointing his finger at the screen, "but if we don't get going on this new album next week, I'm out."

"Out? What do you mean, out?"

"You heard me."

"Children, children," said Alex smoothly.

"Did Maddy see these pictures?" asked Fionn quietly.

"Yes!" said Caspian in exasperation. "She's fine with it. She knows there's nothing going on."

Fionn looked doubtful. "You sure about that?"

"Let's stick to the music, guys," Alex intervened. "Who cares about Caspian's love life?"

"I do actually," said Fionn. "As annoying as she is, I don't want anyone hurting Maddy." He narrowed his eyes. "Again."

"Leave it, Fionn. What's past is past. Maddy knows that," said Caspian.

"Right."

"I wanted to run something by you all actually. Rosa plays cello, as you know. She played on a few of the songs and I think she's brilliant."

"We can see that from the photos," said Ethan smartly.

"I'd like her to play on a few of the tracks," went on Caspian, ignoring the jibe. "It puts the songs on another level."

"How many tracks?" asked Fionn.

"Three? Four? I won't know until we're in the studio."

Alex gave them a thumbs up. "I'm fine with that."

Fionn looked dubious. "How does Maddy feel about it?"

"About what?" asked Caspian.

"Having Rosa working with us."

"She's fine with it."

"Right."

"What's your problem, Fionn? What are you implying?"

"You know what I'm implying."

Ethan clapped his hands loudly for attention. "This is a band meeting. Caspian's love life is not on the agenda."

Caspian scowled.

"Right, see you all next week. No excuses." Ethan's screen went black.

"What's with him?" asked Caspian.

Alex shook his head. "You really can't see it? He's so pissed with you. All this time with barely any updates on your progress. Jax has been breathing down our necks. It's been non-stop stress."

Caspian looked irritated. "I had to work, to have the space to create."

Alex waved, cutting him off. "See you next week." His screen went black.

"I've got to go too," said Fionn.

"Cool, man."

Fionn paused. "Maybe do something with Madison this weekend. She'd like that."

"How do you mean?"

"Surprise her. It will reassure her."

"Reassure her?"

"How would you feel if the internet was plastered with pictures of Mads with some gorgeous guy? Them, this guy comes to work with her on an album?"

Caspian shrugged. "I would see it for what it was."

Fionn snorted. "Yeah right."

"I would!"

"Who would ever want to cheat on you, I suppose." Fionn laughed. "You're something else."

Caspian shut down his laptop and found Madison drying her hair in front of her dressing table. Her towel was wrapped around her body, covering her from her breasts to her thighs. Her blonde hair was half wet, and she arched her arm to shake out the droplets as she held the hairdryer close.

"I know I say it every time, but I wish Mona and Angelica were here constantly," she said, referring to her hairdresser and stylist.

Caspian kissed her bare shoulder. "Do you want to get away for a couple of days?"

"Away?" She turned around, her blue eyes startled. "Away where?"

"I don't know. The Cotswolds or somewhere. Just us."

She eyed him warily. "Why?"

"We haven't seen each other properly in ages and from next week I'm going to be consumed with the new album."

She looked at the mirror and locked eyes with him standing behind her. It was apt, really. How they were communicating through a looking glass, reflections of their true selves.

"Okay, let's get away. I'll call Cora to arrange it."

He kissed her neck. "Great. Don't bother packing much. I don't plan on leaving the bed for most of the weekend." He walked away and closed the door of the bedroom. Madison dropped the hairdryer onto the ground with a thud. There was so much left unsaid, she couldn't focus. All the hurt, all the betrayal, locked away in the recesses of her mind, came flooding to the forefront. Tears filled her eyes. It was easier to push it away again: to conceal the truth.

Fionn was lost in thought when Emilia walked into the room.

"You look worried," she said, sitting down beside him on the sofa and sliding her arms around his waist.

"Caspian drives me crackers," said Fionn broodily. "He treats Maddy so badly."

"Why do you say that?"

"He was photographed in France with that cellist, you know, the one who played at the party."

"Rosa?"

"Yeah, Rosa."

"Rosa and Caspian? I can't believe it." Emilia looked shocked. "Surely not."

"Oh, he says it was all innocent, but I don't believe it. I just feel sorry for Maddy, that's all. As irritating as she is, she's still an old friend."

Emilia traced her finger up his arm. "I knew Rosa when she was little."

"What?" He sat upright. "How?"

"Remember when we first met, I told you that I shagged a film composer?"

Fionn nodded.

"Well, that composer was Rosa's dad: Johann Weber. We were together for years."

"What age was he? He must be ancient!"

"Hey, you're no one to talk about age," she mocked.

"Fair enough."

She sighed. "Twenty years older than me. Oh, but I didn't notice. He was so cultured, so self-assured. I was head over heels in love." She closed her eyes and rested her head on Fionn's shoulder. "I lived with him for a few years. During that time, I was a second mother to Rosa and to her brother, Stefan. We were so close."

"What happened?"

"Johann moved on, met other young musicians, and I moved to America. At the time, the children would spend summers with their mother. When I left that July, I left without saying goodbye. I still regret that."

Fionn said nothing.

"So when I met Rosa at the christening, I was overjoyed. I would love to rekindle our relationship. She was a sweet little girl and I'm sure she's just as nice now."

"Caspian wants her to play on the album. He said that she brings a whole new level to the music. She's going to move back to London apparently."

Emilia smiled. "That's wonderful news! She could do with a purpose. I must contact her."

Fionn didn't look too sure.

Emilia leant up and kissed his nose. "She's a nice girl and so talented. You mustn't worry."

# CHAPTER FORTY-ONE

Rosa waited until 5pm French time to call Johann as it would coincide with his breakfast in L.A. She imagined him by the pool, sipping a black coffee and eating half a grapefruit with a teaspoon. He answered immediately.

"Rosa?"

"Hi, Daddy."

There was a pause.

"Daddy, I need to ask you something."

"Go on."

"I'm moving back to London. I've got a job. Well, sort of. Anyway, I need somewhere to stay and Mamma suggested your place in the city."

"My apartment?"

She swallowed. "Yes. Just until I'm back on my feet."

"Where will you be working?"

"With a band."

"A band?" He snorted. "Years at the best music schools in the world and you're joining a band. God God."

"It's a well-known band called Doctor Eckleburg. Have you heard of them?"

"No."

"Caspian, Raphael's son, is the lead singer."

Johann relaxed slightly. "Oh, yes. The blonde boy."

"Yes, and he wants me to accompany the band on a few tracks. They're going to pay me well and I have lots of bills to clear. This could be lucrative."

"I don't know, Rosa. I really want you to grow up and take responsibility for your life. Giving you an apartment like this is an easy way out. You need to know hardship."

Rosa closed her eyes. The irony of his words hurt her.

"Please, Dad. Please. Just until I'm back on my feet."

Johann paused for what seemed like an eternity. "You can stay there for few weeks, but that's all. I'm coming back to London soon so I'll need it myself."

"You're coming back?"

"Yes, there's a film coming up that I'm doing. British director. All very hush hush."

"Okay, well by then I should be sorted."

"It's just for the short term, Rosa."

"Of course."

"No parties."

"I don't party anymore."

"I'll send you the details of the property management company. They'll give you the keys."

"I'm so grateful."

"What's this Caspian like then? Is he similar to Raphael?"

Rosa felt her heart fill. "Yes and no. I mean, he looks like him, and he's one of those people that gets engrossed in his work, but he's different in other ways. He's so talented, Daddy. I hope you get to meet him."

"Hmmm."

"It's good to talk to you." She bit her lip. "I'm sorry for all that I've done. I promise I'll be better."

"This is your last chance," he warned, "but I'm glad you called. Good luck with your new venture."

"Oh, Dad! Wait, I forgot to tell you. Guess who I met at Anouk's christening?"

"Who?"

"Emilia Thomas."

There was silence.

"Oh, Dad, she's just the same. She composed the music for Raphael's new film that's coming out. You know, *Josephine.* I was so glad to see her."

Johann said nothing.

"I'm hoping to meet her properly when I'm back in London."

"Okay, well, I have to go. There's another call coming through."

"Oh. Okay."

"Call me when you're settled. I'll send an email to tell them that you'll be occupying the apartment for a while."

"Bye, Dad."

"Bye."

The line went dead.

Rosa threw her phone on the bed. Why did her dad clam up like that when she mentioned Emilia? Surely that was all ancient history. Why did they split that time? There was never any explanation.

She pushed it from her mind and her face broke into a huge smile. She had direction. In a few days, she would have a purpose again. She texted Caspian.

***All good. See you next week.***

Then she set about booking a flight to Heathrow. She would need an extra seat for her cello.

Just as she was about to click on a Monday evening flight, her phone rang. It was Caspian.

With a beating heart she answered the call.

"Hey, Rosa."

"Hi."

"Just wanted you to know that there are some photos online if us that day in Amiens. Someone papped us."

"Sorry?" She didn't understand.

"Photos of me, you and Anouk. Someone trying to make money out of a non-story."

"Oh."

"So, just to let you know. I think we were trending for a while." He paused. "Just forget about it, okay? So, when can you make rehearsals?"

"I don't know, Wednesday? I need time to settle in." Her mind was racing.

"Where will you stay?"

"My dad's place, near Primrose Hill." She bit her lip. "Did Madison see the pictures?"

"Yes, but she's fine about it," he lied.

"Right."

"We're used to this kind of thing. Press speculation. *Schadenfreude.* People love to see other's misfortune. It's a fundamental human flaw. They think that Maddy and I have it all so they're just waiting for one of us to mess it all up."

"You're sure Madison is okay with my playing on the album?"

"She's delighted," he said breezily. "Text me when you're in London. I'm really looking forward to working with you."

Rosa ended the call and immediately accessed Twitter. There was nothing unusual trending: just the latest reality TV show and some political scandal. She typed 'Caspian Cole' into the search bar and sure enough, there were grainy pictures of their day out. Anouk's face was blurred out as Raphael was no stranger to suing the press when it came to his family. One showbiz headline read:

***Cole is at it again!***

Another one read:

***Will Ryan be cryin'?***

She clicked on the link and read the article rapidly. It was mostly speculation about him and then a short paragraph on her. She cursed silently. They had her name and her background. Johann would not be pleased. She hoped he wouldn't hear of it.

She exited the article and clicked on 'Latest'. There was a photo of Caspian and Madison in Gloucestershire, walking hand in hand down a street. The headline was 'Reconciled?'.

Rosa exhaled slowly. She was not used to this invasion of privacy. Being a cellist meant that you were known in certain circles, but you didn't have to deal with constant voyeurism and judgement. Using her fingers, she zoomed in on Madison's face. She looked beautiful, her blonde hair loose over her shoulders and her tanned face smiling. Caspian had his hand up, shielding the photographer, a scowl on his face.

She threw her phone away. She thought about Caspian far too much and he was spectacularly off limits. It was the classic case of wanting what you couldn't have. She liked him because he was nice to her. That was it. The sooner she forgot about him, the better.

# CHAPTER FORTY-TWO

Constance O'Connor walked down Grafton Street, her arms laden with shopping bags. Her husband's 59th birthday was only two days away and she had come into town to pick up some spices from a Moroccan shop near Stephen's Green. They were having a small dinner party, nothing like her soirées of old, as Covid had changed how people did things irrevocably. She planned to make lamb tagine with pomegranate couscous and she needed preserved lemons from a deli in town. It was also an excuse to hit the sales and pick up some new shoes.

She was due to meet her best friend, Diana McCarthy, for lunch in the famous Shelbourne Hotel at two. Diana and Oscar McCarthy were their oldest friends. They lived in Killiney, a short distance from her own house on Sorrento Terrace. They had one son, Colin, a fashion guru and influencer, who lived in Cork. Colin and his husband, Val, had adopted a baby boy in 2019 whom they called Orlando. Known as Daddy One and Daddy Two, they doted over their son and visited Diana and Oscar as much as possible in Dublin for 'bonding sessions' as Colin called them. In truth, it was so Diana would babysit, leaving Colin and Val to go out on the town.

Walking past St. Stephen's Green, Constance entered the hotel, smiling at the concierge as she passed. Diana was already seated in the restaurant, reading the menu with her glasses perched on her nose.

"Good afternoon, Constance," she said, surveying the bags. "Have you spent your husband's advance already?"

"Most of it," answered Constance cheerfully. "I love mid-season sales. They didn't exist in my day. It was just January and July." She took a seat and shoved the bags under the table. "It's good to see you, Di. I love your hair."

Diana made a face. "God, I don't know about that. Colin convinced me to go even more blonde than usual and I feel like an aged Marilyn Monroe."

"How is Colin? Is he all set for Orlando's birthday party?"

"Oh, you know Colin. He's super-organised. The marquee was delivered yesterday and he has gardeners pruning the garden as we speak. It's like his wedding *part deux*. Oscar is in Brussels which is a blessing. He hates when Colin has parties. The whole house is rearranged and he can never find anything afterwards."

"I'm sure it will be a triumph. Will there be a big crowd?"

"My sister's family are coming up from Cork and, of course, Val's parents, although Colin has a tempestuous relationship with Val's mother."

"Oh?"

"He hates her dress sense and you know how important that is to him." Diana sighed. "She's also very bossy."

"It'll be a wonderful party. Aonghus and I are really looking forward to it," said Constance genuinely. "Of course, we won't stay all night. Aonghus' birthday bash is on Sunday so I don't want a bad head for that."

"When are the kids coming home?"

"Fionn and Clio are coming home tomorrow and I still haven't cleaned the house. I wouldn't mind, but Clio is bringing her beau. He'll think we're frightful slobs."

"How long will they stay?"

"Until Tuesday." Constance hugged herself in delight. "Filthy house aside, I'm just beside myself. I love when the family gets together."

"How's Fionn getting on? There hasn't been any new music in ages."

"He's in great form. Covid brought them to standstill. There were lots of Zoom rehearsals which just didn't work. It was all out of sync, dreadful sound. Then they played at Caspian's sister's christening in France."

"The Baptiste girl? How exciting."

"Yes," said Constance, her eyes sparkling. "He said he'd never seen anything like the gardens and the house was to die for."

"I'd love to be have been a fly on the wall at that."

"Anyway, Caspian has just finished the new album. They're going to start recording it soon in Abbey Road! Imagine!"

"Wonderful!"

Constance buttered a bread roll. "He's very excited. It has taken ages to reach this point. It's been very frustrating for the rest of the band. Caspian's such a perfectionist."

"Any news of the wedding? I met Louise Ryan last week and she said Madison is frustrated. They seem to have been engaged forever."

"Nothing yet as far as I know. Cliona gets the brunt of it. Maddy calls her up complaining about his procrastination. He's as indecisive as Hamlet."

"Poor Clio. She's always been the shoulder to cry on."

"Anyway, maybe now that the album is ready, Caspian will get in gear. Fionn could do with an injection of cash too. He always said if he made a few bob that he'd install proper heating at home. I must remind him."

Diana arched a perfectly manicured eyebrow. "You know, if you laid off the shopping a bit, you could probably fund that yourself."

"Diana!" Constance looked horrified. "I've never saved money in my life and I don't intend to start." She bit into her bread and chewed. "My darling granny used to say that there's no pocket in a shroud and she was absolutely right. It's futile to amass hordes of money, you can't take it with you to the grave. Plus there's inheritance tax and all that nasty business, so I'm sparing Clio and Fionn that at least."

A waiter appeared. "Shall I take your order?" he asked.

Diana smiled. "Two crab risottos, please."

"And a bottle of Sancerre," added Constance.

Cliona and Alex caught the afternoon flight and were in Sorrento Terrace by five. The dining room table was set for four people, and the cats, Greymalkin and Paddock, were sound asleep on sunny spot on the windowsill. Dust particles were clearly visible in the rays of sunshine that streamed into the room.

Constance squealed when she saw her daughter.

"Clio! My love!" She hugged her fiercely. "And Alexander. What a pleasure to have you back under our roof."

Aonghus sidled up to them and kissed Cliona's forehead. "My best girl!' he said in delight. "I've missed you."

"Hi, Mum! Dad!" Cliona beamed at her parents. "It's so good to be home."

Alex kissed Constance's cheek and shook Aonghus' hand. "Thanks so much for putting me up."

"Not at all, my love," said Constance. "I bought a brand new bed at IKEA for Cliona's room so you'll be staying in luxury."

"What was wrong with my old bed?" said Cliona, affronted. "I quite liked it."

"I drove out there for a look and the beds were so cheap and gorgeous looking. I felt it was time for an upgrade. I got beds for all of us."

Her husband raised an eyebrow. "Don't forget the ten pasta jars, three lamps, the label maker, champagne flutes, and four shelving units."

"Oh, Aonghus, they were just a few extra bits."

"I don't know who you think will put those units together," he continued. "I'm completely impractical and assembling them requires a logical brain."

"So, the beds aren't even assembled?" Cliona put her head in her hands.

"Fionn has a logical brain," said Constance hotly. "I'm sure he'll help his old mother out when he comes tomorrow."

Alex laughed, his red hair flopping over his eyes. "As luck would have it, I have a logical brain," he said. "Leave it with me." He handed Constance a jar. "I brought you some honey from our farm."

"How lovely!"

He nodded. "Dad is all about the bees."

"And rightly so," said Aonghus. "They're declining at a tremendous rate."

"Come and sit down, my darlings. I have a stew in the oven and Daddy just opened a bottle of red."

The next day, Constance was sewing her favourite silk kimono when there was a knock at the door.

"Get the door, Aonghus!" she called. "It's probably Fionn. He's due around now."

She heard the front door open and bang again seconds later. Then the sitting room door opened and Aonghus walked in with a strange expression on his face.

Fionn appeared with a brown bag over his shoulder.

"Hey, Mum." He dropped the bag and hugged Constance tightly.

"My darling boy!' She kissed him over and over. "I should have a red carpet out for you now you're so famous."

"Well, I was wondering where it was…" He smiled.

Aonghus opened the door wider to reveal a woman standing on the threshold, looking uncomfortable.

"Mum, this is Emilia Thomas." Fionn pulled her to him. "Is it okay if she stays?"

Constance sat up straight. "Of course, sweetheart. We have the futon."

"No need," he said cheerfully. 'She can sleep with me."

"Oh?" Constance felt flushed.

"Yes." He took off his jacket. "Don't worry about dinner. We'll probably go out."

"Really? I made a chicken pie."

"Well, you've an extra guest and I didn't warn you…"

"You know me, darling. I always make enough for a small village.' She took a gulp of wine nervously and coughed.

Aonghus turned to an embarrassed Emilia. "Can I get you a drink?"

"I'm fine, thank you."

"She'll have a whiskey, Dad." Fionn took her hand and led her to the couch. "I will too."

Constance sat down on the armchair, startled. "So, how do you two know each other?"

"We met at a party," answered Fionn. "Emmy here is a film composer." He squeezed Emilia's knee.

"Wow," said Aonghus, impressed. "That's no joke." He handed Emilia a tumbler of whiskey. "Have you written music for many films?"

"A few," said Emilia, clearly mortified.

"Her latest project is that *Josephine* film that Aurora Sinclair is in."

"Gosh, that looks great." Aonghus smiled at her. "Which instruments do you play?"

"Violin and piano, mostly."

"Fantastic!"

Constance, uncharacteristically quiet, watched them talk. Her eyes kept darting from Emilia to Fionn and back again. She was itching to google her and check her age. She guessed late thirties.

"So, have you been to Dublin before?" asked Aonghus.

"Once. This was a last minute trip and I'm so sorry for imposing like this."

"Oh, we don't mind," said Aonghus pleasantly. "This house is like a hotel anyway. Lots of people coming and going. Cliona and Alex are here. They just popped into town for a date night."

"Last minute trip?" said Constance, looking directly at Emilia.

Fionn looked up. "Yes, I convinced her to come as I couldn't bear to be separated from her."

"Right." Constance looked at her husband in alarm. "Well, I'll just go and change my clothes. I didn't realise we'd have a guest."

"Oh no, please don't," said Emilia earnestly. "I don't mind in the slightest."

Constance gave a strangled laugh. "Fionn, you remember that we have to pop over to Orlando's birthday tomorrow?"

"Yeah, Emmy doesn't mind."

Emilia looked uncomfortable. "We got Orlando some Kinder chocolate in the duty-free."

"Oh, that's nice." Aonghus beamed at her.

Fionn took Emilia's hand and led her to the sofa.

"Aonghus, love. Help me in the kitchen." Constance got up and made eyes at her husband. "Now."

"Do you need help, Mum?" called Fionn. "What do you need?"

"It's okay, darling. Daddy can help."

Constance typed 'Emilia Thomas' into Google and started to read.

*Emilia Thomas is an English composer and musician. The recipient of such accolades as an Academy Award for Best Original Score and three Golden Globe Awards.*

*Born: December 10th, 1977, Birmingham, United Kingdom*

*Height: 1.59m*

*Current films: Josephine*

*See also* ***Johann Weber; Raphael Baptiste***

"Jesus, Mary and Saint Joseph." Constance dropped the phone onto the table.

"What's wrong, love?" asked Aonghus.

"She's almost forty-five."

"She looks well for it."

"What?" She looked up. "Are you mad? She's far too old for him." Aonghus took her hand. "Now, now. It's only in its infancy. Don't worry about that, for God's sake."

"Oh Aonghus, don't be daft. Of course I'm worried. He didn't warn us. I thought he was coming home on his own."

"Connie, don't." He kissed her gently. "Fionn is a big boy and he knows what he's doing."

"Does he?"

"Yes,' he said firmly.

"He hasn't a clue what he's doing," she said in despair. "When I think of all the times I prayed to St. Martin that he'd settle down and this is what happens. I'll never be a granny."

Aonghus pulled her close. "You're jumping the gun, sweetheart. They've only just met. Remember us in the early days? We were love's young dream. It's a brief time. Let it run its course."

"But what if they stick together, even when the excitement fades?"

"Then so be it." He kissed her curls. "Now, go upstairs and put on something suitable and be nice to that poor girl in there."

Emilia refused top up of wine and placed her knife and fork together on her plate.

"That was delicious," she said softly. "Thank you."

Constance forced a smile. "I'm glad you liked it."

Aonghus and Fionn had done most of the talking throughout the meal, arguing about rugby and Brexit. Constance had barely touched her food.

Every now and then, Fionn would kiss Emilia's hand or stroke her arm. He was clearly besotted.

"So Emilia, what's your next project?" asked Aonghus amiably.

"Raphael is working on a new script too so I'll probably work on that."

"Is it difficult to write scores? There must be an awful lot of work in it, with all the different instruments."

"Well, I've been at it a long time."

Constance's face tightened and Emilia noticed straight away.

"I studied at Oxford and then I had a wonderful mentor," she continued. "I spent a long time in LA too."

"Sounds fascinating."

"She is, isn't she?" said Fionn, kissing her cheek. "Fascinating."

Constance stood up abruptly. "I'll just clear some plates."
"Are you feeling okay, Mum?" asked Fionn, jumping up.
"What do you mean?"
"Clearing plates? I've never seen you do that. That's normally Clio's job."
She forced a smile. "I'll be back in a sec."

A few minutes later, Constance squirted some Fairy Liquid into the sink and watched it fill with sudsy water. She needed some space to think. It was crystal clear that Fionn was enthralled by this woman. He couldn't keep his hands off her. She switched off the tap. He was so young, he didn't realise the implications.

The kitchen door opened with a creak. "Just leave the plates on the counter, love," she said dully.

"Constance, may I speak with you?"

She swung around to find Emilia standing awkwardly near the table.

"Oh, I thought you were Aonghus."

"I'm sorry for turning up out of the blue like this."

"That's fine. No problem." Constance reddened.

"I can tell that you're shocked. I would be too if I were you."

"Shocked?"

"At my age."

Constance wiped her hands on a tea towel. "You're right," she said eventually. "I am shocked. I'm sorry if that's difficult to hear, but Fionn's only twenty-eight."

"I know." Emilia walked forward. "Believe me, I know. I feel just as uncomfortable as you."

"Really?"

"Yes." Her face was earnest.

"Then why are you here?"

"I don't know. It's all been so sudden and he's so insistent."

"Yes, he's always been pushy when he wants something." Constance's face softened. "When he was nine he wanted a Nintendo computer. You know, the hand held ones. They cost a fortune so we tried to dissuade him. In the end, he got what he wanted after an incessant barrage of pleading."

"Well, the same thing happened to me." Emilia smiled sadly. "You don't need to tell me that it's crazy. I know how this will end. It's all a novelty now but wait until he wants to settle down and have children. I may be too old."

Constance said nothing.

"It's just he makes me happy. Even though we've only known each other for five minutes, he makes me feel alive. All I want is your blessing. I know it's a lot to ask, but he adores you and I don't want to come between you."

"I'm just worried."

"I understand."

"He's so young…"

"Yes."

The two women stared at each other.

"Fine. I'll make an effort." Constance walked over and hugged her. "It's not in my nature to be sullen. You will be like Emmanuel and Brigitte Macron. Now, please play the piano for us. I'd love to hear something other than pop songs."

# CHAPTER FORTY-THREE

Alex and Cliona arrived home around half ten.

"We went for ramen in Dundrum and then to the cinema," said Cliona, placing some shopping bags on the floor.

"Wine?" asked Fionn, appearing out of the kitchen.

"No, I'm okay."

"I'd love some tea," said Alex.

Emilia was in the background, clutching her glass nervously.

"Clio, this is Emilia." Fionn took Emilia's hand and pulled her forward. "Emmy, this is my little sister, Cliona."

"Hey, Emilia," said Cliona warmly.

Alex smiled. "Good to see you again."

"Come on, Fionn. Help me make some tea." Cliona linked arms with her brother and led him away. Alex started talking to Emilia about the christening in France.

"So, what did Mum say?" asked Cliona when they were safely in the kitchen.

"She was grand."

"Really? I mean, she's middle-aged."

Fionn looked annoyed. "Why is everyone so obsessed with her age? She's young; I'm young."

"It's just she's at a different stage of life. Stop being so defensive."

"Look," he said, putting his glass on the table and facing her. "I know it's only been a couple of weeks, but I'm in love with her, Clio. No messing. She's amazing and everything I want."

"I believe you."

"Good."

"Just be careful. You may end up breaking her heart."

"I won't."

"You say that now, but down the line you might want kids or a younger woman might catch your eye. Then she'd be cast aside."

"I won't."

"Look at Ashton Kutcher and Demi Moore. Look at Ralph Fiennes and Francesca Annis. Will I go on?"

"Why do you always act like you're my mother?" He smiled, but it didn't reach his eyes. "I'm more worried about you and my bassist, to be honest. When that goes down the swanny, it'll be awkward."

"It won't."

"Says you," he scoffed. "*What if someone younger catches your eye*?" he mimicked. "Now back off. I'm allergic to negativity. Let's enjoy life and screw convention. What is it that Dad always says? When he gets pissed and quotes Joyce?"

"*Non serviam.*"

"That's it exactly. I will not obey." He grinned. "Now, the kettle's boiled. Get cracking on the tea for your boyfriend."

Fionn woke up in his childhood bed and opened his eyes. Emilia was asleep on the pillow beside him, her eyelashes fluttering. In sleep, her face was peaceful. The lines around her eyes that she hated were not as pronounced. Her slender arm was outside the duvet, clutching the blankets close to her chest.

He couldn't stop thinking about her. It didn't seem like a few weeks since they'd first met; it felt like years. When she spoke, her voice was like music. Everything she said was interesting. She'd been so many places and met so many people. Every time she played an instrument, he became mesmerised. She was the whole package.

He got that his mother was concerned. It was an unconventional relationship. He couldn't deny it. However, her age meant nothing to him. He didn't think about tomorrow. He lived for the present.

Leaning over, he kissed her nose. Then he stole out of bed, put on some sweatpants and a t-shirt and left the room.

Constance was making eggs and bacon when he entered the kitchen.

"Morning, darling," she said, popping some bread into the toaster. "Would you like a fry?"

"No eggs, just bacon."

"Coming up." She filled the teapot with boiling water and placed a tea cosy on top. "Did you sleep well in your new bed?"

"Yeah," he answered, opening The Irish Times Magazine. "It didn't look that comfortable, but actually it was great."

"Alex is a saint to put all those beds together. He was hours at it yesterday."

Fionn didn't reply. He scanned an article about Madison and her new rumoured collaboration with Savannah Morris. Her beautiful face looked haughty in the photo, her blonde hair tumbling around her face. On her left hand was a giant diamond, clearly visible.

"Maddy is changing track with her music," he announced. "She spent a couple of weeks writing songs."

"Yes, I saw that." Constance buttered two slices of toast. "It will be good for her. It might give her some self-confidence."

"Self-confidence?" Fionn scoffed. "She has plenty of that."

"Ah, you think that, but our Madison is very insecure. She's quite fragile really."

Fionn said nothing. He just stared at the photo.

Constance poured some tea for him and some for herself. "Why was Caspian pictured with that beautiful young girl in France? Rosa Weber? It dominated the tabloids for a few days."

Fionn's expression darkened. "He went over to Raphael's place to finish the album, or so he says. Rosa happened to be there. They're just friends, by all accounts."

"She's stunning. I went to see her mother in Wexford in the nineties. What a voice."

He nodded.

"That must be hard for Maddy," she continued, sipping her tea cautiously as it was steaming hot.

"Bigtime. I know Madison and she's definitely not okay with it."

Constance buttered some toast, making sure to cover every inch of the surface. Then she added a dollop of apricot jam and spread it generously around.

"Has he any notion of marriage?"

Fionn shrugged. "Who knows? Nothing rushes him."

"Well, he'd want to get a move on. I've an outfit picked out in Arnott's and everything."

Emilia was awake when Fionn returned to his bedroom. She was sitting up on the bed, hugging her knees.

"Morning," he said, leaning down and kissing her on the mouth. "Sorry if I taste of bacon. Mum made some breakfast."

Emilia licked her lips. "Oh, I'd love a bacon sarnie. Does she have any left?"

"Oh, Mum always over compensates. There's plenty."

She pulled him down on top of her. "Fine, make love to me first."

Fionn pulled off his t-shirt and pulled her naked body close.

Constance ordered a taxi for the six of them to go to Orlando's party.

"Mum, Killiney's only ten minutes away!" said Fionn.

"Daddy's hip is troubling him," she explained. "It's also spitting rain and I don't want my hair to be flat."

She checked the lamb tagine she'd prepared that morning, lifting the lid of the pot and inhaling the aroma. "That preserved lemon makes all the difference," she said, closing her eyes. "This will taste divine by tomorrow when the flavours will have had time to develop."

"I can't wait," said Fionn. "I love your tagine."

# CHAPTER FORTY-FOUR

Colin's parents' house was a two-storey mansion in the exclusive suburb of Killiney.

A small marquee had been erected on the lawn and a jazz band was playing some Ella Fitzgerald. Multi-coloured balloons were tied to the trellis surrounding the door and a four-tiered cake was perched on a table inside, safe from the spatters of rain that fell intermittently from the sky. Britney the dog was in the conservatory, jumping and barking in excitement at the commotion outside.

Constance knocked on the front door. Aonghus, laden down with bottles of wine and presents, stood by her side. Cliona and Alex loitered behind, as did Fionn and Emilia.

Diana McCarthy answered the door, looking frazzled. "Come in, come in." She ushered them inside. "Colin's all stressed out. The dog is peeing all over the floor. He thinks she's regressing. Orlando is experiencing delayed terrible twos and the caterers got the order wrong so now we're having chicken cacciatore instead of boeuf bourguignon."

"How awful," said Constance. "Poor Colin."

Diana fanned her face. "That's not all. He ordered a custom-made outfit for Orlando, plus one for the dog, and Britney's doesn't fit! She's been comfort eating since Orlando arrived and Colin is distraught. My poor sister is currently trying to open the seams and let the doggy sailor suit out a bit."

Emilia tried to follow her chatter. "Fionn," she said in an undertone. "Who's Britney?"

"Colin's dog."

"Oh."

"So, as you can imagine, Colin is around like a lunatic, making sure everything is up to his habitual ridiculously high standards." Diana ushered them inside.

Fionn waved to the occupants of the kitchen. A woman with blonde curls and blue eyes looked up from sewing a small white suit with a navy trim.

"Hello," she said, smiling warmly. "I'm Helen, Diana's sister."

"Hi," said Fionn. "How's the re-sizing going?"

"Not great." She bent her head again and inserted the needle carefully. "I'm not the best seamstress.'

"Well, you're a million times better than me," said Diana, appearing behind her. "I don't excel at anything domestic."

Helen laughed. "Yes, you're right there."

A girl with long brown hair was breastfeeding a baby at the table. "Hi, I'm Lydia, Colin's cousin," she said with a small wave.

Alex smiled. "Hello. What's your baby's name?"

"Eva." She stroked the baby's cheek as she fed.

"Congratulations."

Lydia smiled.

Helen held up Britney's suit. "How does this look?" she asked, her face red from concentrating.

Lydia gave her a thumbs up. "Great, Mum."

"Would you like a drink?" asked Diana. 'We have beer and wine."

"Some white wine would be lovely," said Fionn. "Emmy? Wine?"

Emilia nodded.

"Same," said Cliona.

"Beer for me," said Alex with a grin.

"You know our choice of tipple," said Constance. "Don't worry, Di. I'll serve us. You've enough to do."

Suddenly a small girl with blonde hair rushed into the room, shrieking. "Shut the fuck up!"

"Sienna!" Lydia looked up sharply. "No bad language! We've talked about this."

"Sorry, Mom." She beamed up at her mother, not looking remotely sorry.

"This is my grand-niece, Sienna," said Diana. "Don't be fooled by her angelic looks."

"Shut the fuck up!" shouted Sienna and stuck her tongue out at Diana.

Constance laughed and ruffled Sienna's hair. "How adorable! Fionn used to always say 'shit' when he was little. Like once, my mother, God rest her soul, made a chocolate cake. Now, she was many things, but a good chef was not one of them. The cake was dry and we really struggled to eat it. Fionn was a toddler at the time and he pipes up, 'Cake, shit!". Remember, Aonghus? What we laughed."

Fionn leant down and waved. "Hey, Sienna. Do you love your new sister?'

"No," she answered rudely and ran off.

"Fair enough," said Fionn with a laugh. "I remember not being impressed with Cliona in the beginning either."

"Where's your daddy?" Lydia asked her daughter as she circled the island unit. "I need to change into my dress."

"Daddy's watching TV with Xav," said Sienna. "Basketball."

"He's watching the Knicks?" Lydia dislodged a sleeping Eva and some milk dribbled down her chin. "Well, he can look after the baby while he's at it. Honestly! Do I have to do everything around here?"

"Oh Lord,' said Helen, rolling her eyes. "Cue yet another fight between my daughter and her hubby. Change the record."

Lydia stalked out, Eva in her arms, and nearly crashed into Colin, who was carrying a box of glasses.

"Hey, watch it cuz," he said, the box wobbling in his arms. "These are Waterford Crystal." He walked into the kitchen. "Why does Lydia have her angry face on?"

Helen popped a grape in her mouth. "Luca isn't pulling his weight with Eva."

Colin placed the box on the counter. "Yawn. I'm sick of their domestics. How did the alteration go, Auntie Hel?"

Helen held up the little suit and Colin inspected it. "Not as bad as I anticipated. Right, has anyone seen Britney? We need to do a fitting right now."

Helen shrugged. "The last I saw of her she was peeing up against the potted plant in the hall."

"What?" yelled Colin. "Not the Bergenia!"

Diana massaged his shoulders. "Sweetheart, you're so tense. It will be a lovely day. Don't stress so much."

"Mum, have you noticed that it's raining outside? I mean, I'm a good person and I deserve good karma."

"The weather is meant to clear up soon."

"I'm sick of it," he went on. "I've been impeccably behaved all week. I did loads of good deeds without expecting anything in return. Just like before my wedding."

"Like what?" asked Cliona curiously.

"Well, I smiled at ten random strangers when I was in town shopping, spreading the love. Then, when I was in M&S, I helped an old lady reach the nachos on a high shelf."

Cliona laughed.

"Then," continued Colin, ignoring her, "I made Val breakfast in bed two days in a row – pancakes with maple syrup and berries – *and* I also made a donation to a Go Fund Me page."

"Oh? What page?" asked Constance.

Colin reddened. "Well, my friend Barnaby at work has been saving for a nose job for ages and I wanted to help him on his way to achieving some self-esteem."

"Christ," said Fionn, shaking his head.

"And, last but not least, I am owed years of good karma for all the free babysitting I've done for Luca and Lydia over the years. I mean, I've practically raised Sienna and Xavier myself and when Eva is off the boob, I'll practically be a father to her too."

Britney appeared with a half-eaten baguette between her teeth, her tail wagging.

"Britney!" shouted Colin. "Not another carb is to pass your lips, do you hear me?"

The dog scampered away, the half-eaten baguette trailing behind her.

"Get back here!" yelled Colin in hot pursuit.

"Right, we'll give you some space," said an amused Fionn, accepting a glass of wine from Constance.

"Emilia?" Constance held out a glass.

"Thank you." She took the glass from her outstretched hand, her eyes wide at the chaotic atmosphere. Unused to large families and children, she shrank into the background.

"Just shout if you need anything." Diana looked frazzled. "There's plenty more booze so please help yourselves."

# CHAPTER FORTY-FIVE

An hour later, the rain mercifully stopped, and blue skies peeked through the clouds. Constance and Aonghus walked hand in hand around the garden, stopping every now and then for a chat with various people. Diana appeared looking cool in a white chiffon blouse and white jeans.

A waiter handed them three flutes of champagne. Constance took a sip and sighed. "Oh, this tastes good."

Diana moved closer. "So, who's Fionn's girlfriend? I didn't know that he was seeing someone."

Constance gulped her champagne and coughed dramatically, turning away from her friend.

"She's a composer," interjected Aonghus smoothly. "Her name is Emilia Thomas."

"Oh?" Diana sipped her drink. "Where did they meet?"

"In France," said Aonghus cheerfully. "Sparks flew and here we are."

"You never mentioned it," said Diana directly to Constance and she reddened.

"We didn't know," said Aonghus. "He arrived home with her out of the blue."

Constance sighed. "She's in her mid-forties. I know you're dying to ask."

Diana raised an eyebrow. "Really? I would have said late thirties."

Constance shook her head. "Mid-forties. I nearly died when I read it online. He's smitten with her. I've never seen him so animated."

"But surely he sees the problem..."

"No. He refuses to listen. He's such a strong-willed boy. Always has been."

"Why do you call it a problem?" asked Aonghus. "They seem so happy. I think you're being dramatic."

Diana looked over at Fionn with his arm around Emilia, telling a story that made her laugh.

"The odds are stacked against them, Aonghus. She suits his needs now, but down the line, that will probably change. He'll want kids."

"Maybe he doesn't want kids," said Aonghus loyally.

"Well, I do!" said Constance in indignation. "I'm dying to be a granny. Fionn just has to procreate. It would be an abomination if his bloodline ended with him." She drained her glass.

"Look, you're both making a mountain out of a molehill, if you'll pardon the cliché," said Aonghus firmly. "Let the boy be happy. Be happy for him. What will be, will be."

Cliona appeared with Alex in tow, her long brown hair blowing in the sea breeze. "Mum, Dad, there are loads of delicious canapés in the marquee."

Alex nodded. "The mini beef wellingtons are incredible."

"Thanks, darlings." Constance flashed them a smile.

A tall blonde man holding Sienna in his arms appeared. "Hey, you guys. I'm looking for Colin." He had an American accent.

"We haven't seen him in a while," said Aonghus. "I'm Aonghus."

"I'm Luca." They shook hands.

Constance stared at Luca admiringly. With his blonde hair and height, he was easily the best-looking man at the party. She held out her hand. "Hello, I'm Constance," she said with a smile. "Aonghus' better half."

"Hey," he said with a smile. "I'm Lydia's better half, although she'd probably disagree."

"Daddy, shut the fuck up!" yelled the little girl.

"Hey, stop that right now, potty mouth." Luca kissed her forehead.

"She's got a great grasp of language," said Constance admiringly. "Such diction."

Luca smiled and it lit up his whole face. "You're like the only person ever to say that. We get calls from school all the time about her behaviour. She really has an awful tongue."

Constance loved how he pronounced it 'offal'.

Aonghus sipped his champagne. "What part of America are you from?" he asked.

"New York."

"Oh, we adore the Big Apple," said Constance in delight. "One of my favourite places in the world is Central Park in autumn. I suppose you would say 'fall'."

Luca smiled.

"Do you live there now?" asked Aonghus.

Luca shook his head. "I live in Cork. My wife, Lydia, doesn't want to move to the States."

"Quite right too," said Constance. "Ireland is the ideal place to raise a family."

The jazz band were playing *Well did You Evah?* and Aonghus hummed along.

A man wearing a grey suit appeared, a can of beer in his hand. It was Val, Colin's husband, followed closely by a small boy with blonde curls.

"Hey, Val," said Constance. Bending down, she added, "Hello, Orlando! Happy Birthday!"

The little boy grabbed onto Val's leg and hid his face. He was very cute in a navy and white sailor suit.

Val stroked his curls. "Say hello, Orlando!"

The child shook his head and buried his face behind his father's thigh.

A woman wearing a burgundy brocade suit appeared. "Val! We need you for a family photo."

"Okay, Mam." He waved goodbye to the group. "Duty calls, lads. See you later." He ambled off.

"Val's mother looks nothing like him," observed Constance, watching the rather stocky woman march off.

"She's constantly telling Colin what to do regarding Orlando," said Diana. "She thinks that no baby should have designer baby cologne. Colin was really cross about that. She also berated him for having a nappy alarm. She told him that God gave him a nose for a reason."

"Surely Orlando is potty trained by now," said Constance.

Diana shook her head. "Colin read a book about elimination communication and it's proving a challenge."

"What's that?"

"It's based on the assumption that babies naturally signal when they want to go. You figure out their cues and respond. The problem is that Orlando has no cues whatsoever." Diana sighed. "A bit like Britney. Between the dog and Orlando, we're immersed in pee."

"Are you still eager to be a granny?" said Aonghus to Constance with a smirk.

After Orlando had blown out the candles on his cake, a DJ set up some decks and played nineties music. Cliona grabbed Alex's hand and pulled him onto the dancefloor.

"Backstreet's back!" she shouted, wiggling around the floor.

"If you say so," he said grinning.

Constance and Aonghus followed, Constance's multi-coloured skirt flowing as she twirled around. Orlando and Xavier were playfighting with two sticks, ketchup all over their faces, and Sienna was drinking Coke and eating Buttons from a packet.

Lydia was sitting on Luca's knee and they were whispering to each other. Every now and then, Luca would stroke her bare arm, his finger trailing lazily up to her shoulder.

"Do you want to dance?" Fionn asked Emilia. They were sitting on a wall by the garden pond.

"No, I'm not a good dancer."

"Come on," he pleaded. "It'll be fun."

She shook her head. "Honestly, I'll step on your toes." Her eyes looked sad.

"Hey, what's wrong?" He tilted her chin upwards. "You seem far away."

"Nothing."

"Emmy?"

She sighed. "I don't belong here, Fionn. I feel like a freak."

"What?" He rose up angrily. "A freak?"

"You know what I mean. Everyone is looking at us and judging us."

"So?"

"And they're right! I'm too old for you."

"Oh my God, are we back at this again?" He put his head in his hands. "Why do you keep bringing this up?"

"Because it makes me feel bad. I feel like a sad old woman parading around with my toy boy. I feel so wrong. Like this is all so wrong."

"This morning, in bed, did that feel wrong?"

She waved him away. "That's different."

"When you screamed my name, was that wrong?" He grabbed her shoulders. "We're good together. We're meant to be together. Why can't you see that?"

Emilia bit her lip.

"Emmy!"

"Fionn, I…"

"You and me, we're staying together, okay? So, forget this conversation."

She closed her eyes. If only it were that simple.

"Emilia! Say you'll never mention it again."

She nodded.

"Say it."

"I won't mention it again."

Fionn kissed her hard on the lips. "Good. Now, let's dance. Step on my toes all you want."

# CHAPTER FORTY-SIX

The next day, Aonghus found Constance standing at the huge bay window in the sitting room, her face pensive. He walked up behind and her and wrapped his arms around her waist. "What's wrong?" he whispered into her curls.

"Look," she said, pointing outside.

Fionn and Emilia were out by the cliff edge. Fionn bent down and kissed her slowly and lingeringly, brushing tendrils back from her forehead.

Aonghus put his hand on his wife's shoulder. "Stop worrying."

Constance reached up and squeezed his hand. "He's bamboozled by her, darling. You saw them last night on the dancefloor. Of course I'm worried."

"The course of true love never did run smooth. We always knew he'd be unconventional. Fionn has had his own mind since infancy."

"I know," said Constance dolefully.

"We can't interfere," he went on gently. "He will find his own path."

"It's just I can see it all ending in tears."

Aonghus kissed her forehead. "Come on, let's have an early birthday drink. Blot out the anxiety."

Constance shook her head. "Gosh, no. If I start now, I won't make it to dessert. I'm still a bit fragile from Orlando's party."

"A glass of champers will help us immeasurably," he said, ignoring her. "I spotted some chilled Veuve Clicquot in the fridge."

"Oh, go on so."

Constance, pink faced after three glasses of bubbly, busied herself making pomegranate and lemon couscous to go with the lamb tagine she'd made the day before. She made a mental note to remove the preserved lemons and the bay leaves from the pot before serving.

"Cliona, darling," she called. "Will you set the table with the best silver cutlery and my wedding china plates?"

Cliona, who was lying on the sofa with Alex, groaned.

"It's always the same. *Cliona, Cliona, Cliona.* She never asks Fionn."

"I'll help," said Alex, kissing her nose.

A banner with 'Happy Birthday' was stuck to the architrave with some sellotape but had dipped in the middle. A few balloons floated aimlessly around the room and the gravelly voice of Leonard Cohen played on the speaker. A bottle of Château Neuf du Pape was decanting in a glass jug on the dresser, next to a large chocolate birthday cake adorned with chocolate curls and shards. The photo book Cliona had made of her father's life was carefully wrapped in gold paper and a balloon was tied to Aonghus' chair.

The door opened and Constance appeared, carrying a bowl of yoghurt mixed with chopped mint.

"We're almost ready. Clio, take out the good champagne flutes for a toast."

Cliona looked at Alex and rolled her eyes. "Cliona, Cliona, Cliona," she mouthed.

"Don't be cheeky," said Constance mildly. "Your brother is hard at work washing up."

"Fionn's washing up?" Cliona looked incredulous.

"Yes, Clio. I just finished." Fionn appeared in the doorway with Emilia in tow.

"Congratulations," she said seriously. "You must be traumatised from the whole experience."

"I'm okay." He grinned.

Aonghus, who had been dispatched to the shop to buy some napkins, arrived home. He walked into the sitting room and whistled. "Clio, darling, you are a superstar. The place looks lovely." He kissed her on the cheek. "And chocolate cake! My favourite."

Cliona hugged him close. "Happy Birthday, Dad," she said. "I love you."

Emilia, who was standing behind Fionn, watched this exchange with a sad expression. She had been just as close to her own father. She remembered hugging him and telling him about her exploits at Oxford. How proud he had been of her achievements. If only he'd been alive when she had won her first Oscar. His absence had marred that moment, but she told herself that wherever he was now, he knew about it and was proud of her.

"Let's do presents before we eat," said Constance.

Aonghus sat down at the head of the table and picked up Cliona's gift. He held it up to his ear and shook it, and then winked at her. "Nothing rattling anyway."

He tore open the wrapping and threw it to one side. "What's this? 'Aonghus O'Connor: 1963-2022'. Jesus, Cliona, I'm not dead. 2022 is very finite."

Cliona blushed. "No, no. It means that the book chronicles your life between these dates."

"I know." He winked again and opened the book. "Me as a baby. Me at school." He peered closer. "Gosh, that's Nana O'Connor. Where did you find that picture? She died soon after that, you know. I can't remember her at all."

Fionn moved behind his father and looked over his shoulder. "Is that Uncle

Tiernan?" he asked, pointing to a young boy with grubby knees holding an ice cream.

"Yes, I remember that day actually. We went to Inch strand in County Kerry on our holidays. There was a woman selling ice creams from her house."

"Where did you dig up all these photos, Clio?" asked Fionn, impressed. "You're unreal."

"Boxes in the attic," she said. "I sifted through hundreds of them."

"Well, bravo, my darling," said Constance. "I would never have the patience for such a task."

Aonghus closed the book. "I'll look at this properly later," he said, moving on to Fionn's offering. It was a bottle of Jameson Rarest Vintage Reserve, nestled in a wooden case.

"Wow," said Aonghus. "This is impressive."

Fionn nodded. "I went to this specialist place near Covent Garden. They assured me that it was the best. Look, there's a certificate and all."

"Thank you, son."

"It's from Emilia too."

"Thank you, Emilia." Aonghus beamed at her.

Constance tapped her fingers on the oak table impatiently. "Open mine, sweetheart. I can't wait."

There was an envelope on the table with 'Aonghus' written in Constance's flamboyant scrawl.

He tore open the top and pulled out a travel itinerary. "Dubai?" he said in shock.

"Yes!" said Constance in excitement. "Imagine us in the desert at sunset or on top of the Burj Khalifa! The shopping there is to die for and apparently the gold over there is for nothing if you go to the right souk."

"Connie, we were saving up to replace the roof."

"Forget the roof," she said dismissively. "You're only fifty-nine once. We can always save up when we get back."

"But we…"

"Just say thank you and start packing. We leave on Tuesday."

Aonghus glanced at Fionn who was laughing. "Did you expect anything less from her?" he said, shaking his head.

Emilia cleared her throat. "The Museum of the Future is very interesting," she said in her quiet voice. "I was in Dubai a couple of months ago and I went there one morning to pass a few hours. The plan to combat Climate Change was particularly reassuring."

Aonghus smiled warmly at her. "I'll definitely check it out."

"Now, dinner is ready. Everyone take a seat while I bring in the food. Cliona? Come and help your old mother."

"Fionn is just as able…"

"He's taking care of drinks."

"I am?"

"Pour some red, darling. There's a gorgeous red decanting over there."

# CHAPTER FORTY-SEVEN

Rosa put her cello carefully into the back seat of Raphael's car. Her suitcase was already in the boot so all she had to do now was say goodbye.

Isabelle stood on the steps, Anouk balanced on her hip. "We're sure gonna miss you," she said, her eyes teary.

Rosa nodded. "I'll miss you too." She kissed Anouk's forehead. "Come and visit me when you're in London."

Isabelle hugged her with her free arm. "Thanks for all your help."

"Thank you for taking me in." They stepped back from one another. "I'll look after Anouk on the night of the première. Then you can relax and enjoy it."

"You've got a deal." Isabelle rubbed her shoulder. "Now, I'm going to take this little one inside and give her some breakfast. I hate goodbyes."

Raphael appeared from the front hall.

"Martin will take you to the airport and I have organised a car to pick you up when you get to London."

Rosa hugged him. "Thank you for everything."

Raphael hugged her back. "Good luck with this new venture. You and Caspian, you will create great things. I'm sure of it."

She reddened slightly. "He thinks far too much of my playing."

"Not at all. You could be the best in the world if you settled." He handed her an envelope. "This is for all the birthdays I missed. Just to keep things going until you're paid."

She gasped. "Oh, you don't need to do that. I was going to ring Mamma later."

"Take it." He opened the car door. "Safe journey and text me later."

She got into the car, clutching the envelope. Opening it slightly, she could see a wad of fifty pound notes.

Raphael rapped on the window and she jumped. "Thank you for looking after Anouk. She will miss you." Then he banged the roof of the car and walked back into the house.

Madison's alarm went off at 6am. Blearily, she turned it off and turned over. Ten minutes later, another alarm went off and she sat up, disorientated. Caspian, who was lying next to her, groaned. "Either get up now or throw that phone away."

She willed her eyes to open. Boris, her personal trainer, would be here in exactly thirteen minutes. She had no time to lose.

Groggy, she pulled her legs out of the bed and got into a sitting position. Her head was pounding and it felt like she hadn't slept at all.

"Oh, Caspian. Why did we lose control like that?" She rubbed her temple.

"Sssssh." He put a pillow over his head and turned away.

They had gone to stay at a friend's house in the Cotswolds, down the road from Elizabeth Hurley's place. Caspian had been attentive and, as promised, had made love to her over and over. She would have enjoyed it if it weren't for the fact that she felt that he was overcompensating. On the Saturday night, they'd ordered in some sushi and Caspian had opened a bottle of Domaine de la Romanée-Conti Montrachet, and, uncharacteristically, she'd drunk half of it. Then, they'd moved on to vodka and tonic. The last thing she remembered was singing her new song for him as he attempted to accompany her on an imaginary piano.

She couldn't remember the last time she'd been drunk. The calories alone would set her back for days. Not to mind the suffering she'd endured on the journey home.

"Come back to bed," he murmured.

"I can't. Boris will be waiting."

"One day won't make a difference, Mads. Come back to bed."

"You have to be up soon for rehearsals."

"Not for another few hours."

She got up and walked into the bathroom.

Caspian just didn't get it. He didn't get the pressure, the fear. He could be photographed looking below par and no one would bat an eye. If she was seen to be anything less than her usual standard, it would be plastered across every platform. The inequality and downright discrimination infuriated her. Men could age and still be considered gorgeous. She thought of all the famous women she knew of a certain age and how the majority of them had trout pouts and pulled back eyes.

No, she would not be targeted. She would beat the media at their own game. If she looked as flawless as possible, then they'd leave her alone.

Caspian's phone buzzed an hour later, waking him up from a deep sleep. He rubbed his eyes.

Just as he was about to check the message, the bedroom door burst open and Madison appeared. "Fionn just called. As a precaution in case you sleep through your alarm." She pulled off her lycra crop top.

Caspian rolled his eyes. "I'm up. Jeez."

She opened the curtains and light streamed into the room. "God, that workout was hard. I still feel hungover two days later."

Caspian sat up. "I've never seen you drink that much. What happened?"

She looked away. "Sometimes you just need to let off steam, I suppose." The bathroom door closed.

Caspian sat up and reached for his phone. There were three messages: one from Fionn, one from his mother, and one from Rosa. He clicked on Rosa's one straight away.

***Hi Caspian, on the way home. Have some organising to do but should be good for Wednesday. Rosa.***

He felt excitement in the pit of his stomach. The addition of the cello would be a gamechanger. He knew it.

He texted back saying that he was just heading off to the first rehearsal. She replied instantly.

***Good luck. I'm sure they'll be blown away.***

Emilia checked her makeup in a pocket mirror as her taxi pulled up outside a large Georgian building near Regent Street. 'DM Music Management' was written in black lettering over the door. Film composers tended to be represented by smaller specialised agencies and so operated in a narrow world. Emilia's agent, Dorothea Maxwell, had been in the business for years. She had vast knowledge of the art of film scores, and had a knack for cajoling and diplomacy. Emilia had signed with her after the gigantic success of *Mary,* her first film. Together, they had had ups and downs: the ups being the awards and accolades that Emilia had received for her work; the lows being the score that had been binned by Warner Bros for a Marvel film ten years before. Dorothea knew everything about Emilia's art and took the intense competition between agencies in her stride. When Raphael asked for Emilia, all those years ago, it was the beginning of a beautiful collaboration. Everyone in the film business knew that directors tended to build up relationships with composers: Spielberg and John Williams, Richard Attenborough and George Fenton. Emilia and Raphael were now names that were synonymous with each other.

Emilia knocked on Dorothea's door before entering.

"Come in," came the familiar voice.

"Hi, Dorothea!" Emilia smiled.

"Hi, Emmy. Good to see you."

Dorothea had a short red bob and heavily kohled eyes that accentuated their vivid green colour. Small and slim, she wore pencil skirts and heels, coupled with crisp shirts and sometimes a jacket. She looked professional and tough, which was an image she tried hard to maintain. A few years older than Emilia, she had worked her way up from the bottom, first as a secretary, and then as an assistant at a rival agency. Then, at the age of twenty-five, she took the plunge and set up her own business, taking important clients with her. Being a woman in a patriarchal world had been challenging, but she'd overcome it.

"So, I've had a request from a new director." She always got straight to the point.

"Oh?"

"Bonnie Grant."

"Really?" Emilia looked confused.

"She usually works with Johann Weber, your old flame."

"Don't call him that."

"Anyway, she doesn't like his score. She sent him amendments and suggestions, but he wouldn't budge. Then the test audience hated it. It's been axed and she asked for you."

"I can't take his place." It came out as a whisper.

Dorothea knew the story. She and Emilia had shared war wounds over a bottle of Pinot Grigio early on in their relationship. She knew how important Johann Weber had been to her client.

"This is business, Emmy. If you don't do it, she'll find someone who will."

"I don't know. Raphael is pitching a new script at the moment. He'll want me to do it."

"You have time."

"What's the deadline?"

"A month. It's the studio who want to get the ball rolling. You're the replacement composer. I have the temp track here."

"A month? I can't write a score in a month."

"Read the synopsis of the film." Dorothea slid a sheet of paper towards her. "I smell an Oscar."

Emilia scanned the typed paragraph. "A disabled man in Glasgow defies the odds and goes on to be an award winning athlete."

"He's the underdog: working class, workplace accident, depression followed by rehabilitation. A new purpose, a talent. Uplifting message. It has it all."

Emilia bit her lip. She felt it too. That gut feeling.

"It will be awkward with Johann."

"Why? You haven't seen him in twenty years."

"Yes, but I *know* him. I know how insecure he is. When he hears that I'm replacing him on this film, it will crush him."

"Not your problem, Emmy. Anyway, he should be retiring soon. He must be seventy if he's a day."

"Stop." Emilia tried to look reproving. "He's not that old."

Emilia read the overview again. That feeling was there: that urge to create. She could be a modern Vangelis. This could be huge.

"Fine, let's set up a meeting."

Dorothea smiled. "Wonderful. I knew you'd see sense."

# CHAPTER FORTY-EIGHT

The Forge, Doctor Eckleburg's studio and hang out, was situated near Camden Docks in north London. Caspian walked into the main room with a bag full of manuscripts over his shoulder.

"The wanderer returns!" Fionn appeared from the back room and clapped. "Is it a mirage?"

Alex followed, holding a cup of coffee. "Good to see you, Caspian."

Caspian dropped his bag on the ground. "Where's Ethan?"

"Having a smoke." Alex sipped his coffee.

Caspian pulled out a wad of sheets and rifled through them until he found a song called *Unknown.*

"I'd like to start with this one." He handed the arrangements to Alex and Fionn.

Alex scanned the song. "It's quite upbeat."

Caspian nodded. "It's not all ballads and sadness. I promise."

Alex picked up his bass guitar and plucked out a few notes, humming. Fionn took a seat at the drumkit. He twirled the drumstick in his fingers while he waited, brushing his brown hair out of his eyes with his free hand.

Ethan arrived back into the room, putting his aviator sunglasses on his head.

"Hello! Have we met?" He shook Caspian's hand. "Pleasure to meet you."

"I have music here for you," said Caspian, ignoring his sarcasm. Ethan took the music and scanned it. "Seems okay." He turned around to bend down and kiss Stella. "Do you want anything?" he asked her. She shook her head.

Caspian sat at the piano and played the melody of the song with his right hand. Then he started to sing.

*Never alone*
*I feel you*
*Forever unknown*
*I need you*
*To stay with me now*
*Never let go*
*Speaking your wisdom*
*Guiding my life*

He brought in his left hand and gave some bass to the tune.

*I can feel you*
*Up above*
*Shine on me*
*Send me your love*

Alex started to play along, stumbling slightly as the tempo was fast. Ethan played a riff on his guitar, harmonising with the piano. Finally, Fionn started to beat out a rhythm. The end result was riddled with mistakes and experimental sounds, but it was definitely something.

Fionn kicked the bass drum and they all jumped. "Sorry," he said, grinning. "My foot slipped."

Caspian frowned. "Let's focus on the melody. It needs work around the bridge."

After three hours of various versions, the song started to come together. Even Stella was humming it as she made some tea. Ethan rolled a joint and lit it, inhaling deeply.

"This grass is unbelievable," he said, coughing slightly. "Canadian."

Alex accepted the joint as it was passed along. "I would never have survived Covid without this. Our neighbour grew pots of it in his attic."

Caspian refused a drag. "So, Rosa is coming on Wednesday."

"Rosa? Your piece on the side?" Ethan laughed and then coughed violently from the grass. "Wait until you hear her play," said Caspian, ignoring him. "I was blown away."

Fionn refused the joint too. "How many songs will she accompany us on?"

"Four, maybe five. Her input changes everything."

"When will we see the songs?" asked Ethan.

"Wednesday," said Caspian. "We'll all work together, just like we did today. Take things slowly."

"Don't let Jax hear you say that," said Fionn. "He told the roadies to clear their calendars as we'll be heading off on tour soon."

Caspian scowled. "That's ridiculous."

"Today went well," said Alex, changing the subject. "I like the song. I think it's relatable."

Caspian picked up his bag. "I'm going to head home. Had a busy weekend."

"We saw," said Alex. "Did you go to Bath?"

"No, a friend's place near Stroud. Beautiful part of the world."

"See you tomorrow," said Fionn. "I'm going to hang around and practise a bit."

"Well, have fun," said Ethan. "We're going to head home too."

Caspian stuffed his sheet music into his bag. "Enjoy your evening, guys."

And he was gone.

Fionn stayed on for two hours, practising single strokes and double strokes until his arms ached. Even though he'd kept up the practice during lockdown, his arms were not as fit as they used to be. Playing a concert live on stage was a different experience. He needed to train up again. Emilia had asked him to dinner as she was inviting her best friend, Alfie, and his family. She was in London for the day, meeting her agent, so she said to wait until eight.

He glanced at his watch. It was half six. Time to get going.

He called an Uber and changed his t-shirt. He was sweaty after the drumming, but he didn't have time to shower. He sprayed some deodorant on and fixed his hair. His phone pinged, indicating that his driver was a minute away. He turned off the lights, locked the door and walked out onto the street.

The driver had little English and for that he was grateful. It was hard to wind down after an intense day of rehearsal. Caspian was slow and full of himself, but he had an undeniable talent. He just hoped the addition of Rosa wouldn't rock the boat. He could see how the pretty cellist would appeal to Caspian, with her music degrees and famous heritage. He just didn't want Madison to get hurt.

The traffic was particularly bad on the M25 so Fionn didn't pull up outside Emilia's place until half eight. He jumped out of the car and ran around the back. Emilia was barefoot in the kitchen, stirring a pot of chilli con carne with a glass of red wine in her other hand.

"I'm so sorry I'm late," he said breathlessly, kissing her full on the lips.

"Hey, careful, you'll spill my wine." She beamed at him. "Alfie and Miranda are in the sitting room."

"The twins are called Ava and Annabella, right?"

"No, Ava and *Arabella,*" she corrected.

"Right."

"Take in this bowl of crisps," she said, emptying a large pack of salted chips into a glass bowl. "Dinner is almost ready."

"Did you cook?" asked Fionn in surprise.

"Not exactly." She blushed. "Alfie made it and I'm reheating it."

Fionn laughed. "I like your style." He walked out into the hallway and pushed the sitting room door open with his shoe.

A pretty blonde woman was sitting on the armchair. Two blonde girls were playing Jenga on the floor. A man with greying hair and a quizzical look was standing by the piano.

"Hi, I'm Fionn." He smiled broadly.

"Hello, I'm Miranda." The blonde woman got to her feet and shook his hand. "Lovely to meet you."

The girls waved distractedly as the tower of bricks was about to collapse. Ava bit her lip in concentration as she extracted a rectangular piece with extreme precision.

Fionn turned to Alfie. "Hello," he said, holding out his hand.

Alfie paused for a moment and then shook it. "Good to meet you," he said formally.

"Emilia said you made the chilli," said Fionn, sensing some froideur. "Thank God for that. She's not the best cook in the world."

"She's not that bad." Alfie looked guarded.

"Are those crisps?" Miranda glared at her husband. "I'm starving." She took the bowl and placed it on the coffee table. Suddenly the Jenga tower collapsed with a crash.

"Bugger!" shouted Ava.

"Ava!" said Miranda. "Watch your tongue."

Emilia entered the room with the wooden spoon in her hand.

"Dinner is served," she announced.

"But we've barely had time to eat the crisps," said Arabella, stuffing her face frantically.

Alfie took the open bottle of wine off the mantelpiece and walked out of the room. "I'll just get the rice," he called.

"What's with him?" asked Emilia, her eyebrow raised.

Fionn shrugged. "I'm guessing that he doesn't approve."

Miranda put her hand on his arm. "It's not that, honestly. He's just protective of Emmy."

"I'm not a child," said Emilia hotly.

"He'll be fine. Another few glasses of red and he'll relax a bit."

Miranda was right. Two glasses and two bowls of chilli later, Alfie was in much better form.

"Emilia says that you play the cello," said Fionn. "We have a cellist joining us on this album. Caspian is obsessed with the instrument."

"Well, it's the best part of the strings section," said Alfie, earning him a soft punch from Emilia. "I mean, violins are cool and all, but the cello is far superior."

"You're deluded." Emilia rolled her eyes.

"Okay, maybe on an even par then." He laughed. "Superior to violas."

"Everything is superior to them."

They both laughed quietly.

"Why?" asked Fionn curiously.

"Oh, it's well known that violas are the joke of the strings section."

Emilia nodded. "I mean, I know the best viola players in the world, and they're geniuses, but we still tease them."

"It's an orchestra thing." Alfie peered at the sediment at the bottom of his glass.

"That's a sign of a good wine. What are we drinking again?"

"Oh, just a Côte du Rhône from Tesco." Emilia laughed. "You can take a girl out of Solihull and all that."

"Well it's not bad at all." Alfie refilled his glass.

They left at eleven.

Emilia stacked the bowls and put the glasses on the kitchen counter.

"Let's leave this until tomorrow. I can't face it now."

Fionn didn't argue. He put his arms around her waist and pulled her to him. Immediately her legs went to jelly. She kissed him slowly, savouring the moment.

"How did your rehearsal go today?" she asked.

He nibbled on her ear. "Good actually. Caspian is a genius, there's no denying it. He just has that *je ne sais quoi,* or as we say in the motherland, *níl fhois agam.*"

"The motherland?"

"Ireland."

"My agent meeting went well, thanks for asking."

"Oh sorry, I meant to text you but the day ran away from me."

"I've been asked to compose the score for the next Bonnie Grant film. It's about a disabled man in Glasgow."

"Sounds uplifting."

"It is. He defies the odds in the 50s and goes on to be an athlete."

"Bonnie Grant is Scottish, isn't she?"

Emilia nodded. "From Inverness."

"Have you worked with her before?"

"Never. That's why I'm surprised that she requested me." She looked away, a sad look on her face. There was no point telling him about Johann and the huge significance of this venture.

"Are you going to do it?"

She faced him again and smiled. "I'm going to try. The time frame is limited so it may not work out."

"How do you write scores? It's such a mammoth task."

"I don't know. It's all about perspective and inspiration. I believe in gut feelings. Today, when I heard the synopsis of the script, I felt something. Here." She pointed to her stomach. "I knew it was for me."

"Like how I felt when I met you." He kissed her again.

Emilia said nothing.

"Come on, let's go to bed." He picked her up into his arms. "I'll wash up in the morning."

Fionn left at half seven for rehearsals.

Emilia tried to go back to sleep, but the sunlight streaming in the crack in the curtains gave her other ideas. She would start with the overture. Something inspiring, something to reflect the achievement of the main character when he defies the odds. Sport carried such pride and honour, win or lose, it was people coming together and working towards a common goal. This man, cast aside by society, would go on to have the nation behind him. He would cause people to question their preconceived ideas and teach them not to judge so quickly. Her score would have to reflect this, gradually building up to a spinetingling tune that would incite unity and patriotism.

She walked downstairs and put on the kettle. Fionn would be busy all day and for that she was grateful. He was lovely and fun to be around, but she needed to work. He didn't understand the process of writing music on this scale. In order to be in with a chance of success, she would have to get in the zone.

Minutes later, she placed a steaming cup of tea on the windowsill and took a seat at the piano. She automatically played the Chariots of Fire theme. It was one of the pieces on the temp track which was designed to inspire her to write something similar. She closed her eyes and saw the men in white, running along the beach in slow motion. The music was iconic, with its melodic hook and recognisable rhythm. Her hands moved up and down the keyboard. This sweeping tune was synonymous with glory and nationalistic pride. She had to channel something just as legendary.

She played a few keys idly, her brain whirring, when the door opened and Alfie appeared.

"I knocked," he said as way of a greeting.

"Oh, I didn't hear." She smiled. "Just playing around with melodies for that film. I didn't realise you were coming over this morning."

"Chariots of Fire. Reminds me of the Olympic Games in '84. Remember?"

"Yes, the BBC used it for its coverage. God, what age was I? Eight?"

"Long before your boyfriend was born."

"Alfie!"

Alfie looked her straight in the eye. "Emmy, what are you doing with him?"

"I'm sorry?"

"I can't get my head around it. He's funny and nice, but he's not on your level. Not even close."

"So?"

Alfie started to pace. "Emmy, you're cultured, mature, worldly…"

"He's cultured. His dad writes books on Beckett and Yeats and people like that."

"He's a millennial. He plays in a rock band. They'll be off on tour soon. Are you going too?"

"Don't be fatuous."

"What do you talk about? Snapchat? TikTok?"

"Are you trying to be funny?"

"No, I'm not. But surely you see that this is on a road to nowhere. It will never work."

"Why are you so involved in my life?" Her eyes started to flash. "You never like my boyfriends."

"That's not true."

"You hated Johann."

"He's a thoroughly unlikeable person."

"You didn't like Tobias, Luciano or Miguel."

"Again, all thoroughly unlikeable."

"I'm entitled to be happy, Alfie. You have Miranda and the girls. What do I have? A few trophies made of bronze? I want to be loved."

Alfie stared at her for a moment. "You're right. I'm sorry. I shouldn't interfere."

Emilia slumped down on the piano chair. "I get why you're concerned," she said in a low voice. "I'd be lying if I said I didn't share your opinion. However, I'm happy. He makes me laugh and I like waking up next to someone."

Alfie walked over, pulled her to her feet and hugged her tightly. "It's probably jealousy, Emmy. I never did get over you."

She laughed. "Stop that right now."

"It's true. You'll always be my muse."

"Alfie!"

"I'll never mention it again." He put his hand on his chest. "Scout's Honour."

"Speaking of Johann," she began.

"Oh God, what now?"

"He wrote the score for this film." She looked up. "It was axed and now they want me to take his place."

Alfie whistled. "Wow."

"I didn't tell you because I knew you'd be delighted."

"Of course I'm delighted. This is karma for the way he treated you."

"No, it's not. It's just a coincidence. To be honest, I'm surprised our paths haven't crossed sooner. Film composing is a small world."

"Does he know?"

She shrugged. "I suppose. I don't know."

Alfie laughed. "Oh, Emmy, you must write a masterpiece and win all sorts of awards. Put salt on the wound."

"You're awful." She couldn't help but smile. "Seriously, let go of your bitterness. I've moved on."

"Yeah right," he said cheerfully.

Emilia yawned. "You know, I'd love a nice coffee."

"Oh, you would."

"Maybe a cinnamon bun?"

Alfie rolled his eyes. "Fine, but I want to hear your thoughts on this score when I get back. It is now our most important task. I'm your lucky charm after all."

She squeezed his hand. "You are."

# CHAPTER FORTY-NINE

A sleek BMW pulled up outside Johann Weber's London apartment on Primrose Hill. The driver got out and opened the back door for Rosa. She gathered her bag, putting her airpods back in their white case and marked the page on her book. As arranged, the representative from the property management company was waiting at the front door.

"Hello," he said in a clipped tone. "I'm Peter Norris."

"Rosa Weber."

"Delighted. Good trip?"

She nodded.

"Follow me, please."

Minutes later, she entered her father's flat. It had been cleaned the day before and the surfaces gleamed. The driver, red faced from lugging her cello, placed it in the vestibule before going back to bring up the rest of Rosa's bags.

"So, the code is for the main door only." He held up two keys on a ring. "Then, use these to access the property." He pointed to the front door. "If you have any problems, my number is on this."

He handed her a business card.

"Thank you."

Peter nodded and left.

Rosa tried to remember if she had ever been in this apartment, but couldn't.

Her mother's words rang in her ears.

*That's where he brought his whores all those years.*

She winced.

Placing the keys on the hall table, she surveyed the scene. A black leather couch and a rectangular mahogany coffee table. No television. Her father never watched television.

The Steinway took up most of the sitting room area, its bronzed lid gleaming in the sunlight. Each wall was covered with books, all lined up perfectly on the shelves. A framed painting of an orchestra was just above the mantlepiece and it was signed with an indistinguishable scribble.

The kitchen was small but she gratified to see a Nespresso machine. She didn't see her father cooking much when he was staying at this place. The cups and plates were stacked neatly in the cupboard and the fridge was empty except for some white wine and bottles of Evian.

The master bedroom looked out on the street. It had a decidedly masculine feel to it, sparsely decorated in dark brown and black with a large painting of a boat on the wall over the bed. The room reminded her of her father, so she closed the door and went to the guest bedroom down the hall. There was a double bed, a wardrobe and seemed to be used as a makeshift storeroom for music books and instruments. She liked it immediately.

She fished her phone out of her bag and texted her father. Then, she texted Caspian to say that she was on *terra firma*, then a message with lots of hearts to Isabelle. Finally, she texted Emilia, saying that she was back in London and if she was free to meet up sometime?

Emilia texted back straightaway with clapping hands emojis. The text that followed suggested a lunch date in a few weeks when she wasn't so busy with work.

Rosa sent back a heart eyes emoji.

Isabelle sent a short message saying that Anouk was looking for 'Osa' all morning. Rosa bit her lip.

Her father texted her next, with a brief message that read:

*Good. No parties.*

She threw the phone away.

Taking her bag, she brought it to her bedroom and unzipped it. The clothes spilled out and she frowned. Maybe she would unpack later. It seemed like a tedious task after such a long day.

The Steinway called to her when she re-entered the sitting room so she took a seat at the stool and opened the lid. The ivory keys were smooth as she played an arpeggio. It needed to be tuned but only to a trained ear, so she started to play some Beethoven followed by Chopin's Nocturne op.9 in B Flat Minor. Closing her eyes, she played from memory, her fingers moving rapidly up and down the keyboard.

The sound of traffic outside halted her performance so she stood up again, feeling listless. She would be feeding Anouk now if she were still in Amiens. She debated whether to Facetime Isabelle, but decided against it. It might confuse Anouk.

Suddenly her phone pinged and she jumped. Caspian's name appeared on the screen. She accessed the message.

*Great you're here. Want to meet for a drink?*

She sat down on the sofa. It was pretty lonely in the apartment. However, the photos she saw online dissuaded her. She didn't want a repeat performance.

*I'm pretty tired. Lots if unpacking to do.*

He didn't reply for ages. Finally, the phone pinged.

*Tomorrow?*
She sighed. He was insistent.
*Meeting friends tomorrow.*
A little white lie wouldn't hurt.
*Ok, see you bright and early on Wed. Drop a pin and I'll send a car to pick you up.*
She sent a thumbs up emoji.

Walking into the spacious bathroom, she grasped the edge of the sink and hung her head. Slowly, she looked up to see her reflection in the circular mirror. She still had that travelling look: dishevelled hair and tired eyes. People had told her all her life that she was pretty, but she didn't really see it. All she could see were flaws. Her lips were too plump, one nostril was slightly bigger than the other. She hated the dimple on her chin. Insecurity was a lonely emotion, exacerbated by overthinking, so she turned away. The night stretched interminably in front of her and she opened the sliding doors and walked out onto the balcony. The flare of the lighter flame illuminated her face for a moment as she lit a cigarette and inhaled deeply. Immediately, she felt calm. The nicotine raced through her veins and took the stress away. She knew she shouldn't smoke as it was a horrible habit, but it was her thing. Cigarettes were always there for her and they never let her down. Blowing a large smoke ring, she listened to the bustle of people and traffic on the street below.

Wednesday morning dawned. Rosa's alarm went off and she sat up groggily. She rummaged through her bag which was still discarded on the bedroom floor. Eventually she found a green shift dress and brown sandals. She brushed her teeth and pulled a comb through her long hair. A touch of kohl around her eyes and some lip gloss and she was ready.

Caspian, true to his word, sent a car. An electric Mercedes pulled up at exactly 9am. She hoisted her cello case onto her back and pocketed the keys of the apartment. Closing the front door, she made her way to the lift. Minutes later, she emerged out into he sunshine and the driver of the car opened the passenger door.

"Thanks," she said smiling, opening the back door and putting her cello along the back seat. Even though the distance between her apartment and the studio was less than a mile, she needed transport for her cello.

Ethan played a harmonic on his electric guitar, his brow furrowed as he concentrated on the complicated finger movements. The rest of the band watched him intently.

His performance came to an end with a squeal of a high E and he opened his eyes.

"What do you think?"

Alex clapped. "It's great. Really good."

Fionn nodded. "I especially like the middle part."

Caspian frowned. "Is it a bit Slash-esque at the end?"

"Slash?" Ethan's eyes narrowed. "What do you mean?"

"Like, I can see you playing your guitar on a cliff edge or in a desert with the wind blowing through your hair. It gives me those vibes."

"So, you hate it."

"I don't hate it. I just don't want to be compared to Guns n' Roses."

Ethan threw his guitar down, took out a cigarette and stomped off.

"Fucking hell, Caspian." Fionn glared at him. "You need to work on your people skills."

"We've got to be honest. I can't lie about something like music."

"Some diplomacy wouldn't hurt."

Caspian ignored him and started to play the same riff in a more simplistic form on an acoustic guitar. "It's good, I'm not saying it's not, but the end needs work. Like this." He played a mellow version of Ethan's denouement and looked up. "What do you think?"

Alex shrugged. "It's not bad."

"It's better, isn't it?"

Alex looked uncomfortable. "It's different."

Fionn banged his drum. "Stop being a prick, Caspian. We get that you love yourself but don't belittle others."

"I'm not belittling others," he said in annoyance. "Music is higher than that. It's not about opinions or competition. It's a collaborative experience to produce the best sound we can."

"Just be nice."

Caspian ignored him and played the riff again. The sound was interrupted by his phone ringing. Alex peered at the screen. "It's Rosa," he said.

Caspian dropped the guitar immediately and bounded over to the phone.

"Hello? You're outside? Great. See you in a sec." His face lit up. "She's here."

"Clearly." Fionn gave him an old-fashioned look.

"I'll just go and get her." Caspian strode off purposefully.

Ethan arrived back and picked up his electric guitar. "He disrespects me. He disrespects my music."

Fionn walked over and patted Ethan's back. "Don't worry about it. He's the same with us all."

"I'm just sick of it. Who made him the boss? Bringing this Rosa girl here because he wants to jump her bones."

"He says it's her music…" Alex interrupted.

"Bullshit. He fancies her." Ethan put his guitar strap over his shoulder.

"Look, that's none of our business. Let's get through rehearsals and be nice to that poor girl." Alex started to tune his guitar. "This is the hardest part: building on a melody, making it the full package. But we've got to stay focused."

Ethan glowered and turned away.

# CHAPTER FIFTY

Rosa stood on the curb of Montague Street, her cello propped against her side. The Forge didn't look like anything from the outside, just a large warehouse with peeling paint and boarded up windows. Despite its derelict appearance, fans knew it was Doctor Eckleburg's studio and two girls sat on the pavement, cameras poised, waiting for a photo of the band.

The main door opened and Caspian appeared, smiling broadly.

"Rosa!" He made a move to embrace her, but stopped himself just in time as the girls on the footpath jumped up and started snapping.

"Hello," she said shyly, her long hair blowing in the breeze.

Suddenly, five more people appeared, all with their phones poised. Word on the street was that Doctor Eckleburg was back rehearsing and the perfect place to spot them was in Camden.

"Caspian, Caspian," one called. "Can I get a selfie?"

Caspian ignored her and picked up the cello. "Come in, come in. Sorry about the selfie brigade. It happens."

"Not at all. I'm quite flattered. We don't get any such adulation in the classical music world."

Caspian placed the cello against the wall in the corridor and locked the door. Then, he pulled her into his arms and he kissed her cheek lightly. "Welcome home," he murmured into her hair.

He smelled like sandalwood.

Then, as quickly as he'd held her close, he pulled away again. "Imagine if I'd done that outside. We'd be plastered all over social media again."

"Imagine," she echoed, blushing.

"Follow me. The band are here." He picked up the cello once more and walked down the corridor.

"Great."

Another door led to a large room which, in turn, led to the studio. Caspian gestured for her to enter, holding the door open.

"Look guys, it's Rosa!" Caspian deposited the cello next to the piano.

Fionn waved his drumstick in salute. Alex walked over and held out his hand. "A pleasure," he said, shaking hers firmly.

Ethan gave a nod and a wave, and then glared at Caspian.

"Hello," she said nervously, her dark eyes darting around the room.

"How was your trip?" asked Alex conversationally.

"Good," she said.

"London will be a big change from Amiens."

Rosa nodded. "Yes, it certainly will."

"So, I think we should start with this song today. It's called *Another Life.*" Caspian pulled some sheet music out of his bag. "Remember?" he said directly to Rosa, 'it was the first song we played together in France."

Rosa nodded. "I think so."

Caspian grabbed a chair. "Will this do? Is it the right height?"

She nodded again. "It should be fine." She opened her cello case and took out the instrument. Taking a seat on the stool, she positioned the cello between her legs. Twisting the pegs, her ear close to the strings, she tuned it.

Ethan studied the music, playing a few chords. Alex did the same, trying to follow Ethan's lead. Caspian took a seat at the piano.

"This song is a dream, a fantasy. It imagines a life where one can be with someone they've lost. It's mainly in a minor key, see this." He played an arpeggiated intro in A minor.

Ethan strummed a few chords.

"I'll start, then I'll sing, and that's where you come in." He pointed to Ethan. "Alex and Fionn, your cue is at the start of the bridge. Then, just after the chorus, Rosa." He smiled at her.

With theatrical movement, he played the intro and then started to sing.

*Imagine you and me*

*Together and free*

*In another life*

Ethan joined in slowly, strumming the chords gently. Caspian nodded in approval and continued to sing until the bridge.

"Ready?" he called. Alex and Fionn nodded. The key changed to a C major as Caspian built up to the chorus. Alex stumbled slightly, and Fionn switched from snare to cymbal, but despite the stalling, it sounded good. Rosa watched Caspian's fingers as they moved along the keyboard. She was a trained cellist and had played to huge audiences in famous auditoriums all over the world. Yet the butterflies in her stomach were zipping around.

She raised her arm and got ready to play. The chorus came to an end, reverting to A minor and she was off.

The rich, vibrant sound reverberated around the room. Ethan raised an eyebrow and glanced at Alex. Fionn stared at Rosa as she played. Caspian had been right. It added a wonderful depth and emotion to the song.

Together they played until the end, making mistakes, rectifying them, listening for places that they could bring their own individual expertise to the process. Then, it was over.

Caspian hung his head for a moment and looked up.

"That was definitely something," he said.

Fionn nodded in agreement. "That's a hit. No doubt about it."

"Can we play it again? I think I have an idea for the instrumental after the second chorus," said Ethan, testing a few notes on the neck of his guitar.

"Sure," said Caspian. "Rosa?" He looked at her quizzically. "Do you mind if we take it from the top?"

She smiled. "Of course not. Let's do it."

It was after five when they finished and Rosa's arm ached. She hadn't played that much since her orchestra days. Alex was the first to leave as he was meeting Cliona in Soho. Ethan left next, shaking Caspian's hand begrudgingly.

"Look man, I know we don't always see eye to eye, but that was great."

Caspian patted his back. "See you tomorrow."

Fionn took off his wristbands and rubbed his skin. "I've got to go too. It takes so long to get to Emilia's place."

Rosa's eyes widened. "Emilia?"

His blue eyes met hers. "Yes, Emilia."

"Are you two…" Her voice trailed off.

"Yes, we're together."

"Oh." Rosa didn't know what to say.

"So, I'll be going." He picked up his hoodie.

Rosa put her cello into its case. "May I leave this here until tomorrow?"

"Of course." Caspian smiled. "It's quite large to be lugging around."

She propped the cello against the piano, just like Caspian had done initially.

"Have you plans this evening?" he asked. "You're welcome to come back to ours for some food."

Rosa shook her head. "I'm meeting an old friend," she lied. "Thanks though."

Caspian looked disappointed for a moment. "Let me walk you out."

Rosa led the way and soon they were back on the busy street. The girls waiting for photos had left and the summer sun was still blazing in the sky.

"I really enjoyed today." She paused. "Thanks for inviting me along."

"A pleasure."

"See you then." Rosa backed away.

"See you."

She turned and walked down the street. Caspian continued to watch her until she turned the corner.

Later that evening, Rosa sat on the rattan chair on the balcony, smoking her second cigarette after a takeaway pizza.

The music they had practised was playing in her mind and she hummed out loud. Even though it had been gruelling in places, she had really enjoyed her day. It was fun to play with other musicians and see how songs unfolded. She was accustomed to symphonies that had been written hundreds of years ago so it was exciting to be part of a creative process.

She checked her phone but the screen was blank. A part of her willed Caspian to text; he filled her thoughts constantly. She fancied him. There was no doubt that he fancied her too. She could see it in his eyes. The way he had pressed her to his body in that dark corridor. She could still smell traces of his scent on her dress. That was why she had to remain professional and not allow them to be alone. She stubbed her cigarette on the railing and shook her head. How she had changed. In the old days she wouldn't have thought twice about sleeping with him. Conscience certainly does makes cowards of us all, she thought.

Madison sat at Caspian's piano and pressed middle C. She could play the melodies of the songs she had written with Savannah with one finger and sing along. She was due to return to Norfolk in week or so to continue working on the album. Ross, her manager, was insisting and had instructed her personal assistant, Cora, to clear her diary to facilitate this. This new persona that Madison was creating would explode on a global level. Initially, he had resisted her ideas. Her girl-next-door pop girl image had made them both millions. Why change a good thing? Then, when Savannah agreed to come on board, he'd relented. With a multi-Grammy winner and musical legend, how could it fail? *Possess Me,* the song Savannah had written for the *Josephine* film, was climbing the American billboard chart steadily. Madison's voice could be heard in supermarkets, advertisements on television, on radio airwaves all over the world. It was tipped to go all the way to number one again when the film was released in a few months. However, he was anxious to give the fans a taste of what was to come afterwards. He rang Savannah and asked if there was one new song that they could record and release, to whet people's appetites. Savannah, disgusted at his lack of respect, hung up on him.

Madison played a melody again and then glanced furtively behind her shoulder. She didn't want Caspian to come home and find her playing the piano like a five-year-old. Todd was in his own apartment down the hall. She was all alone.

Trembling, she played the chorus of the first song they'd penned. She sang along quietly.

Then she played it again, singing louder this time. She closed her eyes and sang at the top of her voice, the piano forgotten. She didn't notice Caspian walking into the room. When she finished, he clapped loudly and she jumped.

"That sounded great," he said genuinely.

She stood up abruptly. "How long were you there?"

"Not long." He smiled. "It really sounded good."

She closed the piano lid with a bang. "You should've said you were home."

"Why? You were in the zone." He walked over and kissed her head. "When are you heading back up to Savannah's?"

"Soon. I'm waiting for Cora to confirm."

He put his bag on the ground. "How long will you be away?"

"I'll be there for a week." She looked annoyed. "Why are you so interested? Do you want rid of me?"

"No." He made a face. "I'm entitled to know your plans. We live together, don't we?" He took some orange juice from the fridge and took a sip.

She regarded him suspiciously. "How did you get on today?"

He wiped his mouth. "Good. Rosa came and it changed everything."

Madison tried not to feel jealous. "Is she playing on many songs?"

"A few." He put the bottle back in the fridge.

"Does that mean she'll be touring with you?" Her heart started to thump.

"Jeez, Maddy, I haven't thought that far ahead."

"You said she was unemployed."

"Yes, at the moment, but I'm sure she'll be snapped up soon. She's classically trained. She should be in a great orchestra. Not with a rock band."

"Hmmm." She stood up. "I've a Zoom call with Bethany in a minute."

"Will you be long? I'm hungry."

"Giorgio made some salmon earlier. Wrapped in pastry for you, plain for me."

"Great." He gestured for her to continue. "I'm going for a shower. See you later."

# CHAPTER FIFTY-ONE

The next two weeks were wonderful and frustrating in equal measure. Caspian, always a perfectionist, insisted that they play each song over and over until something clicked. Ethan warned Caspian that weekends were sacred.

"No Sundays," he said, "we'll burn out, mate."

Fionn rang Emilia after practice and suggested that she come to London for a change. "We could go for dinner and maybe to a show?"

"Sorry, Fionn. I'm consumed with this score. Next weekend?"

"So, I'm guessing you don't want me to come down?"

"Maybe not this weekend."

"You said that last week."

Cliona called over on the Saturday afternoon with tea and cakes. She opened the ribbon the box she'd bought at an artisan bakery down the road. Macarons, eclairs, mille-feuilles and mini genoise sponges lay in rows. Rehearsals were invite only as the music was classified until they got to a recording studio.

"Anyone going out tonight?" asked Alex. "Clio and I are going to a gig near Shoreditch. This young ska band."

"They're amazing. Mad Professor signed them on his label," added Cliona.

"Nah, mate. I'm exhausted. Stella and I are having a night in." Ethan put an unlit cigarette in his mouth. "See you all on Monday." He fished his lighter out of his pocket, ready to spark when he got outside.

"Fionn?" asked Alex.

"I don't have plans. However, I don't really want to hang out with my baby sister, no offence."

Cliona stuck out her tongue.

"Rosa?"

She shook her head. "I'm pretty tired too."

"Are you okay?" asked Caspian in concern.

"I'm fine. It's just I'm not used to these long days. Looking after Anouk was far easier."

Caspian walked over immediately and sat down beside her on the sofa. "Are you enjoying it? We can slow it down if you like."

Her brown eyes met his. "I'm absolutely fine. Just dreaming of my pyjamas and a takeaway."

"Maddy has plans tonight. We have dinner and drinks with our friends, Aurora and James."

"Oh, that's nice."

"We could meet up tomorrow? Maybe brunch at our place?"

Rosa shook her head. "I can't."

He looked at her contemplatively. "Why do you always refuse?"

"I don't."

Caspian sighed. "I give up. So much for hospitality."

Rosa got to her feet. "Thanks," she said shyly. "I'm honoured to be a part of this."

Fionn, whose mouth was full of éclair, gave her a thumbs up.

Alex smiled. "You've been such a great addition. I hate to say it, but Caspian was right."

"Oh?" said Caspian.

"The cello brings it to another level."

Fionn walked as far as the Tube with Cliona and Alex.

"I'll leave you here," he said when they got to the station.

Alex's phone rang. "I have to take this," he said, walking away.

"You're sure you won't come for a dance?" Cliona hugged Fionn.

"No. I'm actually quite tired. I might FaceTime Mum and soak up some adoration."

"She was complaining about how you never ring her."

"I do. Just not every day like some people."

Cliona paused. "Rosa seems nice."

Fionn nodded. "She's very nice. Very understated. Incredibly talented."

"And so pretty."

"Yeah." He shook his head. "You see it too?"

Cliona nodded. "He's smitten."

"How's Maddy about it?"

"She doesn't say much, but I know she was really rattled after those photos went viral."

"Look after her."

"What? Am I hallucinating? Are you being nice to Maddy?"

Fionn pushed her backwards gently. "I just don't want her to get hurt. I'd still put chewing gum in her hair in a heartbeat though, and don't forget it."

Cliona laughed. "Have a nice weekend. Ring Mum."

"Yes, Sir!"

The next week passed quickly and soon enough it was Friday again. Caspian had barely seen Madison due to their schedules so Madison asked her personal assistant, Cora, to organise a date night as she was leaving for Norfolk the next day to work on her album. Cora booked The Ivy for eight and Bethany had already tipped off photographers that Madison and Caspian were going out on the town.

"We need some exposure," she explained. "It's been all work and no play."

Bethany didn't like to add that sooner or later more pictures of Caspian and Rosa would surface. She'd done everything in her power to prevent the publication of an image taken three days before. Caspian walking down the street in Camden, a laughing Rosa by his side. The body language said it all. Injunctions took a lot of energy so she wanted to quell any rumours and reassure the fans now that all was well.

Madison let Mona work her magic, styling her blonde hair into waves and making up her eyes with glittery shadow. Her stylist, Angelica, laid out an outfit. As she slipped into her short green dress, she felt exhausted. In the old days, going out in public with Caspian would fill her with excitement and a sense of power. She knew he adorned the walls of many a teenager's room, with his handsome face and hair, so it gave her a thrill to be seen on his arm. Now, she felt jaded. She couldn't get Rosa off her mind. All week he'd come home, raving about how much the cello added to the album, and her heart had twisted in misery. This date night was Bethany's idea and, in truth, all she wanted to do was go to bed.

The front door banged and Caspian appeared, pulling off his t-shirt and throwing it on the floor. "Sorry I'm late. Things ran over." He smiled at Mona. "Don't mind me," he said, closing the bathroom door behind him.

"Look up at the ceiling," Mona commanded, ignoring him. Madison did as she was told. John, her driver, was waiting outside in the Mercedes. Todd, her bodyguard, had already called the restaurant in advance to check security.

The Mercedes pulled up outside The Ivy on West Street. A group of paparazzi stood to the left of the main entrance, their cameras around their necks. They'd been tipped that Paul Rudd was expected too, so they hung around patiently.

Todd jumped out and did a quick recon, before opening the back door for Madison. She swung one smooth brown leg out, her four inch black heels hitting the ground with a crack, as the cameras started to flash. Standing up, she squared her shoulders and straightened her dress.

"Maddy! Look this way, Maddy!"

Passers-by stopped and looked. One girl screamed when she saw who it was.

“Madison Ryan! It’s Madison Ryan!” Todd stepped forward and prevented her from getting close.

Madison ignored the girl and waited for Caspian to appear beside her. He looked gorgeous in a black shirt and black pants. A crowd started to from, people’s interest piqued by the shouting and bustle. Caspian took her hand and led her into the restaurant, holding his hand up at the paparazzi as he walked past.

When they were seated, Madison got a message from Bethany with screen shots of photos posted online. One particular shot was very flattering, with Madison looking leggy as she walked past with her head down.

She could see that Bethany was typing. Then her phone pinged.

***Job done.***

Madison sighed. She willed the night to go quickly. She couldn’t wait to clean her face, wash her hair and snuggle under her duvet. She had an early start in the morning as she was going to Savannah’s.

Caspian ordered an Old-Fashioned and drummed his fingers on the table.

“So, how was your week?” he asked conversationally.

Madison sipped her water. “Oh, you know, busy.”

“Same.” He rearranged the cutlery in front of him. “Are you excited for tomorrow?”

“I suppose. It’ll be nice to see Savannah again.”

“You two are a strange combination.”

“Oh?” Her blue eyes were icy.

“It’s like chalk and cheese.”

“Why? Because she can play instruments and I can’t? Because she’s respected in the industry?”

“Calm down, I didn’t mean that.”

The waiter appeared with menus and Caspian’s drink.

“Thanks,” said Madison, glad of the distraction.

Caspian knocked it back. “Another, please.”

The waiter nodded.

# CHAPTER FIFTY-TWO

Fionn decided to go to Surrey after practice. Emilia promised that she would be free at the weekend. He texted her with his estimated arrival time.

She was working at the piano when the taxi arrived. He walked into the sitting room, his back aching from the car ride, his stomach rumbling.

"Hey," he said.

"Hi," she answered without looking up.

"Good day?" he asked, walking over to her and kissing the top of her head.

She looked up and nodded. "I didn't realise you were coming down."

"I texted you."

"Oh."

"We've six songs in the bag. I'm exhausted from it though."

"Hmmm." She wasn't listening; instead, she played the left hand of some symphonic sounding tune on the piano.

"I haven't seen you in ages. I've missed you, Emmy."

Emilia looked up and smiled, then continued to play some notes, writing down various melodies and crossing out bits.

"What's for dinner?" Fionn patted his stomach. "I'm ravenous."

She put down her pencil. "Dinner?" she repeated. "How do you mean?"

"Dinner. Food. Generally some meat and vegetables."

"Oh, I haven't even had lunch. It's been a busy day." She turned back to the sheet music and crossed out more notes.

"I had a busy day too." He rubbed his arm. "I'm wrecked from all the drumming. All I had time to eat was a sausage roll from the deli down the road."

"Hmmm," she said, not listening.

"I just thought that as you're here all day and don't have to commute for two hours that you'd have something for us to eat. I texted you to say that I was on the way."

Emilia put down her pencil and stared at him. "You expected me to have dinner ready?"

He nodded. "It's only fair. You can't expect me to do it. I made the effort to come down."

"Why should I be the one to do it? Is it because I'm a woman?"

"No," he said crossly. "I'm as much a feminist as the next person. It's as I've said: you're here all day and I'm commuting. I'm exhausted and I'd kill for a homecooked meal of some kind."

Emilia shook her head in disbelief. "I'm working, Fionn. I've been working for nearly eleven hours straight. I don't think about anything else when I'm composing. Surely you understand that."

"I've been working for almost as long."

"There's a difference."

"How so?"

"You're a drummer in a pop band."

"And?" His voice was dangerously low.

"It's very different."

"I never realised you were such a snob."

Emilia stood up indignantly. "I'm not a snob!"

"Well, the inference from your previous comment is that composing a film score is far more demanding than playing drums in a pop band."

"It is! You can't deny it."

Fionn threw up his hands. "I'm going back into London. A big bucket of KFC should do the trick." He stalked out, banging the door behind him.

Emilia didn't stop him. She needed to get back to her score. Nothing else mattered when she was working like that. Alfie chided her for her single-mindedness, but she couldn't help it.

She thought about texting him to apologise, but she didn't even know where her phone was. Her brow furrowed, she got lost in the music once more.

Fionn called the Uber driver who had just dropped him off. He refused to come back as he had another booking.

"You must book through the app," he said before hanging up.

Fionn pressed the app but it kept buffering, trying to find any driver nearby. He refreshed the button over and over, but nothing turned up. They were deep in the countryside so he imagined the chance of securing a ride was small. He walked into the nearby village and headed straight for the pub. Pushing open the heavy door, he immediately smelled the stale alcohol in the large room. A barmaid smiled at him and asked what he'd like.

"A pint of Heineken and a menu." He took a seat at the bar and scanned the food on offer.

"I'll have a burger and chips," he said as the barmaid placed the pint on a beermat in front of him.

"Bacon and cheese on the burger?"

"Sure, why not?"

There were a few punters sitting at the bar watching football on a large screen. Two families sat at large tables by the window, the children all glued to phones and the parents sitting in silence.

Emilia was like a stranger to him. He didn't like being second best. Adored by his mother since birth, he wasn't used to playing second fiddle.

The way she had belittled his drumming. His expression darkened.

The burger arrived, covered in cheese and sauce. The chips were chunky and doused in salt.

He stuffed two into his mouth immediately and took a big gulp of beer.

When he had finished, he tried the Uber app again. Still nothing.

He beckoned to the barmaid. "Can I order a burger to go?"

"Coming up."

He had another pint while he was waiting, tapped his card and left. On the road back to Emilia's house, he felt his animosity diminish. Maybe he had overreacted.

He pulled his key out of his pocket and opened the front door. Placing the tray of food on the kitchen table, he went to the sitting room. He found her in the exact same position by the piano, her head down over the sheet music.

She looked up with tired eyes. "Oh, you're back." He couldn't be sure but she seemed annoyed.

He walked over purposefully, took the pencil from her hand and pulled her to her feet.

"You need some food and some rest."

"No, no," she protested.

"Yes, yes." He picked her up easily into his arms, shocked at how light she was. "This is ridiculous unsustainable behaviour. Now, no arguments."

She let her head rest on his strong shoulder. "Fine."

"I got you a burger and chips and I want you to eat every bite." He carried her to the kitchen and lowered her gently onto a chair. Then he tore the tinfoil off the tray.

She baulked when she saw the size of the meal. "I'll never eat all of that."

"You will." He kissed her nose. "Now, white or red?"

"Water, please. I never drink when I'm working."

Fionn took a long glass from the cupboard and poured some water from a glass bottle in the fridge.

"Sorry I was so cranky," he said, placing the glass on the table. "I just miss you. I haven't seen you in ages."

Emilia chewed a chip and swallowed. "I'm sorry too. I should have warned you about how I am when I'm working. I lose all sense of time and place. Everything takes a backseat."

"Including me?"

She looked up. "Including you."

Fionn leaned back against the kitchen counter. "I'm not sure how I feel about that."

Emilia took another chip. "I can't help it. Once I crack it, I'll be better."

Fionn said nothing. How he wished he was at home in London. She clearly didn't want him around.

"How about an early night?" he suggested. "You look exhausted."

She shook her head. "Alfie's calling in a while."

"Alfie?" Fionn stood up straight. "Why?"

"He always works with me on these things. He calls himself my lucky charm." She smiled.

"Tell me this is a joke."

"Why?"

"You don't have time for me, but greet Alfie with open arms."

"We went to university together. He gets my methods and helps me. What's wrong with that?"

"Because what would a drummer know about it, I suppose." Fionn glared at her.

"Hey, stop. Don't be like this." She stood up and walked over to him. "I'm sorry I can't be there for you at the moment."

"Well, excuse me for thinking that my girlfriend would like to see me on a Friday night after a long hiatus."

She closed her eyes. Cajoling his ego was the last thing she felt like doing. Did he not realise the pressure she was under?

She inhaled deeply and forced a smile. "I'll ask Alfie to drop you home. At this time of night, it won't be so busy on the roads. I'm sure he won't mind."

"Are you serious?"

She nodded. "It would be best. I really appreciate your coming down, but I need to work." She leaned up and kissed his cheek. "A few more days will mean a lot."

"I don't believe this." He pulled back.

"Please, Fionn. It's all I can do at the moment."

An hour later, a stony faced Fionn stared straight ahead as Alfie sped along the M25.

The only sound in the car was the sound of Google Maps as its avatar instructed them to Fionn's address.

Eventually they pulled up outside the apartment building.

Fionn took his coat and opened the door. "Thanks," he said gruffly.

Alfie gave him a thumbs up. "She's impossible when she works. Don't take it personally."

Fionn slammed the door. Why did he feel like a child being dropped home by his friend's dad? It was the first time he felt different to her. The first time he felt like there was a gap. In outlook, in passion, in equality. The power dynamic had shifted in her direction.

# CHAPTER FIFTY-THREE

Madison left for Savannah's house early the next morning. Caspian kissed her thoroughly before she left.

"Call me later," he said in a sleepy voice.

She nodded. She knew it was madness to leave him alone with Rosa around, but she had to work.

*You've got to trust him.*

It was just so hard. When he had been unfaithful before, it had been easier to accept. It was just sex with girls he didn't know. Groupies. But Rosa was different. She had it all: beauty, talent and a famous heritage. She just hoped he wouldn't act on it.

Her therapist had warned her against overthinking and pre-empting disaster. The brief was to remain in the present and never to try and mindread others.

Todd opened the door of the car and she got in. John smiled from the driver's seat. There were two messages from her manager about a concert, but she ignored it. She need to concentrate on her new venture. Fingering the giant diamond on her finger, she twisted it around and around. She had no control over certain things and worrying about it was pointless. Caspian loved her and was going to marry her. She had to believe that.

Caspian slept until eleven. After two cups of coffee and a slice of toast, he texted Rosa.

***Want to call over?***

She didn't respond for ages.

***Sorry. Can't. Meeting Stefan.***

He frowned.

***Stefan??? Something I should know?***

She didn't answer for an agonizing three minutes.

***My brother!!!***

He breathed a sigh of relief.

***Well, have fun.***

Rosa groaned and pulled a pillow over her head. She hated lying but what could she do? He didn't realise how much she liked him. Watching him sing and play music, his whole being immersed in his art, only intensified her desire. The day before, he'd leaned over her shoulder to read the music on the stand in front of her and it took all of her self-control not to kiss him then.

She cursed the gods for playing with her like this. She had vowed to turn over a new leaf and not go around destroying people's lives, and instead of giving her a nice single man to fall in love with, they had given her Caspian. Unattainable and forbidden.

The day stretched ahead of her. Caspian had wanted to rehearse throughout the weekend, but Ethan had refused. He had to go to Amsterdam for his sister's 30th birthday so the band took a well-earned break. Now she had two free days and nowhere to go. She had texted Emilia, hoping to meet for lunch, but it fell through. She was working and couldn't leave the piano. She remembered her father like that: focused and obsessive.

Saturday in London. One of the biggest cities in the world. Surely there was something to occupy her time. She got out of bed and walked into the bathroom. A quick shower, followed by a coffee and a cigarette sounded nice. The day was hers.

The next day, Caspian played the four songs they'd practised on his piano, tweaking things slightly as he played. Another two weeks and they would be ready to record. He hadn't felt excitement like this in years. He knew the songs would be hits. It was like Mary had blessed his endeavours.

He played *Another Life* again, but instead of thinking about his birth mother, his thoughts drifted to Rosa and that first night she'd joined in with him on her cello. Her presence changed everything. She was so naturally talented, she didn't need to be told anything twice. She emulated him effortlessly, even when he changed something mid song. He loved how her brow furrowed in concentration when she played.

*Rosa.*

He checked the time. It was close to noon. She had mentioned meeting her brother the day before, but nothing about Sunday. He scrolled back through their messages to each other until he found the pin she'd dropped for the driver on the first day of rehearsals. Primrose Hill was about four miles north of his apartment. It wouldn't take long on his bike.

Ten minutes later, he was cycling up Kensington High Street towards Notting Hill Gate, his blonde hair completely covered by a New York Yankees baseball cap. The hat, coupled with giant shades, made him unrecognisable as he weaved through the traffic.

Rosa was painting her toenails when the intercom buzzed. Puzzled, she replaced the top on the varnish and walked over to the security camera screen by the door.

"Oh God," she said, recognising Caspian straight away.

She debated what to do. What could he want?

He pressed the buzzer again, more insistently this time, so she allowed access.

Minutes later, there was a knock on the door.

"Hey," said Caspian with a grin when she opened it. "I left my bike in the foyer. Hope that's okay."

"Your bike?"

"Yeah. I try to cycle when I can. Better for emissions."

"Right."

"So, can I come in?"

Rosa paused for a moment. "Okay," she said, opening the door further to facilitate his entrance.

He strode in and screwed up his nose. "This place smells like a chemical factory."

She giggled. "I was painting my toes."

He looked down at the red varnish on her tanned feet. "Very nice. Suits you." He looked around the room. "Nice place. Is this your dad's?" He took off his cap and shook out his hair.

She nodded. "He stayed here quite a bit when he was working."

"Nice piano." Caspian ran his finger along the sleek wood of the Steinway.

"Piano is Daddy's main instrument. Tea?"

"Sure. Not much milk."

"I remember that from France." She went into the kitchen and filled the kettle.

"How was your lunch yesterday?" he asked, looking at the books on the shelf.

Rosa didn't dare look at him. "Wonderful. It was great to catch up."

"Is Stefan older then you?"

"Yes, by two years. He's married too. Far more together than I."

"Don't mention marriage." Caspian sighed. "I'm on borrowed time with that."

He accepted the cup of tea and took a sip. "Wow, this is good."

She smiled. "So, why are you here?"

"I wanted to ask you about a song." He put his cup on the table and walked over to the piano. "May I?"

She nodded.

He lifted the lid. "You know this part in *Another Life*," he began, before playing a few bars.

"Yes," she said, "it's where I join in."

"How about this instead?" He played it again, but with a slight difference.

She got up to take a better look. "Play that again."

He did as she asked and she watched his fingers intently.

"Ah, I see." She nudged him sideways on the rectangular stool and sat down next to him. She could feel his leg against hers as the narrow seat didn't have much room.

Closing her eyes, she started to play the song from the beginning of the chorus adding in his changes at the start of the second verse. "I actually like it," she said, when she'd finished.

"You play piano really well." Caspian looked at her in admiration.

She turned towards him, her face only inches from his. "I hated my music teacher when I was little, however, she taught me a lot."

They stared at each other.

"I wish I had my cello here." She tore her eyes away.

"We could go to the studio."

"We could."

"Come on, let's go and jam. I can't think about anything else."

Rosa pressed the pedal with her foot, unsure of what to do.

"An hour, tops." He smiled.

She relented. "Okay. Let's go."

Caspian put on his hat and glasses, and then put up his collar to conceal the rest of his face.

"You look more obvious now," said Rosa.

The sun was shining when they emerged onto the street. He kept his head down and walked at a brisk pace towards Regent's Park.

"We should've cycled," he said over the traffic.

"I don't have a bike."

"You could've gone on the handlebars."

"Hardly." She laughed.

"Why not? I carried many a girl on my bike when I was younger."

"Well, that's one way to get papped."

He laughed too. "I guess you're right."

A few minutes later they arrived at The Forge. Three teenagers were sitting outside, all scrolling through their phones. One looked up and gasped.

"Caspian Cole is here!"

All three jumped up and asked for selfies. Caspian pushed open the door and shoved Rosa inside. Then he closed the door and locked it.

"Sorry, but I hate when fans do that."

They walked into the main room and Rosa put her bag on the sofa.

"Come on, let's practise." He took a seat at the piano. "Your cello awaits."

"Okay, let's go." She sat down, put it in position and held up her bow.

# CHAPTER FIFTY-FOUR

They went through all the songs they'd practised over and over. In the end, Rosa joined Caspian at the piano, sitting on the same seat. Sandalwood filled her nose and she closed her eyes for a moment.

"Are you okay?" he asked softly.

She opened her eyes and looked at him. "I'm really okay. Thank you for inviting me here. I haven't felt this motivated in years."

"It's you who I should thank. You've done the same for me. Giving me another sphere of music to explore and harness. I can never thank you enough." He paused. "I just wish…"

He stopped.

"You wish?" Her eyes were huge.

"I wish I'd met you before." He leaned closer. "I wish we'd crossed paths years ago."

"Oh?" Her stomach flipped.

"Imagine our first album had you played on it."

She felt a wave of disappointment. What did she expect? That he'd admit his feelings to her? That he wished they'd met years ago so that she would be his girlfriend now and not Madison?

"Let's play chopsticks," she suggested, breaking the mood. "Play it faster and faster until we can't play anymore."

"I bet I can play faster than you." He smiled.

She put her fingers on the keys. "Let's go."

Fionn found them like this ten minutes later, Rosa laughing and Caspian playing a non-descript tune at breakneck speed.

"Hello?" he shouted.

Rosa jumped. "Oh, hi."

Caspian looked around. "Fionn! I thought you were at Emilia's."

Fionn's expression darkened. "Well, I'm not."

Rosa got up sensing that Fionn was irritated. "I'll just go for a cigarette," she said, grabbing her bag and exiting the room.

"All okay?" Caspian regarded his friend. "You look angry."

"Where's Madison?"

"Norfolk."

"That's convenient."

"How so?"

"Well, it gives you the perfect opportunity."

"What are you saying?"

"You know exactly what I'm saying. I come down for a practice and find you here, cosying up on the piano stool."

"Shut up, Fionn."

"I know you fancy her. A blind man could see it."

"Fuck off."

"Come on, Caspian. You can't keep your eyes off her."

"Just shut up." Caspian stood up.

"And she likes you too."

"And? What do you want me to say? That we're having an affair?"

"Well, are you?"

"No!"

"Not yet."

"Not ever. Raphael asked me to make friends with her. She's lonely."

"He didn't mean spend every waking moment with her."

"I don't."

"Come on. You rehearse all day. You two are always the last to leave."

"No, we're not."

"Look, Caspian. I don't care about you and her. I only care about Maddy. You've treated her so badly before, she doesn't deserve it again."

They didn't notice Rosa coming back into the room.

Caspian banged his fist on the piano sending a cacophonous sound around the room. "There's nothing going on! Nothing. I like Rosa as a friend. That's all. Now leave it."

Rosa cleared her throat loudly. "Sorry, I didn't mean to interrupt."

Fionn glared at her. "You haven't." Then he turned on his heel and stalked off, banging the door behind him.

"What's wrong with him?" Rosa looked startled.

"Fionn? Nothing."

"What did he say?"

Caspian ran his fingers through his hair. "Rosa, I..."

She bit her lip. "I'd better go." She half-stumbled as she left, her head cast down.

"No, Rosa. Don't go." Caspian followed her. "Come back."

"Rosa!" Caspian caught up with her at the front door. "Rosa, stop!"

"What?" She turned to face him.

"Fionn's taking out his relationship troubles on me. That's all."

"You were arguing about me. I heard my name. Does he not want me on the album?"

Caspian grabbed her shoulders and forced her to look up at him. "Are you mad? We're delighted with your input."

"So, why then?" She stared into his eyes, challenging him.

Caspian paused for a moment. "He thinks there's something going on between us."

His fingers were pressing into her shoulders as he spoke.

"And you told him we're just friends." She looked at him intently.

"Yes."

"So, what's the problem? Caspian? What's the problem?"

Bending his head, he took her face in his hands and kissed her mouth urgently. She tasted like coffee and cigarette smoke. He pulled her to him, moulding her body to his, kissing her hard. Rosa put her arms around his neck and pressed up against him. He pushed her up against the wall and deepened his kiss, lifting her slightly so that her legs left the ground.

"This," he said thickly, kissing her neck. "This is the problem, Rosa."

She couldn't think. Clutching his hair, she hungrily pulled his mouth onto hers once more. This was going too far, but she didn't care. She reached down and tugged at his jeans.

"Stop." Caspian pulled away, his breathing ragged. "This is not what is supposed to happen."

She nodded, her breasts heaving. "I'm sorry."

"Don't be sorry." He looked annoyed. "I'm the one who's sorry."

"I'd better go," she said in a breathless voice.

"Yes." He turned away. "Yes, go."

Rosa straightened her dress, feeling cold. Caspian kept his head down and refused to make eye contact.

"Bye then." She waited.

Caspian turned away. "Bye."

The door slammed.

"Fuck, fuck, fuck," said Caspian, punching the wall. Why did he lose control like that? He was engaged to Madison and Rosa was the key ingredient of his new album. Now he had jeopardised it all.

# CHAPTER FIFTY-FIVE

Savannah dug up some potatoes, brushed the soil off them and put them in the basket. Madison watched her from the gate.

"Six? Will that do?" Savannah wiped her brow.

"Yes. Now, stop overdoing it for a few new potatoes. It's too hot for this kind of work."

Savannah put her hands on her back and titled her face up to the sun. "This weather seeps into my bones and makes me strong. Why not take our food from the land? You won't taste a nicer potato."

"I'm not into carbs," said Madison. Then she saw Savannah's face. "But I'll eat yours," she added hurriedly.

They walked down the field towards the house. "That tree is my favourite," said Savannah, pointing to a huge oak full of verdant leaves. "Oaks have been associated with strength and longevity for hundreds of years."

"It's a nice tree," agreed Madison.

"Those ash trees break my heart," went on Savannah, pointing to three wilted trees with brown discolouration of the bark.

"What's wrong with them?"

"Ash dieback. It's a terrible fungal disease that destroys them."

"Oh."

They walked into the kitchen and Savannah put the basket of new potatoes on the counter.

The air smelt of rosemary and apples as a shoulder of pork in the oven had been cooking slowly for three hours.

"Let's go back to the piano until dinner," said Savannah. "Even though you seem distracted."

Madison filled a glass of water at the Belfast sink, her face hidden. "Oh?"

"Your singing last night, it had a depth I've never heard. A rawness. A pain."

Madison drank the water slowly and steadily.

"Has something happened?'

"No."

"Madison, we can't write music together if you're keeping something from me."
"I'm fine."
Savannah walked up behind her and touched her shoulder. "Turn around."
Madison slumped her shoulders.
"Tell me."
"Caspian doesn't love me anymore," she said in a small voice.
"Why do you think that?"
"He's refusing to marry me."
"Refusing?"
"He won't set a date."
"You said this the last time you were here, what's different?"
Madison started to sob. "He's slipping away. I can feel it. There's this girl."
"Go on."
"She's everything I'm not. Classically trained, beautiful, interesting."
"You could be good at piano if you learned."
"Oh, stop." Madison wiped her eyes viciously. "I can barely play *Twinkle Twinkle*."
"You're beautiful."
"Yes, but she's dark and exotic looking with big brown eyes."
"And you're very interesting," said Savannah gently. "Don't be so hard on yourself."
Madison looked up. "I'm too much for him. I'm too extrovert, too loud, too public."
"Will you stop this self-flagellation, please." Savannah looked stern. "Why are you the problem? Maybe it's him. In fact, I'm sure it's him." She put her arm around Madison. "Remember what I told you? The first time we met?"
"That I have no sense of value?"
"No, not that." Savannah suppressed a smile. "I said that someone like you needs someone quiet and understated. Someone who will let you shine, but be there for you when the lights dim."
"Caspian is understated."
"Come on, you know that's not true. He's not Raphael's son for nothing."
"So what do I do?"
"You either fight for what you want or let it go. You're the only one who can decide your path."
"Fight?"
"Stake your claim. Don't push them together. Fight back."
"I suppose."
"You're his fiancée, you have that vulgar ring on your finger."
"You couldn't just say ring." Madison grinned.
"No, I'm afraid not." Savannah laughed. "Now, come on. This album won't write itself. Let's channel this sadness into a ballad that will go straight to number one."

The minute Rosa got home, she stripped off her clothes and stepped under the shower. So much for turning over a new leaf. She had reverted back to her old ways in a millisecond.

Why was she so weak? She rubbed some shampoo into her hair.

Now things would be awkward. How could she turn up at rehearsals and pretend nothing happened? It was like all the times before. She had destroyed multiple relationships by taking what wasn't hers.

Even after she'd towel dried her hair and put on her robe, she could still smell the sandalwood on her skin. Her mind flashed back to that dark corridor. His lips on her neck, his strong body grinding against her. Opening the sliding door to the balcony, she went outside and lit a cigarette.

He had said that she was just a friend, and then he had kissed her like that. She wasn't a fool. She knew he wanted her, just as he knew she wanted him. It had been inevitable.

But what now? Continue as normal? She blew a smoke ring and sat back on the rattan chair.

That was the only option. Forget it ever happened. She didn't want to give up the band. It was the first time she'd felt needed in years. They looked up to her, trusted her.

All her life she'd played with fire, unconcerned with the effect her actions had on other people. Her time in France had changed that. She wanted what Isabelle and Raphael had: a closeness, a family bond. She wanted her own version of Anouk and a nice garden with willow trees. A quiet life, a fulfilling life.

This was never going to be a reality if she continued to take what didn't belong to her.

"Help me, Fortuna," she whispered, staring at the stars.

Caspian sat in the studio with his head in his hands. He hadn't planned on kissing her. Not like that. Raphael had said that she was vulnerable and he had disregarded it. He had allowed his primal instinct to take over and now he couldn't get her off his mind. Her lips. He had never kissed lips like it. And her body. He had been so close to going all the way. Yanking up her dress and making love to her against the wall.

He couldn't gauge how she would react now. Could they still work together?

Her cello stood close by, reminding him of her contribution to his art. How he needed her to be there. The album would have to be abandoned if she pulled out of the process. She was the magical ingredient. He knew it, they all knew it.

As for Madison, if she knew what he'd done. She'd never forgive him. And rightly so.

He looked up. It had to be sorted out.

He took out his phone and wrote:

***I'm sorry. I don't know what happened. Can we forget about it?***

He read it out loud. Short, to the point and effective.

He pressed 'send'.

Hopefully she felt the same way. Their music should transcend everything. One kiss shouldn't be the reason to give it all up.

Except he didn't want to forget about it. Not at all.

Rosa exhaled slowly when she read his message. He was right, of course. They should forget about it. They should pretend it never happened.

She replied:

***Of course. See you tmrw.***

She would go to work, play the songs and go home. It was as easy as that. She would forget about him and he would go back to Madison. She had no right to interfere in their relationship. How many times before had she been responsible for heartbreak? Sleeping with married men and never thinking twice about the devastation that ensued when the secret got out?

Caspian was Raphael's son. He would be in her life forever. They could not risk a romantic entanglement like that.

# CHAPTER FIFTY-SIX

Alfie pulled up outside Emilia's house the next morning with a bag of food. He had tried to call her but there was no answer. This wasn't unusual: Emilia rarely had her phone. Still and all, he had to check that she was okay.

Using his back door key, he walked into the kitchen and placed the bag on the table. There were unwashed cups on the draining board and one had congealed milky tea at the bottom. A plate with a half-eaten burger lay discarded on the table. Mouldy bread and dirty plates lay on the counter.

"Emmy?" he called.

He found her sound asleep on the sofa, surrounded by sheets of music.

"Oh, Emmy." He shook his head.

He knew better than to tidy up. When she was working there was order to the chaos. He took a woollen rug from the window seat and draped it over her. Then he set about cleaning the kitchen.

Emilia woke up an hour later. She moaned and stretched, lifting her arms up into the air. She glanced at her watch. It was after ten.

"Damn," she said in annoyance. She had slept in.

Her teeth felt furry and her neck ached from the awkward sleeping position, but otherwise she felt energised. She had cracked a huge part of the score last night. A complicated instrumental section that was dramatic and designed to heighten the emotional impact of the scene. It was coming together. Slowly, but surely. The deadline didn't seem like such an impossibility now.

Barefoot she walked into the kitchen to find all of the mess cleared up and freshly baked croissants on a cooling rack. A pot of coffee was bubbling on the hob, a pot of gooseberry jam and some butter were on the table along with two plates and knives.

Alfie appeared in the back door, some wildflowers in his hand.

"Oh, you're up."

"What are you doing here?"

"I called over with supplies and found you asleep so I cleaned the kitchen. The croissants are frozen ones from Waitrose and the jam is from the market."

"Oh, Alfie." She looked at him fondly. "What would I do without you?"

"You wouldn't." He grinned. "How's it all going? I couldn't call last night as Arabella had a temperature."

"Oh, is she okay?"

"She's fine. I texted you to tell you."

"I have no idea where my phone is."

"I guessed as much. Coffee?"

She nodded. "I want you to listen to something when we finish. It's in its infancy but I think it has potential."

"I'm not doing a thing until you eat something."

She picked up a croissant and took a big bite. "Thanks for looking after me."

"I've always been a mother hen type. Now, pass the jam."

They ate in silence for a minute. The birds chirped outside and Emilia spotted a chaffinch and a blue tit on the bird table by the kitchen window.

"The swifts are back," she said conversationally.

Each summer, swifts would nest under the eaves of her old stone house. Then they would fly overhead, screeching loudly, indicating that they were nesting nearby. Their arrival signalled the beginning of summer; their departure meant that the nights were closing in.

"You and your swifts. How many years has it been now?"

"Eight? Nine? I'm not sure."

"Noisy little buggers."

"Oh no, I love to hear them. They fly at such speed and with such grace, of course, they have to announce it."

"How's Fionn?" Alfie put a dollop of jam on his second croissant.

Emilia shrugged. "Annoyed, I'd imagine. He's frantically busy with the new album and there has been no window for us to meet. He's sulking now."

"Well, he is at that age."

"Alfie!" she chided.

"How long more will the score take?"

"Honestly? I don't know. A week?"

"Good. You're exhausted. Now, eat up and I'll listen to your latest offering."

"Be honest. My mind is so boggled now, I can't see or hear straight."

"I promise."

Emilia played the last few notes and hung her head. She hoped Alfie could hear the potential. When she played the piano, she could hear the strings, the percussion and the brass in her head. She could visualise the conductor guiding the musicians along, and the thundering sound of all the instruments in unison. She opened her eyes to find Alfie wiping his eyes.

"Emmy, that's just perfect." He took a tissue from his sleeve and blew his nose. "I'm so proud of you."

"Are you sure?" She looked at him beseechingly. "You wouldn't just say it?"

"I wouldn't just say it." He smiled. "I'd like you to think that my streaming eyes and nose are due to hay fever, but it wouldn't be true. This is a modern classic. You've done it."

"Oh, Alfie." She smiled. "You're always so kind."

"I mean it, Emmy. This is wonderful."

After a sleepless night, Rosa exited the Camden Town tube station and walked towards The Forge. Her mind was racing. She had contemplated ringing in sick, citing a tummy bug, but pushed that thought from her mind. For once in her life, she wasn't going to run away. She could handle this. She could forget it ever happened.

As she neared the studio, she heard her name. Turning around, she saw Fionn jogging towards her.

"Rosa, wait up!"

"Hi," she said, unsure of what to say. She sensed that he didn't trust her.

"Look, I'm sorry you got caught in the crossfire yesterday."

"Oh?"

"I was out of line."

"It's fine. I didn't really hear much."

"So we're cool?" He held out his hand.

"We're cool." She shook it.

He opened the door and stood back to let her through. She closed her eyes as she passed the spot where Caspian had kissed her. The rest of the band were tuning their instruments.

"Morning!" said Fionn loudly over the sound of guitars. "How are we all today?"

Ethan sipped his coffee. "Good. Had an early night last night so feeling good."

Fionn walked up to Caspian who was sorting through sheet music at the upright piano.

"Hey, man."

Caspian looked up, a sober expression on his face.

"Hey, I'm sorry for yesterday. I was out of order."

Caspian nodded. "It's fine. Just forget it."

"Cool." Fionn patted his back. "Thanks."

Alex smiled at Rosa. "Did you have a nice weekend?"

She nodded, a slight blush creeping up her cheeks. "Very nice, thank you."

Caspian had his back to her and had made no effort to greet her. She picked up her cello and positioned herself on the chair.

"Right, let's get going." Caspian took a seat at the piano. "We're almost there. Jax wants us recording by next week."

"Next week?" Ethan looked incredulous. "That's too soon."

Caspian ignored him. "Let's take it from the beginning and run through what we have to date."

Fionn got into position and raised his drum sticks. "One, two, three, four…"

# CHAPTER FIFTY-SEVEN

The week passed quickly. On Friday evening, after a long day of rehearsals, Caspian closed the lid of the piano.

"Let's wrap this up," he said curtly. "I need to go."

"What's the hurry? Isn't the old ball and chain up north?" said Ethan.

Caspian didn't answer. "I'll see you all in the morning." And he left.

Rosa felt the familiar hurt in the pit of her stomach. He had not said one friendly word to her all week. Just a few nods and 'yeahs', but nothing of substance. It made her feel used. Worthless. Cheap, even.

"What's with him lately?" said Ethan crossly.

Fionn said nothing as he suspected it was to do with Rosa. He had been watching them all week, deliberately avoiding each other.

Alex shrugged. "Who knows with him. He's never been one to talk about his personal life."

"Maybe he's missing Maddy?" said Ethan.

Rosa went pink.

"Maybe," said Alex dubiously.

"Can we continue without him?" asked Fionn, tapping his drumsticks. "My girlfriend is ghosting me so I've time to stick around."

"How can we continue? The piano is the main part of most of our songs." Alex made a move to remove his guitar from his shoulder.

Rosa looked up. " I can play piano."

"You can?" Alex looked surprised.

"Yeah."

"He took the piano music," said Fionn.

"It doesn't matter. I can play from ear." She walked over to the piano and lifted the lid. "It won't be as good as Caspian but I can give it a go."

"Who's going to sing?" Fionn looked mischievous. "Ethan?"

Ethan snorted. "Not likely."

"Alex?"

"No."

Rosa laughed. "I can sing. Not as proficiently as Mamma, but I can stay in tune."

"I saw your mamma on Sky Arts last week," said Alex. "My dad is a huge fan."

"That's nice."

Sitting up straight, she played the intro to *Mary*, Caspian's ode to his birth mother. It was a simple song, similar to Elton John's *Your Song*, with a catchy melody and a memorable chorus.

They all stared at her in awe.

Then she started to sing.

*It was the summer of '94*
*You sang a song*
*Of love and lore*
*Your eyes so blue*
*Your hair bright gold*
*An angel face*
*You'll never grow old*

Alex joined in, adding depth and groove to the song, followed by Ethan, who strummed an acoustic guitar. Finally, Fionn brought it all together, providing the pulse of the track.

Rosa's voice was sweet and true, and gave the song a new identity. No one could question Caspian's star quality when it came to singing, but Rosa had a certain edge to her voice too.

No one noticed Caspian standing in the doorway. He had come back for his hoodie which he'd left on the sofa.

Rosa launched into the second verse, making small mistakes but righting them straight away. Her sweet voice soared above them all. Caspian felt something indescribable. It was one thing to write a song and sing it: a song of such a personal nature lost its emotional punch after practising it ad nauseum. The tears he'd shed when penning the lyrics were a distant memory to him now. Hearing someone else interpret the tune gave it a new lease of life. It was painful to hear, heartrending and wonderful all at once.

*Rosa.*

He couldn't sleep properly. He thought about her constantly and had even started writing a song about her. She filled his mind, his world, his existence. He knew he'd behaved abominably all week, but he had to do it. If he acted on this, he could lose her forever. Their families had been connected for decades. Raphael was her godfather and Caspian was pretty sure that he would not be in favour of a romantic liaison between his son and his goddaughter. He had asked him to look out for her, to be her friend, certainly not to break her heart. Madison was another reason. She was his future wife and didn't deserve this treatment. Not after all the previous misdemeanours. Rosa was spectacularly off limits and he had to accept it.

He consoled himself with the notion that artists working together on a common goal often fell in love. It was a shared passion for something that gave the illusion of compatibility. Lead actors in film roles often blurred the lines between fantasy and reality, having affairs during filming. These relationships often fizzled out when the spell was broken. This was exactly what was happening here. He was entranced by her because of their mutual musical talent. It would be madness to risk everything for a few weeks of sex.

He backed away silently, leaving his hoodie where it was. Announcing his return would break the spell. But he couldn't stay any longer. He couldn't stand and watch her from afar, playing his music, channelling his innermost self.

Savannah adjusted her glasses and made a quick change on the sheet music. Pozzo was asleep at her feet and Lucky was curled up on the couch. It was close to eleven and it had only just got dark. Madison waited until she played the intro to the chorus once more and then started to sing. It was a song they'd written about betrayal. How rare it was to find pure, unbridled love.

"You sing this with great passion." Savannah nodded in approval. "I think it will be a big hit."

"Well, it's a subject I'm familiar with."

"Oh?"

"Yeah." Madison sighed. "I never seem to be enough for one person."

Savannah stood up and gestured for Madison to come to the kitchen with her.

"Let's have some camomile tea," she suggested.

Madison nodded. "I'd like that."

Savannah filled the old cast iron kettle and put it in the Aga. She took two pottery mugs from the dresser and popped two teabags into each cup, waiting for the hot water when it was ready.

"Before Caspian, was there anyone really special?" she asked, taking a seat at the table.

Madison raised an eyebrow. "Have you not googled me?"

Savannah rolled her eyes. "What do you think?"

"Well, there was Cal Scott. He was my first real boyfriend. He's the lead singer of The Southsiders, a boyband from Dublin."

"Did you love him?"

"I thought I did." She smiled. "All the girls would scream his name when we went out together, and he was very handsome. I liked photos of us in magazines, things like that."

"What happened?"

"He cheated on me. I ended it." She looked up. "There was no one really special until Caspian after that."

"Do you love Caspian?"

"Why do you always ask me that? Yes, of course. We're engaged."

"Do you trust him?"

Madison paused. "How do you mean?"

"Do you trust him?"

The kettle started to whistle. "The water's ready," said Madison, changing the subject.

Savannah got up and filled the cups with water. She placed the mug in front of Madison.

"You're about to embark on a marriage built on mistrust. I think you need to reflect on that."

"I'm not embarking on anything. He won't set a date."

"Madison, look at me." Savannah looked stern. "You should not live your life looking over your shoulder. Caspian needs to commit to you fully. Unless you have trust, then the relationship is doomed to fail."

Madison put her head in her hands. "Stop."

"You know I'm right."

There was a pause. "Remember the girl I mentioned?" said Madison in a small voice.

"Go on."

"Her name is Rosa Weber." She looked up. "He met her at Anouk's christening. She plays the cello and has famous parents."

"I know who she is."

"I can feel him slipping away."

"Talk to him. Tell him your fears."

"He just denies it. He tells me what I want to hear. They're just friends. He needs her to play cello on his new album. Then, we fall into bed and try to bandage things that way."

Savannah sipped her tea. "You have to make a decision, Madison. Is this the life you want? The next time we meet, I want to see a definite direction. One where you put yourself first. Never settle, that's all I can say."

Saturday dawned: the last official day of rehearsals. Rosa turned off her alarm. She had set it for 6.30am as she wanted to get to The Forge earlier than the others to practise on her own. Abbey Road was booked for Monday morning and she was nervous about the whole affair. Her time at the orchestra had irrevocably conditioned her to desire perfection. No one understood the pressure. All the bows had to go in the same direction, following the first violin to the letter. One error and you'd let the whole orchestra down. One mistake was all it took.

Doctor Eckleburg were far more laid back and she enjoyed the human connection: the space to dream and write music. An orchestra was a huge group of talented musicians, but it was not conducive to creativity.

She had a quick shower, brushed her teeth and pulled a brush through her long hair. A navy knee-length dress and some gladiator sandals and she was all set. She put her phone and her cigarettes in her bag and headed out into the emerging sunshine.

Caspian had deliberately and successfully avoided contact with her all week. He was using the classic move: diffusing an emotionally charged situation by indifference. Only once did they share a smile. Alex mentioned a Jackson Pollack print he'd bought for his mother's birthday and they had both immediately thought of Anouk's white dress. But as quickly as he'd smiled, it had disappeared again. She felt stung by his behaviour, missing their closeness and the chats they had, but she knew it was necessary. She was here to do a job, not fall in love. Caspian was taken. That was that.

Fionn had given her a spare key to the studio the week before. She pushed open the old door and walked down the gloomy corridor. There was a light on in the studio.

She walked into the large room and stopped dead. Caspian was standing by the window, some sheet music in his hand.

"Oh, I didn't realise you were here."

He didn't reply for a moment. Instead, he looked at her with an inscrutable expression.

"I came to practise," he said eventually. "Monday will be busy so I wanted to check a few things."

"Me too." She put her bag on the sofa. "I was first chair in the orchestra and we had to be flawless. Conductors and orchestra managers spent their days breathing down our necks and mistakes weren't tolerated."

Caspian put the music on the top of the piano. "I'll go home then. You need to be alone."

"You don't have to…"

"I do." He looked at her with a sad smile. "I have to go, Rosa."

"I know you regret what happened…"

"It was a stupid thing to do. I've spent over a year of my life writing this album and you're the key ingredient to its greatness. I can't risk losing you."

"So, it's only the music you care about. I should've known."

"No, it's not just that. There's Maddy for one. And Raphael. I like you too much to risk losing you." He picked up his hoodie. "I'll see you on Monday."

She felt her eyes fill up. She turned away, but not before he saw a tear roll down her cheek.

"Rosa, are you okay?" He was beside her in an instant. "Hey, I'm sorry. I shouldn't have brought it up." He pulled her into his arms and stroked her head. She let him hold her as she sobbed.

"We were good friends, you and I," she said tremulously. "Now, you won't even look at me."

"I can't," he said, his eyes closed.

"You can. We can forget what happened and move on. How can I play on your album when you act like you hate me?"

"I don't hate you." He exhaled in frustration. "Jesus Rosa, you know that."

She rubbed her nose with her hand. "I don't care about anything else, but I want us to be friends. I liked having you around."

He took a tendril of her hair and put it behind her ear.

"Okay, let's start again."

"You promise?"

"I promise."

"I don't have many friends in London. Mostly my own fault, but it's still lonely. Don't shut me out."

Caspian made a Sign of the Cross on his chest. "I swear I won't."

"Want to practise *Another Life*?" she asked, rubbing away the tears. "I think it's one of the best songs."

Caspian let her go and nodded. "Okay. Let's do it." He arranged the music on the piano stand.

Caspian took off his shoes the minute he got home and went straight to the drinks cabinet. Pouring a large whiskey, he walked to his piano and took a seat.

He played the beginning of a ballad called *Lost One* and sighed. Inspired by Rosa, he had penned it a few days before. The lyrics told of a girl who couldn't find her way in life. Who kept falling into the same traps, over and over again. In the end, love sets her free.

He refilled his whiskey glass and knocked it back.

# CHAPTER FIFTY-EIGHT

Savannah walked Madison to the car. John was just closing the boot and Todd was standing sentinel by the door.

"The Brut Squad are back," said Savannah drily.

"I can't go back to the real world without them."

Savannah rolled her eyes. "We're not going to argue about this again." Her expression softened. "You've done some great work this week. Your voice keeps getting better and better."

"Thanks." Madison gave her a hug. "I couldn't do it without you."

"Yes, you could." Savannah looked at her sternly. "Why do you constantly believe that you need others to succeed? You have the power inside of you."

"Like Dorothy in *The Wizard of Oz*?"

"Exactly." Savannah grinned.

"I get what you mean and thanks for all the advice. I'll work on it."

"Caspian, the wedding, me – it's all incidental. Madison Ryan is the one in control. You've got to believe that."

Madison arrived home two hours later to find Caspian asleep on the couch and a near empty bottle of whiskey on the coffee table. He had slept in his clothes and the air smelt like alcohol.

"Open the windows, Todd," she said, wrinkling her nose.

"Yes, ma'am."

She put her bag on the ground. Boris, her personal trainer was due in an hour as she had missed her workouts all week. She always hated the first session after a break. Her muscles would ache and burn from the strain. However, she knew it was a necessary evil.

Giorgio didn't work on Sundays so he'd left a plate of prepared fresh fruit in the fridge and a prawn salad for dinner.

Caspian stirred and opened his eyes. "Maddy?" he said in a husky voice. "You're back?"

She nodded. "Just now. What happened you last night?"

He sat up and rubbed his temple. "I don't know."

"Did you drink all of that by yourself?" She pointed to the bottle.

"Not all." He felt a wave of nausea. "Can you get me a glass of water?"

She did as he asked and placed it on the coffee table. "What was the special occasion?"

"We're going to Abbey Road tomorrow."

"That's good."

He gulped the water down thirstily.

"I'm just going to change into my workout gear."

He nodded and sat back on the couch with his eyes closed.

"Caspian?"

He opened one eye. Madison was back from a run and was standing over him. "I thought you'd be up."

He sat up straight.

"Come into the bedroom." She walked away and gestured for him to follow.

He picked up the empty glass on the coffee table and attempted to drink the last drop of water left.

"Caspian!"

He got up reluctantly and felt lightheaded. "Coming."

He found her lying on the bed, wearing a terry robe. She patted the bed. "Come here."

He lay down next to her and she pulled his head onto her chest.

"I missed you," she said softly.

He kissed her lightly and moved sideways, lying down on the soft pillow. "I'm glad you're back."

"Let's hang out today. Go to a gallery or something."

He closed his eyes. "That sounds good."

"Did you hear that there's a Cézanne exhibition coming to the Tate in September?"

Caspian opened one eye. "Since when are you an art buff?"

"I just thought you'd like to know."

He leant up and kissed her neck. "Thanks. I'll definitely check that out." He closed his eyes once more and promptly fell asleep. Madison stroked his hair, her diamond ring glistening in the morning light.

Caspian slept until three and when he woke up, he went straight to the piano and worked on last minute adjustments to a song while Madison had a long Zoom call with her manager. Jax sent an email with all the details about Abbey Road and the meeting time for the next morning. Fionn texted into the band WhatsApp group with an excited emoji.

Madison left the meeting and closed the Mac.

"I can't wait to get into the studio. Wait until you hear what we've written."

Caspian smiled. "I look forward to it."

"Savannah is so bossy and we don't see eye to eye, but she's a genius." She got up. "I'll just take the cling film off the prawns."

"You do that." Caspian smiled wearily. "I might not eat much. My stomach is in a bad state."

"Why did you drink all that whiskey?" She unscrewed a bottle of San Pellegrino. "After that weekend in Gloucestershire, I'm never drinking again. I was so sick."

"I might join you in your sobriety." He got up from the piano. "God, I need to lie down again."

Madison scowled. "We haven't seen each other in over a week and now I have to eat dinner alone?"

"I'm sorry." He disappeared down the hall.

"Todd?" she called. "Todd? Do you want some prawns?"

Todd appeared in the doorway. "No, ma'am. I don't like fish."

The buzzer went off. "Check who that is," said Madison, spearing a single prawn with her fork.

Todd checked the camera. "It's Mr O'Connor, ma'am."

"Fionn? What could he want?"

Todd shrugged. "Will I deny access?"

Madison shook her head. "Let him in. Even hanging out with Fionn is better than being alone."

Fionn arrived into the apartment five minutes later. He held up his arms like he was being strip-searched. "No weapons."

"Ha, ha. I've told you before, never trust anyone. Least of all you."

"Ah, I wouldn't murder you. Where's Caspian?"

"In bed. He drank a whole bottle of Jameson last night."

"Really?" Fionn took a seat at the table. "That's not like him."

"I know." She chewed thoughtfully. "Maybe it's because this album is at the recording stage. It's probably really emotional for him."

Fionn looked at her plate. "Is that your dinner?"

She nodded.

"Where's the bread?"

"Carbs? I'll forget you said that."
"So, all you're having to eat are a few crustaceans and some salad."
"Low calorie and healthy."
Fionn got up. "Can I make a coffee?"
"Go ahead." She took a sip of water. "So, are you nervous about tomorrow?"
Fionn popped a Nespresso capsule into the machine and pressed the button.
"I don't feel nervous at all. I'm excited to see the studio."
"Caspian is too. He feels you are all making history by recording there."
Fionn resumed his seat at the table. "It's a big deal. My mum is beside herself. Abbey Road is one of her favourite albums. She wanted us to pose on the zebra crossing but I can't see Caspian doing it."
"No," said Madison with a smile. "Not a chance." She put her cutlery together on the plate. "He's banned me from calling down. He doesn't want the paparazzi around."
"I get that. We just want to record the album in peace."
"What's it been like having an extra member of the band?" She fiddled with her fork.
"Rosa? It's been fine. She's very quiet and works hard."
"That's nice."
He looked at her intently. "Are you stressed about her?"
"What? No. Why would I be stressed?"
"You can tell me."
"No. I mean, not at all." She took a frantic sip of water. "So how's your old lady?"
"Don't call her that."
"Sorry, how's Emilia?"
Fionn's expression darkened. "I don't know. She's shut me out completely."
"Why?"
"She's working on a huge deadline. Some film score. I haven't seen her properly in weeks."
"I was wondering why you called over. It's because you've been abandoned."
Fionn sat up. "Hey, enough cheek from you. I'm here to see Caspian actually. I wanted to chat about tomorrow."
"Yeah right."
"Jax sent an email and I want to discuss a few things."
She laughed. "You're so easy to rise."
"Says you." He laughed too.
"Do you want some prawns? Giorgio made enough for two. Caspian is too sick to face them."
"Nah, you're okay. I'm meeting Clio and Alex for dinner."
"Clio never mentioned dinner. How come you're invited and I'm not?"

"Because I've been abandoned, as you say. Clio also thought you'd like to spend time with Caspian as it's your first night back."

"Well, that doesn't look likely. He's so hungover."

"Plus, a circus follows you wherever you go. We just want a quiet bowl of linguini in a local restaurant."

"I can be discreet."

Fionn looked unconvinced. "Whatever you say, Maddy Ryan. Whatever you say."

# CHAPTER FIFTY-NINE

Two Range Rovers arrived at number 3 Abbey Road the next morning. Caspian and Fionn were in one, with Ethan and Alex in the other. Rosa was waiting at the entrance, smoking a cigarette. Caspian had offered to pick her up on the way but she'd declined as it was only a ten minute walk from her apartment. Abbey Road Studios, the world's first purpose built recording studio, looked like a white Georgian townhouse from the front. A plaque to Sir Edward Elgar was erected on the left of the front door, in homage to the famous composer whose masterpiece, 'Land of Hope and Glory' was the opening performance in 1931. It housed iconic spaces like Studios One, Two, Three and Four, along with the Penthouse, the Gatehouse, and the Front Room.

"Morning," said Caspian warmly. Rosa stubbed out her cigarette.

"Hi." She saluted the rest of the band. "Morning."

Fionn took a selfie in front of the front door. "For my ma," he explained. "She's a huge Beatles fan."

Jax was in the foyer when they walked in.

He shook Caspian's hand vigorously. "I'm not going to lie, but I really thought you'd cancel on me."

"I wouldn't do that," said Caspian haughtily.

"So let's get cracking. Studio Two is all set up for you."

Caspian nodded. "Okay, we're ready." His stomach flipped slightly. There was something moving about standing in the famous studio. Something special. If only the walls could speak.

"The Beatles recorded in this studio, you know," said Jax as they walked along. "Along with Pink Floyd, Adele, Ed Sheeran, Oasis."

"And now Doctor Eckleburg," said Fionn.

They walked down a stairway to a large room with parquet flooring and cream walls.

"There are two isolation booths," went on Jax, pointing to the end of the room, "and the Control Room is up there." He pointed to the upper floor. "Brian Mulcahy is the producer. He's up there with Peggy Browne, the senior sound engineer. Give them a wave."

Caspian looked up through the glass window and saw a small bald man with tattoos on his arms giving them a thumbs up. A tall woman with platinum blonde hair stood next to him, earphones on her head.

"Brian worked with U2 in Ireland and Emmylou Harris in the States, among others. A legend."

Jax stopped at the piano in the centre of the room. "This is a Steinway upright. Will it do?"

Caspian nodded.

Brian Mulcahy came bounding down the steps.

"Hey, guys," he said in a south Dublin twang which bordered on American. "Love your work, love it."

Caspian shook his hand. "Good to meet you." The rest of the band followed suit.

"I'm excited to work with you guys, I have to say. It's all happening."

Caspian nodded.

"I just want to say that I respect you and your creativity. My job is to help bring your vision to life."

Peggy Browne skipped down the steps and waved at the group. "Hey everyone, I'm the sound guru."

Caspian sat down at the piano and arranged his music on the music stand.

"The songs I've written are inspired by my birth mother. She died when she was nineteen; I never knew her. I wanted to connect with her so I wrote some music to reflect my thoughts and feelings. This song is called *Mary.* It's about her when she was young."

Brian rubbed his chin. "Keep going."

"Anyway, it goes like this." Caspian played a melody with his right hand, and then sang along with it.

Brian nodded. "That's good. Needs some work, but good. Are we tracking the band together or separately?"

Caspian looked at the other members of the band. "We talked about this and we'd like to play as a band but with overdubs. Tracking it live causes too much bleed."

"Agreed."

"So, the focus will be on the drums, bass and piano initially, put down the foundation."

"Sounds good," said Brian.

"We'll all play at the same time to get that authentic feel. Then we can overdub the solos and vocals later."

"How long will it take?" Jax looked worried. "This place costs a fortune."

"Money should not be a part of this," said Caspian disdainfully. "Don't even mention it. This is art, this is our legacy. I don't care how long it takes."

"Well, you're booked for a few weeks so we should do it." Brian took out his phone. "Yeah, I'm working with Noel Gallagher next. Three weeks tops." He clapped his hands. "Right, we've no time to lose. Cindy Brophy will mix and master the tracks when we're done."

"I'd like to be involved in that," said Caspian.

Brian laughed. "Good luck with that one. She hates when artists stand over her shoulder."

"But I want…"

"Relax, I'll supervise the process, and nothing will be bounced without my say so."

Caspian scowled. "We can talk about this again when the time comes."

"I'm just saying, don't mess with Cindy." Brian grinned. "Right, let's tune up and jam."

Rosa's cello had been delivered early that morning and stood on a stand by a wooden chair with an upright back.

Caspian stretched his arms up into the air revealing his taut stomach. "This is a big moment, right guys?"

Fionn sat down at the drumkit. "Bigtime."

Brian tapped on the window of the sound booth and gestured for them to put on the headphones.

"Jax, can you wait outside?" asked Caspian.

Jax held up his hands. "Hey, of course. I'll leave you to it."

The subsequent days were long, but fulfilling. Brian was excellent at his job and allowed the band to experiment with sounds while expertly guiding them through the process. They recorded the rhythm section first. Fionn, Alex and Ethan were given headphones where they could listen to a click track and asked to play together. Caspian sat in the control room and sang into a vocal microphone to guide the band. Fionn's performance on the drums was the critical element and Peggy made them play the same song over and over until the foundation was laid.

The overdub of Rosa's cello was next, so she warmed up playing various parts of Doctor Eckleburg's songs. Brian complimented her on her excellent sense of pitch and well-honed technique.

"Your mother is Cassandra Rosso, right?" he said. "Great singer."

Rosa resisted rolling her eyes. She wanted to shirk that identity and be recognised in her own right.

Peggy Browne, the senior sound engineer, placed two microphones down on the carpet.

"Play something," she said, putting on her headphones. "I'm just going to walk around and find the sweet spot."

"The sweet spot?" said Caspian.

"Where the mic picks up the complete sound." Peggy adjusted the microphones and walked around Rosa as she played. Then she took off her headphones. "Can I move your chair?"

Rosa nodded and stood up and Peggy moved the chair to the right.

"We need to remove the rug underneath her too," said Peggy.

Brian and Ethan pulled back the carpet leaving enough space for Rosa's chair and the two microphones. "Play something else," said Peggy, putting back on her headphones and walking around. Rosa repeated the same piece from before.

"Okay, I've got it." Peggy placed the first microphone about six feet from the cello and three feet off the ground.

Caspian listened intently. He watched Peggy work and made notes of what she said.

"Right, everyone out." Peggy looked at Caspian and Ethan who were the only members of the band in the studio.

Ethan took a cigarette from its box. "Good luck, Rosa," he said, climbing the stairs to the exit.

"I'm going to the control room to track the mics," said Peggy.

"Can I come?" asked Caspian.

Peggy nodded. "Rosa, play about twenty seconds of the first song and then stop."

Rosa nodded. Brian was already upstairs. Caspian and Peggy joined him and closed the soundproof door. She gave Rosa a thumbs up so she played a snippet of the first section of *Another Life.*

Peggy waved her hands in front of her, signalling for Rosa to stop. She then listened back to the recording. The door opened and she bounded down the stairs.

"The on-axis mic sounds wrong," she explained. "I'm just going to move it closer."

When she was back in the sound room, she gave another thumbs up. Rosa played the same piece again. Peggy listened back and both she and Brian agreed that it worked.

Caspian watched Rosa play, her slender arm moving like lightning. There was nothing like the rich, emotional sound of the cello. It moved him in ways he couldn't describe.

Peggy pressed a few buttons and moved a few knobs before signalling for Rosa to stop.

It was when they got to a song called *Nothing Much* that Brian halted the proceedings.

"I think we need to add a solo melodic line here, just in the middle of the song."

He played it back.

"I haven't written one," said Caspian.

"Maybe Rosa could improvise," said Brian. "Come up with a line for the middle section. It will develop the musicality, man."

Caspian looked down at her. "She probably could. I'll pop down."

"I need a coffee and a cigarette," said Peggy. "Take your time."

Caspian went down the stairs and signalled for Rosa to remove her headphones.

"Hey," he said softly.

She smiled. "Is it going well?"

"Like a dream." He pulled up a seat next to her. "We were just talking about *Nothing Much* and we think a solo line in the middle section would lift it."

"A solo line?"

"Of cello. Do you want to play around with it?"

Rosa bit her lip. "My training was focused on the interpretation of classical compositions. We rarely compose ourselves."

"Try it," he said encouragingly. "You've so much to give. Give it a go."

"Oh, I don't know." She blushed. "I'm not sure."

"Pretend I'm not here." His voice was gently persuasive. "Play some of your favourite classical pieces and let the inspiration flow."

She closed her eyes and started to play Cello Suite No.1 Prelude, her head moving with the bow, with sweeping arpeggiations. Caspian watched her in awe. Then she went on to Haydn, playing the Cello Concerto in C Major, the rich emotional sound filling the room.

"Wait, let me play the piano." He started to play *Nothing Much* and she tried to adapt her notes to harmonise with him. The result was chaotic, lots of flats and discordant melodies. Some of the notes on piano were too high, so Rosa transposed them to a lower key. Then something clicked. Caspian held up his hand. "Play that again."

She bit her lip. "Was it like this?" Her bow moved across the strings, playing D and E-flat.

"Yes." He played the piano. "See? It fits. Try it again."

She obeyed and suddenly they were in sync and the music filled the room. Peggy arrived back from her coffee break and whistled. "That's decent," she said approvingly.

Rosa beamed at her. "I didn't think it was possible."

"Anything is possible," said Peggy. "If you want it badly enough."

Rosa's eyes connected with Caspian's for a moment until they both looked away.

"Right, let's record this and finish for the day." Peggy gestured for Rosa to get in position. "I'll have to track the mics again. Same as before."

Brian walked down the steps carrying a polystyrene cup of coffee. "We need a small selection of alternative harmonic layers in different registers for the overdubbing."

Peggy sighed. "Did I say finish for the day?"

Brian laughed. "You know me, Peg. I tear the arse out of it."

The lead vocals took time as Caspian kept changing small parts of songs, before reverting back to the original. Peggy put him in one of the booths for greater controls of tones and to lessen noise bleed. She had listened to the scratch vocals that he'd recorded during the tracking, and had vocal ideas of her own. Caspian initially refused to engage with her, lead vocals were his domain. Then he heard Peggy bitching to Brian over the talkback mic, and nearly walked out. After some skilful conflict resolution, he listened to her suggestions on melodic nuances and found that he agreed. With his eyes closed, he sang into the microphone with every fibre of his being. His only thoughts were of Mary, his muse.

Brian clapped his hands. "That's a wrap, guys," he announced. "Next we get Cindy and we're almost there."

He was referring to Cindy Brophy, a specialised engineer, who was booked for the mixing and mastering stage. There was also another engineer called Rufus Harrington who would come on board to arrange the tracks on the album.

The Range Rovers dropped them off one by one each evening. Rosa had refused a lift in the beginning as she lived so close, but Caspian had insisted. He didn't want her walking through the streets alone at night. Madison was rarely home when he got back to the apartment. When she was, he couldn't wind down enough to listen to her chat. His mind was filled with music and doubts, wondering if they could've done a song better. Finalising anything was frightening as it was the end. Fionn had chided him to let go, but he couldn't. He wanted perfection and he wouldn't rest until it was achieved.

# CHAPTER SIXTY

Alfie used his key to enter Emilia's house. The kitchen was empty except for some used cups on the counter. A half-eaten slice of toast lay discarded on a plate and the bananas in the fruit bowl were black.

He found her in her pyjamas, sitting on a chair in the garden.

"Well?" Alfie tried to gauge her expression.

Emilia looked up. "Dorothea called."

"And?"

"They loved it!" Her face broke into a huge smile. "They have a few tweaks in mind, but it's almost good to go."

Alfie pulled her to her feet and hugged her tightly. "I'm so pleased. You deserve it."

Emilia felt elated. She had poured her soul into the score and when the test audience reacted favourably, Dorothea had called her straight away. The overture, an anthem for the unifying power of sport, fit perfectly with the theme.

"We must celebrate," said Alfie. "Champagne at ours?"

"I'd love to but I should go to London to see Fionn."

"London? You hate the city."

"I know, but I must make an effort. He's recording at Abbey Road at the moment."

"Ring him and ask him to come down instead. Far less stress and did I mention champagne?"

She laughed. "Okay. I'll do that."

Alfie regarded her. "Did you miss him?"

"Who?"

"Fionn. Did you miss him when you were apart?"

She shrugged. "I didn't have time to miss him."

"Red flag, Emmy."

"Oh, stop. You just can't be happy for me, can you?"

"That's a bit harsh."

"It's true. You haven't approved of him since the start."

"No, and I'm not going to patronise you by lying. However, I want you to be happy and if it means hanging out with a millennial, then so be it."

Emilia rang Fionn twice. Each time the phone rang out and went to messages. She guessed that he was in the studio so she sent a quick text for him to call her as soon as possible.

He called an hour later.

"Hey." His tone was cold.

"Hi, Fionn. How's Abbey Road?"

"Busy."

"I wanted to tell you my good news. The score was accepted."

"That's nice."

"Is that all you have to say?"

"Well, what do you want me to say?"

"Anyway, I was wondering if you'd like to come down tonight. Alfie has champagne and we're going to celebrate."

"Wait a second, I don't see you for weeks and now I'm meant to drop everything and travel two hours to see you?"

"Don't be like that."

"Sorry, Emmy. It's a bit much."

"I didn't mean it like that."

"Look, I don't know when I'll be free. We're working day and night here."

"Keep in touch then."

"I will."

"Bye, Fionn."

"Bye."

That particular day at the studio ran over time. Peggy could not get the right sound quality for Ethan's guitar solo so there was a lot of re-tracking and playbacks. Eventually Brian shouted "Cut!"

"I can't listen to another note," he said, yawning. "Night, guys."

Caspian, Rosa and Alex ended up in the same Range Rover going home. Alex got out first.

"Good work today," he said, with a thumbs up.

"See you bright and early," said Caspian.

The car pulled off again. Rosa could barely keep her eyes open.

"You played really well this afternoon," said Caspian as they sped along.

"Thanks. You too."

"Brian is quite opinionated."

"Yes, but he's good."

Caspian frowned. "I don't know. Producers can be a bit bossy sometimes."

Rosa yawned. "I don't agree. I think he's just what we need. His suggestions make so much sense."

The car moved along the street, stopping intermittently at traffic lights.

"When will we be finished?"

Caspian drummed his long fingers on his thigh. "A few days? Maybe a little more?"

Rosa looked away. "My dad called. He's coming back to London soon so I'll have to move out. He doesn't want me there long term."

"Where will you go?"

"I'll probably leave London. After the album is done, I've no reason to stay."

He said nothing.

"Mamma wants me to go to Florence. I might do that."

"With your talent, you could go anywhere."

She felt the tears well up in her eyes as the car reached her apartment building.

"Well, night then." She gave a little wave.

"Will you be okay?" He looked at her in concern. "Have you food in?"

She forced a smile. "I'll be fine. I've some leftover pasta from last night."

They stared at one another.

"Goodnight, Rosa," he said reluctantly.

"Goodnight." The car pulled away.

The apartment was quiet when he got home.

"Hey Todd, where's Maddy?"

"In bed. She's not feeling so good."

"Oh?" He walked into the bedroom to find Madison lying on the bed with a bowl next to her.

"Mads, what's wrong?" He was beside her in a flash.

"I don't know. I can't stop getting sick. It must've been the sushi last night."

Her hair was bedraggled and when he put his hand on her forehead, it felt clammy.

"What can I do?"

"Nothing." She wiped her nose miserably with a tissue. "I've emptied my stomach so now all that's coming up is yellow stuff."

Caspian made a face. "Do you want some water?"

"No. Whenever I drink anything, it comes back up." She closed her eyes. "If I die, make sure Savannah records our songs and releases them."

"You won't die." He felt a pang. She looked so vulnerable. "I'll be out in the sitting room if you need me."

She nodded. "See you later. I won't hate you if you sleep in the guest room tonight."

"It's okay…"

"Seriously, Caspian. You might pick up this bug."

Fionn rang Emilia for the seventh time. Again, she didn't pick up. He cursed himself for being so cranky when she'd called. She had been delighted about her score and instead of being nice, he'd been sullen and rude. He contemplated getting a taxi to her place, but he was too tired. They were due at the studio first thing in the morning so it wasn't feasible.

He called her again.

Nothing.

He threw his phone on the bed.

Emilia poured herself a glass of wine and took off her shoes. Fionn had called umpteen times but she'd ignored it. She didn't want a scene. He was hurt, she got that, but the pressurised time was over now.

She traced the rim of her glass with her finger. She had a feeling in the pit of her stomach: a familiar feeling that she had grown accustomed to over the years. It was the same pattern with all her previous lovers; everything went great until it didn't. Alfie had hit a nerve when he'd asked her if she had missed Fionn. She had to admit that he hadn't really crossed her mind. The night he'd turned up unannounced had annoyed her rather than pleased her. Now she was starting a new project: Raphael's new film about Yeats. Would she have time to devote to a younger lover?

The next afternoon, there was a knock on the door. The clang of the brass knocker reverberated through the house. She was playing her violin, having a workout as she called it, an exercise she tried to do most days to keep her arms supple. Barefoot, she walked out into the hall and unlocked the latch.

Standing on the doorstep was Johann Weber.

She held onto the door handle, stunned.

"Hello, Emilia."

He looked the same, only older. His hair had gone completely grey and there were lines on his face, but his eyes were exactly the same. They regarded her with intensity.

"How did you find me?" Her voice sounded strange, strangulated almost.

"Bertie. He's never been one for discretion."

"Why have you found me?"

He smiled. "I'm getting older. Time is running out. I wanted to meet you again."

"You did?"

"I did." He stepped closer and she could smell his aftershave. It brought back so many memories in an instant.

"May I come in?"

She bit her lip. "Into my house?"

He nodded.

"Okay." She stood sideways and he walked into the hall.

"Nice floor," he said. "Are those Winckelmans?"

"The tiles? Yes."

"I have them in Hertfordshire."

"Yes, I remember." She took his coat and hung it on the rack. "Would you like some tea?"

He nodded. "Yes, please. I'd forgotten how good English tea is. I've been based in America for nearly fifteen years."

She went into the kitchen, filled the kettle and switched it on.

"I like your hair," he said in approval. "Blonde suits you."

She didn't react; instead, she took two cups from the dresser and popped teabags into each one.

"Congratulations on the score for Bonnie."

She went pink. "Oh, you know, it worked out in the end."

"I didn't jump through hoops for her and she couldn't handle it." He sat at the table. "Of all the composers to take my place, I'm glad it was you." He winked. "My protégée."

Emilia poured the boiling water into the cups, clearly uncomfortable.

"What are you working on now?" she asked brightly.

"This and that." He accepted the cup from her. "And you?"

"The same." She sipped her tea. "I met Rosa a couple of months ago. She looks so well."

Johann's expression changed. "She's on thin ice with me."

"She's been working hard on that album."

"For a rock band?" Johann snorted. "All that fine training and she's a session cellist for a band."

"You shouldn't be such a snob."

"You know what I mean, Emmy."

"How's Stefan?" she asked politely.

"Wonderful. He's married to a lovely girl called Claudia and works in finance. He's never caused a day's trouble."

"Rosa will find her way."

"Will she? I despair for that girl."

"Of course she will. Talent like that always wins out."

They stared at one another.

"When was the last time we met?" asked Johann, watching her.

"It was in LA." She turned away. "A long time ago."

"I'm sorry if I hurt you."

"It's fine."

"I never meant to."

"Of course."

"It's just artists cannot be tamed. We are put on this earth to love and lose, and then to create art from these emotions. Staying with one person would create mediocrity, a stagnancy that would not be conducive to inspiration."

Emilia looked out the window. "So, why are you here? Really?"

Johann walked up behind her and kissed the back of her neck. She closed her eyes.

Putting his arms around her waist, he swivelled her around to face him.

"You know why I'm here."

The next morning, Fionn went outside and tried calling Emilia again. This time it went straight to messages.

"Fuck," he cursed under his breath.

He couldn't imagine her turning off her phone on purpose. She was too mature for that. It was far more likely that she had forgotten to charge it.

If he wasn't so busy, he'd go down to her house and make it all up to her. But time was money and Jax was piling on the pressure to finish things.

He tried calling her one more time.

# CHAPTER SIXTY-ONE

Madison had never felt so awful in her life. The thought of food made her retch and her skin felt sweaty. Her mother offered to fly over and look after her, but she declined the offer. Ross, her manager, sent flowers and phoned her.

"There's gastroenteritis on the rounds, Maddy love," he told her. "Stay in bed and get well soon." Todd was on hand for whatever she needed. The days were long and filled with intermittent naps. She couldn't wait to get dressed and have her hair styled. To feel human again. Caspian called in to see her each night when he got home. He looked exhausted and she could tell from his lack of communication that he was consumed by the music. Idle chit chat was futile, he simply would not engage. She encouraged him to continue to sleep in the one of the guest rooms as she didn't want him to catch what she had. Not when he was in the middle of such an important stage.

By the fourth day, she was able to get up. She donned a velour Juicy Couture tracksuit and her Ugg boots, and ventured out to the living area. The cleaner had been that morning so the place was gleaming.

"Morning, ma'am," said Todd with a salute. "Good to see you up and about."

She still felt slightly queasy so she half-smiled and took a seat at the large kitchen island.

Giorgio, her chef, appeared from the larder.

"Miss Madison," he said in his Italian accent. "I'm so happy to see you."

She nodded. "Thanks."

"Can I make you some breakfast? Eggs? Avocado? Salsa?"

She put her hand over her mouth and made a run for the toilet.

"What did I say?" said Giorgio.

Brian Mulcahy took off his earphones. The hard work was done. In truth, he'd doubted their progress as Caspian had been difficult, but it had worked out.

Jax called as they were packing up and Fionn put him on speaker.

"I've booked a table at Libertine as we've got to celebrate," he shouted, "courtesy of Odyssey Management."

Everyone cheered.

"Dress code is smart so go home and doll up." Jax hung up.

Brian stood at the top of the stairs. "Are you up for a party?"

Fionn shrugged. "Why not? I could do with a beer." He took out his phone and texted Emilia.

***Finished! Heading out for drinks. Want to come up?***

He sent the message and put his phone away. He was tired of looking at messages with one grey tick indicating that they hadn't been delivered.

Rosa picked up her bag and made a move to leave.

"Have fun, guys." She gave a small wave.

Caspian stared at her.

"You're not coming?" said Ethan.

She nodded. "Clubs aren't really my thing."

"Ah, Rosa. You've got to come. It's so important to wind down together," said Alex. "Just for one drink."

"No, seriously."

"Rosa! Enough of this. You're coming." Ethan looked stern.

Fionn watched her as she glanced furtively at Caspian who turned away.

"Let's go," said Alex. "The cars are waiting outside."

Caspian waved them away. "You go, I'll follow."

Rosa followed Ethan out the door, Alex and Fionn behind her.

Rosa was dropped off first.

"You have thirty minutes," said Ethan. "We'll call you when we're outside."

Rosa groaned inwardly as she entered the foyer of the building. That last thing she wanted was to go to a noisy club and make small talk. She could text the others and feign sickness. A period pain. No one could argue with that. Just as she was about to text, a message came through from Ethan.

***Don't even think about pulling a sickie.***

She laughed. The lift pinged and she walked out. She opened the door of the apartment and screwed up her nose. The half-eaten curry that she'd had the night before lay congealing on the counter. She threw it in the bin and closed the lid. The clock on the wall told her that she had a bare twenty minutes to get ready. A big pile of dirty laundry lay behind her bedroom door and she cursed her laziness. It left her with very little to work with. She opened the wardrobe and rifled through the dresses. They were all cotton summer dresses. Every day, boring clothes that she wore on a normal day. Jax had specifically said to dress smart. A flash of red caught her eye and she pulled out a tight mini dress she'd purchased for a concert three years before. At the last minute she'd changed her clothes as wearing a short skirt was difficult when playing a cello. She held it up against her and looked in the mirror. The red colour looked nice with her dark hair. She threw the dress on the bed and started to get undressed. She didn't have much time.

Caspian arrived home to find Todd in the kitchen.

"Where's Maddy?" he asked.

"In bed."

Caspian walked into the bedroom and Madison gave a small wave.

"Hey, you." Caspian sat down next to her. "How are you feeling?"

"Tired." She yawned. "I just can't seem to shake this."

"We finished the album today."

"That's great! I'm so happy for you."

"Jax has organised drinks at Libertine." He looked down. "I mean, I don't have to go."

Madison shook her head. "Of course you should go. You need closure."

"But you're so sick…"

"I'm fine. I can call you if I need you." She attempted a smile.

Caspian reddened. "You won't believe this but I left my phone at the studio."

"What? Can you go back for it?"

He shook his head. "There's no need. I won't be long and if you need me, just call Fionn or Alex."

"Okay." She slumped back on the pillow. "I'm sick of being sick. I'd love to go out on the town."

He leaned over and kissed her cheek. "Next time."

Libertine, one of London's most exclusive clubs, was famous for its sophisticated clientele and glamorous interior. Jax had called ahead and booked a table in the VIP section. The club manager was waiting when the car pulled up.

"This way," he said, leading them into the club through a side door. Cliona and Stella were already at the reserved table, both drinking margaritas and chatting. Ethan slid into the space next to Stella and Alex sat next to Cliona. He kissed her lightly on the lips.

A woman appeared at the table. "Hi, everyone. My name is Matilda and I'm your hostess for the evening."

"We'd like some drinks," Jax said loudly. "A rum and coke for me."

"I'll have a Jameson," said Fionn. "Straight."

"Those cocktails look good," said Ethan. "I'll have one."

"Me too," said Alex. He turned to Rosa. "Would you like a margarita?"

She shook her head. "Just a Pepsi for me."

He nodded. "No problem."

Rosa rummaged in her bag until she found her cigarettes.

"Through that door over there," said Ethan helpfully. "I'll join you in a sec."

"Thanks." She walked over to the smoking area. She should never have come. She was tired and her back ached from the high heels she was wearing. Her red dress was tight and uncomfortable, and the music was too loud.

She instantly felt calm when she inhaled her cigarette. Leaning her head back against the cool wall, she sighed. One sociable drink was acceptable. Then, she would sneak away and get some sleep.

Five minutes later, she stubbed out her cigarette and re-entered the club.

"Rosa? Rosa Weber?" came a familiar voice. She looked around. A small man in a Hawaiian shirt and skinny jeans approached her.

"Radoslav?"

"It's me, baby!"

She gasped. Radoslav Rehák had been her friend when she worked for the London Symphony Orchestra. A Czech viola player, he was a notorious gossip. Even though they'd vowed to stay in touch after her departure from the orchestra, the texts had fizzled out. The last time she'd heard from him was after her dramatic flight to France. He asked her about the rumours of an affair with an older man, but Rosa had ignored it. Heartbroken, she'd left him on 'read'.

"You look great, Rosa. That dress is fab. Why are you back in London?"

She suppressed a smile. He didn't wait around for information.

"I'm playing a few tracks on the new Doctor Eckleburg album."

Radoslav's eyes widened as he took in the group sitting at the table behind her. "The rock band? Oh my God, is Caspian Cole here?"

"No, not yet." She turned pink.

"Are you a session cellist now?"

"I suppose."

"Lucky you." He sipped his cosmopolitan. "It's the same old ding dong at work. Although I'm thinking of making a change myself." He leaned in closer. "The Beeb have headhunted me and I fancy playing at the Proms."

"They headhunted you? A viola player?" she mocked.

"Hey, enough of the viola gags. We're the cream of the string section."

"Right.' She grinned. "So, are you here alone?"

"No, as it happens. A few of the others are over there." He pointed to a crowded corner. "Some old faces, some new." He nudged her. "That hot violinist you took home one night is here."

Rosa frowned. "Who?"

"Come on, Rosa. Surely you remember Nikolai? Nikolai Markov?"

She peered closer at the tall dark-haired man in the gloomy club. "Maybe."

"He was one of your last victims as I recall."

"Do you keep detailed notes on all the scandal at work?"

"Only in here." He jabbed his head. "Anyway, he was heartbroken when you didn't call him back. He told me over shots one night. I must tell him that you're here."

"Oh, don't!" Rosa shook her head. "I'm not in the mood to small talk tonight."

"Ah, come on. I know he'd be thrilled to see you."

Rosa held up her hands in protest. "Honestly, Rad, I don't want to. It's been too long. Plus, I'm going home soon."

But Radoslav wasn't listening. Instead, he dragged her towards Nikolai who turned in surprise.

"Rosa?" he said in his deep voice. "Rosa Weber?"

She forced a smile. "Hi, Nikolai."

He leaned in awkwardly to kiss her cheek. "You look exactly the same. How long has it been?"

"I'm not sure…"

"Over a year anyway." He gazed at her. "How's life?"

"Oh, you know, okay."

"Things didn't work out at Southbank?"

She reddened. "No."

"I heard that." He moved closer. "Can I get you a drink?"

She shook her head. "I have a drink back at our table."

"Our table?"

"Over there." She pointed across the room.

"What orchestra are you playing with now?"

"I'm not." She held her head up. "I'm working with a rock band. Doctor Eckleburg. Have you heard of them?"

Nikolai laughed. "Of course. I like their music."

Radoslav cleared his throat. "I'm off for a refill. Nikki? Another pint?"

Nikolai shook his head. "I'm okay."

"Rosa?"

"I'm fine."

Nikolai stared at her intently. "You seem different."

"How do you mean?"

"The last time we were out together you were doing tequila shots until three in the morning. You sprinkled salt on my chest and licked it off as I recall."

"I did?" She looked down. "Sorry about that."

"Don't be sorry." He tilted her chin up. "It was one of the best nights I've had in London."

"Nikolai, I…"

"Don't say anything. I know why you didn't answer my calls."

"You do?"

"It was bad timing."

She said nothing.

"You got fired and had to cut all ties. I get that."

"Yes," she said, relieved. "That was it."

"It's so good to see you again." He smiled at her.

She relaxed slightly. He really was handsome. She had good taste, even when she was pissed out of her mind on José Cuervo.

"So, tell me about your new life as a rock star." He drained his pint and placed the empty glass on the table.

"I'm just a guest on a few tracks. Hardly a rock star."

"But it must be such a different experience. I envy you."

Alex tapped her shoulder.

"Excuse me," he said apologetically, "but here's your Pepsi. It's going flat over there."

"Thanks." Rosa smiled at him. Nikolai nodded in salute.

"Alex, this is Nikolai Markov. I used to work with him at the LSO. Nikolai, this is Alex Ryder, the bassist in Doctor Eckleburg."

Nikolai shook his hand. "Good to meet you."

"Likewise."

Radoslav arrived back with Nikolai's pint. "That barman is divine," he said, putting his hand on his heart. "I'm definitely asking for his number. Oh, hello. You're Alex Ryder."

"Yes, hello." Alex smiled. "And you are?"

"Radoslav Rehák. I work with Nikolai here." He grinned. "And we used to work with Rosa."

Rosa made a face. "Please don't bring that up."

"Nikki and Rosa here were the Romeo and Juliet of the orchestra. Star crossed lovers or something like that."

"Hardly." Rosa went crimson.

Alex patted Rosa's back. "Brian and Peggy just arrived so I'll head back. Let me know if you want another drink."

Nikolai tapped her glass with his finger. "What's with the Pepsi anyway?"

"I don't drink alcohol anymore."

"What?"

She nodded. "It just gets me into trouble."

"In my case, good trouble." He smiled again and her heart jumped.

She struggled to remember that night they spent together, but only flashes of memory existed.

"I'm going back to flirt with my barman some more," said Radoslav.
"Thanks for the drink," shouted Nikolai after his retreating back.
Rosa didn't notice Caspian arriving through the side door.
"So, what's the orchestra up to these days?" she asked politely.

# CHAPTER SIXTY-TWO

Johann kissed Emilia's shoulder and got up out of her bed. Naked, he walked into the bathroom and shut the door.

She stretched and sighed, her body sated from the sex. It had been so easy, so familiar. They had slipped into their routine of old, their bodies remembering the moves as if it were yesterday. Johann was older, there was no denying it, his skin sagged around his neck and his once taut torso was flabbier now. His legs looked more knobbly but his eyes were the same. All he had to do was look at her and she was lost.

Her phone was on the bedside locker, out of battery for almost two days. Leaning down, she plugged it in to charge. She was hopeless when it came to that sort of thing. The apple logo appeared, indicating that the phone was rebooting. The screen came to life and lots of notifications came through. Most were from Fionn.

She bit her lip. Like lightning, she scanned the messages: apologies for his rudeness, asking to see her. She typed a reply quickly and pressed 'send'.

Johann came out of the bathroom and smiled.

"You know, I'd forgotten how wonderful you are," he said, climbing under the duvet again. "It's like we've never been apart."

Emilia kissed him softly. 'I know."

He pulled her head onto his chest. "You're like a fine wine."

"Don't say that."

"It's true."

Emilia let herself be. Lying on him like this was bliss, listening to his steady heartbeat, inhaling his skin. It was so comfortable, so nice. Loving Johann was hotwired into her brain and, like an addict, she was helpless against him. Her relationship with him had defined her in many ways. He had been there during her most transformative moments. After years of wandering and searching, she was right back where she started. That chemistry, that pull, had never happened with anyone else. No one could ever measure up. Even after all this time.

Fionn read the text from Emilia for the sixth time.

***We need to talk.***

That sounded ominous. He scowled and didn't text her back on purpose. Not that she'd notice. He downed his whiskey.

Jax, who had just done a line of cocaine in the bathroom, arrived back to the table.

"More drinks?" He didn't wait for an answer. "You, more drinks," he said rudely to the hostess, Matilda.

Alex shook his head. "I'm only half way through this."

Cliona held up her glass. "I'm fine too."

"Have them. You're not paying." Jax's eyes glittered and his nostrils flared.

The music was loud and the bassline was deep. Strobe lights illuminated the crowd which was wall to wall with people drinking and dancing. Ethan got up, an unlit cigarette in his mouth, and walked in the direction of the smoking area. Stella followed, her long blonde hair trailing down her back.

Caspian arrived and slid into the seat that Ethan had vacated. "Sorry I took so long."

Jax saluted him. "Drink?"

"I'll have a beer."

"Peroni?"

"Sure."

Jax snapped his finger at Matilda. "Bottle of Peroni."

Caspian looked around the table. "Where's Rosa?"

Alex pointed to the far side of the room. "Chatting to that tall hunky guy for that last while."

Caspian's eyes travelled around the room until he spotted her long dark hair.

"An old flame from the LSO. Seems nice enough."

Caspian stared at them. "What's his name?"

"Nikolai something? I can't remember."

"Right."

"Looks like there's some unfinished business there," continued Alex.

"Oh?" Caspian stared at Rosa, a muscle flickering in his cheek. Fionn watched him intently.

Matilda arrived with the drinks. "Jameson," she announced, putting it in front of Fionn.

"And a Peroni." She blushed as she put the bottle of beer near Caspian, who didn't even acknowledge her.

Nikolai leaned closer and whispered something in Rosa's ear. She threw back her head and laughed. He leaned over again, closer this time.

Fionn watched Caspian's knuckles go white as he gripped the bottle.

"Maddy's still sick, I hear," said Fionn, swirling his whiskey around the tumbler.

Caspian nodded.

"It's a pity she couldn't make it tonight."

"Yeah." He didn't take his eyes off Rosa. That dress unsettled him. He liked her in a t-shirt and jeans: normal clothes that she wore to the studio.

Brian and Peggy both did a shot of sambuca. "Yuk," said Peggy, wiping her lips. "I don't know why I do it to myself."

"It's the theatre," said Brian, grinning. "Lighting the flame, downing it in one go."

"Looks like Rosa's going to get lucky," said Cliona smiling. "I'm so happy for her. She deserves some fun."

Caspian looked tortured. He took a vicious swig of beer and set the bottle down on the table with a clatter.

"Are you okay?" Cliona looked at Caspian in surprise.

"I'm fine," he said, forcing a smile. "Never better."

"I texted Maddy but she didn't reply. How is she?"

"Still sick," he replied, watching Nikolai put his hand on Rosa's back. "To be honest, I should go home to her." He got up.

"But you just got here," said Cliona in surprise.

"I know, but I'm exhausted."

He walked away purposefully. Rosa sensed him as he walked past. She turned and was about to wave when he disappeared into the crowd. He didn't even stop to say hello.

"Back in a sec," said Nikolai, heading in the direction of the toilets.

Radoslav arrived back with drinks. "Was that Caspian Cole?" he asked in excitement. "God, he's dishy."

Rosa nodded. "That's him," she said wistfully.

"What's he like? In real life?"

Rosa's expression softened. "Lovely. He's just lovely."

"You must introduce me sometime. I'd love a selfie. Do you think I'd get to meet Madison Ryan too? I'm a huge fan."

Caspian stopped in the toilets on his way out. He lined up at the urinal and unzipped his jeans. Nikolai walked in with another man of a smiliar height.

"Can you believe Rosa Weber's here? Man, I didn't think I'd ever see her again."

Caspian's ears pricked up.

"What's her story?" the other man asked, unzipping his jeans. "Still as wild as ever?"

"I'm not sure. She was fired soon after I started. We only ever had one night together and it was some night."

The other man laughed. "Tell me more."

"She's feral, man. We didn't stop all night. She has the most amazing lips. Imagine them around your..."

Caspian pressed the hand dryer and the noise mercifully drowned out the end of the sentence. Nikolai glanced in his direction, but didn't recognise him.

"I'm going to take her home tonight, that's for sure." He zipped up his pants.

"She's gagging for it," his friend agreed.

They left the room.

Caspian felt like punching the wall. He should've intervened and told them to shut their filthy mouths. He should've said something.

But why? She didn't belong to him.

He turned on the tap and threw some water on his face. He couldn't let her go home with that creep.

He fixed his hair and straightened his shoulders. He owed her that much.

# CHAPTER SIXTY-THREE

Caspian strode right up to Rosa and tapped her shoulder.

"Rosa, I need to talk to you."

"Why?" Her brown eyes looked wary.

Taking her hand, he led her to a corner. There was a flash of a camera as a girl took his photo with her phone.

He turned around angrily. "Hey! Don't do that."

"Can I take one with you? Please."

"No." He glared at her and turned to Rosa. "We can't talk here. Come on." Taking her hand again, they walked through the crowd. When they reached an emergency exit, he pushed the doors open and they were outside the back of the building. She leaned up against the wall, resting her head against it. He moved in front of her, his face inches from hers.

"What's the story with that guy?"

"What guy?" The aroma of sandalwood lingered in the air and she felt herself sway.

"That violinist you were talking to."

"Nikolai? Nothing. There's no story."

"Is he an old boyfriend?"

She blushed. "I wouldn't say boyfriend."

"But you had sex with him."

She stood up straight. "Why are you asking me this?"

"He's a creep. Stay away from him."

"It's none of your business."

Caspian leaned closer. "I heard him talking about you. He said some things."

"What things?"

"Personal stuff, about your night together. He's also planning to take you home."

"Well, that's not going to happen," she said angrily. "Anyway, what's it to you? I can do what I want."

"I just wanted to warn you. He's not a nice guy."

She stared at him in disbelief. "Are you my dad now? Is that it? Because believe me, he never cared about what I got up to."

Caspian held up his hands defensively. "Look, I've made you angry. That wasn't my intention."

"Then why did you bring me out here to insult me?"

"Insult you?"

"Yes, insult me. You've pretty much said I'm a slut."

"No, I didn't."

"Easy pickings for someone like Nikki."

"I didn't mean it like that. I'm just worried about you."

"Why?"

He paused and chose his words carefully. "I care about you."

She hit his chest with her fists. "Just back off. Leave me alone."

"Rosa!" He fell backwards and she continued to hit him.

"Hey! Stop." He grabbed her wrists and pulled her arms down by her sides.

"I'm a big girl, Caspian. I can make my own decisions. I don't need you poking your nose into my life."

"I'm not."

"Good." She stared at him defiantly, her chest heaving. He leaned closer instinctively, as if to kiss her, and she closed her eyes in anticipation. Suddenly, he pulled back.

"Look, forget it," he said ruefully. "Go back inside."

"Where are you going?"

He put up his hood and walked away. "For a walk."

"How will I get back in?"

He didn't answer.

"Caspian!"

He turned the corner and walked towards Oxford Street. He needed to clear his head. A red bus flew past and he covered his nose so as not to inhale the fumes. All the shops were closed as he walked past, with some doorways housing the homeless in sleeping bags.

He had to compartmentalise his feelings. He had Madison. She was beautiful and loving and familiar. Rosa was a fad: a flight of fancy. She was not what he wanted or needed. Why should he care who she went home with?

But he couldn't stop thinking about it. He couldn't stop imagining them together. How dare those creeps talk about her like that? Reducing her to a sexual object. She was so much more. Sweet, talented, beautiful, funny.

He turned right onto Regent Street. He didn't know where he was going but he had to move. Away from Libertine. Away from her.

# CHAPTER SIXTY-FOUR

Madison had never felt so sick. Every time she tried to get up, her head started to spin and she'd fall back onto her pillow. There had been a rapid decline in under an hour and she felt weak. Her abdomen hurt on the lower left side so she told her PA, Cora, to call her doctor.

"What if I have appendicitis and it bursts?" she said fearfully.

Cora rang the doctor's private number as it was out of hours and she promised to come straight away.

"Will I call Caspian and tell him to come home?" asked Cora.

Madison shook her head. "He doesn't have his phone. Let's wait until the doctor comes."

Doctor Prisha Kumar arrived exactly half an hour later. She was the head of an exclusive private clinic that Madison and other celebrities attended. She had been out for dinner with her husband when the call came through. Leaving the restaurant, she drove to Kensington straight away. She could charge handsomely for the interruption.

"Hello, Madison," said Prisha, putting her leather bag on the end of the bed.

"I think I'm dying," said Madison. "I feel so awful."

Prisha, who was used to Madison's drama, put on some rubber gloves. "Tell me how you've been all week."

Madison groaned. "So sick. I think I had food poisoning first, and now I'm afraid my appendix is going to burst."

"Lie back." Prisha felt Madison's abdomen, pressing gently until Madison screamed.

"Ow!"

Prisha pulled back. "So, tenderness on the lower left side."

Madison nodded.

"When was your last period?"

"I think I have it now, but it's weird looking brownish blood."

"Has the vomiting eased?"

"Yes. It's only every now and then and it's this weird greeny yellow stuff. I haven't eaten in ages."

"Can you give me a sample?" asked Prisha, holding up a bottle.

Madison groaned. "I suppose." She swung her legs over the side of the bed and sat up. "Wow, I feel dizzy."

"I'll help," said Cora, springing into action. "Lean on me."

She held Madison's arm as she walked slowly towards the bathroom. The door closed.

Prisha took some boxes out of her bag and put them on the desk.

Madison returned with a specimen bottle half-full and handed it to the doctor. "I don't have much fluid in my body at the moment."

She lay down on the bed in relief, exhausted from her short trip.

"Madison, you're pregnant." Prisha held up the indicator.

She sat bolt upright. "What?"

She nodded. "I tested the sample as I had to rule it out. Abdominal pain could be problematic. I'd like to admit you for a scan right away. Can you get someone to help you pack a bag?"

"Look, I think you've made a mistake. I'm not pregnant. It's not possible."

She patted her shoulder. "News like this can be a shock, but we need to get you into hospital to check what's going on."

"What do you mean, going on?"

"How bad is the pain? Give me a number between one and ten."

Madison winced. "Definitely a ten."

"Then we need to move."

"Todd!" she called, her head spinning.

"Yes, ma'am?"

"Caspian doesn't have his phone. Call Fionn or Alex and find him."

"Yes, ma'am."

The doctor closed her bag. "I can call an ambulance but I'd imagine you'd prefer a more discreet mode of transport."

She nodded. "John, will take me."

"We need to leave as soon as we can."

Cora put a nightdress, underwear, a toothbrush and paste, a hairbrush and a phone charger into a small bag.

"My moisturiser!" said Madison through gritted teeth.

Cora nodded. Todd knocked on the door.

"Yes?"

"Miss Madison, Alex's phone is off. Fionn didn't answer."

"Ring anyone." Her eyes filled with tears. "Please Todd, I need him."

"Right away, ma'am."

Prisha closed her bag. "Let's move. They're expecting us."

Fionn felt his phone ring in his pocket and was surprised to see Madison's name.

"Hello?" he said curiously.

"Fionn, this is Todd. I need to speak with Caspian."

Fionn looked around. "He isn't here. He left a while ago. Ring his phone."

"He doesn't have it. Is there any way we can contact him? Is he with someone we could call?"

Fionn shook his head. "Not that I know of, Todd. I thought he went home."

"Well, he's not home yet."

"What's wrong, Todd?"

"I'm not at liberty to say, sir."

Fionn sat up straight. "Is it Maddy?"

"If you see Caspian, please tell him to call me straight away."

"Todd, what's going on?"

"I'm not at lib…"

"I get it." Fionn hung up the phone. He yanked Ethan's sleeve. "Have you seen Caspian lately?"

Ethan shook his head. "I think he left."

Alex arrived back from the toilets. "Alex, did you see Caspian in there?"

"No. Why?"

"I'm looking for him."

"I'd say he went home. He said he was tired."

Fionn got up. "I've got to go."

Cliona blew him a kiss. "See you soon, big bro."

Jax downed a shot of tequila. "See you," he called and sucked a slice of lemon.

Fionn walked towards Rosa. She was deep in conversation with two men.

"Rosa?" Fionn tapped her shoulder and she turned around.

"Hi, Fionn."

"Have you seen Caspian lately?"

Her face went pink. "No, I haven't seen him for ages."

"If he rings you, please tell him to call me."

Rosa held up her phone. "My battery is dead," she said.

"Okay. Thanks anyway." Fionn half ran to the door, booking an Uber on his phone.

Cora put a fleece blanket around Madison's shoulders and Todd lifted her like a child. Her face was white and her body felt limp.

John was waiting at the car with the door open. Prisha got into the back with Madison and tied her seatbelt.

"I'll leave my car here," she told Cora, pointing to the BMW parked next to the wall. "I can pick it up later."

John rang ahead and was instructed to pull up at a back entrance of the hospital. Todd lifted Madison onto a waiting wheelchair and long silk scarf was draped over her famous blonde hair. A nurse was waiting to push her inside. John took the bag from the car and followed, with Prisha filling the emergency doctor in Madison's history.

They got inside and Madison was taken to a private room. Prisha put her bag on the ground and helped her into bed. Her face contorted with pain as she gingerly lay back on the pillow.

Prisha held Madison's hand. "Squeeze as hard as you like," she said.

"What are they going to do?"

"It's a transvaginal ultrasound," she explained. "It will detect what's going on in your uterus."

"How do you mean, what's going on?" Madison whispered. "You must have an idea?"

"Let's just wait and see." Prisha's face betrayed nothing.

Cora had volunteered to wait at the apartment for Caspian to come home. She had called Bethany and informed her of the situation. Madison's condition and hospitalisation needed to be kept under wraps.

The doorbell buzzed and she ran to the CCTV screens, hoping to see Caspian outside apologising for not having his key.

It was Fionn.

She buzzed him in and waited. Maybe he had news of Caspian's whereabouts.

She opened the door and Fionn walked in with a worried face. "Where's Maddy?" he asked.

Cora ignored his question. "Have you seen Caspian?" she asked.

"Where's Madison?" Fionn said again. "Can I see her?"

Cora shook her head. "You know I can't say anything, Fionn."

"Bullshit. I don't care if you signed a million NDAs, I want to see Madison."

Cora bit her lip. "I can't."

"I'm practically family, for fuck's sake. I know how sick she's been. Where is she?"

Cora relented. "She's been taken to hospital."

"What? Why?"

Cora shrugged. "Abdominal pain."

Fionn started backing out the door. "Where is she?"

"The Portland."

The door slammed.

Fionn called another Uber and there was mercifully a Kia Sportage a minute away. The driver pulled up and Fionn jumped in.

"The Portland, yeah?" said the driver. Fionn nodded.

The car pulled off, speeding past Hyde Park before turning north until it reached Great Portland Street. It screeched to a halt at the entrance and Fionn got out. He called Madison's phone and Todd answered.

"Yes?"

"Todd, I'm downstairs. Can you bring me to Maddy?"

"Who told you where she is? " asked Todd sternly.

"That doesn't matter. I want to see her."

Fionn hung up the phone. A pregnant woman in a camel coat was looking at him strangely. Her husband was escorting her inside, carrying a small Louis Vuitton suitcase.

He entered the hospital through the main doors and looked around for Todd. He debated whether to ask at reception, but decided against it for privacy reasons. Suddenly Todd appeared out of the elevator.

"I asked Miss Madison and she said you can come up."

Fionn put the phone back in his pocket. "What's wrong with her, Todd? What's going on?"

Todd crossed his bulky arms and said nothing. They entered the lift and he pressed the fourth floor.

Prisha was talking to a man wearing scrubs in the corridor when the doors opened.

"Which room?" Fionn asked Todd.

"That one," he said, pointing to the door behind Prisha. Fionn walked past and was about to open the door when Prisha turned around. "Hey, you can't go in there!"

Fionn ignored her.

Madison was lying on the bed, her face ashen. She was wearing a hospital gown and her hair was in a blue cap. A nametag bracelet was on her wrist and she was hooked up to a blood pressure monitor. The machine beeped intermittently.

She looked up. "Fionn?"

He nodded. "Hey."

She started to sob. "Oh Fionn, where's Caspian?"

He ran over to her and took her hand in his. "I don't know, Mads. I don't know." His heart constricted.

"I need him," she whispered. "Get him, Fionn."

"I don't know where he is. I'm so sorry." Fionn stroked her wrist.

"I'm so scared."

"I know."

"Caspian should be here. Where could he be?"

Fionn rubbed a tear from her cheek. "Will I do instead?" he asked softly.

"You?" Her blue eyes widened.

"Yes, your mortal enemy."

She gave him a watery smile. "I suppose."

"Good."

The consultant who had been talking to Prisha entered the room.

"How are you feeling, Madison?" he asked, checking the screen of the monitor over her bed.

"My tummy hurts," she said breathlessly. "I feel like it's going to burst."

He turned to Fionn. "Are you the father?"

Fionn did a double take. "Father?" His eyes met Madison's. "No, I'm not."

"Then I have to ask you to leave," said the consultant, not unkindly.

# CHAPTER SIXTY-FIVE

Fionn walked up and down the corridor, his heart thumping in his chest. Cora had texted to say that Caspian had not come home yet. She promised to ring the minute he turned up. Fionn tried Cliona and Alex again, asking if they'd seen him. At this stage they were at home, tucked up in bed, and had not seen or heard from Caspian.

"Why do you ask?" asked Cliona suspiciously.

"No reason," said Fionn, hanging up.

Ethan and Stella hadn't seen him either. Jax was the same. He rang Rosa but it went straight to messages. Then he remembered that she'd said that her battery was dead.

Bethany appeared out of the lift, her phone in her hand.

"Hey," she said to Fionn. "How's Madison doing?"

He shrugged. "I don't know. They're doing tests."

"I'm keeping an eye on all the socials and there's nothing yet."

"Why would there be? No one knows."

"You'd be surprised." She looked around. "Where's Caspian?"

"Gone AWOL. We can't contact him." Fionn rubbed his temple. "Can you get someone to check The Forge? He sometimes goes there to practise."

"I'll make a few calls." She walked away.

Prisha came down the corridor and Fionn tried to gauge her expression. "How's Maddy?"

"She's gone for surgery."

"What? Why?"

Prisha ignored him. "Any sign of Caspian?"

"Nothing."

She walked away.

Bethany walked back over to Fionn. "Not a word to anyone, okay? Don't make contact with anyone."

He sat down and put his head in his hands.

Caspian stopped before he got to Leicester Square. The crowds were huge and he was sure to be recognised. He felt bad for how he'd behaved. Leaving her alone like that. It's just he had to leave or he would've kissed her. He reached into his pocket for his phone and then remembered that he'd forgotten it at the studio.

"Damn," he muttered under his breath.

The Range Rovers were waiting in the Q-Park near Libertine. He'd just walk back and get a lift home. Cutting across Brewer Street he turned left up Lexington Street in the heart of Soho. His head down and his hands in his pockets, he weaved through the crowd. Shops filled with souvenirs and Chinese paraphernalia were still open and brightly lit, with Chinese lanterns draped across the doorways. Soon he was on Oxford Street again, and heading in the direction of Winsley Street.

Libertine was still busy, with queues of beautiful people waiting outside. Security guards stood at the doors and you could hear the bassline of the music emanating out. He spotted a doorman and headed in his direction. He needed to find Jax to call the car.

Suddenly he saw Rosa walking out of the main door and heading in the direction of Oxford Street. She seemed to be alone. Changing direction, he walked quickly, gaining on her easily. Just as she was about to cross the road opposite TK Maxx, he pulled her sleeve. She jumped and turned, putting her hand on her chest.

"Caspian! You frightened me."

"Are you heading home?" he asked.

She nodded.

"Why are you walking? There are cars to bring us home."

"I felt like some air." She paused. "Did you want something?"

He ran his fingers through his hair. "I'm sorry for earlier. I shouldn't have interfered like that."

"No, you shouldn't."

He held up his arm. "Taxi!" he yelled. A black cab came to a halt. "Come on, let's drop you home."

"There's no need."

"I want to, Rosa."

Rosa sighed and stepped into the taxi, sitting on the leather seat. Caspian followed.

"Primrose Hill," he said, knocking on the glass partition. The car drove off, narrowly avoiding a group of women on a hen night.

They travelled in silence. Rosa stole glances to the right and saw a pensive expression on his face. She didn't want to talk. Not again. She felt like they'd had the same conversation over and over.

About fifteen minutes later, the taxi pulled up outside the apartment building. Caspian handed the driver a fifty pound note and they got out.

"Can I come up?" he asked, putting his hood up over his blonde hair.

She stared at him. "Up to my place? Why?"

"I don't want any weirdness between us."

"I'm not sure. It's late."

"Just for a few minutes. I don't really want to be papped on the street."

She relaxed slightly. "Of course. I didn't think." She took her key out of her bag and they walked into the building.

Caspian remained silent until they were safely in the apartment.

Rosa took off her heels and threw them in the corner. "Sorry, but my feet are so sore." She padded into the kitchen and switched on the kettle. Taking a clean cup off the draining board, she popped in a teabag. "Would you like something to drink? I'm going to have some tea."

Caspian shook his head. "Have you anything stronger?"

Rosa walked over to the dresser. "He has whiskey in here, I think." She opened the cupboard. "Yes, lots of whiskey."

"I'd like one."

She poured a generous measure into a cut glass tumbler and handed it to him.

"So, why are you here?" she asked, sitting on the sofa opposite him.

Caspian took a large slug of whiskey and coughed. "I don't want us to fall out."

"We haven't."

"I just feel that things have changed."

"They have." She regarded him steadily. "We're not kids. You know that there's something between us. When you kissed me, I felt it. You felt it too."

"It's complicated." He fiddled with a stray thread on his jeans. "Raphael is my father. He'd kill me if he knew I'd behaved like that."

She shrugged. "Don't worry about it. Our time is over. The album is done. I'll be leaving soon."

"How soon?" he asked quietly.

"Soon." She smiled sadly. "I have to find direction."

"Don't go."

"What?"

"Don't leave.'

"I have to. There's nothing in London for me now."

"You've got me and the band."

She stared at him.

"Rosa, I don't want you to leave."

"Why?" Her eyes challenged him.

He got up and crossed the room. Sitting down next to her, he cupped her face in his hands and kissed her. Then he pulled back. "I'm in love with you. I love you so much I can't see straight."

Rosa closed her eyes. "Stop," she whispered.

"Look at me." He grabbed her shoulders and shook her gently. "Look at me, Rosa."

She opened her eyes.

"I love you."

She shook her head. "You say that but there's no such thing. Not when it's me."

"I think about you all the time. When I wake up, when I sleep. I dream of you, Rosa. I've tried to fight it." He bent his head and kissed her again, more urgently this time. He lay her down on the sofa and pulled the strap of her red dress to one side. "Your skin, I've never touched skin like it." He kissed her shoulder blade and then trailed his tongue over the pulse in her neck.

"That night we slept together, that night in France. It felt so good waking up beside you."

She tugged at his top, pulling it up and exposing his strong back. He put his arms over his head and allowed her to remove the t-shirt completely. She sat up and tried to open her dress.

"Here, let me," he said, pulling the zip down in one movement and yanking it up over her head. She unclasped her bra and flung it to the side while he took off his jeans.

Lying back on the cushions, she removed her black lacy thong. He gazed at her.

"You're so perfect." He kissed her hip bone, her ribcage and then her breast.

Pulling off his boxers, he positioned himself between her legs. Kissing her deeply, he began to thrust, moving slowly and deliberately. Rosa gasped in pleasure, clutching his hair. He buried his face in her neck and moved faster, inhaling her soft skin.

"Rosa..."

She urged him deeper. Afterwards, he rested his head on her breasts, his body heavy on hers.

"Caspian?" she said softly.

"Hmmm?" He had his eyes closed.

"I love you too."

# CHAPTER SIXTY-SIX

Fionn must have fallen asleep because it was Cora who shook him awake and told him that Madison wanted to see him.

"Where is she?" he asked, disorientated.

"Back in her room."

He knocked on the door before entering. "Hey, Maddy," he said softly.

She was lying on the white pillow, her hair fanned out. Her face was pallid and her cheeks were tear-stained.

"Mads, what happened?"

She stared out the window, her lip trembling.

"Maddy," said Fionn, taking her limp hand in his. "Please tell me. I'm so worried."

She inhaled shakily. "I had an ectopic pregnancy."

"A what?"

"It's when the baby starts to grow in the wrong place. Mine was in one of my fallopian tubes." She started to cry. "They operated and removed it."

'Oh, Jesus." He stroked her hand. "Oh, Maddy, I'm so sorry."

"I never knew. I never knew that I was pregnant."

He rubbed the inside of her wrist.

"And now it's gone before I ever got a chance." She was openly crying now, her small shoulders hunched.

"Who can I call? Your mum?"

She shook her head. "No, not Mum."

"Caspian should be here soon. I can go and search for him if you like."

"No," she said dully. "It's fine."

"But he needs to know."

"Does he?" She looked up. "It's over now."

Fionn said nothing. He just rubbed her arm.

"Can you stay with me?" She looked up at him. "I don't want to be on my own."

"Of course."

"And you won't be mean to me?"

He laughed. "Now, you know I can't promise that, but I'll try."

She laughed too. "Why are you always so mean to me, Fionn? You never let me away with anything."

He shrugged. "Maybe it's the classic boy pulling the girl's pigtails in the schoolyard situation."

"Meaning?"

"Nothing." He lifted her hand to his lips and kissed it. "Now, get some rest. I won't go anywhere."

Caspian groaned and lifted his head. "I have to go."

Rosa stroked his hair. She had been expecting this.

"Maddy will be wondering where I am."

Suddenly she felt exposed so she pushed him away. Sitting up, she grabbed a cushion and positioned it in front of her breasts.

"So, go then."

"Hey, what did I say?" He moved closer and wrapped his arms around her. "Rosa?"

"This was a mistake."

"No, it wasn't." He kissed her shoulder.

She put her head in her hands. "Of course it was. You're engaged to Madison. You're living with her."

"Yes, but not for long more." He fell to his knees in front of her. "I'm going to tell her it's over. You and me, we're staying together."

"You say that now…"

"I mean it."

"Caspian, It's not as easy as all that. You're about to break her heart, destroy your life together. It's not a simple thing."

"Things haven't been right between us for ages. She knows it, I know it."

Rosa stood up and faced him. "All my life, I've been second best. With everyone I love. I can't be second best with you."

Caspian stood up too. "You won't be."

"It's all or nothing, Caspian. I can't give you anything else."

He pulled her to him and kissed her deeply. "I promise I won't hurt you."

"When will I see you again?"

"It will take me a few days to sort things out, but when I do, I'll come for you."

She buried her head in his shoulder. "You swear?"

"I swear."

Caspian got home and opened the door quietly, planning to creep in and go straight to the guest room. To his surprise, all the lights were on.

"Maddy?" he called cautiously.

Cora, who was asleep on the couch, sat bolt upright.

"Jesus!" He jumped. "Cora? Why are you here? It's two in the morning."

She stood up and straightened her dress. "Madison's in hospital."

Caspian stared at her. "What?"

"She's at the Portland."

"What happened?" He ran his fingers through his hair. "Is she okay?"

"She's okay now. We couldn't contact you."

"I left my phone at the studio."

"I'll just call John to pick you up. She's on the fourth floor. Under the name Emily Brontë."

Caspian felt his world spin. "What happened?" he asked urgently.

Cora looked at him pityingly. "You'd better ask her yourself."

Fionn opened his eyes and winced. His neck was cramped from sleeping on the armchair. Madison was wide awake, staring out the window at the misty sky.

"Hey, you." He rubbed the back of his neck and yawned. "Was I snoring?"

Madison shook her head. "Not really."

"How are you feeling?" He took her hand in his.

She started to sob. "Oh, Fionn. It's such a mess."

"I know, I know."

"I never knew. I never got a chance. Now, it's gone and I don't know how to feel."

"You're going to be fine."

"Was it my fault?" She looked at him anxiously.

"Of course not. Nature is cruel sometimes. You couldn't have known."

"Maybe it was that sushi I ate last week."

He shook his head. "That is just a bonkers thing to say."

"Really?"

"Yes! The baby grew in the wrong place. I can't really remember my Leaving Cert biology, but I'm pretty sure babies grow in wombs, not tubes."

"But why?"

"I don't know." His face softened. "Awful things happen all the time. We can't control it."

"I just feel so cheated. So empty."

"I'm so sorry."

Suddenly the door burst open and Caspian walked in with a nurse in hot pursuit.

"You are not permitted to just walk in," she shouted. "I don't care if you're Elton

John himself. You need to leave."

Caspian stopped dead when he saw Fionn. "Why the hell are you here?" he shouted.

Fionn stood up. "Maddy needed someone. You were nowhere to be found."

"Well, I'm here now." The message was clear.

"No, Fionn. Don't go." Madison clutched his sleeve.

"I have to," he said, gently removing her hand. "I'll be back in the morning."

Caspian nodded curtly at him as he walked past.

Madison looked up, her eyes wet with tears. "Where were you?" she whispered.

"What happened?" Caspian ignored her question.

Madison looked out the window. "I had an ectopic pregnancy."

Caspian swayed backwards, such was the shock. "You had what?"

She started to cry. "It's when the baby grows in the wrong place. That's why I was so sick. They operated and took it all out."

"There was a baby?" The colour drained from his face.

She nodded.

"How far along?"

"Seven or eight weeks? I don't know."

He closed his eyes. "How did it happen? We're always so careful."

"That weekend in the Cotswolds. I don't remember much about that Saturday night. It must have been then."

Caspian didn't know what to say. Rosa, their time together, his promise, all seemed like a lifetime ago. He could barely look at Madison who looked wretched: with blotchy skin and dark shadows under her eyes. She had been carrying his child. Like Mary had carried Raphael's all those years ago. And like Mary, she'd been all alone. He couldn't think. He took her hand and rubbed it.

"Where were you?" she asked quietly. "Why didn't you come home? Fionn said you left the club early."

Caspian went red. "I needed some air. I went for a walk."

"Until now? It must have some walk."

He couldn't quite meet her eyes. "I needed some headspace."

She leaned over and inhaled his neck. "Why do you smell of perfume?"

He moved backwards violently. "What do you mean?"

"You know exactly what I mean." She sat up straight, her hospital gown falling down on one shoulder. "You were with her, weren't you? With Rosa?"

"No," he lied.

"Caspian, I know you were. I know it."

"I wasn't. Christ." He got up and started to pace around the room.

"You look guilty. I know when you're lying."

He hung his head.

"Just tell me the truth," she said wearily. "Please don't lie anymore. I'm so tired of lies."

No one spoke for about a minute. The beeping of the blood pressure monitor was the only sound. Eventually Caspian looked up.

"I was with Rosa." He forced himself to look at her. "I'm sorry, Maddy."

"With her? How do you mean, with her?"

"I'm sorry," he repeated.

"We're engaged," she spat. "You put a ring on my finger and swore loyalty to me." She jabbed her chest.

"I know. I didn't mean for this to happen."

"For what to happen?" Her eyes glittered.

He inhaled sharply. "This is not the time."

"Oh, I think it's exactly the time."

"Madison, we've just lost a child. This should be about you and me."

"There is no you and me, don't you see? There hasn't been in a long time." She put her face in her hands. "I knew it. The minute you laid eyes on her, I just *knew* it."

"Knew what?"

"That she'd be the type of girl you'd want."

"That's ridiculous."

"Is it?" Her eyes flashed. "She's classically trained, beautiful, has famous parents, speaks a zillion languages. Exactly your type. God, you're so full of shit."

"Can we stop talking about Rosa?" He banged his fist against the wall. "This is about us. What has just happened."

"Please leave."

"Madison, don't do this."

"Get out."

"No."

"*Get out!*" She threw a pillow at him. "*Get the fuck out of my life!*"

Todd burst in the door with Fionn in pursuit.

"Maddy? Are you okay?" Fionn was by her side in an instant.

"No, no, no." She started to rock back and forth.

"What's wrong?" Fionn pulled her close. "What's the matter?"

"Caspian," she whispered. "Caspian and Rosa."

"What did you say?" Fionn stiffened.

Caspian pushed him aside. "You need to go, Fionn."

Madison lifted her head. "No, it's you who needs to go."

"Don't, Maddy." Tears rolled down Caspian's cheeks and he took her hands in his. "It's not just you. I've lost something too."

"Get out of my life," she said through gritted teeth. "Get out."

"Please, Madison."

"Todd!" she screamed. "Get Caspian out of here! Now!"

Todd squared up to Caspian. "You heard the lady, move."

Caspian turned to her. "Madison, tell Todd to let go of me."

"Take him away, Todd. Now!" The whole world was collapsing around her. She couldn't breathe.

Todd forcefully pulled Caspian from the room.

"Let me go," he yelled. "Todd, let me go!"

A nurse appeared. "What's going on?"

Madison started to scream. "Everyone get out! Get out!" Her screams got louder and more high pitched. Her lungs felt like they were going to burst and her heart was racing. She started to shake violently.

"Maddy! Maddy, what's wrong?" Fionn jumped up in alarm.

"Move out of the way! She's having a panic attack," said the nurse, pressing the call button. "Everyone out."

Fionn backed away. The nurse started talking to Madison, soothing her and calming her down. A doctor came running down the corridor and went straight into the room. The door slammed.

Fionn took the lift downstairs and met Todd in the foyer. "Where's Caspian?" he asked.

Todd scowled. "John has taken him home."

Fionn nodded. "Thanks."

He opened the door of a parked taxi outside. "Kensington."

The car pulled off.

# CHAPTER SIXTY-SEVEN

Caspian went straight to a bottle of whiskey and poured a huge glass.

He couldn't process the situation. Making love to another woman while his fiancée was in hospital. Swearing loyalty to Rosa when Madison was carrying his child? Now, there was no longer a child, but a gaping emotional wound that may never heal. He had never seen Madison look so heartbroken, so miserable. He had done that. He had caused all of this with his self-centred behaviour. How could he break up with her now? What kind of bastard would do that?

Rosa was at home, unaware of the terrible turn of events. She had believed him when he'd promised to come back for her. She trusted him. Now that trust would be decimated, destroyed. He couldn't be with her now. Not after this. She deserved better than him.

There was a loud buzzing noise. He knocked back the whiskey and walked to the camera screens over the door. Fionn was outside.

He pressed the intercom. "What do you want?"

Fionn looked up at the camera. "Let me in," he mouthed.

Caspian hesitated for a moment, but then allowed access.

He opened the front door and went back to the sitting room. A few minutes later, the door slammed and Fionn walked into the room.

"Where were you?" he roared.

"Don't."

"Cut the crap. Were you with Rosa tonight?"

"Leave me alone."

"What did you do?"

Caspian poured another glass of whiskey. "It's none of your business."

"Actually it is." Fionn rounded on him and grabbed the glass from his hand. "I had to step up and be there for Mads. It should've been you."

"I didn't know…"

"You went out knowing that she wasn't feeling well."

"She told me to go. She said that I needed closure." He sat down on the couch, his face contorted in pain.

"Closure?" Fionn towered over him.

Caspian rubbed his temple. "Can you please leave?"

"Were you with Rosa?"

"No."

"Say it."

"No."

Fionn yanked him to his feet. "Were you with Rosa?" he repeated dangerously, holding him by the scruff of the neck.

Caspian locked eyes with him. "What do you want me to say? None of it matters now. We lost our baby."

Fionn contemplated punching him in the face, but relented. "You're not worth it," he said, releasing him. Caspian fell back on the couch, his face etched with misery.

"Maddy's better off without you. Ever since the beginning, you've made a fool of her." Fionn headed in the direction of the door. "Well, it's over. You're not going to hurt her anymore."

Rosa woke at seven am the next morning. Her hair still smelled of sandalwood. She closed her eyes and imagined his lips on her skin. The warmth of his body as he moved inside her. She couldn't believe it. That he'd admitted his feelings like that.

She unplugged her phone from its charger and checked it for messages. The screen was blank. She felt disappointed until she remembered that Caspian didn't have his phone. He'd left it at the studio. Feeling brighter, she got up and stretched. She debated whether to have a shower, but decided to wait. She liked having his scent on her body. It made her feel closer to him. She wondered if she'd see him. Maybe he'd call around later on.

Switching on the coffee machine, she took a cup from the rack on the counter. Her cigarettes were on the table, so she took them and her coffee outside into the sunshine.

Fionn went back to the hospital first thing. Even though visiting hours were not until the afternoon, he rang Todd to sort it out. Madison was sitting up when he entered the room, drinking a cup of tea. Her eyes were puffy with dark circles underneath. Her mane of blonde hair looked lank and dishevelled.

"Morning," said Fionn warmly. "You look better."

She raised an eyebrow. "Really?"

"Yes." He sat down on the chair next to the bed. "I brought you some grapes and magazines."

"Thanks."

"I was going to bring sweets but I figured you wouldn't eat refined sugar."

She nodded. "I never eat sweets." Her voice sounded hoarse. He wondered if she'd been crying all night.

"I was thinking, can I call Clio? She could come and see you."

Madison shook her head. "I don't want anyone to know."

"Your mum?"

"No."

"Madison, you need support. You can't just go home and forget this ever happened."

"Of course I can." She tapped the teaspoon on the side of the cup. "That's exactly what I'm going to do. My schedule is jampacked. I can't afford to take time off."

"Mads…"

"I never even knew that I was pregnant. So why should anything change?"

He sighed. "You know you're being crazy, right?"

She looked up. "Why? Why, Fionn?"

"You can't just recover overnight from something like this. You need time. Your body needs time. You can't just go back to normal."

"I've told Cora to ask Caspian to leave," she said, changing the subject. "I want all traces of him gone by the time I get home."

"Maddy, is that a bit hasty?"

"No."

"Look, I'm pretty mad at him too, but he's grieving. You must talk this through."

"No, Fionn. I want him gone by the time I get out of here."

"You can't go home to an empty apartment."

"It won't be empty. I'll have Giorgio, Bethany, Mona, Cora and Angelica. John and Todd. How could someone like me ever be alone?"

"Maddy…"

"Look, I want Caspian out of my life. I don't want to see or hear from him again."

Caspian spent the night staring at the wall. His head hurt, his chest hurt. As dawn broke over the horizon, he fell asleep only to wake again when Cora arrived. She eyed him warily.

"Are you okay?" she asked.

He rubbed his eyes. "How's Maddy?"

"A bit better."

"What time can I go to see her?"

Cora reddened. "She doesn't want visitors."

"I'm not a visitor, Cora."

"She was very clear. No one is to come to the hospital."

Caspian stood up. "I'm going for a shower and then I'm heading over there."

"Caspian, she doesn't want to see you."

"I don't care."

"In fact, Todd is on his way over here to evict you."

"Evict me? Are you serious?"

She nodded. "Madison wants you out."

"Well, I'm not going." He started to pace. "I have to see her, Cora."

"I can't help you." Cora looked uncomfortable. "Madison's my boss and I do what she says."

Caspian had a quick shower and changed his clothes. This was a kneejerk reaction. She was angry. He didn't blame her for that, but he didn't deserve to be shut out completely. He needed to be with her. She was the only other person in the world who understood how he felt. He had to talk to her, to hold her. To connect with her.

They had created a life. He had right to be a part of that.

"John, take me to the hospital," he ordered. John, who was drinking a cup of tea with Cora at the kitchen table, shook his head. "I'm afraid not."

"Cora, can you call me a taxi?"

She shook her head too. "Our hands are tied."

"Christ."

In the end, he walked. The hospital wasn't far and the fresh air was therapeutic. He pushed Rosa from his mind. All he could think about was Madison and the trauma she went through alone. He didn't think he could ever forgive himself. Ever.

As he approached the hospital, he baulked slightly. He tried to put himself in her shoes and imagine how he'd feel if the roles were reversed. He'd feel disgusted, appalled. And rightly so.

Steeling himself, he continued walking up the street and through the main doors.

# CHAPTER SIXTY-EIGHT

Bethany had been working all night to keep any rumblings of Madison's hospital admission under wraps. However, when Caspian Cole arrived at the Portland at around ten the next morning, a camera phone clicked quietly as he strode in the doors. Seconds later, the photo was on Twitter and the 'likes' started to mount. It was spotted by a tabloid journalist who immediately made a few calls. Soon, there was a small group of photographers assembled across the road from the hospital. Madison's management were contacted, asking why she failed to appear at a scheduled appearance on BBC4 radio. Anonymous phone calls were made to the hospital, asking about Madison and Caspian. Patients and personnel were approached and offered huge sums of money to spill the beans. The media world woke up that morning to a breaking story and they would stop at nothing until it was exposed.

Todd was standing at the door of Madison's room when Caspian arrived.

"Don't even think about it, sir." He crossed his beefy arms.

"Look, Todd, I have to see her. Tell her that I won't leave unless she lets me in."

He shook his head. "The brief was not to let you near her."

"Then I'll wait." He sat down on a chair opposite the door. A nurse walked past and her eyes widened slightly when she saw him. Madison's room was in the VIP section of the hospital so it was no surprise to see celebrities. However, Caspian's sheer presence was dominating and soon there was a steady flow of nurses, doctors and cleaning staff walking by for a look.

The door opened and Fionn walked out. Caspian jumped to his feet.

"What the fuck are you doing here?"

Fionn eyed him coldly. "I could say the same about you."

"Maddy said she didn't want any visitors."

"She meant you."

Caspian lunged towards him but Fionn was too quick. He stalled the punch with his forearm and pushed Caspian backwards.

"She doesn't want to see you, man. I think you'd better go."
"I'm not going."
"For once, think about her and not yourself. She needs time to process what's happened. Another scene here could drive her over the edge."
"I've been told to pack my things."
"What did you expect?"
Caspian looked bleak. "I didn't expect this."
Fionn patted his back. "Go home. She'll see you when she's ready."
Caspian nodded. "Tell her I'm sorry."
Fionn shook his head. "You know I can't say that. This is between you two. Just go home."
Todd stepped forward. "I'll escort you out."
Caspian held up his hand. "There's no need." He walked away, his face cast down.

At four pm, Bethany walked purposefully out of the lift.
"Where is he?" she asked, looking around.
"Who?" asked Fionn.
"Caspian."
"He left ages ago."
She scowled. "I can't believe him sometimes."
"Why?"
"We're in the shit because Caspian doesn't think."
"What happened?"
"He was photographed walking in the main door of a maternity hospital this morning." She held up her phone to show him the picture. "Someone leaked that Madison was supposed to record *Desert Island Discs* today. People are talking as to why there's a no show."
"Ah, you need to calm down. People don't know anything; they're speculating."
"Calm down? Ross said they've been calling all morning, looking for comments. Caspian and Madison are trending."
"Trending?"
"Someone even made a photo of what the baby will look like." She held up the phone again showing a photo of a gorgeous blonde baby.
Fionn's expression hardened. "Don't let Madison see that."
Bethany put her phone in her pocket. I've already seen reels on Instagram with pictures of Madison and comments about her weight. Comparison photos, that sort of thing."
"But she's so thin," said Fionn.
"Oh, people are saying that she has a belly. They see what they want to see. One

unflattering angle is all it takes."

"What can we do?"

"I'm trying to get a super injunction. I can control the tabloids but not social media. We have to move fast."

Fionn cursed under his breath. "We must keep this from Maddy."

"How?" Bethany looked at him as if he were stupid. "The minute she gets out of here there will be a barrage of posts and comments. I think we should tell her and prepare her."

"No!" Fionn stayed firm. "She doesn't need this."

"So what do you suggest?"

Fionn threw up his hands. "I don't know."

Todd cleared his throat. "If I could make a suggestion," he said in his deep voice.

They all looked up.

Madison gingerly touched her stomach. Her whole body felt fragile, like it could shatter into a million pieces at any given moment. She couldn't remember much. They had scanned her the minute she'd arrived. The obstetrician had inserted the transducer inside her vagina to check the pelvic organs. She had flinched at the intrusion, instinctively tightening her muscles. His brow furrowed, he had moved the nozzle around purposefully. She remembered the screen. It seemed dark and the patterns didn't make much sense to her. Then they told her it was ectopic: that the foetus was growing in her fallopian tube. That she needed emergency surgery.

The world had slowed right down.

Things were hazy after that. The surgery had went well, her obstetrician told her. They had caught it just in time and saved the tube.

She started to cry silently. She'd never lost anything like that. Even though a baby hadn't been in her life plan, now that it was gone, she felt empty.

Caspian's betrayal didn't even come close to the pain she felt when she thought of her loss.

His behaviour had been inevitable. She had always known it. Deep down.

She never felt more alone in her life.

Cliona texted Fionn.

***Call me now.***

He sighed. How could he lie to his own sister?

He knocked on the door of Madison's room and opened it. She was in the exact same position as before, staring into space.

"How are you feeling?" he asked.

She shrugged.

"Clio is trying to contact you. She texted me to know where you are. I told her that you don't have your phone. She's suspicious."

Madison didn't respond.

"Mads, she's your best friend. I think you should tell her."

She shook her head. "Don't."

"She will be there to support you. You need that."

Madison started to cry. "If we talk about it, it makes it true. I don't want it to be true."

"But it is true," he said gently.

She wiped her nose with the back of her hand.

"You have so many people who love you: Clio, your parents, my mum and dad, Ross, John, Todd." He paused. "And me."

"You?" She smiled through her tears. "That's going too far."

He grinned. "Maybe just a little. Don't think for a second that I wouldn't put more chewing gum in your hair given half the chance."

She gave a shuddering sigh. "Tell her about the baby. Nothing else."

"Okay."

He walked down the corridor. There were six missed calls from Cliona and two from his mother. None from Emilia. His face hardened.

He called Cliona first.

"What the hell is going on?" she said immediately. "People are saying that Maddy's pregnant. Others are saying that she's in intensive care."

"She's okay. That's all you need to know."

"That's all I need to know? I'm her best friend, Fionn. When did you become her confidant all of a sudden?"

"She had an ectopic pregnancy. They got it in time and she should make a full recovery."

"Oh my God."

"She's really upset and doesn't want to talk to anyone."

"Yes, but her friends and family should be told. Mum rang and said that Louise Ryan is up the walls with worry. That's just not on, Fionn. She's her mother, for God's sake."

"Chat later, Clio." He hung up.

Emilia's text remained unanswered. He knew he should respond, but he couldn't focus on her right now. Not when Madison was so vulnerable. He put his phone away.

# CHAPTER SIXTY-NINE

Emilia made toast with apple and rhubarb jam. She put the plates on a tray with two cups of tea and the newspaper. She felt young again, carefree. Filled with optimism and hope.

They had barely left her bed for over two days. They'd shared a bath, just like they used to, and she'd washed his hair with her white musk shampoo.

"I like the grey," she said, sponging away the suds. "It suits you."

Fionn hadn't answered her text and all she felt was relief. She didn't want to engage with him now. Not when she was so happy. She couldn't think about anything else but the man in her bed.

She kicked opened the door and found him sitting up with half-moon glasses on his nose, reading his phone.

"How's Raphael?" he asked conversationally.

She carefully put the tray on the bed. "He's well. Canal + have signed to partly fund his next film. He's negotiating with Paramount next to seal the deal."

"We fell out, you know."

"Yes, I know." She took a bite of her toast.

"He didn't vouch for me. That time with the score."

"I'm not sure he could have done much about it."

"Of course he could have. Directors are powerful."

She said nothing.

"Rosa tells me that she stayed with him for a while."

"Yes."

"That was kind of him."

"He's a good person." She sipped her tea. "Your toast is getting cold."

Johann looked at her for a moment. "You're so beautiful, do you know that?"

She blushed. "Don't say that."

"It's true." He reached out and stroked her cheek. "My Emmy."

Prudence Cole rang her son for the tenth time. Again, it rang out. Unaware that his phone was in the studio, she started to imagine the worst. Her neighbour had sent a link to a story that had gone viral. That Caspian and Madison were having a baby, but there were complications.

"Come on, George," she said to her husband. "We're going to London."

Caspian picked up his phone. The screen was full of notifications: texts, missed calls, voice messages. Most of them were from his mother, Prue, who was clearly distraught. There were some from Louise Ryan and three from Jax. Bethany had also called and left a furious WhatsApp message about his visit to the hospital.

He rang Prue first.

"Hey, Mum."

"Caspian, where have you been?"

"I left my phone at the studios."

"I've been ringing Madison too and there's no answer. What's this story about a baby? What's going on?"

Caspian felt his chest tighten. "We lost a baby. Madison is in hospital. She had an ectopic pregnancy."

There was silence.

"We didn't know. We didn't know until it was too late."

"Oh, darling. I'm so sorry."

He started to weep silently. "Mum, I've made such a mess of things."

"I'm sure you haven't."

Caspian wiped his cheeks with his sleeve. "I have."

"Where are you now?"

"At Abbey Road."

"Well, we've just come off the M25."

"You're in London?"

"Yes. We'll come and pick you up at your place. George is just putting it into the Sat Nav now."

"I'll be about an hour."

"That's fine. We can wait."

"Thanks, Mum." He couldn't wait to see her. "Thanks so much."

Louise Ryan didn't pick up and he didn't leave a message. He didn't know how much Madison had told her. They'd never been that close. He definitely didn't want to cross the line there. Not when Madison hated him so much already.

He ignored Bethany and Jax's message was short: he wanted all of their gear moved out of the studio as soon as possible. Caspian texted Alex and Ethan. He couldn't bring himself to text Fionn.

Then, his finger hovered over Rosa's name. He could just organise for her cello to be delivered to Primrose Hill. He wasn't sure if he could face her. Not now. When he thought of her, he hated himself. He knew it wasn't fair but he couldn't help it. With all that was going on inside his head, he didn't have room to cope with what had happened between them.

He knew it was unforgivable to shut her out, but he needed to process what had happened.

.

Rosa checked her phone constantly, hoping for a message from Caspian. It felt like their night together was a dream. He hadn't been active on WhatsApp so she wondered if he'd picked up his phone from the studio. It had been almost three days: three long days. She longed to see him, to hear his voice, to touch him. To pass the time, she opened her Twitter app and started to scroll. There were articles about Salman Rushdie being stabbed and updates on the war in Ukraine. Suddenly she saw a picture of Madison and her stomach lurched. It was an old photo of her at the Met Gala. Beneath it was a celebrity gossip blog that had been posted by a fan called Pink Bubble with a headline that read:

***Maddy's Baby Shock***

Rosa clicked on the link straight away. It had another old photo of Madison leading Caspian by the hand as she walked through a crowd of photographers. She started to read.

***Madison Ryan, pop icon and fashionista, is reportedly pregnant with Caspian Cole's baby! Yes people, there's a bun in the oven. Ryan, 26, has been engaged to Cole, also 26, since 2020. A source close to the couple said that Madison is 'over the moon' and plans to have her baby at the exclusive Portland Hospital, where Duchess Meghan had Prince Archie. Only the best for our Princess of Pop.***

***Ryan's last public appearance was three weeks ago when she sang Possess Me live on Jimmy Kimmel Live. Judging by her skin tight dress, the pregnancy is in the early stages.***

***Cole was seen entering the Portland Hospital on the 15th August last. An insider said that he was attending the first ultrasound scan. The couple have refused to comment.***

***Imagine how cute their blonde baby is going to be!***

***Have they picked a name? Will there be a nod to the famous grandfather?***

***Leave some suggestions in the comments below.***

***Click to subscribe for more celebrity updates.***

***PinkBubble.com***

Rosa exited out of the article. She struggled to make sense of what she'd just read. Surely this was misinformation. Caspian and Madison having a baby? It couldn't be true. He would never have brought her home that night. It was impossible.

She checked what was trending and sure enough, Caspian and Madison or 'Madian' as they were known by fans, was trending with 123k posts. She clicked on the tweets and gasped. The photo of Caspian walking into the Portland was posted again and again. She googled the hospital. Sure enough, it was a private maternity hospital.

It couldn't be true. He promised that he'd come for her.

She bent down and picked up the phone. With a shaking hand, she called Caspian's number. It rang out so she tried again. Just as she was about to give up, she heard his voice.

"Rosa." He sounded weary.

"Is it true?"

Silence.

"Caspian, is it true? Is Madison pregnant?"

"Madison is in hospital." His voice broke. "She was pregnant but she lost it."

"What?"

"She was rushed in while I was…" He paused. "With you."

Rosa's hand flew to her mouth.

"Is she okay?"

"She'll be okay."

"Thank God."

"She asked me why I couldn't be contacted that night."

"You didn't tell her, did you?" Rosa felt nauseated.

"I didn't say the words, but she knew."

"Oh my God."

"I have a lot to sort out. I mean, this changes everything."

"Oh." She knew what was coming.

"I can't commit to anything right now. I hope you understand."

"Of course."

"I can't abandon her."

"No, no. I understand."

"I was going to tell you in person."

"There's no need."

"I'm sorry."

The line went dead.

She felt numb. It was all surreal. Lying in his arms that night felt like a dream.

Her phone pinged indicating that she had a message. It was from Caspian.

***I'm sorry.***

She burst into tears.

# CHAPTER SEVENTY

When Caspian arrived at the apartment he shared with Madison, he noticed ten boxes neatly stacked by the front door. Cora was instructing a man to carry them downstairs.

"What's going on?"

"We hired a company to come in and box up your things. We can't move the piano until Wednesday so I'd appreciate a forwarding address."

"Are you joking?"

"No." Her tone was brisk. "Madison will be coming home soon and all traces of you must be gone."

"Cora…"

"Don't shoot the messenger, okay?" She held up her hands. "I'm just doing my job."

Caspian stared in horror at his sheet music which had been stuffed into a box in no particular order. His clothes and shoes filled four more boxes, and the rest was an array of personal items such as books and records.

"She can't do this," he said in disbelief.

"It's Madison's apartment so she can." She sighed. "I can help you find alternative accommodation if you want. I'll make a few calls."

"It's fine. My parents are coming to pick me up."

"Your things will be put in storage until you have another residence. I'll email you the details."

Caspian turned around and walked out. How quickly memories can be erased. In just a few hours, all remnants of him had been removed from their home.

Prue jumped out of the car before it had a chance to stop completely.

"Hold on, woman!" shouted George.

Prue grabbed Caspian and hugged him tightly. "Are you okay?"

"Not really."

She noticed the moving van and the boxes. "What's going on?"

"Maddy's kicked me out."

"What?"
"Can I come home with you?"
Prue took a deep breath. "Of course, my darling. But what is going on?"
"It's a long story."

The next day, Rosa stared at her cello. It had been delivered first thing. She touched the slender neck lovingly, trailing her finger down the sleek maple. She knew it was strange to rely on an inanimate object, but it had never let her down. It was her comfort: when she played music, her troubles melted away. She couldn't stay in London now. She had no friends, no job, no purpose. But where could she go? Her heart ached when she thought of moving again, staring fresh. How many times had she packed her bag and travelled to a new place? She yearned for stability, for structure. She thought for one brief moment that Caspian would give her that.

Now, that was all a distant memory.

Cruel Fortuna had intervened and destroyed any chance they had. From the start, it was cursed. She should have known.

There were four unanswered texts from Nikolai on her phone. She had deliberately left them on 'read', hoping that he'd get the message.

She marched over to the drinks cabinet. Reaching inside, she felt around the back of the cupboard until she found the gin. Pulling it out, she unscrewed the cap. The smell hit her nose and she nearly gagged. Her lips touched the bottle and she lifted it up to take a gulp, but at the last moment, she stopped. It reminded her of that night she'd crashed David's car. She had been out of control, crazy. Did she want to be like that again?

She put it back in the cabinet, her heart twisted with misery.

Later that evening, she took her cello from its case and positioned it between her legs. She sat up straight with her back away from the chair, automatically remembering her music teacher's warning about good posture. With the endpin on the ground, and the cello resting against her collarbone, she lifted the bow with her right hand. Closing her eyes, she put her left hand in the middle of the strings, using her first finger to stop the string of the first fret, and drew the bow across the string in a smooth motion. Vivaldi's Cello Concerto in D Minor filled the room. Then she changed to Bach before Brahms Symphony No.3. Her arm ached from the continuous movement, but she kept going. Finally, she launched into *Another Life* and started to cry.

# CHAPTER SEVENTY-ONE

Bethany was well prepared for the day Madison left the hospital. She hired a private van with blacked out windows and arranged for it to be parked by the delivery entrance at 5.30am. Madison was asked to wear a hat with all of her hair concealed, large glasses and an overcoat. Todd shielded her as she sneaked out the door and got into the van. Cora and Bethany were already in the back, and they smiled at Madison as she strapped herself in.

"Good to see you," said Cora.

Madison took off the hat and shook out her hair. Todd got into the back with the others as he was afraid of being recognised in the passenger seat. He was frequently photographed with Madison and so was a red flag for any press or photographers hoping for a scoop. Despite the super injunction, photographs could still be published online and were likely to earn a hefty price. John drove off, manoeuvring the van expertly through the dawn traffic.

Madison put her head back against the seat rest and sighed. The doctors were pleased with her progress. There was no sign of infection and the latest scan had shown a healthy tube. They had reassured her that there was no reason why she wouldn't go on to have full-term healthy pregnancies in the future. She was due back in four weeks for a check-up, but, overall, they were happy. They told her to expect some soreness and vaginal spotting and to rest for three weeks. One midwife had been particularly kind. She knew Madison was feeling low so she took her hand and explained that the foetus could never have developed in the tube and it would have been a huge risk to her life. Even though she knew that to be true, it still didn't make it easier to accept.

The van sped along the motorway, weaving effortlessly in between trucks and family cars.

"Where are we?" asked Madison suddenly. "This isn't Kensington."

Bethany, who had been busy typing on her phone, looked up. "We felt that you'd be better getting away for a while."

"Away? I don't want to go away."

"Don't worry. It's all been organised."

"What has been organised?" She was getting angry now.

"Where better to convalesce than on a farm in Norfolk?" Bethany smiled. "Todd came up with the idea."

Todd nodded.

"Savannah's place?" Madison felt panicky. "Why are you sending me there?"

Cora rubbed her arm soothingly. "Just until things die down."

"Die down?"

"There have been rumours, some speculation."

"About?"

"You and Caspian."

Madison winced when they said his name.

"Savannah said to bring you up to her place. No one will look for you there. They'll expect you to go home to Dublin."

Madison didn't reply. She just closed her eyes and willed herself to sleep. Her head ached and all she wanted to do was go to bed.

Pozzo and Lucky started barking madly as the van approached. Savannah had just been at the chicken coop and was carrying a bowl of fresh eggs. The sun was shining on the barnyard, illuminating the rusty hoops and stakes propped against the shed.

John got out and nodded curtly to Savannah. Opening the boot, he took out Madison's bag which had been carefully packed by Cora. Todd got out and held out his arm for Madison to lean on as she emerged into the daylight.

Bethany and Cora followed, shielding their eyes from the sun.

"Good morning," said Savannah.

Madison tried to smile, but her stomach hurt and she felt sick.

"Would you like to lie down?" said Savannah in concern.

Madison's lip trembled. "Yes."

"Take her upstairs and turn right," said Savannah to Todd.

"Right? But my room is on the left."

"I've made up my room for you. It's bigger and has a nicer view."

"Oh, Savannah, there's no need..."

"Don't argue," she ordered.

Todd helped Madison inside and John followed with the bags.

"I'll be up in a minute with a cup of camomile tea," she called. Then she turned to Cora and Bethany and said in an undertone, "How is she?"

Cora looked grave. "In a bad way. She's not really talking to anyone. The nurse said she's barely eating a bite."

Bethany nodded. "We need her fighting fit as soon as possible. She needs to get back on stage and reassure the world that Madison Ryan is absolutely fine."

"I'm sorry?" Savannah looked at her. "Fighting fit?"

"Yes," went on Bethany. "Madison is a brand. She's an icon. We can't have her looking sickly and depressed. Fans will be obsessed with this story. She needs to make an appearance that will show the world that she's strong."

Cora nudged Bethany. "Let's get back in the van."

Savannah looked at Bethany coldly. "Madison is not a brand. She's a human being. She will stay here as long as she needs and she certainly will not be focusing on reassuring her fans. What nonsense."

"It's not nonsense…"

"It's codswallop. Now, if you don't mind, I'm going inside."

Bethany glared at her. "This is my job. This is what I'm paid to do. Madison appreciates how I manage her image. You'd do well to remember that."

"If Madison thought less about her image, she'd be far happier. Afraid to eat, afraid to live! Under no circumstances are you to come up here again. Madison will go back when she's ready."

"How dare you…"

"I've told her a million times to get rid of people like you." Savannah gave her a withering look.

Bethany opened her mouth to retort, but Cora pulled her away. "Bye, Savannah! Thanks." She pushed Bethany into the back of the van and pulled the sliding door.

Savannah turned on her heel and went into the house, Pozzo and Lucky by her side.

Savannah's bedroom was indeed bigger and had a double bed. The bedclothes were decorated with different breeds of dogs. Madison lay down on the bed and her eyes travelled around the room. There were lots of pictures of Savannah: on stage, on holiday, with Mick Jagger, singing with Paul McCartney, playing piano in the Royal Albert Hall. There was also a large portrait of a younger Savannah, painted by her late husband, Andreas Sharman. The large window looked out on the meadow with the orchard on the left and the aviary on the right.

Todd stood back. "Can I help you with anything else, ma'am?"

Madison shook her head. "Go back to London with John. I'll be fine here."

"London?" He looked shocked. "I'm not going that far."

"Go home, Todd," she said firmly. "I'm perfectly safe."

He hesitated for a moment, but then nodded and left the room. Madison lay back and sighed. The car journey had exhausted her.

Savannah knocked on the door.

"Come in."

The door opened and she walked in with a steaming mug of tea. "This will help you relax," she said, placing it on the bedside locker.

"Thanks."

"Are you hungry?"

Madison shook her head.

"I'm making a chicken and mushroom pie for dinner."

"That's nice."

"Cora said that you're not eating much."

"Really? I hadn't noticed."

Savannah sat down on the edge of the bed. "Have you seen Caspian?"

Madison flinched. "Don't mention that name."

"What has he done?"

She started to cry. "I don't want to talk about it."

"That's okay." Savannah squeezed her hand. "Just drink your tea and rest."

# CHAPTER SEVENTY-TWO

"I need to go to London," said Johann over breakfast.

Emilia munched on her cereal. "Oh?"

"I have to meet my agent," he continued, shaking the paper so as to read the bottom of the page.

"Your agent?"

"Yes."

"Why?"

Johann put down the newspaper. "To discuss my retirement."

"What?"

He smiled. "I'm retiring, Emmy. It's time."

"But you're so young."

"I'm sixty-five."

"Look at John Williams."

"I've made my decision."

"Well, I think you'll be a loss to the composing world." She put her hand on his arm. "A huge loss."

"I've peaked, Emmy. You saw how my last score didn't cut it. I'm past it."

"No, you're wrong."

He kissed the back of her hand. "You're too kind. Thanks for boosting an old man's ego."

"I'm not."

"I'll go to London after breakfast and be back for dinner."

"I can come with you if you want."

"Not at all. I have to check my apartment and meet my agent. Tedious to say the least."

"If you see Rosa, invite her down for dinner."

"Really?"

"Yes of course. She's family."

He sipped his coffee. "I'd prefer not to tell her about us. Not yet."

"Why?"

"Let's just enjoy each other, without anyone else taking the attention. One thing Rosa is very good at is taking attention."

"You're too hard on her."

Johann didn't reply. Instead, he kept reading the paper.

Rosa was smoking on the balcony when the front door opened and her father walked in.

"Daddy?" She dropped her cigarette and stamped on it.

"Hi, Rosa."

"I didn't know you were back."

Johann surveyed the room. "This place is a mess." He cursed in German.

"Sorry, if I'd known you were coming…"

"That's not the point. I wanted it to be kept clean regardless of my being here or not." He took off his coat. "I plan to use this place from now on."

"Oh."

"How did the recording go?"

"It's finished."

"I hope that you're not touring with that band."

"No." Her heart ached. "Definitely not."

"Good. You're a talented cellist." He walked over to the piano and touched a ringed stain with his finger. "Is this from a cup?" he shouted. "What's the rule about drinking near instruments?"

She blushed. "I'm sorry. I must've forgotten."

Johann regarded her. "Are you planning to stay in London?"

"I don't think so."

He looked relieved. "Good. This was never a long term arrangement."

"I know, Daddy."

"Where will you go?"

"Florence."

"To Cassandra?" He looked incredulous.

"Well, I can't impose on Raphael again. My options are few."

"If you're going to Italy, I'll give you the number of my great friend, Fabrizio. He worked with Morricone. He might have an opening for you in Verona."

"Really?"

"But you must take it seriously. I've put my neck out for you so many times."

"I know, I know."

"If you screw this up…"

"I promise I won't." She crossed her heart. "I've changed, Daddy. I want to do well."

He opened his arms. "Give me a hug. It's been so long."

She ran into his embrace and clung to him. "Thank you."

He kissed her forehead. "Make me proud, Rosa. That's all I ask."

Emilia was making a toasted cheese sandwich when Alfie walked in.

"Emmy! Where have you been hiding? I thought we were going to work on that Yeats score?"

She tried to close the lid on the machine but the bread was too thick. "Yes, I know. I'm sorry. Things have been crazy."

"Is your boyfriend here?"

She went pink. "Not exactly."

"Not exactly? Do tell." He took an apple form the fruit bowl and bit into it.

"Fionn and I, well, we're over."

"Quelle surprise." He rolled his eyes. "I'm sensing that he's been replaced. Who's the lucky guy?"

"Johann." She didn't dare look at him.

"Say again?"

"Johann. He turned up here last week, out of the blue, and we've been together since."

Alfie nearly choked on the apple. "You're kidding me. Say you're joking."

"Why?"

"You do remember how he treated you, don't you?"

"He's different now. He's older, less flighty."

"Listen to yourself, Emmy. Once a creep, always a creep."

"That's just not true."

Alfie threw the apple in the bin. "I can't believe you let him back into your life."

"Why not?"

"He doesn't respect you."

"Shut up."

"Wait for it, he'll break your heart."

"Get out!" She pushed him backwards. "Get out now!"

"Emmy!"

"You're always interfering. Always telling me what to do. Well, I don't need you anymore. I'm a big girl."

"Fine." He straightened his shirt. "I'll go."

Her chest heaved with emotion.

"But mark my words, he'll hurt you." Alfie shook his head. "Without a doubt."

"Get out!" she shouted, slamming the door. Turning around, she put her back against the wooden panelling before sliding down onto the tiled floor. Holding her knees, she started to sob.

# CHAPTER SEVENTY-THREE

Madison stayed in bed for days, preferring to blot out reality. Savannah cooked delectable meals, but the plates returned untouched. There was an emptiness, a loneliness that she couldn't shake. The world seemed dreamlike with no sense of time.

Then, slowly, she started to recover. She began to enjoy the delicious food that Savannah made: moussaka made from homegrown aubergines one day, wild mushroom risotto the next. Eating regularly made her stronger and soon she was out on the farm, breathing in the fresh air and helping with the chores. There was no heavy lifting, the doctor had been clear about that, but she could gather the eggs from the chickens while they were still warm, and pick the apples from the trees. Every day they would walk down the garden and around the field. Blackberries dotted the hedgerows, ripe and luscious. Savannah would pick them and pop them in her mouth, much to Madison's horror.

"You could be eating slugs! At least wash them first."

"I always loved Seamus Heaney's description of blackberries," said Savannah, ignoring her. "A glossy purple clot. How wonderful is that?"

Savannah taught her how to play chess and the games went on for hours. Sometimes they talked about the old days, when Savannah was touring around the world. Madison listened, wide-eyed, about wild nights with Stevie Nicks and jamming with Bob Dylan.

"How did you give it all up?" she asked Savannah one night.

"It's an empty life, making you think you're the centre of the universe, when you're really just a pawn."

"I wish I could leave it all behind."

"So, why don't you?"

"I want to release our album. I'm proud of it."

"Well, in that case we'd better finish it then."

So, they went back to the piano, practising the original songs for hours. Madison sang with all of her heart, and often cried while doing so. Savannah told her to write down her feelings.

"You should keep a journal," she advised. "I kept one for years. I'd write random thoughts, feelings, peeves. It was great raw material for songs later on."

Madison did as she was told. She found it difficult at first, writing down her innermost thoughts, but then it became addictive. Cathartic. Verbalising her emotions was powerful and reassured her that everything was going to be okay.

One day in the second week, an Uber pulled up in the yard. Pozzo and Lucky heard it first and barked the house down.

"Who could that be?" said Savannah in annoyance. "I hate uninvited visitors."

"It's not journalists, is it?" said Madison fearfully. "Have they found me?"

Savannah reached behind the larder door and pulled out a shotgun. "Leave it to me," she ordered, walking outside.

The driver's eyes widened when he saw Savannah emerge holding the gun menacingly.

"Bloody hell, mate. Hurry," he shouted.

Fionn got out of the car and it sped off down the drive with Pozzo and Lucky racing after it.

"Whoa, whoa, I come in peace,' said Fionn, holding up his hands.

"Who are you?" shouted Savannah.

"Fionn O'Connor. A friend of Madison's."

"Fionn?" said Madison in delight, bolting out of the house and straight into his arms. "It's so good to see you," she said, hugging him close. "How did you find me?"

"I have my ways," he said, grinning.

She took his hand and led him to Savannah.

"Savannah, this is Fionn. I've known him since I was little."

"What brings you here unannounced?" Savannah lowered the gun.

"I wanted to check if she was okay." He squeezed her hand. "I can see that she is."

"Come inside," said Madison, beaming. "We've made lentil and lemon soup for lunch." She turned to Savannah. "You don't mind if Fionn stays for lunch, do you?"

"Of course not. Come inside."

They walked into the house, and Fionn had to duck slightly as the ceilings were so low. The soup was bubbling on the Aga and fresh yeast bread was cooling on the wire rack.

"Your house is lovely," he said admiringly. "When was it built?"

"The 1830s," she answered. "It was a tenant's house on the estate nearby which is now part of the National Trust. Some earl lived there."

"My parents live in a Victorian house too. Mum calls it a money pit as there's always maintenance to be done."

"Yes, I agree with that." Savannah took out three bowls from the dresser. "Where do your parents live?"

"Dublin."

"Fionn plays drums in Doctor Eckleburg," said Madison quietly.

"Ah, I see." Savannah put the salt and pepper mill on the table. "Who knows that you're here?"

"No one," he said immediately. "I got an Uber straight from my apartment. I didn't even tell my sister."

"His sister is Cliona, my best friend," explained Madison. "Has she been asking about me?"

Fionn nodded. "Everyone thinks that you've gone back to Dublin. She's dying to talk to you but understands that you're not ready."

"I feel bad for shutting her out."

"Sometimes it's all you can do."

She bit her lip. "Have you seen Caspian?"

Fionn shook his head. "He's gone AWOL too. We think he might have gone home."

"To Banbury?"

He nodded. "Jax wants us to meet the tour manager, but Caspian won't answer his calls."

"Where's Rosa?" She forced the words out.

Fionn accepted a slice of bread from Savannah. "No one knows. She left the band group chat without explanation."

"How do you know Caspian's not with her?" Her heart felt sore.

"I don't," he said gently, "but someone said he's up with Prue and George."

She took a shaky breath. "I shouldn't care, but I do."

"Of course you do. It's only natural."

"The thought of them together..."

"Don't think about it." He buttered his bread and took an enormous bite. "Wow, this is yum."

Savannah, who had been listening intently to the conversation, smiled. "There's plenty more so eat up."

After lunch, Fionn and Madison went for a walk. The breeze had picked up and she shivered, pulling her cardigan tightly around her.

"When will you be back?" he asked casually.

"Soon. I need to get back to normal. Plus that première is coming up."

"Doctor Eckleburg is in crisis. We were living in one another's pockets for months, rehearsing, recording, and now? Nothing. The album has been mixed and mastered, and Caspian isn't around to approve it. Jax was hoping to release the album soon to harness the Christmas trade, but it doesn't look likely."

"The hard work is done, surely."
"Yes, but we have to make music videos and plan a tour. It's only the beginning."
"It's going to be weird between us now that Caspian and I are over."
"Why would it be weird?"
"Awkward then."
"The band is my job, that's all. My personal life is separate." He pulled her to him and hugged her. "My loyalty is to you, Maddy Ryan."
She let him hold her, feeling calm and safe. "Did we ever think we'd see the day?" she said into his chest.
"What do you mean?"
She looked up. "That we'd be friends. Like, real friends."
"I was always your friend." He looked mock-wounded.
"Yeah right, you were such a meanie to me."
"It was a sign of affection." He pushed a lock of her hair behind her ear. "Come on, let's get back."
She linked arms with him and smiled. "Tell me all the gossip from home. I'm sure your mum has been ringing you with all the news."
"Well, you've been the main subject of conversation to be honest."
"Me?"
"Louise rings Mum all the time. She really wanted to come and stay with you."
Madison went red. "I must seem like an awful person."
"No," said Fionn carefully. "It's just she's your mum and it's natural for her to want to help you."
"We don't see eye to eye most of the time. I couldn't handle that. Not when I was so low."
"How about we go home to Dublin soon and visit? You and me. We can go for pints in Dalkey, have dinner with Mum and Dad, and spend time with your parents."
"I'd love that." She really meant it.
"Good. Now we'd better get back or she might shoot us."

Fionn left at five.
"You mind yourself, okay?" He hugged Madison tightly. "We're all there for you when you come back to the real world."
"I know." She kissed his cheek. "I'll be back soon."
"You seem so different here," he said thoughtfully. "You eat bread and cheese and apple pie. I swear I haven't seen a carb pass your lips since 2002."
"Shut up," she said mildly.
"What I mean is, this way of life suits you. You should retire and buy a farm."

"I'd be a terrible farmer."

"I don't know. I could see you driving a combine harvester."

"Stop being silly."

He leaned in to kiss her cheek, but swerved slightly and kissed her lips instead. "I'll see you soon."

And then he was gone. The car drove off, leaving a confused Madison standing immobile in the yard. It must have been a mistake, to kiss her like that. Did he stumble? She wasn't sure.

She walked into the house to find Savannah seated at the table topping and tailing some green beans.

"Fionn just left," she said, taking an apple from the bowl.

"He seems like a nice boy," said Savannah, throwing the ends in a bucket. "Very cheerful."

"That's just Fionn," she said with a shrug. "He's always like that."

"You seem very close."

"Oh, we're not really. I mean, he's always teasing me and making me look stupid. Lately though he's been nicer." She thought of the kiss and reddened slightly. "I suppose it's because of all that's happened."

"Hmmm." Savannah smiled knowingly.

"What's for dinner?"

"Venison with poached pears and a green bean salad."

"I'm going to miss your food when I go."

"I can teach you some recipes."

"Me?" Madison laughed. "I never cook. Giorgio does it."

"Then maybe you should learn." She threw the last bean into the steamer. "Food is life. My whole day revolves around what I'm going to eat."

"My whole day revolves around how I look."

Savannah smiled. "I see that you're getting back to normal."

# CHAPTER SEVENTY-FOUR

Emilia woke early and left the bed quietly. She had thought of a melody and she had to play it. She crept down to the piano and started to play. She was still playing when Johann walked into the room two hours later.

"I missed you," he said.

"Sorry, I just had to write it down."

"Is this an original piece?" he asked, peering over her shoulder.

She nodded. "It's for Raphael's new film."

"Ah, yes. The one about Yeats. I've heard about that."

"Do you really like it?" She turned around on the stool.

He smiled. "Wonderful. I wish I could've written something like that myself."

"You've written far better scores."

"Not for years." He played a few notes with his right hand. "I just wish I could go out with a bang. Write a score that will be my legacy."

Emilia rubbed his arm. "You should say it your agent. Surely there's something out there."

Johann's face was impassive.

"Your swansong," she said lovingly and she started to play the same tune again.

He watched her fingers flying up and down the keys. "I'll make some tea," he said, ruffling her hair.

Caspian sat in his father's armchair, his face sombre. The cup of tea Prue had made lay untouched on the coffee table. She always added too much milk and he didn't have the heart to tell her.

Bethany had managed to keep the story out of the papers and for that he was grateful. Losing a baby was a private affair; no one needed to read about it in *The Daily Mail.* He loathed that side to fame: the one where you were fair game for the public to judge, ridicule or scorn. Yes, he wrote songs and performed for thousands of people, but he was also a human being.

Prue put a china plate of Hobnobs on the table. "Your favourite," she said softly.

Caspian tried to smile. "Thanks, Mum."

"Any word from Madison?"

He shook his head. "She's gone off the radar for a while. It's probably best until the speculation dies down."

"What will you do?"

"I'll go back to London. Find a new place to live."

"Can you salvage the relationship?"

He stared into space.

Prue pressed on. "I'm fond of Maddy, I've always been fond of her. But from what you've told me, you haven't been happy for a while."

He looked up. "I betrayed her. I knowingly made a choice and slept with someone else. That makes me an absolute bastard."

"Yes, but why did you do it?" She took his hand. "Why did you make that choice?"

"I couldn't get Rosa out of my head."

"Why?"

"Because I'm…"

"Yes?" Prue waited.

"I'm in love with her."

Prue sat back. "There you have it."

"Yes, but I can't be with Rosa now. Not after all of this."

"That's your choice, darling. Staying away from that girl may ease your guilt, but ultimately it won't bring back that child or save your relationship with Maddy. That was brokena long time ago." She stood up. "The first thing you need to do is to find Madison and talk to her. You need to tell her the truth. She deserves that."

"They won't let me near her."

"They will in time. Let the dust settle a bit." She looked out the window. "Then tell Rosa how you feel. If you love her, then don't let her go."

"I can't, Mum. You don't understand. She's fragile, more fragile than most. I've really hurt her and who's to say I won't do it again? I love her too much to risk it."

"Love is a risk, Caspian. No one knows how it will turn out. You've got to take a chance."

"I can't think about it. Not now." He crumbled the Hobnob with his fingers. "Rosa is better off without me. What kind of life would we have together? One where I'm on the road and she's at home?"

"Anyone you love will have to put up with that."

"Yes, but she's not that type of girl. She needs stability. Someone who will be there every morning when she wakes up. She never had that, you see. She's been let down so many times."

Prue sighed. "That's not your fault."

"Yes, but I promised her that I'd come back for her. I swore that I'd sort things out and come back."

"You weren't to know."

"Can you imagine the media storm when it gets out that Maddy and I have split? The press will be out for blood. I can't do that to Maddy: to be seen with another woman so soon after what's happened. She deserves more." He frowned. "Rosa would be hounded. They'd dig up everything they could about her. I can't expose her to that. She has to be protected."

Rosa heaved her cello out of the taxi. She had sent her clothes and belongings ahead of her with DHL, stating her mother's address for delivery. She had also texted Cassandra and warned her of her imminent arrival. The text she got back informed her that Cassandra was in Moscow and would be back in a few days.

The airport was busy as she queued at the check-in desk. A school tour was ahead of her: fifty excited teenagers on the way to Florence. The flight attendant checked them in as a group but they had to show their passports to get their boarding cards. She waited patiently as they filed up to the desk, brandishing their IDs and chatting excitedly.

She had booked a separate seat for her cello, just like she always did. She never checked it in: she couldn't bear it if something happened to it. She had read horror stories about celli in the baggage compartment. Going through airport security always took longer, but she didn't mind. She had a window seat for the instrument and a middle seat for herself. That way no one could damage it and it didn't obstruct any passengers.

When she landed at Amerigo Vespucci airport, Cassandra had instructed her driver to be there waiting. They loaded the cello into the backseat and she got in the front. The driver was friendly and they chatted the whole way into the city. It had been ages since she'd used her Italian. Speaking it gave her a sense of identity; a sense of pride. Maybe Italy would be the answer: maybe this would be a new beginning where she could leave behind her troubles, once and for all.

Cassandra's home was a magnificent penthouse on the Piazza Della Santissima Annunziata, a historic Florentine palazzo built in 1574. It had eighteen bedrooms and was only a short walk from the Santa Maria del Fiore cathedral where Cassandra sang hymns each Christmas. Rosa arrived and greeted the cleaner who had just finished mopping the beautiful mosaic floors. Her bedroom had been prepared with fresh sheets and towels, and a vase of pink lilies had been left on the dresser. She went out to the little balcony and lit a cigarette. The sun was hot so within a minute under its glare, she had to seek shade under the stone architrave of the French windows.

She had a meeting with Fabrizio the next morning. Soon she would be back in an orchestra, playing to packed auditoriums. Her session with Doctor Eckleburg seemed like months ago. It had certainly been lucrative; she had paid off her debts and still had enough left over to live comfortably. However, Caspian and all that followed would haunt her for years to come.

She felt cold, paralysed. Maybe because she was so accustomed to being cast aside. She had blocked his number on her phone. She didn't want the temptation of calling him or texting him. She needed to make a clean start. She'd also deleted Instagram, Twitter and TikTok, terrified that she'd see posts about him and Madison. The timing always seemed wrong with every man she'd been with. There were always obstacles, always reasons why she was never put first. She had believed that Caspian was different. That their relationship was special, unlike any she'd had before. But now their union was forever tainted by what had happened that night.

What had he said?

*I'm sorry?*

She blew a perfect smoke ring.

She was done with love. Finished. The fates had sent her numerous signs. She was not cut out for relationships. Caspian was the last straw in series of disastrous attempts.

She took the high speed train to Verona the next day. Fabrizio Frino was the leader of the Arena di Verona orchestra and choir which was based in The Verona Philharmonic Theatre. After an hour and a half she arrived at Verona Porta Nuova. She hailed a taxi outside the main door.

"*Teatro Filarmonico, por favore.*"

The car sped off.

One of the oldest theatres in Verona, The Teatro Filarmonico was designed by the famous architect, Francesco Galli da Bibbiena. Rosa paid the taxi driver and stepped out onto the pavement. The main entrance was through an internal courtyard. She walked up the path and through the imposing neoclassical façade with tall Doric columns.

The horse-shoe shaped theatre with its golden opulent interior had a chandelier, ornate tiers of boxes decorated with gold leaf, and red velvet drapes and seats.

Fabrizio Frino, a small man in his seventies with a balding head and thick glasses, was standing on the main stage.

"Rosa Weber." He peered at her over his glasses. "Welcome."

"Hello." She gazed at the auditorium.

"Your father spoke highly of you."
"Well he's desperate that I get a job."
He laughed. "Well, we'll see about that. Will you play something?"
She nodded.
"The cello is over there."
"I'm going to play an excerpt from Prokofiev's Sinfonia Concertante."
"An excerpt? That's a relief. It's quite long."
"Too long," she said with a smile. "A test of endurance." Taking the cello, she positioned it between her legs and tuned it. Raising the bow, she began to play.

Later that night, after a bowl of linguine, she sat out on the balcony and smoked a cigarette. Fabrizio had offered her a job as second chair. It was a demotion, she had always been the principal cellist, but she was grateful that he'd hired her at all. If she worked hard and impressed him, she would progress to first chair eventually.

Isabelle texted her, asking if she would look after Anouk while she and Raphael went to London for the première. They wanted her to come to Amiens as it would be a familiar environment for Anouk. She agreed straight away. Isabelle booked a flight immediately and sent on the details.

The thought of seeing Anouk made her happy. She wondered if she'd remember her.

Automatically she thought of the tomato sauce on the white Benetton dress and her heart felt sore.

She called Johann and told him the good news.
"Wonderful," he said in relief. "When do you start?"
"Two weeks."
"Make it count."

The next day she went for a walk down by the river, wrinkling up her nose at the stench of the dried up riverbank. The incessant sun caused the Arno to evaporate and the resulting sludge smelled horrible. The Ponte Vecchio looked the same as it did the last time she walked past. She bypassed tourists posing by the wall overlooking the famous bridge, and headed in the direction of the Museo Galileo. When she reached the Piazza della Signoria, she paused in front of the statue of Fortuna. The impassive stone face stared out beyond her, focused on a point in the distance, far out of anyone's reach.

By the time she got home, the sun's heat had lessened. Her skin was already turning golden brown, even though it had only been a couple of days. Cooped up inside all summer with the band, she'd rarely been out in the sun.

She walked into the cool atrium of the apartment and noticed three large Louis

Vuitton cases near the wall.

"Mamma?" she called.

Cassandra emerged from the kitchen, dressed in black with a red belt, and a huge diamond bracelet on her wrist.

"*Rosa, tesoruccia,*" she said in her thrilling voice. She opened her arms and pulled Rosa close.

"You're home early."

"*Si, si.* I wanted to see you."

"You did?"

"*Si.*" She linked arms with her. "Come, we will have a *caffè freddo* on the terrace. I want you to meet my new lover. He's American." She pointed to a young black man in a hat sitting at the garden table. "Rosa, this is Jamal. Jamal, my daughter, Rosa."

Jamal stood up. "Good to meet you, Rosa." He smiled broadly and held out his hand. She shook it and sat down.

"Jamal is a jazz musician," said Cassandra. "I saw him play in New York. Oh Rosa, he's *meraviglioso.*"

"I'm sure," said Rosa.

"Your mamma here asked me to come to Italy. First time I've been."

"Wait until you see the Duomo," said Cassandra, kissing his hand lovingly. "I can't wait to show you my country."

"If you girls don't mind, I might go and change." He stood up.

"Of course."

"See you later." He lifted his hat in salute and walked off.

"*Mamma,* how long have you know him?"

"Eight days. Isn't he wonderful?"

Rosa poured some coffee onto ice cubes. "He seems nice but it's all very fast."

"At my age, you don't wait around. Also, I would appreciate if you left him alone."

"Meaning?"

"You know what I mean."

"*Mamma!*"

"Well, I have to say it." Cassandra sat back. "How have you been, *bella?* You seem sad."

Rosa stirred some sugar into her coffee. Her mother, despite her absenteeism and general neglect, had excellent emotional intelligence and always knew when she was upset.

"I'm fine."

"Don't lie to your mamma."

"I really am. I got a new job with the Arena di Verona in the Teatro Filarmonico."

"How lovely. I sang there last year for the Settembre dell'Accademia."

"Daddy rang this man called Fabrizio…"

"Fabrizio Frino."

"And he was really nice. I got second chair."

"You will progress to first in no time." She smiled. "Do you know that a very young Mozart gave a concert in the Sale Maffeiana and the audience was astounded by his talent? It was called the Sala Grande back then."

"Is it that old?"

"*Si, si.* Hundreds of years. It burnt down in the 18th century and was bombed in the war, but is still going. Reconstructed of course, but still with the essence of the original *teatro.*"

Jamal arrived back, minus the hat, wearing shorts and a t-shirt. "What time is dinner, Cass? I'm starving."

"Soon. We're having gnocchi."

Rosa finished her coffee. "I can go out and give you some space."

"Not at all." Cassandra squeezed her hand. "Let's eat together and talk."

The chef made gnocchi with mushrooms and thyme leaves. Cassandra kept the table entertained with her stories of her travels. As Rosa watched her gesticulate, her face animated and warm, she felt so cheated. Her mother was so enchanting, the life and soul of any gathering, but she always just out of her reach. She was never someone she could call her own. She belonged to the world.

When Cassandra produced the limoncello, Kamal stood up. "I'm beat, you guys. I'll call it a night."

Cassandra kissed him passionately on the lips. "I will be up soon."

Rosa watched her fill two small glasses with the yellow liqueur.

"I'm glad your father helped you," said Cassandra, handing her the drink. "I didn't agree when he abandoned you like that."

Rosa closed her eyes briefly. Of course she would blame Johann. All her life her parents had competed, both shirking responsibility by holding the other accountable.

"Your father will never change. He's selfish."

"You're one to talk," said Rosa bitterly.

"Rosa!"

"Well, it's true. Yes, Daddy was awful to me after Southbank, but at least he was there. You disappeared, you didn't even answer my messages."

"I'm not good with phones."

"You've never been there for me. I sometimes wonder why you had children at all."

"I love you, Rosa. I love Stefan too."

"Oh, please."

"I do, *carissima.* I love you madly. It's just I love my art. My purpose on this earth is to create art. In order to do this, I have to be selfish. I have to devote my energy to music."

"Do you ever listen to yourself?"

"Rosa, you're an adult now. You understand that life is complicated. That sometimes we are not the people we set out to be. I realised early on that I was not a mother who would stay at home and be content. I had to go out and make music, to bring joy to people with my voice. God gave me this talent to share, not to hide away." She downed her limoncello. "If Johann had left home to work or to go on tour, no one would have judged him because he's a man. I, however, have been vilified for such an act."

"We needed you."

"I know."

"So why didn't you come home?"

"I have regrets. I won't lie and say that my heart did not break sometimes. But that is then and this is now. I would like us to move on."

Rosa stood up. "There is a hole in my life that can never be filled. You did that." She put her chair back under the table. "I'm going to bed and I fly to France tomorrow."

"France?"

"Yes. After that, I'll move to Verona. Night, Mamma."

"Rosa, please."

Rosa didn't look back.

# CHAPTER SEVENTY-FIVE

Fionn knocked on Emilia's front door. He had practised what he wanted to say on the car journey south. How it was probably best if they cooled things down for a while as he was expecting to go on tour soon. It was a white lie, but necessary. He didn't want to hurt her.

He took his key out of his pocket, but hesitated. Since their fight, he didn't feel like he had a right to just barge into her house. Yet he had come to sort things out and that was just what he would do. Opening the door, he stepped into the gloomy hall. A lack of natural light and the tiled floor rendered it a cold space. Funny that he had never noticed that before. He walked into the kitchen to find a much older man with grey hair sitting at the table who looked up at him with a quizzical look.

"Hello?"

"I'm looking for Emilia." Fionn took in the man's attire: boxers and a t-shirt. He was barefoot too, with dishevelled hair.

"She's upstairs. How did you get in here?"

Fionn held up his key.

"Why do you have a key?"

"Wait a second, who are you?" said Fionn who was getting a bit irked.

"Rather the question should be, who are you?" Johann put his glasses on and regarded him haughtily.

Fionn opened his mouth and shut it again. What was his status now? It felt facetious to say 'boyfriend'. Emilia never liked that term.

"I'm a friend of Emilia's."

"You must be a close friend if you have a key."

"I am. Well, I was."

Johann nodded. "I'll just call her."

Fionn walked to the door. "No need. I'll go up myself."

Johann stood up and pulled his sleeve. "Best not." He walked out into the hallway and shouted for Emilia to come down.

"She's coming," he announced, resuming his seat at the table.

Fionn glowered at him but waited where he was. Emilia came through the door a few minutes later wearing a silk robe and no shoes. Her hair was tousled and she had no makeup on.

"Fionn!" She stopped dead. "Why are you here?"

"You said you wanted to talk."

"I thought you'd text first." She pulled the robe tightly around her.

"Introduce me to your guest."

"Of course." She blushed. "Johann, this is Fionn. Fionn, this is Johann Weber."

Fionn's eyes widened. "Rosa's dad?"

Johann held out his hand. "Yes, Rosa's dad. Do you know my daughter?"

"She played cello on our new album."

"Oh, you're in that band. Doctor something."

"Doctor Eckleburg. I'm the drummer."

Fionn made eyes at Emilia to follow him into the sitting room.

"I'll be just a minute," she said to Johann, closing the door behind her.

Fionn was standing by the fireplace. "Is that your film composer? The one who broke your heart?"

Emilia nodded. "I'm sorry. I didn't mean for you to find out like this."

"Are you two together now? Is that it?"

She nodded again. "We have a big history. He showed up here and it was like the old days. I'm sorry. I like you too much to lie to you."

Fionn exhaled loudly. "Well, I certainly didn't expect to find a man in your kitchen."

Emilia bit her lip. "I'm mortified."

Fionn walked over and hugged her. "I'm happy for you."

She looked up at him in shock. "You are?"

"Yes." He kissed her forehead.

"You're not angry?"

He smiled. "Well, a bit miffed that I've been usurped by a pensioner, but I'll live."

Emilia laughed. "Hey now, don't be ageist."

"You know I'm not ageist." He grinned. "It was really fun, Emmy. I'll never forget our time together."

"Nor I."

"I'll just give you this." He put the key in her hand. "Good luck."

She leaned up and kissed him softly. "Good luck to you too."

Fionn's taxi pulled up outside his apartment building. He got out and tipped the driver.

"Thanks, have a good night." The car drove off.

He walked towards the front door and stopped. Caspian was lounging in the doorway, his hood up.

"Jesus Caspian, you frightened me."

"Sorry. Can I come up?"

Fionn took his key out of his pocket. "Come on."

Fionn's apartment was on the second floor. He opened the door and gestured for Caspian to come inside. The living area was neat and tidy with a pleasant aroma of lavender.

"Mum is obsessed with Max Benjamin diffusers," Fionn explained. "She sends me one every month." He threw his keys on the table. "How have you been?"

Caspian took down his hood. He looked exhausted. "I'm okay. I've been up in Banbury for the past while."

"Jax is looking for you."

"I know." He sat down. "I'm trying to find an apartment."

"Pay someone to do that. You can afford it." Fionn sat on the chair opposite him. "Why did you call over?"

"I need to see Maddy."

Fionn frowned. "I'm not sure if that's ..."

"I have to see her." Caspian cut him off.

"She's in a good place now. Seeing you will only bring it all back."

"I need to see her. Tell me where she is."

Fionn stood up and walked to the window. "I promised."

"Please, Fionn."

He turned around. "She's at Savannah's place."

Caspian stood up. "Thank you."

Caspian called John and asked him to drive him to Savannah's farm.

"You know I can't do that."

"Please, John. This is important."

"Our brief is total privacy."

"Please."

In the end, John relented. Caspian sounded desperate and he remembered the pain when his wife had a miscarriage in the late nineties. He wasn't even factored into the grieving process as the whole thing was brushed under the carpet.

When Todd heard about it, he insisted on going too, just in case there was any hassle.

The car pulled up in the late afternoon. Savannah and Madison were practising a new song at the piano: a song Madison had penned about the end of a relationship. Todd banged on the front door and Savannah scowled.

"Who could that be?" she muttered, getting up and walking out into the hall.

Madison practised her scales, loosening her voice even more to hit the high notes.

The door opened. "Who is it?" she asked, not looking up.

"It's me," came a familiar voice.

Madison's head shot up. Caspian stood in the doorway, his face drawn and pale.

"You." She felt winded. "Why are you here?"

"I need to see you. To talk to you."

"There's nothing to say."

"Maddy, there's plenty to say."

"Really? From where I'm standing, you couldn't care less about me."

"That's not true."

"Then why were you with her? When I was at home, sick in bed?"

"I don't know. I didn't plan it."

"Bullshit. You made a choice."

"Look, I'm not here to fight. I want us to talk about the baby."

"There was no baby. Just a small blob of cells."

"Don't say that."

"It was cursed from the beginning, growing in a place where it couldn't thrive. Reminds me of our relationship."

"Don't say that."

She held up her hand. "I'm not wearing your ring. Did you even notice?"

He nodded.

"I'm not wearing it because it's a mockery. It is a symbol of your deceit. How you led me along and had no intention of marrying me."

Caspian sighed. "I did, Maddy. When I proposed to you, I had every intention of marrying you. I love you."

"But you're not in love with me. The usual story."

"We're just so different, you and I. We're opposites."

"Why? Because I'm shallow and my music is commercial?"

"No. That's not it."

"Then what?" She rounded on him and started to punch his chest. "You make me feel so worthless. I can never forgive you for that." He grabbed her wrists and held them still. She was crying now, her face wet with tears.

"Maddy, I'm so sorry."

"It's too late. Everything you say means nothing."

He pulled her head onto his chest and stroked her hair. "I'm sorry," he repeated.

She sobbed into his t-shirt, her body convulsing. "We could've had it all, Caspian. We could've been so happy."

He kissed her hair.

"What's wrong with me?"

"There's nothing wrong with you," he said sternly. "You're amazing."

"Then why did you betray me?" Her blues eyes looked up at him.

He sighed. "I never meant to hurt you. I know that sounds stupid, but I didn't."

She walked to the window and stared out at the diseased ash trees. What was it Savannah had said? Ash dieback? They had no future, no hope.

"You know, you never wrote a song about me. Not once."

He said nothing.

"Last night, I was thinking about what our baby would've been," she continued, wrapping her arms protectively around herself. "A musician? An actor? Something creative anyway."

He smiled sadly. "It would have been beautiful. Blonde with blue eyes like you."

"Beautiful," she echoed. She turned to face him. "But it was never meant to be."

They stared at each other.

"Goodbye, Caspian."

"Maddy, I want…"

She put her finger to her lips. "Ssssh. Don't say anything else. Just go."

He looked torn. "I'll miss you." He turned to leave. At the door, he looked back. "I really loved you, you know."

She wiped away her tears. "I know."

And then he was gone.

Savannah left her alone for a while, but then knocked on the door.

"Madison?" she called.

"Come in."

Madison was sitting by the piano, her face red from crying.

"He's gone," she stated.

"I guessed as much."

"It's over."

Savannah nodded.

"I thought I'd feel worse to be honest."

"Oh?"

"In a weird way, it's a relief. Isn't that strange?"

"Not at all."

"I mean, I spent so long worrying about how he felt and feeling unimportant because he wouldn't set a date, and now I don't have to care about that anymore." She played a tune on the piano with her right hand. "I'm back to being me. Not someone's girlfriend or fiancée, but just me."

"How does it feel?"

"Liberating."

"Come on, let's have a cup of tea." Savannah gestured for her to follow.

"I'm going to go home," said Madison, taking a seat at the table. "I need to get back to work."

"Are you sure?"

"Yes. It's been long enough. I have to reconnect with my life. My everyday routine."

"It might be difficult, now that you and Caspian are finished. That will attract a lot of attention."

"Bethany will know what to do. That's what I pay her for."

"Just take it slowly," Savannah warned. "You need to take care of yourself."

# CHAPTER SEVENTY-SIX

When they got back to London, Caspian asked John to take him straight to The Forge.

Todd shook his head fervently. "We're not your taxi service."

"Leave it," said John.

When they pulled up outside, Caspian noticed a few fans waiting by the door. He glanced to the right and saw a lone paparazzo smoking a cigarette. He couldn't comprehend these celeb-hungry photographers, desperate for the scoop. How dare they feel they had the right to showcase the most vulnerable moments of people's lives.

"Keep driving, John,' he said wearily.

"Where to?"

"Banbury, please."

Todd turned around in his seat. "We are not obliged to drive you anyplace, sir. I thought I made that clear."

"Leave it, Todd," said John, indicating out onto the street.

Caspian picked up his phone and dialled Raphael's number. He answered on the third ring.

"Caspian, how are you?"

"I'm well. I just wanted to call and tell you that Maddy and I broke up."

"I have to admit that I heard rumours."

"Oh? From whom?"

"Bertie."

"Well, we've split. Amicably, I hope. I just wanted you to hear it from me."

"Was there any particular reason?"

"There were lots of reasons." He inhaled sharply. "She was pregnant and she lost the baby."

"I'm sorry."

"It was all very sudden. To be honest, I can't really believe that it happened."

"Is she okay?"

"As good as she can be."

"Can I do anything?"

"No. I just want to lie low for a while."

"Probably best."

"I'll be in touch."

"Remember you have a refuge here anytime."

Caspian hung up the phone. He didn't mention Rosa; he was sure that Raphael would not appreciate that aspect of the narrative. He remembered when he'd asked him to look out for her, to be her friend. That she needed good people in her life. He felt ashamed of himself.

He pictured her in his mind. Her brown eyes, her slender neck. Her long hair cascading down her back. The way she furrowed her brow when she played the cello.

*Rosa.*

His phone beeped. It was a text from Bethany.

***Read this and tell me if it's ok. Will post with your approval. I think a joint statement is best.***

***Bethany.***

***We have chosen to separate as a couple. We had a wonderful time together, but sadly, our paths have gone in different directions. We need to take some space and we go forward with love and friendship.***

***Thank you all for respecting our privacy at this time.***

***Lots of love,***

***Madison and Caspian x***

He read it twice. He hated this kind of thing, but he couldn't object. He owed it to Madison.

He sent a thumbs up in reply.

That statement would go viral, there was no doubt about that. He thought of Rosa, reading the post, feeling like an outsider.

He texted Bethany again and asked her not to post the statement for a couple of days. Then he called Rosa's number. It rang once and went straight to voicemail. He tried again and the same thing happened. He debated whether to call over and explain. He knew it was madness to see her in person, but he should warn her.

He hated what he had done to her: leaving her in the lurch like that. He had hurt her and that was something he'd promised himself he'd never do. He wished things were easier, that they could be a normal couple, but it was impossible. There were many bridges to cross before he could even try to make amends.

He cleared his throat. "John, can you drop me to Primrose Hill first? There's something I need to do."

When the car pulled up outside Rosa's apartment, it was in darkness. He pulled his beanie hat down over his head, got out and strode up to the main door of the building. He pressed the buzzer over and over, but no one answered. Just as he was about to leave, he heard laughter and voices. A man and a woman were walking towards him. He recognised her straight away.

"Emilia?"

"Caspian, what are you doing here?"

"I'm looking for Rosa. Have you seen her lately?"

The grey-haired man with Emilia looked him up and down. "What do you want with Rosa?"

"I need to talk to her."

"She's not here."

"Where is she?"

"That's none of your business."

Caspian stood up straight. "It is my business. Who are you anyway?"

"My name is Johann Weber. Rosa is my daughter."

"What?" said Caspian, startled.

"I presume that you're Raphael's boy."

Caspian nodded dumbly.

Well, Rosa's not here. She's gone."

Caspian pulled himself together. "Gone where?" he asked.

"Ask her yourself." Johann looked annoyed. "Now, move aside."

"Sorry," mouthed Emilia, clearly mortified.

Caspian watched them enter the building and disappear.

He took out his phone and called her again. It rang once and went straight to messages.

"Fuck," he said under his breath.

John drove straight back to London after he'd dropped Caspian at his parents' house. They'd parted amicably. The trip to Norfolk had been a once off. Caspian was no longer a client and therefore their working relationship was no more.

Madison wanted to be picked up the next morning from the farm so he drove straight home. He only needed five hours sleep to function. His house was quiet as he crept up the stairs. Two more years and he was out. With his police pension and the private one he'd taken out when he'd started working for Madison, he and his wife could make the most of retirement. Their two children were grown and the mortgage was paid. He entered his bedroom and could see his wife sleeping soundly. Removing his earpiece, he took off his shirt and rubbed his tired eyes.

"Johnny?"

He walked over and climbed under the covers. "Don't mind me, love."

He kissed her shoulder and willed himself to sleep.

Savannah helped Madison with her bag.

"Don't be a stranger."

Madison threw her arms around Savannah's neck and hugged her tightly. "Thank you. I can never repay you for what you've done.'

Savannah stiffened first, but then relaxed and hugged her back. "We've an album to finish so I expect to see you after that première."

"Are you sure you won't come? You wrote the song."

"Madison, do you really think I'd walk on a red carpet and answer silly questions about who I'm wearing?"

Madison giggled. "No, I guess not."

"Have you plans for today?"

"A workout with Boris. A zoom call with Bethany and a manicure."

"How dreadful."

"Yes, it doesn't sound appealing."

"Then postpone it."

"I might."

"Take my advice and be kind to yourself. Forget Boris and Mona and Bethany and all those hangers on. You need some time. Take it."

The apartment was spotless when she got home. Cora had a bunch of flowers displayed on the table, and there were cards from various family members and friends on the mantelpiece.

Madison's eyes travelled around the room. There was a huge space where the Steinway used to be. She felt a pain in her chest.

Giorgio was in the kitchen preparing a delectable seafood platter. He had imported Dublin Bay prawns especially and was busy shelling them and placing them on a lettuce leaf.

Cora smiled at her. "How was your trip?"

Madison shrugged. "You know, fine."

"Giorgio is almost ready. Are you hungry?"

Madison shook her head. "Not really. Actually Cora, I might go for a nap."

"Really?"

"Yes. I didn't sleep very well last night."

She walked into her bedroom. The bed was perfectly made, the sheets crisp and clean, the pillows arranged how she liked them. Opening the wardrobe, Caspian's shelves were empty. His aftershave was gone, as was the pile of books on his bedside locker. She could never understand how he liked to read people like Dostoevsky. She couldn't even pronounce his name, not to mind make sense of his work.

She crawled under the covers and lay back on the soft pillow. Turning her head to the right, the bed was empty. She started to cry, the tears flowing fast and full.

Three hours later, she woke up. She checked the time on her phone. It was six. Her stomach rumbled but the thought of prawns was not appealing.

Stretching her arms upwards, she loosened her muscles. There was something so strange about waking up after a short nap. The sky was dusky outside and night was falling, yet her body was ready for a new day. She felt completely disorientated.

Swinging her legs over the edge of the bed and spotted her robe hanging on the back of the door. Todd was in the kitchen when she emerged, sipping a San Pellegrino and watching 'The Great British Bake Off' on his phone.

"Hey, ma'am," he said, pressing pause.

"Hi, Todd." She took a glass and filled it with filtered water. "Don't turn off your show on my account."

"Can I do anything for you, ma'am?" He stood up.

She drank thirstily. "No," she said, shaking her head. "I'm going to make something to eat."

"Giorgio has gone home, but he'll be back right away if I call him."

"It's fine." She waved him away. Opening the fridge, she surveyed the contents. The shellfish platter was covered in clingfilm on the middle shelf. She frowned and her eyes travelled downwards. There was cheese and some tomatoes, next to two tubs of fat free yoghurt. Nothing jumped out at her.

With a sigh, she closed the fridge.

"Call Giorgio so."

Todd nodded and pulled his phone out of his pocket.

"Did Cora leave any messages?"

Todd pointed to a notepad on the coffee table. "She wrote it all down. She said to call her if you need any clarification."

Madison walked over and picked up the paper. Cora had numbered what she had to do. The première of *Josephine* was a priority. The dress had to be fitted, Mona wanted to know what do with her make up. The list went on. Madison scanned the rest and sighed.

She couldn't hide forever.

Her phone rang. Bethany's name flashed on the screen. Madison groaned. She knew what was coming.

"Hello?"

"Hi, Madison. Good to see you back. Just wondering about posting about the split. We need to get in there quickly."

"Go ahead."

"I'll email you the draft and you can confirm. I've already sent it to Caspian."

"Sure."

"Chat later." The line went dead.

# CHAPTER SEVENTY-SEVEN

The next day, the world woke up to the news that Madian was no more. The statement, posted by Bethany the night before, was shared, liked and commented on millions of times. Fans were gobsmacked: only a few weeks before they had believed that there was a baby on the way. To the outside world, Madison and Caspian were the perfect couple. Their followers had formed an emotional connection with their idols and were traumatised by the end of their engagement. The story even made the Six O'Clock News, pictures of Madison and Caspian in happier times on the top left side of the screen.

There was speculation as to why. Sources close to the couple said that the pressures of their careers proved too much. Others said that Caspian dumped her because she was infertile. Some indignant fans wondered if Caspian was having an affair. Old images of him with groupies popped up on Twitter, along with the pictures of him and Rosa.

Bethany sent an email to both Caspian and Madison, organising a Zoom call for later that day to brief them on how to handle the situation.

Caspian contemplated not joining the call, but, in the end, he relented. He knew how much this meant to Madison, keeping her image as untainted as possible.

Bethany admitted them both. Madison looked haunted, her hair dishevelled and her eyes red. He immediately felt terrible and cast his eyes down. He could tell she was back in London: their sofa was visible in the background and the Banksy painting they'd bought together was hanging on the wall.

"Right, let's be clear," said Bethany briskly. "You are not to be seen in public with anyone, and I mean anyone, until you've both made a solo public appearance looking happy and strong."

Caspian rolled his eyes.

Bethany glared at him and continued. "Madison, you must channel the quintessential independent woman. The ideal event is the première next week." She turned to Caspian. "Are you attending?"

He shook his head. "No. It would detract from the film. This is about Raphael's art, not our breakup."

"Good. Also, if you could keep away from girls, vis à vis, Rosa Weber, it would be helpful."

"What the fuck do you mean by that?"

"You know what I mean." She adjusted her glasses. "In fact, you both need to disappear until it settles. It's the only way to quell the media speculation. Caspian, stay at your parents place. I'll post old photos of you walking down a street in Gothenburg to put them off the scent temporarily."

Madison put her hair behind her ear. "What about me?"

"You need to do the same. The première will be your renaissance into the spotlight. You'll look fabulous on the red carpet and everyone will move on and forget."

"But that's over a week away. I can't stay cooped up here until then."

"Your first appearance has to be orchestrated and controlled. Caspian, you too. Somewhere public, on your own, smiling and carefree. Don't fuck this up."

His finger hovered over the 'Leave' button. He hated how contrived it all was. He could take or leave fame. Music was his love and he wanted to share his art with the world. Being constricted and controlled was another side to it: a side he loathed. However, he owed it to Madison. He also didn't want Rosa in the spotlight. From what he knew of her past, he imagined that there were lots of skeletons in her closet. He had to shield her from that.

"Fine."

"Good. Now, I've managed to suppress the baby story. It's no longer trending and the newspapers have not reported on it per se. There's the odd blog on Twitter, but mainly speculation. I'm confident that it will disappear. Soon, the rumours will be gone and we can go back to normal."

Madison felt her stomach lurch. She hated how Bethany spoke about the whole affair: no emotion, business-like, ruthless. Her eyes met Caspian's and they held each other's gaze.

He nodded, the silent message received.

"Bethany?" he said.

"Yes?"

"We're done here."

"Sorry?"

"This call is over." He gestured to Madison to leave the call. They pressed the button in unison.

He rang her straight away.

"I'm sorry, but she's an absolute cow."

"She can be," said Madison carefully. "However, I can't survive without her."

"Really?"

"Yes."

There was a pause.

"How are you feeling, Mads?"

Her voice broke. "Not great."

"I'm sorry."

"Stop saying that."

"I wish I could go back and change that night."

"Well, you can't." She sighed. "Your being there wouldn't have changed the outcome. Our baby didn't have a chance of survival."

"Please stay in touch," he said softly.

"Okay," she lied.

They both knew this would never happen. It was finally over.

Later that evening, the intercom beeped by the front door.

"I'll check that," said Todd, striding over and peering at the screen. "It's Mr and Ms O' Connor, ma'am."

Madison frowned. "I presume you mean Cliona and Fionn."

He nodded.

"Then say that," she said irritably. "Mr and Ms O'Connor sounds like it's their parents."

"Yes, ma'am."

"Let them in." She walked to the mirror in the hallway and fixed her hair. Her eyes looked small and tired, and there was the beginnings of a spot on her chin. Her bronzed skin was pale and her eyebrows needed to be groomed. She turned away from her reflection in disgust.

Todd appeared five minutes later with Cliona and Fionn in tow.

"Maddy," said Cliona, opening her arms. "You poor thing. I'm so sorry."

Madison fell into her embrace and hugged her tightly. "It's good to see you," she said in a muffled voice.

Fionn rubbed her shoulder. "Good to see you back, Mads."

"Although I hear that my brother here went to visit you without me!' Cliona glared at Fionn.

"Her location was top secret,' he protested. 'Plus it was like a warzone up in Norfolk. I nearly got shot."

Cliona took Madison's hand. "How are you feeling?"

Madison inhaled deeply. "Can we talk about other things? I don't mean to be rude but I really don't want to go over it again."

"Of course." Cliona squeezed her hand.

"How's Alex?" Madison didn't really care how he was, but she needed to change the subject.

"It's his birthday today actually."

"Oh?"

Cliona looked uncomfortable. "So I can't really stay that long. We're meeting his parents and his sisters later for dinner. They're coming up from Kent especially."

Madison's face fell. "Of course. You go."

Fionn cleared his throat. "Clio here is going, but I'm not."

Cliona smiled. "Fionn's going to stay for a while. I know it's a pale reflection of yours truly, but he's better than nothing."

Madison's blue eyes connected with Fionn's and her stomach flipped slightly.

"We'll order in some food and watch TV," he said, pulling out his phone. "Will Deliveroo get past Rambo over there?"

Todd bristled.

Madison smiled. "He'll have to check it over, but it should be fine."

Cliona put on her coat. "Are you sure you'll be okay?"

Madison sighed theatrically. "I suppose."

"Hey, Ryan," protested Fionn. "I'm the better option and you know it." He held up his phone. "How about some Indian food?"

She shook her head. "I'm not feeling that adventurous today."

"Nando's?"

"I don't eat fried food."

"Jesus, Maddy. A few chips won't kill you."

"Fine. Nando's. Whatever."

"Todd? What do you want?"

"I'm good, sir."

"Todd, come on. Have some chicken or something."

Madison smiled encouragingly. "Go on, Todd. You'll be taste testing it for poison anyway so you might as well."

Todd nodded. "Okay, I'll have the piri-piri chicken, sweetcorn, fries and slaw."

Fionn typed in the order on the app. "There. All done." He smiled. "I got you two portions of everything, Todd. Even though you treat me like an armed terrorist every time I call over.'

Todd looked embarrassed. "That's my job."

"He knows that," said Cliona soothingly. "Right. I'm off. Enjoy your Nando's."

"I'll escort you out," said Todd.

The door slammed.

Fionn walked into the kitchen. "Mads, have you some nice wine?"

"There's some white in the fridge." She flopped down on the couch.

After dinner, Fionn cleared the plates and poured some more wine for them both.

"I've already had two glasses," complained Madison. "Plus fried chicken and loads of chips."

"Maddy, you had seven chips. I counted." He handed her the glass. "Now shut up and enjoy yourself."

She relented and sat back on the cushions. Fionn flicked the channels on the giant flatscreen, pausing on random shows before flicking again.

"So, what's the plan now?" he asked. "I hope you're not going back to work yet."

Madison felt her stomach heave. She couldn't imagine standing on stage in a skimpy dress, stomping her feet and singing her heart out.

"I don't know." She shrugged. "Ross will expect it."

"Ross can go jump. You're not to even think about it until you're ready."

"It's easy for you to say. People depend on me. My entourage, my fans. A lot of people make a lot of money out of my career."

"So? They can wait."

He sipped her wine. "If only life were that simple."

"It is that simple."

"Oh, Fionn." She looked at him pityingly. "I am the biggest thing in the entertainment industry."

Fionn snorted. "Have you heard of Taylor Swift?"

Madison glared at him. "I'm one of the biggest stars on the planet. A cultural touchstone. My fans need me like they need air. I can't abandon them."

Fionn put his glass own on the coffee table with a clatter. "There you go again. The world will keep turning whether you're on stage or not."

"Oh, typical. I was waiting for you to turn on me." She sat up straight, her eyes flashing. "It was all too good to be true."

"You deserve it sometimes."

"Oh yeah?" She started to tremble. "I've had a shit day. Bethany made me do a Zoom call with Caspian and she kept going on about the baby and …"

His face softened. He took her hand in his, softly caressing her wrist before threading his fingers through hers. She closed her eyes, enjoying his touch, feeling a calmness flood her body.

"Maddy," he said gently. "I'm sorry."

She opened her eyes. "What?"

"I'm sorry," he repeated.

"Are you feeling okay?" she mocked.

He nodded. "I swear on Granny O'Connor's grave."

"It's just you freak me out when you're nice to me."

"I was out of line." He removed his hand and picked up the remote once more. "So, what will we watch?"

She found herself wishing that he'd hold her hand again. It made her feel safe.

"I really don't mind."

"Fine. Let's watch *The Terminator.* It will remind us of Savannah."

Fionn called over again the next day armed with chocolates, popcorn and put on *How to Lose a Guy in 10 Days.*

"On retrospect maybe the title of this movie is a bit insensitive," he said with a grin.

Madison tried to look affronted.

"You remind me of the actress in this," he said, throwing off his shoes and putting his feet on the coffee table.

"I'd like to say that you remind me of Matthew McConaughey but…"

"But I'm better looking?" Fionn stuffed some popcorn into his mouth. "I know. It's the cross I have to bear."

Madison ate three chocolates in a row.

"I'll have to do overtime with Boris tomorrow," she moaned. "You're a bad influence on me."

"Yawn." Fionn patted his mouth theatrically.

She scowled at him and sat back.

"Put your legs up here," he said, patting his knees. "Stretch out and get comfortable."

"Really?"

"Yes, really." He leaned down and pulled her legs onto his lap.

Madison settled back into the cushions. "This is actually nice."

"Yeah, Emilia loved when I let her do this."

"Your old lady."

"If you mean old as in past, then yes."

"What happened?"

"She traded me in for an older model."

"Are you okay?"

"I'll live." He rubbed her shin. "Now, pass the chocolate."

# CHAPTER SEVENTY-EIGHT

A few days later, Madison was reading a fashion magazine when her phone rang. Fionn's name was flashing on the screen so she answered it immediately.

"Hey," she said, smiling.

"Morning. Are you dressed?"

"Yes. Tracksuit and Uggs."

"Great, now put on a wig or a hat or whatever you do to disguise yourself, and come down to the main door."

Madison baulked. "I'm not going outside."

"The paps are gone. In case you haven't noticed, Queen Elizabeth died. You and Caspian have faded into the background."

"Why? Where are we going?"

"It's a surprise."

"Ugh, fine." She got up and walked into her bedroom. There was a box of disguises in her wardrobe for when she wanted to blend into the public. Rummaging through, she pulled out a short brown wig. Her stylist, Mona, was on holidays so she attempted to pin up her hair with hair grips. Bending her bead down, she pulled on the wig and looked in the mirror.

The pixie cut made her neck seem longer. She pulled the sides down over her ears and adjusted the hairline. It really was amazing how hair could define someone. Her blonde mane concealed, she was almost unrecognisable. Picking up her Dior glasses, she put her phone in her pocket and called Todd.

Fionn was waiting in the foyer of the apartment building, chatting to the security man stationed by the revolving door. Todd walked ahead and frisked Fionn quickly.

"God, but you're thorough," said Fionn, holding his arms up.

Madison laughed. "One slip up is all it takes."

Todd stood back. "All good, ma'am."

Fionn held out his hand. "Come on, let's go."

"Where are we going?" Madison put on her giant glasses and pulled her hoodie up around her neck.

"For a walk. You're looking sickly and pale. Some fresh air will do you the world of good."

"Oh, Fionn. I'm not sure that's a good idea."

"No one will recognise you, for God's sake." He grabbed her hand in his and held it there. "Come on."

They walked out onto the street and crossed the road, entering Holland Park from the east side. "Let's visit the Kyoto Gardens," he suggested, holding her hand even tighter. Madison was amazed when no one gave them a second glance as they ambled along. A man and a woman dressed in lycra jogged past, followed by a group of teenagers and an older couple walking their Bichon Frisé.

"I can't believe that we haven't been recognised," she whispered.

"Well, I'm not Caspian," said Fionn reasonably. "I'm just a drummer. No one cares what I look like."

They reached the Kyoto Gardens. Fionn led her to a large pond with a tiered waterfall. The maple trees were a rich red colour and a small bridge crossed the water. Fionn sat down on the stone cobbles by the edge of the pond and gestured for her to join him.

"The water is full of koi carp."

"What are they? Fish?"

"Well, yes. Fish generally live in water."

She nudged him playfully. "You're not allowed to be mean to me today."

"Look, they're brightly coloured. You can see shoals of them zipping around."

"Oh yeah." She peered closer and beamed at him. "They're really pretty." She put her head back and let the sun beat down on her face. "It's so peaceful here," she said with a sigh. "All I can hear is the water gushing from those waterfalls over there. You wouldn't think that you were in the middle of London."

"It is peaceful," he agreed. "I feel like I should be sitting here reflecting on my life and making big decisions."

"I never even knew this place existed. I've lived close by for years and I've never even walked in this park."

"You need to live your life, Mads. You're a slave to the industry."

"Maybe you're right."

A seagull landed on the bridge with a banana skin in its mouth. Its beady eyes travelled around the garden, searching for more food.

"Let's go back to Dublin," suggested Fionn suddenly, "just for a couple of days. I'm sure your mum is dying to see you."

"God, I don't know."

"Come on, let's fly commercial."

"You always fly commercial."

"Like I said, I'm just a drummer."

Madison looked dubious. "If I go home, I have to talk about it. I don't want to talk about anything."

"You can hang out at my house." He stood up. "Mum is mad to see you and give you a hug."

"Bethany did say to lie low."

"Where better than Ireland?"

"Okay, fine. I'll get Cora to organise it."

He lifted up her hand and kissed the inside of her wrist. "Good."

She felt her cheeks redden and he looked at her in amusement.

"Come on, Todd looks bored over there by the maple trees." He stood up. "Race you back to the street."

Later, as she lay in bed, she couldn't stop thinking about him.

Fionn O'Connor. Cliona's older, annoying, infuriating brother. Her mortal enemy.

The chewing gum in her hair incident was only one offence on a long list. He had made fun of her for as long as she could remember. When she was cast as Eliza Doolittle in the school musical, he had laughed at her cockney accent. When she made cookies for Constance as a Christmas present one year, he pretended to choke after one mouthful. When one of her early hits, *Text Me Back*, got to number one on the charts, and everyone was congratulating her, he'd called her a 'loser', making an 'L' shape with his fingers.

Yet, throughout this whole nightmare, he had there for her. When she was alone in the hospital, the day he visited her on the farm, calling over with rom-coms and cheering her up.

*Fionn.*

She closed her eyes and fell into a deep sleep. For once, Caspian didn't haunt her dreams. Instead she dreamed about home: Dalkey Bay at sunset, the orange sun disappearing on the horizon as darkness descended on the shimmering sea.

# CHAPTER SEVENTY-NINE

They touched down in Dublin the next evening.

Fionn had insisted that Todd stay at home. Madison refused at first, but finally relented. They were both going home to their family houses so no public appearances. Fionn explained that travelling without security afforded her more privacy. People would gawp at her walking along with her muscly sidekick. She'd never really thought about it that way.

However, she insisted on wearing a short dark brown wig and huge glasses.

"You look like Velma from Scooby Do," said Fionn.

"Thanks," she said smiling. She was learning that the best way to deal with him was not to react.

They stopped at Sorrento Terrace first.

"Let's go in and say hi."

"Okay."

Fionn walked ahead of Madison and opened the heavy front door. She took off the wig and shook out her hair. "What a relief. Wigs are so uncomfortable."

Constance was in the kitchen, stirring a sauce and singing *Islands in the Stream.*

Fionn crept up behind her and hugged her.

"Jesus, Mary and St Joseph!" she yelled. "Fionn, you rascal. I didn't know you were coming home."

"Sorry, Mum. I should've called first. Have you enough food for two more?"

"You know I make enough for the whole street. Is Emilia with you?" She looked over his shoulder and Madison came into view.

Constance's eyes widened. "Maddy, darling!" She flew over and hugged her tightly. "You poor thing. Clio told me bits and pieces. Awful thing to happen."

Madison nodded. "Yeah, well."

"I'm sorry about Caspian too."

Fionn pulled his mother away. "Mum! She doesn't want to talk about all of that."

Constance blushed. "Oh, you know that I wear my heart on my sleeve. Sorry, love."

"It's okay." Madison smiled reassuringly. "I'd better keep going. I'm sure Mum is dying to see me."

"Will you come back for some food later?"

"Sure. I'd love that."

"I'm making chicken marsala with mash. Don't bring wine, we've loads in the shed."

Fionn helped her to put back on her wig and walked her out to the car.

"See you later," he said, opening the door. "Say hi to Louise and Kevin."

"I will." She rested her chin on the car door. "You know, I don't feel half as bad when you're around."

Fionn raised an eyebrow. "Oh?"

"You're a distraction." She smiled. "A good distraction."

"You're welcome."

She got into the car and he closed the door.

"See you at seven, " he called as the taxi pulled off.

When Madison got home, she pulled off her wig and threw it on the hall table. Bluebell, her old Labrador, bolted towards her and she fell to her knees to hug her.

"Hey, girl. Hey, Bluey. I've missed you, yes I have."

Louise Ryan was having her nails done in the sitting room. "Maddy? Is that you?"

"Hey, Mum."

Katya, the nail technician, tried to stay normal. She was a huge fan of Madison and had all her albums. However, she had to remain professional. She painted the last nail and blew on it gently.

"Don't move, Mrs Ryan," she ordered. "Ten minutes."

Louise stayed sitting with her hands on the table. "I didn't know you were coming home, darling. Mina hasn't made up your bed and she's finished work for today."

"I can make my own bed."

"You can?"

"Yes. Savannah makes me do all sorts."

"Come sit over here. I can't move until the polish is dry."

Constance wouldn't have cared, reflected Madison as she walked towards her mother. She would've dropped everything and pulled her into her arms.

She was used to it. A beautiful house on Vico Road, reminiscent of a museum. An absent father for most of her childhood, a mother who cared more about her highlights and Botox than her own daughter.

"How are you feeling? I wanted to come and stay with you, but that Cora girl said no."

"I needed some space."

"How are you physically? Is it sore?"

Madison shook her head. "Not really. Anyway, how's Dad?"

"Playing golf with Oscar McCarthy. He should be back later."

"I'm going to the O'Connor's for dinner."

"That's nice." Louise looked relieved. "I have a function at the sailing club tonight that I just couldn't cancel at such short notice."

# CHAPTER EIGHTY

Aonghus came home from a lecture in Trinity College and hugged Fionn tightly. "You never said that you were coming home."

"It was a last minute thing."

"Is Emilia with you?"

Constance shook her head behind Fionn's back.

"Emilia and I have split up. We're still friends, but it's over."

"Are you okay?"

Fionn nodded. "Fine."

"Madison's home with him," said Constance, giving her husband a pointed look. "She's coming for dinner later."

Fionn sighed. "Before you buy a hat for the wedding, listen to me. We're friends. That's all."

"Of course," said Constance with a wink.

"Mum, stop. I know you've harboured this fantasy about us since we were kids, but let it go."

"I'm not saying anything."

"How is Maddy?" asked Aonghus. "It must be a tough time for her."

"She's doing really well. She's stronger than you think."

"How's Caspian?" asked Constance.

Fionn went to the fridge and poured a glass of juice. "Okay, I think. To be honest, I haven't really spoken to him."

"I wonder why they broke up?" said Constance with a frown. "You'd think the loss of a baby would bring you closer."

Fionn drank his juice and remained silent.

"Right, I'll open a nice bottle of red," said Aonghus. "Where's the Ripasso, Connie?"

"On the left as you walk into the shed, next to the chianti."

Madison put on a light blue summer dress and silver strappy sandals. She applied some mascara and lip gloss, but nothing else. It was just Fionn. He didn't care what she looked like.

Bethany had emailed about the première of *Josephine* which was only ten days away. She'd outlined the pre-event schedule: a gown fitting with Alexander McQueen, lunch with Ross about the status of new album, hair appointments, beauty appointments. Extra fitness sessions to look good on the red carpet. It sounded exhausting so she put it out of her mind. She was home to relax and enjoy herself.

The doorbell rang. She shook out her hair and applied some more lip gloss.

"Coming," she called.

Fionn smiled when she opened the door. "You look nice for once."

"Wow, thanks."

"Mum is cooking up a storm."

"Great. I'm starving." She stepped outside.

Just as they were leaving, her dad's car pulled up. The electric window lowered.

"Maddy," said Kevin in surprise. "We didn't know you were coming home."

"Hi, Dad." She leaned down and pecked his cheek.

"Hi, Fionn."

"Hi, Kevin."

"You off somewhere?"

Madison wrapped her long blonde hair into a bun and shoved it under a beanie hat. "I'm going to the O'Connor's for dinner."

"Are you okay?" He looked uncomfortable. "Louise told me about what happened."

She smiled brightly. "Grand altogether. See you later."

"Maddy's here," announced Fionn, leading Madison by the hand into the dining room.

"Madison! Good to see you, love." Aonghus hugged her tightly.

"Thanks."

Constance came through another door, carrying a bowl of crisps and a platter of nuts.

"I hope you're hungry," she said, placing them on the coffee table. "I've enough chicken marsala for the whole of Sicily."

Fionn took a handful of pistachios and shelled them one by one.

"Tell us about Abbey Road," said Constance. "The photos you sent looked great. I was so jealous."

"It was long and intense. Our producer, Brian, was brilliant. He's from Dublin actually. Worked with Bono and the lads back in the day."

"What's his name?"
"Brian Mulcahy."
"God Aonghus, I wonder is he related to Maurice Mulcahy from Rathmines?"
"Could be."
Fionn laughed. "I'm sure he's not."
"Everyone knows everyone in Ireland," said Constance firmly.
"Anyway, our sound engineer was brilliant too," Fionn continued. "She really knew her stuff."
"What was her name?" asked Constance.
"Peggy Browne." Fionn glanced slyly at his mother. "You know, I'm sure she's related to Marty Browne from down the road."
"Stop being cheeky!" Constance threw a pistachio shell at him.
"Then, this engineer called Cindy Brophy came down to mix and master the album."
"Is it ready?"
"I think so. Caspian hasn't texted us yet."
"I can't wait to hear it. It will be so emotional. Cliona said there's a session cellist on some of the tracks? How lovely."
Madison looked stricken so Fionn jumped up. "Would you like a glass of wine, Mads?"
She shook her head. "I'm okay."
"Ah, go on. It's worth the calories."
"Fine, but I'd prefer white if you have it."
"Coming up."

After dinner, they had cheese and crackers. Constance smeared some brie on a round wafer biscuit and groaned in pleasure.
"There is nothing like soft brie. Nothing."
"I'm more of a comté man myself," said Aonghus.
Madison yawned. "I think I'm going to call it a night."
Fionn stood up. "Come on, I'll walk you home. It's a lovely evening."
"I was going to call my dad."
"Come on, lazybones. You need to work off the teaspoon of mash you had with your chicken."
"I might get papped."
"Did we get papped on the way over here?" Fionn rolled his eyes. "Just put on your beanie again."
Madison made a face. "Fine." She waved. "Night and thanks. I had a really nice time."

Fionn followed her out the door. "Back in about half an hour."

Constance kicked Aonghus under the table and crossed her fingers in glee.

The moon was full and the large milky orb was reflected on Dalkey Bay.

Madison shivered in her light dress so Fionn put his arm around her shoulder.

"Thanks for bringing me here," she said, snuggling in closer.

He squeezed her tightly. "You're welcome. You need to reconnect with your homeland before you go back into the spotlight. It keeps you grounded."

"You should see my dress for the première."

"I'm sure it's lovely."

"I'm not really pushed about going but Bethany is insisting. She wants me to show the world how happy I am to be single."

"Are you happy to be single?"

"You know, I'm not unhappy. I haven't really thought about Caspian at all."

"Good. It will get easier every day."

"I mean, it hurt when your mum mentioned the cello, but not as much as I thought."

Fionn stopped walking by a stone wall on the cliff edge. "Sit down for a second."

"Why?"

"Just sit down."

She obeyed and he sat next to her, his arm around her again for warmth.

"This is the spot where I shifted my first girlfriend."

"Here?" Madison burst out laughing. "Why would you kiss someone here?"

"I thought the view was romantic." He laughed too. "It was a moonlit night like this one."

"Who was it?"

"Anaïs Le Gall. She was Cliona's French exchange."

"I remember her! She was quite pretty."

"Of course she was pretty."

"Deluded obviously."

"Why?"

"For kissing you."

He regarded her contemplatively. "You know, I always ended up with Cliona's friends. All through school. They couldn't resist her hunky older brother."

"Not all of her friends." She looked up at him. "You never kissed me."

"No, I just attacked you with bubble gum." He reached out and touched a loose tress of her hair that had escaped from the beanie hat. "That's why I brought you to my old hunting ground. To right a wrong."

"Oh?" Her heart started to beat faster.

"All the fighting, all the banter. It was as Shakespeare said, a 'merry war of wits'." He moved his face closer to hers. "I love you, Maddy."

She felt tears well up in her eyes.

"It's always been you. I just couldn't see it."

"Fionn, I …"

"I love you."

She stared at him.

"Will you move back to Dublin with me?" He traced her ring finger with his thumb. "I remember you saying that you want to walk down the aisle before you have to get fillers."

"Move back here?"

"Yes, move home."

"With you?"

"With me." He put his hand on her waist and pulled her to him. "Now, you're about to join a long list of girls who had the privilege of kissing me on this wall."

"A long list? Hardly."

He kissed her then, slowly and deliberately.

"You're a good kisser," she murmured.

"I've been told."

"And your arms are so muscly."

"I'm a drummer."

He moved down and kissed her neck, his lips lightly touching her skin. "You smell so nice."

"Coco Mademoiselle."

Pulling the strap of her dress down her arm, he kissed her shoulder blade and then the top of her breast.

"We'd better stop," he said in a muffled voice. "It's the one time we could be papped."

"Don't stop."

He kissed her again, more urgently this time. Then he pulled back.

"We've got to move. Otherwise I'm not sure I can stop."

She reluctantly pulled the strap of her dress back into position. "Will you still walk me home?"

"Of course." He kissed her nose. "Let's make a move."

They walked the remainder of the journey, hand in hand. There was no need for conversation as there was a sense of familiarity that didn't need words. When they got to the front door, Madison looked at him shyly.

"Do you want to come in for a while?"

"For a cup of tea with Louise and Kevin?"
"No," she laughed.
"Okay, I'd like to come in."
She opened the door and pulled off her hat. Bluebell barked for a moment, but then stopped and rolled over on her stomach.
Fionn bent down and dutifully rubbed her. There was a light on in the sitting room and France 24 was blaring on the television. Madison gestured for Fionn to go upstairs.
"Dad's in there," she whispered. "I'm just not in the mood for small talk at the moment."
Fionn nodded and followed her up the huge staircase.

Madison's room was huge with thick piled carpets and heavy drapes, a four-poster bed and a walk in wardrobe. There was also a dressing table with lights all around the mirror. Sure enough, there was a signed poster of Justin Timberlake on the wall.
"I met him when I was seventeen," she said. "He signed it and it was my most treasured possession."
"I think I remember Clio talking about that. She was so jealous."
She took off her sandals. "Do you want to watch a movie?"
"If you like." He took off his shoes and lay down on the bed. She positioned herself next to him and pressed the remote. A gigantic flat screen lowered down from the ceiling. She clicked on Disney + and started to browse.
"When the film is over I'll head home," he said, rearranging the pillows.
She put down the remote. "You don't have to go."
He pretended to look shocked. "You harridan!"
She blushed. "No, no. I'm not propositioning you. I'm not in the head space right now for anything much. Not since the baby. I hope you understand."
He leaned over and kissed her. "I understand."
"But I'd like you to stay over. I'd like to sleep with you and wake up with you."
"Grand. Have you a spare toothbrush?"
She lay up against him and put her head on his chest. "I do."
"Do you snore?"
"Fionn!"
"I'm messing." He kissed her again. "When will you learn that most of what I say is a joke?"
"So you don't really love me then? Was that a joke too?"
He flipped her over onto her back, lowered his body onto hers and kissed her deeply and thoroughly.
"I don't joke about that."

# CHAPTER EIGHTY-ONE

Fionn got home at noon the next day.

Constance was hanging clothes out on the line so he walked out into the garden.

"Hey, Mum."

"Hi, darling." She shook out the sleeve of one of Aonghus' shirts before pinning it on the line. "Did you just wake up?"

He gave her an old-fashioned look. "You know I didn't sleep here."

She smiled. "I guessed."

"I'm just going to make a cup of coffee." He ambled into the kitchen.

"Fionn O'Connor, you get back here right now." Constance marched up to him. "What happened? Tell me everything."

"There's nothing to tell."

"My eye! You look like the cat who got the cream."

Fionn switched on the coffee machine.

"Have I ever told you details of my personal life?"

She put her hands on her hips. "Fionn!"

"Okay, okay." He reddened. "I was with Maddy."

Constance stared at him in shock. Then she started to scream in delight.

"*Aonghus! Aonghus!*"

Aonghus rushed into the kitchen. "What, Con? Are you okay?"

"My Saint Martin candle came up trumps!"

Fionn looked at her in confusion. "Saint who?"

"Saint Martin of Porres. My mother swore by him. I lit a candle and prayed that you'd settle down."

"But you're not remotely religious. You don't even go to Mass."

"That doesn't matter."

Aonghus cleared his throat. "As yet, I'm in the dark. What is going on?"

"Fionn and Maddy are in love!"

"Mum, you're unreal. I never said anything about love."

"Of course it's love. I've watched you two for years, bickering constantly. I knew there was something more." She squealed and clapped her hands.

Aonghus slapped Fionn's back. "I'm delighted for you, son."

"You must get married and have lots of babies."

"Whoa, slow down, Mum."

"I can wheel them around Dalkey in the buggy. Louise could meet me for coffee."

"Constance!" Aonghus looked stern. "You'll jinx it."

Fionn kissed his mother's forehead. "When I propose, you'll be the first to know."

"How long will you be over this time?"

"Until tomorrow. Maddy has a big week coming up. There's the première of *Josephine.*"

"Oh, fab. I can't wait to see that film."

"Isn't it directed by Caspian's father?" said Aonghus.

Fionn nodded. "Caspian isn't going."

"How's all of this going to work with the band?" asked Constance. "Won't it be awkward?"

Fionn sipped his coffee. "I hope not. If it's an issue, I'll quit."

"Quit the band?"

"Yep. Madison makes enough money for the both if us. I'll be a house husband."

"Husband? Have you proposed already?" Constance squealed again.

"No, Mother. I haven't. It's just an expression."

"I don't care, I'm so happy. It's like all the pieces of the puzzle have come together."

Aonghus met Fionn's eye and winked.

"Will Maddy be over later?"

"Yes. I invited her for dinner again."

"Aonghus, get out the Veuve Clicquot. We have so much to celebrate."

Caspian opened his laptop and viewed another possible apartment. He hadn't left his parents' house in weeks, steering clear of the public or anyone associated with him or Madison. However, he needed a base in London when he went back to work.

Steering clear of Kensington, he'd instructed his estate agent to look in Notting Hill and Chelsea. He'd been sent virtual tours of all sorts of places, but none had suited him. One was too big and another was too small. Not one seemed like a home, a place where he could write music and feel peace.

He sighed. If it wasn't for The Forge, he'd leave London for good. He was tired of city life and longed for somewhere like Amiens. The vast fields, the gardens and the general sense of calm lured him back. Perhaps he'd visit when the pomp and ceremony of the film was over.

The estate agent had written under the latest property that it was coming in at four million.

Caspian shook his head and typed:

***It's not for me.***

Later that evening, he checked his emails on his laptop. Cindy Brophy had sent the stereo file of the album, but he didn't have the headspace to concentrate. Jax wanted a meeting to decide a release date and the first single. Prue had sent on details of the upcoming season at the Royal Shakespeare Company.

***The Tempest with Alex Kingston as Prospero! My treat xxx***

He smiled. She was his rock.

His Steinway had gone into storage and he yearned to play. All his life he had used music as his outlet: when he was sad or happy, angry or despondent. Denied access to his instrument, he felt lost and alone. He was avoiding The Forge as fans were sitting outside the door, waiting for him to arrive so that they could take photos and selfies.

Clicking on YouTube, he typed Rosa's name into the search engine. Various videos popped up. One in particular was from five years before: she was playing solo on a stage in Vienna. Dressed in a black velvet dress, her hair was braided down her back. Accompanied by an orchestra, she played Bach, followed by Elgar and then Schubert. He watched her play, her brow furrowed. He loved how she did that. Miserably, he exited out of the clip and closed his laptop.

The next morning he received a handwritten letter with an airmail sticker. It had been forwarded to his parents' address. The writing was cursive and old-fashioned.

He tore open the envelope.

***Dear Caspian,***

***I hear that you are having a difficult time. I invite you to stay at my house in Paris, you will not be troubled there.***

***My address is on the bottom of this page. I look forward to seeing you,***

***Your grandmother,***

***Agathe.***

He looked at the address. It was somewhere called Faubourg Saint-Germain.

Prue put a plate of toast on the table. "Who's the letter from? God, I didn't think people sent letters anymore."

"Agathe Baptiste."

Prue stiffened. "Oh?"

"She's asked me to come and stay."

"And?" Prue sat down.

"I think I'll go, Mum. The première is tomorrow and I don't want to be in

England for that."

She grasped his hand. "Then go, my love."

"You're not upset?"

Prue shook her head. "I promise."

"I love you so much."

"Me too."

"Don't think for a moment that this affects us. You're my mother, you'll always be my mother. Same for Dad."

"I know, sweetheart. I know."

# CHAPTER EIGHTY-TWO

Paris looked beautiful in the autumn. The trees were shedding their leaves resulting in a russet brown and yellow carpet on the pavements. Caspian gazed out at the buildings and people as his Uber moved along the river towards the 7th arrondissement.

Agathe's house was a townhouse close to Esplanade des Invalides. The red brick building had three storeys, a small garden and a charming courtyard.

Caspian took his bag and walked up to the main entrance. He knocked on the door and a woman of about forty opened it.

*"Bonjour, puis-je vous aider?"* she asked politely.

Caspian gave a small wave. "I'm Caspian, *je suis Caspian,* I'm here to see Agathe."

"Ah, Caspian." She smiled. "We have been expecting you. Please follow me."

He walked into a large hallway with a beautiful tiled floor.

"Madame Baptiste is in the drawing room," she said, gesturing towards a door on the left.

"Thanks," he said with a nod.

Agathe was sitting on an antique armchair by a large window. She looked up and smiled.

"Caspian, hello. It is wonderful to see you."

He liked how she said 'wuuunnnderful' like Maurice Chevalier.

"Hello," he said, walking towards her to kiss her cheek.

"I'm so glad you came."

"Me too."

"Amandine has made some dinner. I hope you're hungry."

"Yes, I am."

He hesitated before sitting on the sofa opposite her. "How have you been?"

She laughed. "Forget about me, how have you been? I read about your break up with Madison."

He sighed. "It's all a bit of a nightmare."

"Raphael mentioned the baby. I'm sorry."

"It was over before we had a chance to think about it."

"How is Madison?"
"Pretty devastated."
"Naturally." She used her cane to stand up.
"May I help you?" he asked in concern.
"Not at all. I'm quite independent." She walked towards the door. "Let's have dinner."

Amandine showed him to his room after they'd eaten. The stairs creaked as they climbed to the third storey. He gazed at the paintings and photographs on the wall as he ascended.
"Madame Baptiste loves photographs," said Amandine, leading him down a dark corridor. "She displays them all over the house."
His room was on the south side of the house and looked out over the small garden. The bed was big with floral sheets and the furniture was mahogany and antiquated. On the dresser, there were lots of framed photos. He looked at them intently, trying to figure out who was who.
"Amandine," he said, pointing to a black and white photo of a young boy on a beach. "Who's this?"
"Monsieur Baptiste, Raphael's father."
"My grandfather?"
"*Oui.*" She smiled.
"Are there any of Raphael when he was young?"
She nodded. "Look, here." He stared at a picture of Raphael with parted long brown hair, a long black coat and Doc Marten boots. He guessed that he was about seventeen. On the right was a grainy picture of Doctor Eckleburg. Caspian picked it up, touched.
"I'll let you get settled," said Amandine, leaving the room.
Caspian put his bag on the ground. He texted Prue to say that he'd arrived safely.
The house was really something. Situated in the historic 7$^{th}$ arrondissement, it obviously had a story to tell. He made a mental note to ask Agathe about its history in the morning.
Lying down on the bed, he closed his eyes. A minute later, he was asleep.

His alarm went off at eight the next morning. He sat up, disorientated.
Grabbing his phone, he turned off the wailing sound and saw that there were two messages from Prue.
Over at the wash basin, he splashed his face with cold water. Agathe was at the dining room table when he got downstairs, looking at an old photo album.

"Ah, Caspian. Come."

He sat down next to her.

"Amandine will bring you some breakfast in a moment. You slept well?"

"Yes, incredibly well."

"*Bon.* Come closer, I want to show you the family."

She opened the book and pulled back the see through paper. "This is Emmanuel Baptiste. He was Louis' great-grandfather, so your great-great-great-great grandfather."

"Wow."

"He made a lot of money in the bank. He built the estate in Amiens in the 1824. This is his son, Jean. He was also in finance. His wife was American. Quite different to us. She made quite the impression in Paris."

"What was her name?"

"Rosemary."

"And who's this?"

"Louis when he was a boy. He arrived quite late and was an only child."

Caspian gazed at the childhood picture of his great-grandfather. It could have been him as a young boy. They had the same bone structure and eyes.

"His son, Claude, was not only a banker, but an active member of the Résistance."

"Really?"

"Yes, he knew De Gaulle personally. When the war was over, he was elected to government."

"So my grandfather was Claude's son."

"Oui, Pierre. We met when we were only eighteen. I was a model for Yves Saint Laurent. He was a banker, like his father. We married after two months."

"You must have been in love."

"Oh, we were very much in love. God only blessed us with one child, Raphael. I lost a daughter before he was born."

"I'm sorry."

"She was born sleeping."

"What was her name?"

"Marie-Claire." She turned the page. "When Claude died, we moved to Amiens. Raphael was just a baby."

"Do you miss living there?"

"Sometimes. I loved the garden in summer." She looked wistful. "Did you meet Marcel?"

"The gardener? Yes."

"Well, his father was our gardener. He cultivated the most beautiful roses in Picardy."

"I must show you something. *Attends.*" She turned the pages of the album. "I have one of Louis' wedding."

"Louis?"

"Yes." She rifled through photos and newspaper cuttings until she found what she was looking for. "Here it is." She put it on the table. "Louis and Elise."

"Was she my great-granny?"

"Oh no, she was his second wife."

Caspian looked up. "You mean Rosa's great-grandmother?"

"She told you about that?"

He nodded and stared at the photo. Louis looked dapper in a suit and hat. Elise looked beautiful in a white suit with a small bouquet of flowers.

"Were they happy?" he asked softly.

Agathe touched the photo. "Oh yes, very happy. His second match far exceeded his first."

"Why?"

"Their love was the real thing. They say that Elise was his true love; that she was the one he planned to marry first."

"Why didn't he?"

"He fought in the First World War and when he came back to Paris she was engaged to another man. George Harding-Jones: Rosa's great-grandfather."

"Poor Louis."

"*Oui,* it was a pity. George was British, of course, so they moved to his family home in Hertfordshire."

"Rosa said that George died young."

"He had a brain haemorrhage at the age of thirty-six. They had one daughter called Alexandra who was Johann's mother."

"How did Louis and Elise meet again?"

"After your great-grandmother died, Louis travelled a lot. Elise moved to New York before the war and he met her there. They came back to Amiens after France was liberated." She took his hand in hers. "Their story teaches us the lesson that life should not get in the way. That you should not miss opportunities."

Caspian gazed at the picture.

"Their destiny was to be together. Their fortune was decided. For centuries humans have believed in fate. The Greeks had Tyche, the Romans had Fortuna."

He looked up. "What did you say?"

Amandine arrived into the room with a tray.

"Ah, wonderful. Breakfast is served." Agathe moved the pile of photos to the side.

Caspian stared at her as if in a trance. She couldn't possibly have known. It must be a coincidence.

Agathe poured some coffee into a china cup. "Tell me what happened with Rosa."

"What?" He jumped.

"I've seen the photographs of you online. Amandine keeps me up to date on your activity."

"Those photos were innocent."

"*Ah bon?*" She gave him a funny look.

He reddened. "She played cello on the album. We were together a lot. That's all."

"So your *rupture* with Madison, it had nothing to do with her?" Her wise old eyes regarded him knowingly.

He sighed. "Well, maybe a little."

"Tell me."

He pushed the album to one side. "I can't. I'm too ashamed."

"I cannot be shocked. I'm too old."

He ran his fingers through his hair. "The short version is, I'm in love with her but I feel like I'll be no good for her. She could do a lot better than me."

"Does she love you?"

"I think so."

"So why are you apart?"

"Madison, the baby, the media. Things are crazy lately. I don't want her dragged into that."

"Those are not reasons."

"I've never felt love like this for anybody." He frowned. "That's what scares me."

Agathe regarded him thoughtfully. "You need to tell her how you feel."

"I can't.'

"You and Rosa? You're meant to be together. It's in your blood." She pointed to the picture of Louis and Elise.

"I don't know where she is." He looked despondent for a moment.

Agathe pushed a cup of coffee towards him. "I might be able to help you with that."

"What do you mean?"

"Raphael mentioned that she's looking after Anouk this weekend while he's in London for the première."

Caspian perked up. "You mean, she's in Amiens?"

Agathe nodded. "She arrived last night. My driver will take you there."

Caspian got to his feet and hugged her fiercely. "Are you sure?"

"I'm sure."

He walked to the door and stopped. "My coffee."

"Forget the coffee." She smiled. "Now go! Go and find love."

# CHAPTER EIGHTY-THREE

Emilia blotted her lips on piece of tissue. Her silver gown was shimmery and figure hugging, with a cowl neck and straps. She had pinned her hair back on one side and she inserted long diamond earrings to complete the look.

Johann whistled when she walked into the sitting room of his apartment. "You look stunning," he said approvingly. "Easily the prettiest woman on the red carpet."

"Hardly," she said, blushing.

"If you're talking to Raphael, please give him my regards. I would love a rapprochement."

"Really?" She sat down and tied the strap of her sandal. "After all this time?"

Johann nodded. "Our feud was for nothing. I see that now. I want to make amends."

"I'll tell him to call you."

"That would be great." He raised his glass of whiskey to her. "Here's to a great night and an Oscar nomination for Best Score."

She smiled. "You flatter me."

"Give my love to everyone. I'll warm the bed for when you get back."

Bertie's car pulled up outside Johann's apartment building.

"I'm not even going to ask what you're doing in this neck of the woods," said Bertie when she got in. "Did we have a relapse?"

"Maybe."

"Emmy!"

"Don't judge me. I'm happy."

"Fine. I'll change the subject. My tux is a bit tight. I gorged on empanadas last week."

"Where were you again?"

"Tijuana. The street food was to die for."

Emilia picked a stray thread off her dress. "I hear Napoléon's heir is coming."

"Yes, Jean-Christophe, the undisputed head of the Imperial House of France.

There will be hordes of press."

"Raphael must be so nervous. You know how he gets."

"Isabelle will calm him down." He opened the top button of his shirt. "My moles tell me that Madison is coming on her own. *Sans* Caspian."

"Really? Good for her."

"Funny how they broke up like that." He gave her a sideways glance.

"Don't look at me. I don't have any inside information."

"I thought you were still *in flagrante* with that young boy."

"Bertie!"

"If you were, I'd have the inside scoop."

The car approached Leicester Square Gardens. Fans were already lining the street, hoping to get a glimpse of the rich and famous. A red carpet was laid out with stanchions along each side. The velvet rope barriers controlled the crowd and kept the entrance clear. There was an army of head-set wearing individuals running around, making hand signals and checking their clipboards.

Emilia checked her lipstick in a pocket mirror. Bertie tied up his shirt again and straightened his bowtie.

Two men in suits with earpieces opened the back doors of the car to let them out. The crowd screamed as Bertie held out his hand for Emilia to hold and together they walked up the red carpet past the photographers and onto the press section. The PR team had lined up a selection of local and international journalists, all divided up into broadcast, print and online groups. A celebrity news reporter wearing a lanyard with E! News was commenting on all the new arrivals. Cameras flashed as they walked past and fans held out their phones, hoping for selfies.

Emilia reached the summit and saw Raphael standing at the top of the steps, Isabelle by his side. He looked handsome in his tux with his dark hair curling over the collar. Isabelle looked beautiful in an emerald gown. Her red hair was wound up in a bun on top of her head and she wore the Baptiste emeralds around her neck.

"Hello!" said Bertie, bowing at them both. "Delighted we're finally here."

The next car to arrive was Madison's Mercedes. She stared out the tinted windows at the crowd and felt a wave of anxiety. She hadn't been seen in public in over a month. Her stomach churned at the thought of walking up the red carpet alone. Fionn kissed her hand.

"You look amazing,' he whispered.

Her gold Alexander McQueen dress was long and slinky with a small train. She had been pleased with her reflection at home. Now, she felt like she was going to get sick. The car stopped.

"Fionn, I can't do it." Her lungs felt tight.

"You can."

"I can't walk up there on my own."

"You will." He kissed the inside of her wrist.

"Will you come with me?" She looked really young for a moment.

He smiled. "I'm a drummer. I hate this kind of thing. Now, go out there and be a star."

Todd opened the door and she put one leg out. Looking over her shoulder, she saw Fionn's encouraging smile. "I love you," he mouthed.

She stood up. There was a roar from the crowd and a barrage of flashes.

"Madison!"

"Maddy!"

"Look this way, Maddy!"

The lights were glaring and for a moment, she couldn't see. Straightening her shoulders, she raised her chin. She could do this.

Slowly she began to walk, smiling brightly and waving at non-descript faces in the crowd. She stopped for photos, posing with one leg forward and one arm on her hip. Then she continued, smiling at the press.

"Who are you wearing, Maddy?" asked one young journalist.

"Alexander McQueen," she replied.

"Where's Caspian?" asked another.

Madison felt herself stumble slightly, but she pulled it together. Her eyes fixed on the billboard of *Josephine* at the top of the stairs, she ignored the question and continued to walk.

*Almost there.*

She turned around and waved at the fans. The cameras flashed. There was a drone overhead filming the event from the sky.

Raphael walked over and hugged her. "Thank you for coming," he whispered in her ear.

She looked up at him. "I hope we can still be friends."

"Always." His eyes were kind. "Come, Isabelle is over here."

Madison followed him gratefully. She could shouts from the crowd, some said Caspian's name, others Raphael's. She blocked it out.

Isabelle smiled warmly at her. "You look awesome. That dress is incredible."

"Thanks. I love your dress too."

She looked down the red carpet and could see Aurora Sinclair walking up wearing a long black dress with feathers. It had a full skirt and a giant bow on the back. Behind her was Jasper Dale, her co-star. He looked chic in a red suit and an open necked purple shirt.

Bertie took Madison's hand and kissed it. "You look divine."

"Thanks, Bertie."

"Sorry to hear about Caspian."

She nodded.

Suddenly there was a huge roar as two Range Rovers pulled up. Extra security guards seemed to be swarming around as Jean-Christophe, Prince Napoléon, and his wife, Olympia Bonaparte, Princess Napoléon, exited the car. Raphael marched down to greet them.

Aurora took her place in the line-up. "I didn't realise Napoléon's heir was coming," she whispered loudly.

"Raphael wanted the blessing of the House of Napoléon," explained Isabelle. "Jean-Christophe's dad, Charles, used to play tennis with Pierre Baptiste."

"Bravo, Raphael," said Bertie. "What a coup."

Raphael approached the line of stars and crew, introducing each person in turn.

Madison held her head up and waited. She could see the cameras poised, ready to take a shot of her chatting to Jean-Christophe.

Raphael smiled at her. "This is Madison Ryan who performed the song for the film."

Madison curtseyed and bowed her head as the camera flashed.

Fionn was lying on the couch watching television when Madison got home. Todd escorted her to the door and then went to his own apartment.

"How was it?" Fionn asked, pausing the show.

She threw off her four inch stilettos. "Really good. I met Napoléon's heir. The film was well-received. I looked better than Aurora."

"Ah, Maddy." He laughed.

"Well, I did. Those feathers were a questionable choice."

"Come here," he said, patting the sofa. "Was the party good?"

"No!"

"Why?"

"You should've been there with me."

"No way." He shook his head. "I hate that side to things. Plus you had to go alone tonight. To show the world that you're perfectly fine without Caspian Cole."

"I *am* perfectly fine without him," she said, kissing his neck and snuggling up close. "I must take off this dress. It's so tight, I can barely breathe."

"I'll help you in a second. I just want to see what happens with Fleabag and the priest."

Later in bed, Fionn suddenly laughed. "Oh, I forgot to tell you. Clio is horrified."

"What? Why?" Madison was half-asleep on his chest, listening to his steady heartbeat.

"She thinks it's, quote unquote, gross that we're together and she's looking for a new brother and a new best friend."

Madison kissed the stubble on his chin. "She'd want to get over herself."

"That's what I said." He bent his head and kissed her deeply.

# CHAPTER EIGHTY-FOUR

Agathe's driver, Philippe, didn't speak English so the journey to Amiens was a silent affair.

The car pulled up outside the house and Caspian took a deep breath. It was close to 8pm and twilight was descending slowly. He remembered learning about it at school, how it was known as the witching hour as the dying light created shadows and played tricks on the eyes. *Entre chien et loup*, the French called it. The irony was he had never seen things so clearly in his life.

"*Merci,*" he said to Philippe who smiled.

He went to the back door and pulled the handle. It was open and he sighed in relief. Coralie only locked it at night.

The kitchen was deserted and so was the living area. A jigsaw lay scattered on the rug, half assembled, and there was a half-eaten bowl of mashed banana on the coffee table.

Climbing the stairs, he went to Anouk's bedroom. The cot was empty, just as he suspected.

That only left one place: Rosa's room.

Sure enough, he could hear them through the door. Rosa was singing a lullaby in Italian to the little girl and Anouk was singing along. He opened the door to find them lying on the bed, Anouk with her small legs in the air.

"Yan Yan!" she yelled in delight.

Rosa sat bolt upright. "What are you doing here?" Her hair was loose and she was wearing a t-shirt that barely covered her legs. He gazed at her.

"I heard that you were here and I had to see you."

She blinked. "I'm trying to get her to sleep."

"Let me help." He took off his shoes and lay down next to Anouk. "Yan Yan and Osa," she said happily.

Rosa lay back on the pillow, stunned. Caspian's arrival was the last thing she expected.

"Keep singing," he said. "Don't mind me."

Rosa took the bottle of milk and popped it in Anouk's mouth. "This might work," she whispered.

Sure enough, ten minutes later Anouk was asleep, the teat of the bottle lodged in the side of her mouth, milk dribbling down her neck. Rosa removed it gently. She gestured for Caspian to get up.

Then she put pillows all around the sleeping child in case she rolled over and fell off the bed.

"We can move her when she's in a deeper sleep," she whispered.

Caspian nodded.

Downstairs, the place was deserted. Rosa picked up the bowl of banana and wiped some cereal off the table.

"Coralie is out for the evening hence the mess."

He walked over to her and took the bowl from her hand. "Forget the mess. Come on."

He led her out into the garden. There was a stone bench next to the pond under a large willow tree. He sat down and indicated for her to sit next to him.

"I should put on more clothes," she said, aware that she was only wearing a t-shirt.

"You're perfect."

They sat in silence. A starling flew above them chirping loudly. Rosa stole a glance sideways. Caspian looked broody, his brow furrowed.

"Where did you go?" he asked suddenly. "No one would tell me."

"No one knew really. I just left."

"I met your dad."

"What?"

"With Emilia."

"You're not serious."

"He refused to tell me where you were."

She pulled the t-shirt down over her legs. "I went to Florence."

"To your mum's place?"

She nodded. "I have a new job in an orchestra, starting next week."

"In Florence?"

"No, Verona."

More silence. Caspian wanted to say so much, but couldn't find the words.

"How's Madison?" she asked.

He looked up. "She's okay as far as I know."

Even more silence. Then they both turned to one another and spoke in unison.

*"Why are you here?"*

*"I love you, Rosa."*

Her eyes widened. "Oh."

"I told you before. Surely you know that."

"I just thought that with the baby and Madison, you'd changed your mind."

He shook his head. "No. When you left and I couldn't find you, I didn't know what to do. Then Agathe sent me a letter to visit her and she said that you were here."

"That's funny. She rang the house this morning for a chat. She asked me how long I was staying."

They both laughed and it diffused the tension.

"I tried ringing you over and over."

She went pink. "I blocked your number."

"What? Why?"

"I had to make a clean start. I had to forget you." Her lip trembled. "I really thought what we had was different. That it was the real thing."

"It was, it is."

"Really?"

He kissed her softly on the lips. "I've never felt like this about anyone. Ever."

"That can't be true."

"It is. You've put me under a spell. It actually hurts when I'm not with you."

"It's too complicated."

"On the contrary, it's not complicated at all. I'm going to move to Verona."

She rolled her eyes. "Stop being silly."

"I don't care about the band, the album, anything. I just want us to be together."

"I can't take you away from your music. I could never do that."

"I love you more."

She stared at him. "So what now?"

He stood up and held out his hand. "We're going to move Anouk into her cot."

She threaded her fingers through his. "She'll probably wake up."

"Be positive. Manifest."

"And then?"

"We're going to Louis' room and I'm going to make love to you."

"Why Louis' room?"

"It's my room when I stay here. I feel like we're like him and Elise. Meant for one another. We'll share the bed they shared."

"Caspian," she said, coming to a halt. "You mean all of this, don't you?"

He lifted her up into his arms, her feet leaving the ground. "I promised you that I'd come back for you. It took me longer than I'd planned, but I'm here." He kissed her softly. "I want to spend my life with you." Then he kissed her again, slowly and thoroughly.

Rosa woke up and for a moment she didn't know where she was. The sun was streaming through a crack in the heavy drapes. Caspian was sound asleep on his stomach next to her, his blonde hair fanned out on the pillow. His body felt warm so she lay close to him and put her arm around his waist. He stirred, clasping her hand in his and holding it to his chest.

"Morning," he mumbled.

"Hey."

He turned his whole body to face her. "I can't believe you're here."

She kissed his chest. "Me too."

"I dreamed of you all the time."

"Really?"

He kissed her nose. "I even watched you on YouTube."

"Oh God." She blushed.

"I'm in awe of what you do. I wish I could play an instrument like that."

She put a lock of his hair behind his ear. "I never did give you those lessons."

"We have forever to rectify that."

Anouk was standing up in the cot when Rosa eventually got up.

"Osa," she said crossly.

"I'm sorry, *amore mio.*" She picked her up and swung her around and around. Anouk squealed in delight.

Caspian jumped out from behind the door and said "Boo!" and she screamed again. "Yan Yan!"

All three went downstairs and Coralie did a double take when she saw Caspian.

"Morning," he said cheerfully.

"*Bonjour,*" she answered stiffly.

Rosa got a cup and filled it with milk. "Come on, Anouk. Breakfast time."

"When will Raphael be back?" asked Caspian, putting a coffee pod in the machine.

"This afternoon. Isabelle texted last night and said they're flying in later."

"Yan Yan," said Anouk. "Drop." She threw her cup of milk on the floor.

"Oh, are we back to this?" He tickled her tummy. "Yan Yan picks it up and you throw it down again?"

"Yeah." Anouk giggled.

Raphael's helicopter touched down at three causing the autumn leaves to fly in all directions. He was a licenced pilot and flew the craft himself. Taking off his earphones, he shook out his hair. Isabelle picked up her tote and her emerald gown which was in a long zipped up bag.

Jean ran over to the helicopter to open the door and help Isabelle down. His hair whipped up in the wind as the rotor blades kept spinning around.

"Madame Baptiste," he said, taking her hand.

"Hi, Jean," she said with a smile. She stepped down onto the lawn.

Rosa was standing inside the French doors with a squirming Anouk in her arms.

"*Maman!*" she called, trying to break free.

Isabelle held her hair in place and walked towards the house. "Anouk, baby!"

She covered her daughter in kisses and beamed at Rosa. "Looks like you guys had a great time."

Rosa smiled. "She was perfect."

"Did she sleep in her crib?"

"Eventually. I had to move her from my bed."

"We have to break this habit. Raph gets so mad at me for putting her to sleep in our room, but what can I do?" She draped her dress on the back of a chair. "The première was awesome. Critics loved the film. Some say it might be nominated for an Academy Award."

"That would be amazing."

"I know, right? Raph deserves it." She bounced Anouk on her knee. "What did you guys do while I was away?"

Rosa blushed. "Jigsaws and things like that. Um, I need to tell you something..."

"Hi, Isabelle." Caspian walked into the room.

"Caspian!" She got up to kiss his cheek. "I'm so happy to see you. I didn't know you were in France."

"I went to stay with Agathe and popped up here for a quick visit."

Rosa stood up and walked towards him. He put his arm around her waist and kissed her head.

"Wait a second..." Isabelle looked from one to the other. "Are you two a thing now?"

Rosa nodded. "Yes."

"Oh my God, that's incredible." She put Anouk on the ground and got up to hug them. "I always thought there was something between you, but I was never sure. Then Coralie said that you slept together and I said you're kidding me, right?"

"Coralie said that?" Caspian looked shocked. "When?"

"When Raph and I were in the States. She said she was looking for Anouk and found her in Rosa's room with you guys asleep on the bed."

"It was innocent, I promise." Rosa went bright red.

"What was innocent?" said Raphael, entering through the patio doors.

"That time Coralie found Caspian in Rosa's bed."

"Oh, yeah." Raphael picked up Anouk and kissed her.

"They're a couple now," said Isabelle in delight.

"Good. Did you see my phone?"

Isabelle picked up her dress. "No. I'm going to take this to Coralie to be dry cleaned. Let's have dinner together later and celebrate."

# CHAPTER EIGHTY-FIVE

Johann was making coffee when Emilia woke up. Her head was pounding so she took some Nurofen, drinking the water thirstily.

"Good night?" Johann looked at her in amusement.

"I think so."

"How was Raphael?"

"Good. The film was highly rated so he's relieved about that." She rubbed her temple. "He and Isabelle left early."

"Did you say it to him about me?"

She shook her head. "There wasn't an opportunity. Sorry."

Johann scowled. "Jesus, Emmy. I asked you to do one thing."

"I said I'm sorry. It was too busy and he wasn't focusing on anything."

Johann pulled himself together. "I apologise. Of course he was."

Emilia rubbed her temple. "Bertie made me drink lots of cocktails."

"How is Bertie?"

"Good form. He's dying to play Yeats in Raphael's new film, but Raph said he's too old."

"He looks about thirty with all that work he's had done."

"Exactly, but Yeats didn't have a shiny face and pulled back eyes."

Johann laughed. "True."

"Now, if you don't mind, I'm going back to bed. Remind me never to mix my drinks again."

Later that day, Emilia went home to Surrey. She needed to change her clothes and work on her score. Staying in London was fine short-term, but she yearned for the lavender fields and tranquillity. Johann assured her that he would be down to her house later that evening.

As she sat in the car on the way home, she couldn't believe how quickly her life had changed. How different Johann could be. Gone was the arrogant self-serving man and in his place was a loving and kind one. She imagined them growing old together, content.

She was just about to step into the shower when her phone rang. It was Dorothea Maxwell, her agent.

"Emmy," she stated matter-of-factly. "You'll never guess. Robert Barron, that snake, has been enquiring about Raphael's Yeats film! Every agent knows it's ours. What the hell?"

"Remind me who this Robert Barron is again?"

"My biggest rival. Word on the street is that he's signed your old flame, Johann Weber. It's all cloak and dagger, but apparently Johann is after the score for himself."

Emilia felt faint so she sat down on the bed. "Johann's retiring. He told me so himself."

"No, he left his old agent and has signed with Barron Management. Rob rang me himself to tell me."

"This makes no sense."

"I'll keep you updated. As if they have a chance of breaking your bond with Raphael. I mean, really."

She hung up the phone. Emilia bit her lip. It must be a mistake. Johann said he was done with composing: he was retiring. It had to be a misunderstanding.

She decided to put it out of her mind. Someone got their wires crossed. She had more important things to do.

She spent the day working on the love theme of the score, or as Alfie called it, the unrequited love theme. She missed him terribly. He had not been in contact since their argument.

She hoped it would blow over; she needed his advice and support.

Johann walked in at seven, his briefcase in his hand. She glanced at it, wondering what could be inside.

"How was your day?" she asked, putting her pencil down.

He smiled. "Boring. I met some old friends and chatted to my realtor in LA about selling my house over there."

"Oh?"

"I want to move back to the UK permanently."

"Really? Why?'

"To be with you."

She stared at him intently. "Who's Robert Barron?"

Johann stiffened. "Sorry?"

"Robert Barron. Who is he?"

"I don't know. Why do you ask?" His face was impassive and he spoke in a monotone. It was then she knew he was lying.

"I know you signed with his agency."

"That's ridiculous."

"Stop! I know that you did."

He put his briefcase on the ground. "Okay, okay. I did meet with him."

"Why?"

"I need some new blood, new energy."

"But you're retiring."

He looked down at his shoes. "Yes, I plan on it. I just want to do one last score before I do. A masterpiece: a legacy."

"Another score?" She felt weak.

"Raphael's film." He looked up and stared at her steadily. "I feel it in my gut that this is the one."

"What?"

"I know it could be the pinnacle of my career. Emmy, it's my last shot. The last few scores I submitted were binned. I can't retire with that hanging over me."

"But Raphael asked me to compose the score. I'm working on it as we speak."

"You love me, don't you? You want me to be happy?"

She couldn't answer.

"Then give me this score, Emmy. Recommend me to Raphael. He'll listen to you. I can incorporate what you've done already and credit you as a co-composer on those pieces."

She turned away.

"I need this, Emilia. Remember how I helped you all those years ago? This is your chance to repay me. It's just one score. Give me a piece of the pie."

"Repay you?"

"I gave you a chance. Without me you'd never have progressed this far. I opened doors for you." He walked towards her. "I love you and I know you love me. Let me have this and I will retire happily."

"Have you finished?"

"Emilia, darling. It's one score. You're young and have plenty of opportunities left. I, however, am at the end of my career. Give me this chance. Please."

She played a few notes on the piano keys in front of her.

"Emmy! I beseech of you."

"Get out of my house." She played more notes, louder this time. "What?"

"You came to my door, to my bed, with one objective: to betray me."

"That's not true."

"Get out of my house."

"No."

"*Get out!*" She stood up and grabbed the closest object to her. A vase went flying through the air and narrowly missed his head. "*Get out now!*"

"Emilia!"

She picked up a cup and threw it at him followed by a plate. "*Out!*"

"You're overreacting."

She picked up the sheet music and threw it up into the air. It scattered all over the room.

"*Get out of my life!*" she screamed.

He picked up his briefcase and backed away.

"I'll call you tomorrow when you've had a chance to think."

A bowl hit the wall beside him and smashed. He covered his head and left.

It was an hour later, after she'd cried every tear in her body, that Emilia sat up straight.

When things seem too good to be true, they generally are. Johann was never going to be the man she wanted. She had allowed herself to be duped, fooled, all because she held on to an ideal memory of what she thought he was. Alfie had been right: he'd hurt her again. Except this time, she felt that there was closure. This was the last wound. Gone were the dreams and fantasies of what could've been. Her heart had closed up and she no longer felt his power over her.

She sat on the piano stool and started to play the love theme again, the emotion of the piece lifting her up. This was her score, her legacy. She would write the greatest music the world had ever seen. Despite his claims that he was responsible for her success, she knew it was wishful thinking on his part. She had made it through sheer grit and talent.

She walked to Alfie's house the next evening. He lived on the other side of the village in a charming thatched cottage. He and Miranda had built an extension out the back of the house when the twins were born, and the resulting conservatory was where the family spent most of their time. Emilia walked up the path and knocked on the door. She could hear music inside, a modern pop song of some sorts, so she guessed the twins were at home.

The door opened and Arabella appeared. "Emilia! How are you?"

"I'm well. Is your dad home?"

She nodded. "He's mowing the lawn. Mummy said we don't need to do it as it's almost October, but he thinks we should."

"May I go out to him?"

"Of course."

Ava was doing her homework on the large wooden table.

"You've a great voice," said Emilia as she walked past.

"Thanks, I love Lizzo."

Emilia smiled and opened the glass door that led to the garden. Alfie was pushing an ancient lawnmower over the grass, humming a tune.

"Alfie!" she called but he didn't hear her over the hum of the mower.

"Alfie!" she repeated and he turned.

"Emmy?" He switched off the machine. "I didn't realise you were coming over."

"I should've texted you first but I wasn't sure that you'd reply."

"Of course I would." He wiped his forehead with his sleeve. "What's up?"

"Alfie, I'm sorry. I should've listened to you. You were right, about everything. Fionn, Johann, the lot."

"No, Emmy." He sighed. "You were right. I'm always poking my nose into your business."

She ran up to him and hugged him briefly. "You're my best friend and I can't survive without you."

"Of course you can."

"No, I can't. You're my one constant. Can we be friends again?"

"We never stopped."

"Oh, Alfie." She wiped away a tear. "I've been so stupid."

"*We are all fools in love,*" quoted Alfie.

"Okay, Jane Austen." She smiled. "Will you come over later and listen to my love theme?"

"Your *unrequited* love theme," he corrected. "Maud Gonne rejected Yeats over and over."

"Yes, I know."

"He loved her and she only wanted to be his friend. He managed to adapt, but never got over her." His eyes met hers. "*Tread softly because you tread on my dreams.*"

"Oh, Alfie."

"It's fine. I'm happy. I love Miranda and the girls. But know you'll always be my one that got away."

Suddenly they heard screeches as a flock of swifts flew overhead. The birds raced across the sky with great speed, propelling through the air with beauty and grace.

"September is late for swifts," said Emilia in wonder. "I thought they'd migrated ages ago."

"Maybe they're saying goodbye," said Alfie.

"Maybe."

They both gazed at the birds as they veered off south at tremendous speed.

"Swifts symbolise change, you know," said Alfie.

"Oh?"

"They are symbols of freedom." He squeezed her hand. "It's time to reset, Emmy. Begin again."

Together, they walked back towards the house as the sun began to set in the west.

# EPILOGUE

*Two years later…*

Anouk twirled around in her silk gown, giggling as the skirt fanned out. She loved playing in her mother's bedroom as it had a three way mirror where you could see your reflection from all angles. Zola barked loudly at the little girl, trying to bite the skirt as it whirled around.

"Stop, honey," said Isabelle sternly, who was fixing her hair. "You'll get dizzy and fall."

Anouk ignored her and continued to spin, stopping intermittently to wobble with dizziness. The pink rose that Isabelle had inserted into the little girl's hair had become loose, and the petals fell silently to the ground as she moved. Raphael strode into the bedroom, his tie undone.

"Can you do this for me?" he asked Isabelle, lifting his chin.

"Sure, honey. Just let me finish my hair."

*"Papa, Papa, regarde-moi,"* said Anouk in delight, twirling around at tremendous speed. Suddenly, she tripped and fell onto the carpet. Zola licked her face in concern.

"See, I told you that would happen." Isabelle wagged her finger. "Now, sit on the bed and stay still. I want you to look nice at the church."

"Zsa, Zsa, we must go. The guests are here." Raphael tapped his foot.

"I'm coming." She got to her feet slowly, her baby bump clearly visible, and walked towards her husband. "Now, sit still." She bit her lip as she wound the tie into shape, pausing to elongate one end. Finally, she was satisfied. "Done." She leant up and kissed Raphael softly.

"*Bon,* let's go downstairs." Raphael straightened his shirt and picked up his jacket. "It's almost time."

Rosa stared at her refection in the mirror. Her white wedding gown was timeless with off the shoulder sleeves, a fitted bodice covered in Alençon lace, and a full silk taffeta skirt with a six-foot train. The lace veil was cathedral in length, held in place with a pearl clasp at the base of her neck. Her long dark hair was in a chignon, and her mother's pearl necklace hung around her slender neck. When Caspian had proposed the year before, they had immediately decided to have the ceremony in Amiens. It was their special place, where they could be themselves without prying eyes.

She moved towards the window and gazed down at the garden. The small marquee stood on the lawn, filled with tables and chairs for the reception. A string quartet were positioned under the gazebo, playing Pachelbel's Canon. The musicians were colleagues from the orchestra, flown in especially.

The guest list was small. When her father was diagnosed with pancreatic cancer the year before, his demise had been swift. Three weeks after hearing the awful news, he had died. The funeral had been a huge affair, with notable faces from the classical music world and the film industry in attendance. Johann was buried in the kirkyard of the chapel on the Hertfordshire estate. Cassandra had sung the requiem, her face covered in black lace, her eyes cast down in sorrow.

Rosa still didn't know how to feel about his death. He was her father but she wasn't sure how much she would miss him. He had intimidated her, made her feel inadequate. She had spent her life trying to prove herself to him.

Funnily enough, since his death, she and her mother had become closer. Cassandra, reminded of her own mortality, made more of an effort with her daughter. Initially, Rosa had been wary. She had been hurt so many times before, it was difficult to allow her mother in. It was Caspian who had encouraged it, who had convinced her to give Cassandra a chance.

She glanced at the clock. It was almost time. She imagined George and Prudence Cole sitting on the groom's side of the chapel, dressed up and nervous, unsure of how to behave on Raphael's turf. Cassandra was already on the altar, warming up her voice. She could hear bits of *Panis Angelicus* faintly through the open window. Gertrude had come over, thrilled that Rosa had finally found her path. She had early onset Parkinson's, but nevertheless had managed the journey. Stefan and Claudia had arrived the night before, as had Agathe. Viola Harte, Mary's best friend, had flown in from Cork with her husband, Brian. Caspian had not visited her in a long time, but felt that it was appropriate that she was present, representing his birth mother. Jean, the stable hand, looked smart in a black shirt and pants. He had Luna and Rajah by the reins outside the chapel, waiting to wish the couple well. Caspian had lost touch with the other members of Doctor Eckleburg following the shock split. After all the legalities had been ironed out and equal royalty rights maintained, he had moved to Verona to be with Rosa. His Steinway took up most of the small apartment, but when they played music together in the twilight, often well into the night, she knew that she'd never been happier.

The band's last album, simply entitled *Lost Love*, was released just before the split. Critically acclaimed, it won a Grammy and a VMA. Caspian refused to attend the award ceremonies so Ethan picked up the gongs for both. Fans found it hard to adjust to the break up. They deluged social media to mourn, deeming it a modern tragedy. The tabloids blamed Rosa, paining her as the *femme fatale* who stole Caspian away from Madison, but soon the gossip faded away. She kept a low profile and there wasn't anything remotely scandalous about playing cello in concert halls around the world.

Raphael's Yeats film had wrapped six months before and was due for release, so the wedding was planned to fit nicely into the break before the endless premieres and promos. She imagined Caspian in Louis' room, fixing his tie and slicking back his blonde hair. It was hard to believe that she would soon be his wife.

There was a knock on the door.

"Rosa?"

It was Isabelle.

"Are you ready?"

Rosa lifted the veil over her head so that it covered her face. Lifting the heavy skirt, she walked out into the corridor.

Raphael was waiting at the foot of the stairs. He had offered to give her away in Johann's place. He smiled as Rosa descended the staircase. "You look beautiful," he said genuinely.

"Thank you." Her heart was racing.

"I am so honoured to be the one to give you away." His eyes were warm.

She leant up and kissed his cheek. "You're my godfather. Of course it had to be you."

Taking her hand, he led her out through the main door and down the path towards the chapel.

Anouk was standing by the door, her hand held tightly by her mother. Zola was lying in the sun, a white ribbon tied to his collar. Jean was standing near the entrance with the horses. Rosa paused to rub Luna's mane.

The string quartet had moved into the church to accompany Cassandra who was singing *Ave Maria* in her thrilling voice.

"Now, baby, throw the petals on the ground like we practised." Isabelle kissed Anouk's head. "When you're done, sit with me, okay?"

"Okay."

Isabelle smiled at Rosa. "It's a piece of cake. Just say 'I do'." She walked into the church, her heels clacking on the marble floor.

Rosa took a deep breath.

"Ready?" Raphael stood up straight.

"Ready."

Anouk skipped ahead of them, throwing rose petals wildly around her. Raphael squeezed Rosa's hand and they entered the church.

Caspian was standing at the altar looking handsome in a suit. George Cole was standing beside him, delighted to have the honour of being the best man. The two gold bands were ready to be presented to Père Bernard when the time came.

Anouk ran up the aisle, throwing the petals in an *ad hoc* fashion, ignoring Isabelle's pleas to slow down.

*Ave Maria* came to an end and the string quartet began the *Wedding March.* Cassandra, looking radiant in pink, sat down by Isabelle and Agathe.

Rosa's dress and train filled the aisle as she moved. Caspian gazed at her as she walked towards him, his eyes locked with hers. He didn't feel nervous. Why would he when this was meant to be? Glancing down at Rosa's right hand, he was gratified to see Mary's mood ring on her finger. He had very little of his biological mother's possessions, so when he had asked Rosa to wear the ring as her 'something old', she had agreed straight away.

When they reached the top, Raphael stopped and put Rosa's hand in Caspian's.

"I wish you every happiness," he said, his voice thick with emotion.

Caspian moved forward and hugged him briefly. "Thank you."

Prudence wiped a tear from her eye. Raphael took a seat next to Isabelle and Anouk immediately sat on his knee.

Caspian took Rosa's hand and they walked up the steps to the altar where Père Bernard was waiting. Lifting the lace veil, he leaned in and kissed her lips softly.

***

Madison stood on the podium, with her head back and her eyes closed. Twenty thousand fans screamed her name, asking for an encore.

She opened her eyes as he face filled the giant screen on the stage behind her.

"Thank you, San Francisco."

More screams.

"This is the last song." She adjusted her microphone. "It's called *Blind*."

The crowd erupted. Madison took a seat at the grand piano on the stage and played the intro. After over a year of lessons and practice, she found that she could play chords quite well. It was Fionn who had urged her to learn, to believe in herself.

"This is a song about courage," she said into her microphone. "How it's hard to see things for what they really are." She played the intro fluidly, her hands moving up and down the keyboard. "Sometimes it's easier to be blind."

Leaning in, she started to sing.

*Close your eyes*
*Pretend it's not real*
*Don't look back*
*Try not to feel*
*Blind to the truth*
*Blind to pain*
*Numb and cold*
*You will remain*

The crowd sang along, holding up their hands and swaying them in time to the music. Madison moved to the chorus and the guitarist and drummer joined in.

*You were not the right fit*
*You messed with my mind*
*We had to just quit*
*We couldn't stay blind*
*Couldn't stay blind...*

The song ended and Madison hung her head. That feeling was like no other feeling in the world. That connection with the fans, that emotional charge. The Liberty Tour was coming to a close after multiple dates and venues around the world. It had a set list of over thirty songs, all grouped into six acts, charting Madison's musical journey. Her latest album, co-written by Savannah, was compared to Joni Mitchell. For the first time in her life, she really felt the music. Deep in her veins.

Standing up, she bowed. More screams. The lights on the giant screen started to flicker, sending laser beams into the night sky.

"Thank you," she shouted, waving her arms and walking off stage. Someone put a towel around her neck and handed her a bottle of Evian. She drank thirstily, her throat raw from projecting her voice.

"Where's Fionn?" she asked Todd, wiping her lip.

"In the trailer."

"Take me to him."

Todd said something into his earpiece and led the way through the hordes of technicians, guests and crew. Cora appeared wearing a lanyard.

"Bethany wants to see you."

"I'll be at my trailer."

Todd held up his arm and shielded her from journalists and photographers.

Fionn was waiting at the door, his arms wide open. She fell into his embrace, inhaling his familiar smell.

"You okay?" he murmured into her hair.

She nodded.

"You were amazing out there."

She kissed him slowly. "I need a long hot bath. My legs ache."

They entered the plush trailer and she threw off her heels. The thick make up felt heavy on her face and her back was damp with stale sweat. He pulled her onto his lap, hugging her close. He knew that she needed silence to wind down so he just held her.

Bethany knocked on the door, a phone in her hand.

"May I come in?"

Madison nodded. "What's up? I said no press."

"I have a picture that you should see."

"Oh?"

Bethany held out the phone. "Of Caspian's wedding."

Madison stiffened.

Fionn kissed her head. "You don't have to look."

"I do actually." She got up and grabbed the phone. "Just to prove to you how little I care."

She focused in on the grainy shot a paparazzo had obtained from sending a drone over the Baptiste estate. It was of Rosa and Caspian at the chapel door. Both were smiling and Rosa's veil was blowing out in the wind. Raphael was to the left, looking proud as punch, and Prue Cole was on the right, wearing a pink hat. Madison zoomed in, her face impassive.

"Are there any more?" she asked in a monotone.

Bethany shook her head. "Just the one."

Fionn took the phone gently from Madison's hand and gave it to Bethany. "Maddy wants a hot bath," he said giving her a pointed look.

"Of course." She backed out the door and closed it.

He pulled her into his arms once more and kissed her nose. "Are you okay?"

She nodded. "I really am."

"It must be hard to see it all the same."

"Not really." She exhaled slowly. "I'm glad it's her and not me. I would've been miserable."

"Are you sure?" For a moment he looked vulnerable and her heart melted. Winding her arms around his neck, she kissed him hard on the lips.

"I love you, Fionn. Only you."

"Oh, you do."

"Even though you ruined my hair.'

He laughed. "Will you ever let that go?"

She laughed too. "Never." She stroked his face. "It's always been you. All those years when I thought I hated you, but it was the opposite."

He stared at her intently. "Do you know what, Maddy Ryan?"

"What?"

"I believe you."

"Good. Now, let's agree on one thing, that dress was horrendous. Lace is so passé."

"Maddy!" Fionn started to laugh.